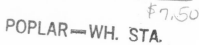

HARDBALL FEVER

Collectors Signature Copy
First Edition

HARD TIMES
CATTLE COMPANY
PUBLISHING

Also by John Carver

WINNING
a football novel

HARDBALL
FEVER

by

John Carver

PUBLISHED BY
Hard Times Cattle Company Publishing

Book Design and Editor: Renee Baker
Front Dust Cover Art:
Chip Erwin
Kyle, Texas
(Original artist illustration digitally enhanced)

All inquiries for volume purchases of this book
should be addressed to Hard Times Cattle Company Publishing at
P.O. Box 941792, Plano, Texas 75094

Telephone inquiries may be made by calling:
972-669-0707 or FAX 972-669-0894
e-mail: Fntngreen@aol.com

To my son Johnny—
whose exploits on the playing
field provided me with more
thrills than anything I
personally achieved.

SPECIAL ACKNOWLEDGEMENT

My special thanks to good friends—

David and Joan Hands,
Kathy Nepple,
Krista France,
my daughter Renee Baker
and my sister Lin Rushing

for proofreading my manuscript and for
their critical encouragement.

HARDBALL FEVER

a baseball novel

CHAPTER ONE

ORCHESTRA MUSIC and polite party conversation drift over the high brick wall built to insure both security and privacy for the Segars family. I park my Pontiac behind a sleek black Lincoln, lock the car door, and hurriedly tramp across the brick driveway which circles in front of the house. A brawny security guard posted at the entry gate stares inquisitively after me. Probably he's wondering how a fellow wearing a threadbare, out-of-style sports coat and driving a ten-year-old car wrangled an invitation to the chic wedding in progress on the opposite side of the tall barrier.

Actually, I'm not sure why I'm here. I certainly don't belong. I received an invitation several weeks ago, but I never planned to attend. My invitation was mailed simply as a family courtesy. The bride-to-be is my wife's sister, but my wife and I have been separated since January. The only common interest we share is an impatient wait for final divorce papers—to dissolve our union and put a definitive end to the hurt we've inflicted on one another these past three years.

A phone call early this morning from Victor LaBranch, the family's bodyguard and self-appointed social director, changed my mind. He was very specific. I was expected to attend. No excuses accepted. Either show up or have my body parts rearranged.

Stationed outside the front entrance to the big house is the Segars' butler, providing a secondary line of defense against entry by uninvited guests. This wedding is strictly by invitation only. No one will be allowed to enter without his personal inspection and approval.

"Good day, Mister Rick, nice to see you again," Felix says, greeting me cordially. The Segars' butler is a prince, one of the few family people I genuinely like.

"Good to see you too, Felix. I'm running late. Got a late start coming out of Dallas. Has the wedding started yet?" I ask foolishly, offering a lame excuse to justify my late arrival. I rummage through my coat pockets, fish out a mutilated invitation and shove it into his outstretched hand.

"No, I expect there's still time to find a seat. The bride's taking her own sweet time. She's making certain she'll be the center of everyone's attention when she arrives," he advises, carefully inspecting my invitation. Satisfied with its authenticity, he hands it back to me. "But please hurry. We don't want to spoil Miss Vickie's grand entrance."

"Yes, I wouldn't wanna get on Vickie's bad side too. I've got plenty of headaches dealing with her older sister's temper tantrums."

"It's too bad about you and Miss Kaye. I always thought the two of you were a nice match."

"Oh, sure. We're a perfect match, and we get along fine, except when she's trying to slit my throat or drive over me with her car. But who knows, maybe she'll be in a good mood today. It's her sister's wedding day. Maybe we can speak to each other without ending up in a cuss fight. How's my wife holding up, being footloose and almost single again?"

Felix's friendly smile quickly degenerates into a sorrowful frown. "Mister Rick, you know Miss Kaye. She just puts a smile on her pretty face and goes on like nothing fazes her, but deep down, she's hurting real bad."

Felix's observation stokes the coals of my own heartache. These past three months have been the most miserable days of my life. It seems so improbable my rich, spoiled wife could also be grieving. She's so self-reliant, so confident, and so damn headstrong. Could I have been so self-absorbed, so preoccupied with my own feelings of self-pity, that I didn't notice her pain? Is it possible she still loves me?

"I'd better get inside before the wedding starts."

"Yes sir. You take care now, Mister Rick. And do everyone a favor—lay off the booze and mind your manners. We'd like Miss Vickie's wedding party to be a friendly family affair, without any unpleasant incidents."

"Felix, you worry too much. I'll be on my best behavior today. You can have my word on it."

"Oh, I almost forgot. Colonel Segars wants to talk with you. He gave me strict instructions not to let you leave until you've checked in with him."

"Segars wants to see me? Good grief, I hope he's not gonna light in on me too. He say what he wants?"

"No sir. He just asked me to make certain you didn't leave without speaking with him. He'll have my hide if you don't check in before you leave."

Clyde Segars is my wife's father. He's a complex person, but all in all, not a bad sort—at least he's always treated me decently. He's definitely not someone you'd want to cross. These days Segars is a respected businessman. He owns a car dealership near the downtown business district and a number of other profitable local enterprises. However, he hasn't always been such a stellar citizen. As a young man during the East Texas oil boom, he manned a taxicab, twenty-four hours a day, seven days a week. Rumor has it Segars made his first real money pimping for prostitutes who turned tricks out of the Blackstone Hotel and by selling bootleg hooch from the trunk of his taxi. Somehow he made the right connections to cash in on the rich bounty of East Texas black gold—probably by furnishing prosperous oilmen with plenty of rot-gut whiskey and loose women. Using his illegal profits, he bought part interest in a wildcat well being drilled near Kilgore. From that point, the story could've had a rags-to-riches fairy tale ending, but Segars was a greedy young man. He shot one of his partners outside a saloon in Longview then hired a crooked lawyer to screw his other two partners out of their share of the oil. Thirty

3

years and no telling how many million dollars later he still operates pretty much the same way.

❖ ❖ ❖ ❖ ❖

IN THE SEGARS' BACKYARD a spirit of serenity prevails. A five-man orchestra softly serenades the wedding party with a familiar pre-nuptial melody. Immaculately trimmed bushes and colorful flowers punctuate the landscape. Giant oak trees block out the brilliant spring sunlight. The garden-like atmosphere, a cloudless blue sky, and warm pleasant weather combine to provide a perfect setting for the outdoor wedding.

A short runway blanketed in red carpet extends from the concrete patio out to a white wooden arbor where wedding vows will be exchanged. The arbor is adorned with strands of greenery and ruby red roses. Beneath the arbor a balding preacher, the groom and three nervous groomsmen have taken their positions, waiting apprehensively for the appearance of the bride and her bridesmaids.

Discreetly, I slide the patio door open and step outside. Wedding guests have been seated. Four eager ushers, wearing white jackets and black bow ties, have stationed themselves on the grassy margin behind the rows of folding chairs.

My arrival causes several anxious aunts and uncles to glance back expectantly. Their faces express their disappointment as they curiously watch me slink across the porch and slip down a crowded back row to take a seat beside Roy Segars, Kaye's portly uncle. Uncle Roy isn't exactly delighted to share my company.

"What tha hell you doing here? This wedding is for invited guests."

"Take it easy, big guy. I have an invitation," I whisper, embarrassed by his outburst. I was hoping to avoid an out and out confrontation with family members.

"Oh, sure. Fat chance of that. I know why you're here. You heard there'd be an open bar and decided to crash the party. If the colonel finds you here, he'll have you horse whipped."

"Simmer down, Uncle Roy. Clyde knows I'm here. Felix checked me in at the front door. I'm a legitimate guest of the family, just like you. Let's not have a scene and ruin Vickie's wedding. As soon as the wedding is over, I'll kiss the bride, have a piece of cake and be outta here," I explain, keeping my voice low, hoping my promise to leave promptly will pacify him. It doesn't work.

"Bullcrap! You don't give a rat's damn about food. You're nothing but a free loading drunk. Now, are you gonna leave peaceful or do you want I should have you removed?"

"Alright, keep your shirt on. I'll leave peaceable," I say yielding to his embarrassing verbal assault. I rise to my feet and lean forward, preparing to shuffle back toward the end of the aisle. "I'm not here to cause trouble."

"Sit down. The wedding's about to start," Roy hisses, grabbing my arm and pulling me back down into the chair.

"But I thought you wanted me gone?"

"Sit still and shut up, Mason! It's too late to leave. Now keep quiet. You're gonna spoil the ceremony. Me and my brother—we'll throw your sorry ass outta here later."

Amplified music and the appearance of a bridesmaid on the patio postpone further conversation. The orchestra switches to a wedding march, and a bridesmaid, her face brandishing a nervous smile, begins a slow, deliberate trek down the carpeted runway. A second later Kaye appears on the patio.

It's been three months since Kaye walked out on me—three lonely, miserable months. Her abrupt appearance accelerates my heart beat. My stomach flip-flops and leaps up to lodge in my throat. Her stunning beauty affects me the way it always has. She takes my breath away.

❖ ❖ ❖ ❖ ❖

WEDDINGS ARE SO dreadfully boring, and they last much too long. I'll never understand why people insist on subjecting their friends and family to a long, drawn out ceremony. When I married Kaye, I slipped the Justice of the Peace a twenty and told him to keep it short and sweet—say just enough words to make it legal. Kaye and I said our "I dos" and headed straight for the nearest motel. Two days and three fifths of whiskey later we sent out for food.

During the exchange of rings, the sun peeked over the tree tops. Now the backyard is flooded in sunlight, and it's hot as hades. I've lost all feeling in my right leg. After sitting on a rock hard metal chair for the better part of an hour, my butt is numb. Uncle Roy saw to it that I sat perfectly still, until the last vow was exchanged. Only by tricking my mind, reminiscing about good times and diligently studying the lithe movements of my wife's shapely figure, did I endure the ordeal. Now I desperately need a drink.

"Bourbon and seven. Make it a double," I advise the bartender, shouldering my way up to the canvassed topped counter and sliding an empty glass toward him.

A gnarled, hairy fist reaches across the portable bar and grabs the unfilled glass.

"Colonel Segars says not ta serve this guy. He can't hold his liquor," the burly man informs the barman and swivels around to face me. "Sorry, Rick. The colonel wants you sober. We don't want no trouble."

"Just one drink, Vic. That's all I'll have. Just one drink, then I'll switch to ice water," I plea diplomatically, trying to conceal the anger rushing up inside me.

"No. I got my orders. Colonel Segars wants ta talk business with ya. Can ya come now?"

"Tell Clyde I'll check in with him later. I haven't paid my respects to the bride and groom."

"You wasn't invited here ta pay no respects, and if you piss off the colonel, you're liable ta be leaving here feet first."

"Alright, I'll come. But before we go, let me say hello to my wife. Wouldn't want her to think I'm snubbing her."

"No way. Colonel Segars gave strict orders to keep you two separated. Says you and her already done too much talking."

"Lemme have a drink then. I truly am thirsty."

Vic eyes me suspiciously.

"Ice water, Vic. One lousy glass of ice water."

"Okay, but then we gotta go see the colonel. And I don't want no more back talk. Ya understand?"

❖ ❖ ❖ ❖ ❖

VIC USHERS ME up a rear stairway and down a long hallway. Signaling me to keep quiet, he knocks twice on an oversized door leading to Clyde Segars' private study. The door cracks open slightly.

"It's Vic. I got Mason with me, like Colonel Segars wanted."

"Hold on a minute while I check," a voice whispers from inside the door. Instantly I recognize the voice on the opposite side of the door. The voice belongs to Ted Gooding, Segars' personal attorney and family advisor. If I hadn't come along to louse things up, Kaye would have married Ted. Things would've been much simpler for the old man.

Vic and I fidget nervously in the hallway, occasionally shifting our weight from one foot to the other. Inside the room I hear faint voices deciding our fate. Abruptly the conversation ends. Seconds later the door swings open.

"The colonel's ready for you. He's in the big study," Gooding advises bluntly. We've known each other since high school, but we've never been friends. Actually, Ted hates my guts, but for the time being, he's apparently decided to simply ignore my presence. Nonetheless, his narrowed eyes don't bother to mask his animosity.

Vic nudges me and motions for me to follow. Without speaking, we cross an outer suite and enter a larger room where Segars and two other men are waiting. Anticipating our arrival, Segars has risen to his feet. He stands behind a huge wooden desk. The two men are seated on the opposite side of the desk facing Segars. Their aggravated facial expressions suggest my appearance has interrupted some sort of spirited argument.

This room is my father-in-law's private sanctum. Hundreds, maybe thousands, of business deals have been arranged here—some legitimate, some possibly not so legitimate. Ted's presence is mostly for show. Legal papers are seldom needed. Most of Segars' bargains are sealed with only a handshake. Clyde possesses the memory of an elephant. He remembers every agreement down to the most minute detail. Even if his memory was flawed, no one would dare challenge him, not with his reputation of doing away with difficult partners.

A wide bay window behind Segars' desk overlooks the garden and the post wedding party in progress below. The other three walls are embellished with wide library shelves, each seven tiers high and skillfully sandwiched between rich panels of golden oak. Each shelf is filled with rows of leather-bound books. Different book sizes have been grouped and placed to precisely fill each shelf. Each book is an expensive, collector-quality edition. Prior to purchase, every book was personally examined and approved by the colonel.

Once, a few months after we married, Kaye swiped a key ring from Felix and brought me here. Clyde was in Dallas that day on business. Giggling like two mischievous school children, we crept up the stairs, sneaked down the hallway and unlocked the big door. I knew it was a mistake the moment we entered. There was something cold and unholy about this magnificent room. I wanted to leave, but Kaye grabbed my arm and pulled me inside, calling me a fraidy cat wimp, challenging my manhood. Against my better judgement I allowed her to coerce me into exploring her father's sanctuary.

For a time it seemed like fun, checking out the book titles in her father's library, snooping through his desk drawers, rummaging through stacks of paid bills. I was astounded by the amount of money required to keep his business and properties intact. When we discovered the secret file closet, I realized my premonition of danger was justified.

The file closet is a narrow room situated between the bookshelves to the left of Segars' desk. Unless you know it's there, the entrance door is almost impossible to detect. Kaye and I stumbled onto it by accident. A black button behind the books on the third shelf from the bottom activates the door. Even now, recalling what we found inside the small compartment makes my skin crawl.

Despite his towering presence in local affairs, Clyde Segars is a short man, slightly overweight, standing maybe five-foot-six. A middle-age pouch around his waistline affirms he has succumbed to rich food and good cooking. Little trace remains of what once must have been a trim thin body, rippling with rock-hard muscles. An inch above his temples, streaks of gray give way to thinning brown hair. My father-in-law is in his early sixties. Normally he's a spiffy dresser, opting for colorful shirts and bright ties, which he believes give him a youthful look. Dressed as the father-of-the-bride in his solid black tuxedo, white silk shirt and black bow tie, Clyde looks much younger.

Segars steps around the desk and offers his hand. Neither of the other men stands nor makes any show of friendliness. Their expressions are solemn, perhaps resentful. Almost certainly I was the subject of a heated debate which was interrupted by my arrival.

"Hello, Rick. Good to see you again. We appreciate your coming," Segars says, shaking my hand vigorously, welcoming me as if I volunteered to attend his exclusive business party.

"Nice to see you too, Mister Segars."

"Rick, these two gentlemen are my partners in a new venture. You probably recognize them—Biff Crawley and Garry Watkins."

Crawley is the owner of an animal rendering plant located in an industrial district near the eastern city limits. His processing plant is notorious for stinking up the east side of town when the wind blows in the wrong direction. Watkins is an elected State Senator, representing the Tyler district. Crawley and Watkins are related—uncle and nephew. Biff is Garry's mother's brother. Something like that.

I can't imagine what interests these three men could have in common. But like they say in Austin, "Politics and money make strange bedfellows."

"Yes, I know both Mister Crawley and Mister Watkins. I've seen their pictures in the Tyler paper many times," I respond, stepping forward to shake the hand of each man. Each man politely accepts my handshake, but neither bothers to stand. Although they often represent conflicting interests, within their individual circles of influence, each of these men commands considerable power. Wealth gives Crawley his edge. Financially, he's definitely a major leaguer—one of very few men in Tyler who can match Segars dollar for dollar.

In comparison to his two partners, Watkins is a lightweight. I know him from college, but we were never what you'd call friends. We traveled different paths. He was a snooty fraternity brat with a sleek sports car and too much money to spend. I was a baseball jock, on scholarship, usually on foot, and always on the verge of poverty.

Watkins is the consummate small town politician—immaculately groomed, light blonde hair, bleached white teeth, polished finger-nails—never worked an honest day in his life. He's the only son of a prominent local physician. Although his family isn't in the class with Segars and Crawley, they're fairly well off. Watkins' father provides the necessary financial backing and the right political connections. Garry's youthful good looks and his ability to pick up on popular causes account for his success at the polls.

"Rick, you must be wondering why we invited you here, so I'll get straight to the point. Biff and I have recently purchased the Tyler baseball franchise. Garry will receive a minority interest for his assistance in our negotiations, but he'll be strictly a silent partner. We're looking for a new manager. Wanted to see if you might be interested."

"The Trojans! You bought the Trojans?" I gasp in genuine amazement, baffled by his offer and wondering why anyone in their right mind would want to own a money-guzzling minor league base-ball club—a club that finished in the league cellar last season.

"Yes. And now we're looking for an innovative new manager—someone who can turn the team around, get our fans coming back to the ballpark."

"I'm flattered you men would consider me for the job, but you folks don't need a manager. You need a miracle worker. There's not a decent ball player on the squad. No one in their right mind would wanna manage that bunch of rag-tags."

"We understand the team has some problems, and we're pre-pared to invest a few dollars to acquire new players. Also, through a stroke of luck, we've secured a slot in the Big State League. Moving up to Class B should mean larger crowds, better attendance."

"Big State League? Yes, you're right. That's a darn sight better than the East Texas League. It also means tougher competition—Waco, Austin, Wichita Falls, Texarkana. If your club couldn't win playing Class C baseball, how do you expect to compete in the Big State League?"

"Better players, good coaching and more effective management should correct most of the problems the club experienced last season. We believe the franchise has a bright future. Biff and I are both civic minded. A winning baseball team will be good for business—bring Tyler some well-deserved recognition. And the publicity from a successful season might help me sell a few cars."

"Clyde, am I hearing this right? You're offering me the manager's job? Why would you want me? You know my history. I've been demoted and fired from my only two coaching jobs."

"Well, maybe—maybe not. Me and my partners aren't exactly together on this, at least not yet. Let's say we're here to feel you out— see what you think about the opportunity. We realize you've had a run of bad luck, but you've played in the big leagues. You have coaching experience. You understand how a professional baseball club works. You can recognize a quality ball player when you see one. And you're family. We can trust you to keep your mouth shut when you're told to."

"Family? Clyde, have you talked to your daughter recently? She's divorcing me. We're waiting on the judge to sign the final papers. She hasn't spoken to me since January."

"Yes, I know all that, but I'm not so sure she wants a divorce. She filed her lawsuit mainly out of spite—to get back at you. If you accept this manager's job and stop drinking yourself into an early grave, I expect Kaye can be convinced to drop her divorce action. All that can be addressed later. The question here is—are you interested in the job?"

"Clyde, your Trojan roster is already plum full of baseball rejects. I'd only add to your problems."

"Yes. Well, to be perfectly honest, you're not our first choice. The manager we had in mind turned us down late yesterday afternoon. With our regular season set to begin in less than two weeks, you might say we're eager to get the matter resolved. You're flat broke, unemployed and on the brink of a divorce. What we're offering here is a chance to turn your career around. You interested in the job, or not?" Segars' razor sharp voice reveals his frustration. He's obviously irritated by my lack of enthusiasm.

Eager? These three aren't eager—they're desperate. Otherwise I'd never have been invited here. Even so, it's apparent the offer is strictly Segars' brain child. Crawley and Watkins don't seem particularly delighted with the prospect of my managing their ball club. That's fine, because I also have reservations. What they're offering is a dead end—baseball suicide. If I accept and wind up being run off like last year's manager, I'll be branded with the stench of a loser. Managers with losing reputations usually have a heckava time landing another baseball job.

On the other hand, I have no prospects for a baseball job, or any job for that matter, and perhaps my father-in-law's intervention might reconcile my marital situation.

"Could I think on this? I need some time to consider the pros and cons."

"Certainly. You can have until Monday to think it over. It's imperative we have an answer by then. We're rather short on time."

"I don't suppose it matters, but I reckon I should ask. How much does the job pay?"

"Three hundred a month plus incentives."

"Incentives?"

"Yes. Three dollars a game for every game you win. A hundred-dollar bonus for a third place finish. Two hundred for a second. Five hundred for first."

"Looks like I'd be working for three hundred a month."

"That'll be strictly up to you. You'll be fired the day the Trojans fall ten games below five hundred."

"With the quality of players you have on board, I might not make it past the first month. Lemme think on it over the weekend, Clyde. I'll get back to you on Monday."

"Good enough. But we need a definite answer by Monday. The season starts a week from Tuesday. Whitey Waters has been managing the club during the exhibition season. He's agreed to take the job full time if you turn it down."

"Clyde, surely you wouldn't give the job to that old geezer. He must be pushing seventy."

"He's seventy-two, but he's still a good baseball man. Whitey and I go a long way back. If you accept the job, he'll be your assistant."

❖ ❖ ❖ ❖ ❖

A ONCE FIERY-WHITE sun is slowly changing to a dull, burnt-orange as I reach the outskirts of Canton. Sporadic stands of tall pine trees cast long shadows across the asphalt roadway. For a Saturday afternoon there's not much traffic. I shift the Pontiac into high gear and push down hard on the gas pedal. The speedometer needle inches past seventy.

Except for his promise to patch things up between Kaye and me, Segars offering me the Trojan manager's job would cause me to bolt for the nearest exit. Many of the colonel's enterprises border on being illegal. Getting mixed up in Segars' family business could land me in jail.

Damn. If she's so upset and heartbroken and missing me so much, how can she look so cool and collected—so ravishing. I'd almost forgotten how beautiful she is. No, that's a lie—she's never been out of my thoughts, not for a moment. Not since the day we stood naked in that ice-cold lake, and I pulled her warm body against me.

Maybe I should've stayed and tried to see her. No, I needed a drink. No way I'd get one there, not with Vic monitoring my every move.

Before I see her again, I've gotta sober up—lay off the hooch. Otherwise, even if her father can convince her to take me back, I'll have no chance of keeping her. When I get to Dallas, I'll call Paul. Once before he helped me stop drinking.

I reach for the half-empty whiskey bottle on the seat beside me, grab it by the neck, raise it to my lips, and take a long swallow. The alcohol burns my tongue then warms my insides as the fiery liquid travels downward into my stomach.

My visit to the Segars' mansion brought back a flood of painful memories. Memories that maybe should've stayed buried. I needed a drink bad. Tyler's a dry city, but a dedicated boozer can always find a bottle—if he's willing to pay the price.

I lift the whisky jug for another swallow. The bottle barely touches my lips when I notice the flashing red lights atop the patrol car pulling up behind me.

CHAPTER TWO

SUNDAY MORNING in the Van Zandt County jail is no picnic. The accommodations rank considerably below four-star. My back aches. I feel like death warmed over. It's not the whiskey. I could handle that. These past three months, since Kaye walked out on me, I've grown accustomed to waking up with a hangover. My grievance is a lack of sleep. Trying to nap on the thin lumpy mattress would've been tough enough, but the black guy locked in the cell next to mine kept me awake most of the night with his wheezing and coughing.

A bright morning sun is beginning to peek through the steel bars of my cell window when the Negro rolls over and sits up. The man coughs to clear his throat and spits the mucus residue on the concrete floor. Muttering something inaudible, he rises to his feet, staggers across his cell, and proceeds to relieve himself into a badly stained open toilet.

"You been here all night, mister?" the man inquires, noticing me lying on the bed in the adjacent cell.

"Yeah, I was here when they brought you in. Must've been about midnight. Don't you remember?"

"No sir. When I go off on a drunk, I don't hardly ever remember a thing. Was I ranting and raving, or was I meek like a lamb?"

15

"You were barely conscious when the two deputies dragged you in and laid you on the bunk. I suppose you were meek like a lamb."

"Good. Sometimes when I've been ranting and going on real bad the judge makes me stay 'til Tuesday. I got a job I gotta be working on Monday. What'd they get you for?"

"Drinking and driving under the influence. My name's Rick," I answer, rolling over to sit up on my bed and face the man. My stomach growls. A malicious pang of hunger reminds me I haven't eaten since yesterday morning.

"Big Luke here. You look familiar, Rick. This your first time in jail?"

"First time in Canton's jail. I'm kinda hungry. You know what time they serve breakfast?" I ask, assuming the man is a regular patron.

"The jailer's wife usually brings in some dry toast and a pot of hot coffee around nine. She ain't much of a cook, so the toast is generally burnt. Judge King, he'll be here sometime before ten to set our fines. Your trial won't take long. The judge likes to be in church for the eleven o'clock service."

"How does the judge feel about drunk drivers?" I ask apprehensively. Luke seems to be acquainted with the local judicial system. It's possible the county has some standard punishment for crimes like mine. Knowing what to expect might ease my anxiety about facing the judge.

"The judge, he don't take kindly to drunk drivers, especially ones from outta town. He could put you on a work gang for a few days, but if you can pay in cash, I expect he'll just pop you with a stiff fine. The county don't collect much in taxes, so they need the money. They got bills to pay like everyone else, so hard cash talks real loud."

Luke's conjecture about my fate deflates my already low spirit. If the judge socks me with a fine and demands it be paid in cash, I'll have no choice except to call Paul and ask him to come bail me out. He'll come, and he won't be critical or ask a bunch of embarrassing questions. I don't know why that should matter. Paul already knows I'm a hopeless drunk. Still, I hate to tell him I've let him down again. He's tried so hard to steer me back onto the straight and narrow.

Regardless of my reservations, I'll make the call. A rough, sleepless night in jail resolved the debate raging inside my head. Now my mind is made up about the Trojan manager's job. It's imperative I get released today. Like the big fellow in the next cell, I got a job I gotta be working on Monday.

❖ ❖ ❖ ❖ ❖

"TWO HUNDRED DOLLARS! Judge, there's no way. No way I can come up with two hundred dollars."

"Two hundred dollars or sixty days, young man. You Dallas people gotta learn you can't come racing through Van Zandt County, driving like a bat outta hell and drunk as a hoot owl. We have women and children to protect."

"Yes sir, and I appreciate your position. But I'm not some rich city slicker from Dallas. I'm just an ordinary working stiff, and I'm broke as a skunk. Maybe we can work something out. How about reducing my fine and giving me some time to pay? I have a job waiting in Tyler. Supposed to start work tomorrow. Wouldn't you rather I pay the fine instead of sitting in jail with the county footing the bill for keeping me fed?" I rationalize, hoping to appeal to the judge's avidity. Big Luke said the county needs money.

"Tyler? Well now, that might make a difference. Tyler's a fine city, full of decent people and so many wonderful old churches. Where'll you be working?"

"For the Tyler baseball club. I'll be managing the Trojans this season."

"Then you're a baseball player?"

"Well, I was a player, played second base for the Cleveland Indians until I wrecked my knee two summers ago. Nowadays I'm trying to make it back to the big leagues as a coach."

"So you don't actually have a legitimate job?"

"No. I mean yes, I do. The Trojan position is a steady job. Regular paycheck once a month. I'll be able to send you something toward paying off my fine the first of every month."

"As I recall, the Trojans played baseball on Sunday last year. You people planning to play on Sunday again this year?"

"Yes, your honor. But we play on Sunday afternoons, after church services are over. All the clubs in the Big State League play on Sunday," I answer dejectedly. I'm fairly certain where this conversation is headed. Luke said the judge likes to be in church on Sunday morning. He failed to mention the man is a religious fanatic.

A troubled magistrate peers down at me from behind his judicial bench. Sincere compassion fills his eyes while he carefully considers my plea. "You have my deepest sympathy, young man. You've cut yourself out a mighty 'tough row to hoe.' But I can't condone your lifestyle—drinking, driving too fast, playing baseball on Sundays. How long has it been since you attended church?"

"Uh, well, I attend when I can. I'd like to be in church every Sunday, but playing baseball keeps me on the road. I move around a lot, from team to team, can't seem to get settled into a regular church," I lie. Actually, I haven't attended a church service in years, not since college, and then only on the occasions when Coach Falk mandated our entire Longhorn ball club attend as a group.

The judge rubs at his chin while he considers my statement. Arriving at a decision, he reaches for his gavel and leans forward. His booming voice resonates through the courtroom as he pronounces my sentence.

"Son, you're headed straight for hell. I'm gonna do you a big favor and give you some time to reconsider accepting that job. Two hundred dollars! Pay the jailer in cash by five o'clock, or spend the next sixty nights in our jailhouse."

Presuming he's had a hand in saving my soul, a sly smile creeps across the magistrate's face. Judge King is obviously pleased with his decision. He slams his gavel down hard against the top of his desk, emphasizing his absolute authority and ceasing any further argument on my behalf.

❖ ❖ ❖ ❖ ❖

KEYS JINGLE, and the shrill ring of steel banging against steel reverberates through the prison as the jailer unlocks the iron door at the end of the corridor and shoves it open. Like a child fascinated with a favorite toy, he swings his huge ring of keys back and forth while he ambles down the open hallway. Evidently he's coming to see me. All the other cells are empty. Big Luke made his exit several hours ago. The judge fined him five bucks and set him free.

"You have a friend downstairs, Mason. He paid your fine," the jailer informs me. He rummages through his keys and unlocks my cell door.

I roll over and sit up on the edge of my bed. The cold shock of the concrete floor against my stocking feet reminds me my shoes are stashed beneath the bed. "Does that mean I can leave now?"

"Yeah, you're free as a bird. But I'd suggest you hurry before Judge King gets wind. He called right before your friend arrived. Told me he'd been worrying over your situation during church service. Wanted to know if you were still here. He's planning to contact the Baptist minister and have him come pray with you. The judge is a good man. Takes his responsibility very serious. If he thought you might leave before the preacher gets in his licks, he'd probably be inclined to change your sentence."

"Hey, thanks. Last thing I need from this one horse town is another sermon. Once I collect my personal stuff and repossess my Pontiac, I'm outta here. Any chance my car can be released today?"

"No problem. Your car's parked in the city pound over on Terrell Street, a block off the square. The keys are in my desk downstairs. How about you get a move on before the preacher shows up. Your pal Matlock is waiting to make sure you get out."

"I'm right behind you. Soon as I slip on my shoes."

Paul Matlock is my AA sponsor. Our Dallas group meets in a small house located in the Lakewood area. The members have a simple goal and only one purpose: "to live one more day—sober." I met Paul almost a year ago inside the drunk tank at the Fort Worth city jail. He and another AA comrade had come to retrieve a friend who'd fallen off the wagon. At the time my baseball career had hit rock bottom. A knee injury ended my career as a major league player. Then my dream of becoming a big league manager vanished—lost somewhere inside the taverns of New York, Boston, Chicago and Detroit—the pubs and night clubs where we celebrated every hit and every victory and mourned every out and every loss.

When Paul found me, I was sleeping off another of what was too frequently becoming "another night on the town." My career had hit the skids. My marriage was on the rocks. My string of luck had run out. The hotshot golden boy, who once could do no wrong, had screwed up his perfect life. After only one season as a rookie member on the Cleveland coaching staff, I'd been demoted and reassigned to serve as an assistant coach for their Fort Worth minor league affiliate. I was working hard at messing up that job.

Paul is a mechanical engineer, educated in Houston at Rice University. When it comes to crunching numbers and applying scientific formulas, he's an absolute genius, but he's a drunk, just like me. Paul was once vice-president of a successful Dallas manu-facturing corporation. His company was listed on the stock exchange. He had the world by the tail—everything going for him—a lovely wife and two terrific children. That was six years ago. Before he hit bottom, he lost his job and his family. All his assets were awarded to his wife in the divorce settlement. Paul wound up dead broke. Best job he could find was pumping gas at a convenience store.

These days Paul's sober. He's employed by a Dallas plumbing contractor, preparing bids for new projects and solving their con-struction problems. Incomewise, he's back in a comfort zone, but since he's paid by the hour, it's unlikely he's reached a financial bracket where taxes are much of a bother. His ex-wife still hates his guts, but his kids are beginning to talk to him again.

"Hi, Paul. Thanks for coming."

"We gotta quit meeting like this, Rick. I can't afford it."

"I'm sorry, Paul. This'll be the last time. Starting today, I'm gonna stop drinking, and I'll pay you back every last cent. I promise. I've landed a job—a baseball job—managing the Tyler Trojans."

Paul's facial expression suggests he's not impressed. He's heard similar promises regarding my drinking habit before.

"This time I'm serious. I'll pay back every dollar. Honest I will," I reiterate, trying to convince him, and at the same time realizing he could care less about the money. Paul's told me many times he doesn't care about money anymore. He swears he's satisfied with being sober and working steady. Still, I feel guilty accepting his charity without offering to pay him back.

"I'm sure you have the best of intentions, Rick, but you don't have to pay me back. Once we have you dried out, I'll expect you to help some other fellow straighten out his life. That's the one obligation I ask you to honor. You sober enough to drive, or you want to ride back to Dallas with me?"

"I'm okay to drive. Haven't had a drink since yesterday. My Pontiac's parked in the city pound. The jailer says it's within easy walking distance."

"Rick, our Sunday night meeting begins at six. You oughta start attending on a regular basis—use the group for support. That's the only way you'll ever lick your drinking problem. Believe me. I've been there. How about tonight? Can you come?"

The prospect of spending a chummy evening with an odd assembly of reformed drunks is less than appealing, but how can I refuse? It darn sure beats suffering through another sleepless night in Canton's penal facility. And without my friend's benevolence, I'd be sequestered here for the next sixty days and forced to listen while an overzealous preacher prays for my miserable soul.

"I've had a rough day, Paul. Lemme run by my apartment and clean up first. I'll meet you there."

"Fine. And no stops for a quick snort on your way home. Okay?"

"No stops, Paul. Trust me. I'll be at the meeting. You can count on it."

My friend and benefactor waits patiently while the jailer hustles me through his checkout routine. I sign the release documents, retrieve my wallet, a few coins of loose change and my car keys then rejoin Paul in the visitor's lobby. We hike side-by-side down a poorly lit corridor, navigate a narrow flight of steps down to the ground floor and exit through a side entrance.

During the short hike we hardly speak, but before we part company on the courthouse lawn, I thank Paul again and shake his hand, promising to see him at the AA meeting.

A cool afternoon breeze ripples the fresh new leaves of the huge oak trees which encompass the courthouse square. Breathing in deeply, a strange exuberance overwhelms me. I pause to savor the gorgeous day and cherish my newfound freedom. Winter is gone. Cold, miserable winter weather is behind us. Fond memories of happier times and baseball games, played and won, on warm spring days flood my mind, making my personal troubles seem insignificant.

A losing team, rag-tag players, poor facilities—if you're playing the game you love, why should that matter? Spring and a brand new season have arrived. It's time to play baseball. I can hardly wait.

Impulsively, I glance back toward the courthouse lawn, wanting to share my feelings of joy. Paul hasn't moved from the spot where we said our goodbyes. His head is lowered. His lips move in silent prayer. He's either asking for divine help or offering up a prayer on my behalf.

❖ ❖ ❖ ❖ ❖

FOR THE PAST THREE MONTHS, since Kaye left me and moved back to Tyler, I've been living in a two-room furnished apartment on Gaston Avenue in Dallas. My apartment is one of four units heartlessly carved out of an aged two-story house, which not long ago was a proud single family residence. Up until the mid-forties this was the home of a well-to-do family who owned and operated a retail clothing shop in downtown Dallas. Now the once affluent neighborhood has degenerated into a sad state of disrepair. Businesses which prospered downtown have relocated to new shopping strips in the suburbs. Most of the original families have moved out. Many of the fine old homes have been converted into rental properties.

The crunch of my car tires grinding down the gravel driveway prompts my landlady's appearance at the window of her ground floor apartment. She pulls back her drapes, peeks out and waves to me. My rent is past due. She'll be knocking on my door shortly, asking why I haven't paid. It's a question I've been trying to avoid, but the answer is elementary. I simply have no money.

I park the Pontiac and step swiftly across the yard to my quarters at the rear of the house. If I hurry, maybe I can avoid her suspicious eyes and sharp tongue for another day. Tomorrow morning when I call my father-in-law, I'll ask for a pay advance. Hopefully, he'll loan me enough money to pay off my Dallas bills. I'd like to depart with a clean slate. Sneaking out, owing a bunch of debts, is not my style.

Once inside, I purposely leave the lights turned off. My landlady is persistent but hardly brave. Faced with the prospect of entering a single man's darkened apartment, she might consider postponing her visit.

My living room floor is covered with week-old newspapers and mini-piles of assorted trash. A plate of half-eaten food and two empty bourbon bottles embellish the coffee table which sits cocked at an angle in front of a shabby cloth couch. I've never been a world-class housekeeper, but Vic's urgent, no-nonsense wedding invitation yesterday morning gave me precious little time to tidy up before I left for Tyler.

My body teems with the stench of my own perspiration. After a restless night in a warm, humid cell and two days without a shower, I stink worse than the visitor's locker room in mid-August. I head straight for the shower, shedding my shirt and pants, leaving them strewed on the bedroom floor where they fall.

Inside the bathroom, I turn on the faucet, adjust the temperature, strip off my shorts and slip inside. The rush of warm water instantly lifts my spirits, temporarily washing away a nagging anxiety that's hounded me since my meeting with Segars yesterday afternoon—a premonition that some terrible tragedy lies ahead.

Heck, why should I worry? What could possibly happen that's worse than what I've been through? Haven't I scooped bottom and tasted the bitter scum? Haven't I wrestled with the devil and survived? Okay, so maybe I didn't win. So I screwed up my knee and messed up my coaching jobs. So I lost my girl. Hey, I'm alive, and I'm back in baseball. The Trojan manager's job is my chance to start over—get my life back on track. It's not too late. I have a dream, and I'm not giving it up.

❖ ❖ ❖ ❖ ❖

AFTER A NIGHT without sleep, the last place I want to go is an AA meeting. The nauseating smoke, the senseless chatter, and everyone seems so damn happy, so satisfied just to be sober. I'd prefer to stretch out on the couch, maybe turn on the radio and listen to a ball game, but I promised Paul I'd attend. It would be shameful to let him down again.

Anyway, if I want my wife back, I need to quit drinking and dry out. Why not start tonight? Tomorrow morning I'll call Segars and accept his job offer. If he knew where I spent my weekend, I doubt if he'd still hire me.

❖ ❖ ❖ ❖ ❖

MY AA GROUP meets in a single story wood frame house on Richmond Street in the Lakewood area. The building belongs to one of our more affluent members. He allows the group to use the place without charge.

A short column of automobiles are lined along the front curb. Even though it's not quite dark, a light shines above the doorway on the front porch. The light indicates a meeting is in progress. Pulling the Pontiac up behind a beat-up '48 Ford at the rear of the line, I park, lock the door, and hurry up the front walk. I'm running late on purpose. I despise these meetings. Everyone is so darn sober, and the conversations are boring. You seldom find anyone who wants to talk sports. All these people seem to talk about is how long it's been since they've had a drink.

Maybe I shouldn't be critical. Most likely every man here slept in his own bed last night.

Inside, the meeting room is filled with the rancid smell of coffee. A thin cloud of cigarette smoke hangs overhead, pushing against the ceiling. A majority of these chapter members are heavy smokers. They use a smoking habit as a crutch, substituting their addiction to alcohol with an addiction to cigarettes. Perhaps smoking is the lesser evil. Dying of lung cancer in a clean hospital bed is decidedly preferable to having your throat slit while you lie alone and dead-drunk in some dark, rat-infested alley.

Paul spots me at the doorway and waves. He grabs Bill Wyler's arm, and they hasten over to welcome me.

"Hello, Rick. Good to see you again. We're glad you could come. Haven't seen you in quite awhile," Bill says cheerfully while he shakes my hand warmly.

"I've been busy. Been out of town interviewing for some coaching jobs," I reply, telling a half-truth.

"That's terrific, Rick. You have any luck? I know you've been out of work."

"Yep, looks like I landed a job managing the Tyler baseball club. I'm supposed to call the owners tomorrow and give them an answer. If they meet my salary demands, I plan to start working right away. The Trojans are only a minor league outfit, but I reckon a job's a job."

"Tyler? Aren't they in the East Texas League with Longview and Marshall? Seems like I remember they had a rough season last year."

"You've got a good memory, Bill. I didn't realize you were a baseball fan. Yes, Tyler played in the East Texas League last season. The Trojans really stunk it up. Finished in last place. But this year they're moving up to the Big State League. That's why the owners are after me. Actually, I'm kinda looking forward to it. It'll be a real challenge to get the ball club turned around."

Wyler smiles and nods his head to agree and mutters something about a recent newspaper article he's read describing challenges in the workplace. He's obviously not a baseball fan. The question he's dying to ask is how I could sink so low I'd pursue the Trojan job. When he realizes he's losing my interest, he recovers quickly.

"I believe we have a chapter in Tyler. Before you leave tonight, I'll get you the name and phone number of a contact person."

25

"Thanks, Bill, I'd appreciate that. I hate to leave this Dallas group. You folks have helped me through some tough times. But now that I have my drinking under control, maybe I can pitch in and help the group down there."

"We'll miss you too, Rick. I'm excited about your new job. I hope you do well. You know you're always welcome here. You staying sober?"

"You better believe it, and I intend to stay that way."

Knowing Paul, I doubt if he's told Bill about bailing me out of the Canton jail. AA members are usually tight-lipped. Nevertheless, Wyler's eyes can't hide his skepticism.

Damn. Why is it so difficult to admit I have an addiction I can't control, a habit that's destroying my life? Why is it so hard to admit I'm a drunk?

From the speaker's podium a gavel raps twice, calling the meeting to order. Paul, Bill and I abandon our strained conversation and scurry to find a seat among the rows of folding chairs which face the raised platform.

"Good evening, people. My name is Jeff. I'm a drunk, and I've been sober for 873 days."

The president's announcement is greeted with loud cheers as members stand and applaud his confession. From their reaction, you'd think the man had just belted a grand slam homer in the ninth inning of the world series.

Perhaps he's achieved a more commendable goal. He's stayed sober for one more day.

CHAPTER THREE

"OPERATOR, I want to place a station-to-station call to Tyler. The number is 5566."

Having squandered the last of my folding money on Saturday's pint of bootleg whiskey, I have only a few coins left. So I'm taking a gamble. Calling station-to-station will cost less, but there's a possibility someone on my father-in-law's staff will answer and put me on hold. That would wipe out the last of my meager funds and eliminate any chance of my paying for this call. Even after Segars comes on the line, I'll need to talk fast.

"Please wait, while I ring," the operator tells me.

Clicking noises echo over the line then a buzzing sound, indicating the phone on the other end is ringing.

"Segars' DeSoto Mart," a male voice answers. The voice is friendly but unfamiliar. It's probably some salesman on the showroom floor. Under my breath I curse at my bad luck.

The operator interrupts, "Deposit thirty-five cents please." I insert a quarter and two nickels into the pay phone coin slots.

"Hello," I say, shouting into the mouthpiece. A delivery truck roars past on the street next to the phone booth. I cup a hand over my unoccupied ear to block out the road noise. "This is Rick Mason. I need to speak to Clyde Segars. Can you connect me?"

"Hey, Rick. Larry Holmes here. Long time no see. How you been?"

For reasons beyond my comprehension, my father-in-law keeps several high school students on his payroll. Maybe it makes good business sense. Maybe it connects him to the younger generation. Maybe the students work cheap. Whatever the case, the DeSoto dealership is a favorite hangout for the Rose City's teenage male population. The young people enjoy the mechanical environment and the occasional thrill of being the first to see new cars arrive. But the primary attraction is that Segars allows a few of his regular student employees to commandeer his wreckers when they respond to police calls. It's not uncommon for as many as five wild-eyed young men to be piled inside one of his oversized wreckers while they speed breakneck to the scene of an automobile accident.

Larry Holmes has been working for the Segars family since his junior high years. Because he's one of a select few who've been sanctioned to pilot a company wrecker, he commands enormous respect among his male peers.

"Hi, Larry. Listen, can we visit later? I need to speak with Mister Segars. This is urgent. I'm calling from a pay phone, and I don't have much change. Can you get him on the line?"

"Sure thing, Rick. I believe he's in his office. Gimme a second, and I'll connect you."

"Thanks Larry. I'll drop in to visit after I get situated. If the colonel hasn't changed his mind, I'll be managing the Trojans this summer."

"You're moving back to Tyler? Well I'll be danged. That oughta start a lot of tongues wagging. When you coming back?"

"Maybe today. It depends on what Clyde has to say. How about putting me through?"

"Oh, yeah. Check you later, Rick."

The phone clicks and seemingly goes dead. My hopes for a quick, productive phone conversation diminish. Larry Holmes is a good kid, but like any other teenager, he can be an absolute klutz. Apparently he's cut me off.

A voice answers as I'm about to hang up. "Hello, Rick. Clyde Segars here. I was wondering if you were gonna call."

"Hello, Clyde. I've been thinking about your offer. If the manager's job is still available, I'd like to give it a shot."

"Wonderful. My partners and I talked it over after you left. I can't say they were delighted with the prospect of hiring you, but we're in kind of a pickle. They finally agreed you were the best candidate available. The job is yours if you want it."

Nothing like being told flat out you're the last possible choice. Oh well, it could work in my favor. Maybe they won't be so quick to fire me when the team does poorly.

"Fine. I'll take it. When do you want me to start?"

"Right away. The team's been on the road playing preseason games at Beaumont and Shreveport. They arrived back in Tyler late last night. Whitey called early this morning. He has a rookie tryout session scheduled for nine o'clock tomorrow morning. Tells me he's gonna be shorthanded. Any chance you can be here to help out?"

"No problem. I have some business here in Dallas to take care of, but there's no reason I can't be in Tyler tomorrow morning."

"Good. Be sure and check in with me the minute you arrive. We can talk more then. I have to go. Got another phone call waiting."

"No. No. Don't hang up. Clyde, I'm broke. I owe on my rent, and I need some traveling money. Could wire me an advance on my salary?"

A long, awkward stretch of silence infers my father-in-law isn't pleased. I can hear Segars breathing while he considers my fate.

"Clyde? You still there?"

"Yes, I'm here. How much do you need this time?" His barbed tone signifies his indignation. No doubt he's recalling past occasions when I've hit on him for a loan and never paid him back.

"Two hundred dollars," I answer timidly. Actually a hundred would do me. I owe my landlady sixty dollars. Another thirty will pay off my remaining debts, leaving me ten bucks for gas, but in matters of finance, I've learned to allow plenty of room for negotiation.

"Two hundred! Good Lord, man. You think money grows on trees down here?"

"That's how much I need. Surely you don't want me worrying about money, not while I'm getting your baseball team ready to compete in a new league?" I rationalize, appealing to his business sense, trying to hold my ground without ticking him off. My father-in-law has a very short fuse.

"Two hundred dollars is a hellava lot of money, Rick. I'm taking a big gamble on you as it is. My partners think I'm loco, hiring an out-of-work coach with a drinking problem."

"I'm a reformed man. No more drinking. Your money won't be wasted on booze. I promise."

"Alright, I suppose I have to trust you. But let's not make this a habit. I can't have you constantly hounding me for money. Payday for the rest of the team comes on the first of each month. Even though you're family, I'll expect you to abide by the same rules. You'll receive your next paycheck just like the players—on the first of May, less this two hundred advance. Do you hear me, Rick? I want to make myself perfectly clear—no more advances."

"Sure, Clyde. I won't let you down. This'll be the last time I ask for money. You got my word on it."

"Fine. I'll hold you to that. Where do I send the money?"

"Western Union Office, on Main Street, downtown Dallas."

"It'll be there today. I'll have my girl take care of it. Anything else? I need to go."

"Thanks, Clyde. I really appreciate. . ."

The phone line goes dead before I can finish, leaving me talking into a disconnected receiver.

If I was having second thoughts about the Trojan manager's job, my brief conversation with Segars does nothing to raise my expectations. I hang up, shove my hands into my trouser pockets, and stroll across the sidewalk toward the Pontiac. My three remaining coins jingle through my fingers, reminding me how perilously close I am to absolute poverty.

❖ ❖ ❖ ❖ ❖

SINCE THERE ARE few Tyler homes where I'd be a welcome guest, I postponed my departure until this morning. By staying one last night in Dallas, I avoid the expense of a motel room and preserve a few of the precious dollars remaining from Segars' advance.

Tyler is less than ninety miles from Dallas, but if you observe the speed limits, slowing to a crawl while you pass through each small town, it's a good two-hour drive. To make sure I'll arrive in Tyler before nine o'clock, I leave Dallas at dawn.

Early morning is my favorite time to travel. Because there's hardly any traffic, you can often cruise along for miles without seeing another car. The cool, damp air carries an exhilarating fresh smell, like the world has been rejuvenated and is anxious to begin a new day. Maybe this manager's job will do that for me—rejuvenate my tarnished career—give me a brand-new start—put my heartaches and disappointments behind me.

Honoring his promise, Segars wired me the two hundred Monday afternoon. The first sixty went to pay my overdue rent. My suspicious landlady accepted my payment grudgingly, arguing that I owed a late charge. When I informed her I'd be vacating the premises immediately, she capitulated and accepted the money without further debate. She seemed delighted with my news—most likely relieved because she'll no longer have to chase me down to collect her rent.

Using the Seven/Eleven pay phone, I called Paul's office to say goodbye, but he was out, probably solving a mind-boggling problem on some construction project. I left a message with his company secretary, promising I'd contact him once I get settled in Tyler. I gave her the phone number of Segars' DeSoto dealership in case he wants to get in touch.

Generally, rookie tryouts are a waste of everyone's time. All the quality players have been scouted, contacted and signed long before now. And since no self-respecting veteran would dare come near the ballpark during rookie tryouts, every player who shows up will be a green amateur. Possibly a few of the rookies will have played a year of college ball, but the majority will be fresh out of high school.

Despite the overwhelming odds, every young man will be gushing with aspirations of catching on with a professional team, hoping to eventually make it to the major leagues. The chances are slim, but occasionally, a raw jewel is uncovered—an honest-to-god baseball player who's been overlooked by the scouts.

Our veterans will report back on Thursday. With our first regular season game scheduled next Tuesday, I have less than a week to check out the players and set a lineup. That's the curse of Class B baseball. There's never enough time. The sole redeeming consolation is that none of the other Big State clubs have it any better. Actually, every minor league team is forced to play the same gut-wrenching game, waiting to see which players become available after teams in higher classifications make their final cuts. The key to a successful season is to make good decisions in the short time remaining.

By Thursday, Whitey and I should have culled through the rookies. Chances are not more than one or two of the youngsters trying out today will be invited to join our roster. Even the ones we do keep won't play much. They'll be paid a minimum salary of eight dollars a game. With a season of a hundred-forty-seven games, that boils down to less than twelve hundred dollars total pay—less than two-fifty a month for working seven days a week—and they'll earn that only if they stick with the club for the entire summer.

Trojan Field is situated some two miles west of Tyler's downtown business district, near the end of Houston Street where it dead ends into the East Texas Fairgrounds. The grandstands, press box, and dressing quarters were completely rebuilt after the aged facility burned to the ground in August of 1948. Even so, the stadium still needs a myriad of minor repairs, but compared to the baseball diamonds some Class B teams call home and considering the bleachers can seat more than four thousand fans, it's not all that bad.

A steel-trussed, metal roof extends from the back of the grandstands out to a point midway above the bleacher seats. Private box seating, which is separated from the bottom row of bleacher seats by a wide aisle, extends along both the first and third base lines. Each private box is equipped with permanent individual chairs. Snuggled against the grandstands on the first base line is the home team dugout. The visitor's dugout is on the third base side. Both dugouts are roofed with galvanized metal—to shield team members from the blistering Texas sun and occasionally from the wrath of angry, over-wrought baseball fans.

Underlying a thin layer of fine sand which blankets the infield is a crust of rock-hard red clay which will peel the hide off your buttocks, like a sharp-toothed knife skins a raw potato. The base paths of Trojan Field are sufficiently hazardous to cause even the most fearless base runner to think twice before sacrificing his body in a hard slide.

Sparse patches of grass struggle to survive in the outfield. By midsummer most of the outfield vegetation will wither and turn the color of pancake batter. In past seasons the scrooges who owned the Tyler franchise initiated a firm ground maintenance policy—water as seldom as possible.

❖ ❖ ❖ ❖ ❖

ALTHOUGH OUR TRYOUT SESSION is officially scheduled to begin at nine, more than twenty cars are already crowded into the parking spaces near the entrance gate. Intermittent, sharp popping sounds of baseballs pounding against leather gloves reverberate from behind the ten-foot-high rock fence which surrounds the field. My dashboard clock indicates it's only eight-thirty. Evidently I'm not the only one who's stricken with baseball fever.

Coasting to a stop, I shut off the engine and hop into the back seat. Whitey has a phobia about missing equipment. He also pos-sesses the only set of keys to the Trojan locker room. With so many strange faces on hand for the tryouts, there's not a chance he'd leave the dressing quarters unlocked. I slip into cleated shoes and workout sweats then lock my car doors and jog to the front gate.

Inside the ballpark a horde of eager, anxious young men populate the baseball diamond. I pause for a few seconds, suppressing a smile while I survey the hodgepodge of mismatched, but colorful, baseball garb worn by the youngsters, musing how each player agonized over his selection of apparel—trying to choose the precise outfit which might attract maximum attention from the Trojan coaches.

Over in right field another group is circled about a tall, rail-thin man who is directing them through a series of throw and catch drills. Thick locks of unruly white hair protrude from beneath the instructor's solid black ball cap. The man in charge is my assistant manager. I trot over to check in with him.

"Good morning, Whitey. Looks like we've got a good turnout."

"Hey there, Rick. Heard a car drive up. I was hoping it might be you. Yep, I expect we may have as many as thirty show up before we get up and runnin'," Whitey replies, welcoming me with a wide smile.

"You have anyone besides us coming to help? Thirty's more than the two of us can handle."

"Nope, couldn't find anyone who was willing. Even contacted the high school to see if Coach Hennig might come, but he begged off. His high school club's battling it out, trying to win their district championship. Told me that's all the baseball he can handle right now."

"How about your regulars? Any of them willing to help out?"

"Naw, that'd be counterproductive. They'd be worried we might run across a rookie who'd steal their job. I'm afraid it's gonna be just you and me, Rick."

"Alright, we'll make do with what we got. I haven't thrown a baseball since last summer. You suppose we can find some volunteers to pitch batting practice?"

"That won't be no problem. I already lined up a couple of pitchers. They're rarin' to go."

The beauty of rookie tryouts is there's never a lack of enthusiasm. Most of the players who tryout have neither the talent nor the personal stamina to endure a long summer of professional level baseball, but every kid arrives here with a dream, believing that deep down inside himself there's a Stan Musial or a Bob Feller waiting to be discovered. It'll take less than an hour to determine which youngsters possess the ability to make our squad. We'll ask those people to come back tomorrow morning for a closer look. But we'll keep the entire group on the ballfield demonstrating their skills until sometime after one o'clock. We owe these young men a good show. It would be bad P.R. to have anyone leave here thinking he got short changed.

Another significant aspect of today's event is to see that every participant leaves here excited about baseball and anxious to tell friends and family how the Trojan coaches liked his style—how he was invited to tryout again next year. It won't necessarily be a lie. With a year of seasoning, possibly one or two of these young players might make next summer's club. Perhaps a few of the hopefuls will coax their family or girlfriends out to watch a game this summer. We darn sure need the fans.

❖ ❖ ❖ ❖ ❖

A FIERY-HOT MORNING SUN beats down from overhead when Whitey motions for me to come observe his batting practice. I'm delighted to accommodate. The insufferable heat and humidity have taken their toll. My butt is dragging. My arms ache from hitting fly balls to our outfielders. I send my players scurrying toward the dugout fountains for a water break and jog over to the batting cage.

"What's on your mind, Whitey? You find us a slugger?" I inquire, dropping down on one knee to rest beside the old man.

"Not really. More like I found someone who can't hit. Take a look at this kid who's up to bat. He's a super little infielder, covers second base like a vacuum."

Whitey and I kneel together to watch a stocky youngster taking his turn in the batting cage. On the pitching mound behind a protective wire shield, a tall red-faced chap performs the pitching chores. Using the sleeve of his jersey, the pitcher wipes at beads of sweat streaming down his forehead then winds and fires a fastball across the middle of the plate. Whitey's squatty kid fouls it off.

"Don't see nothing exciting here, Whitey. This fellow couldn't hit his way out of a wet paper bag."

"You see how he swings his bat, Rick? Notice how he rotates his hands and kinda pushes the bat forward. Never saw anyone who could make such good contact swinging a bat that way."

"I oughta get back to my outfielders. Still have a few guys I haven't checked out yet."

"Humor me here, Rick. I'm formulating a plan. Stay and watch my man for another couple of swings."

"Okay, but if he don't show me something quick, I gotta go."

Whitey cups his hands around his mouth and yells at the lanky pitcher, "Throw him a breaking ball! Give 'em the best you got. Let's see if young Henry can hit a curve."

The red-faced pitcher has fairly good stuff. He throws three consecutive hard breaking curves. Each pitch is a strike, each barely nipping the outside corner of home plate. Taking a full cut, the batter swings hard. His bat catches a piece of each pitch, sending the baseball bouncing foul outside the base lines.

"Whitey, I gotta get back to my outfielders. You might ask that elongated redhead out there to come back tomorrow. The kid who's batting needs to find himself a paying job. He ain't no hitter. That's for sure."

"Hey, batter! The manager wants to talk with ya. Come over here," Whitey yells, ignoring my snide remark.

"Whitey, are you nuts? You're gonna embarrass the kid. What the heck are you up to? You guys kin or something?"

"No, but something tells me this youngun's a player. Wait a minute and talk to him."

Responding to Whitey's request, the young man rushes over. His face is flushed, and he's breathing hard. Not only is this youngster a poor hitter, he's also in sad physical condition. To qualify for our tryouts, a player must be a graduating high school senior or older. This rookie's clean-cut boyish face makes him seem much younger. I doubt if he's celebrated his eighteenth birthday.

"You wanna see me, Coach?" the young man questions, wheezing as if he's short of breath.

"Sure do. What's your name, son?" Whitey asks.

"Henry. Henry French."

"You play ball before?"

"Yes sir. Played for Van High School this spring. We finished second in our district."

"What'd you hit? What was your batting average?" I ask, barging into the conversation, hoping the answer will put an end to Whitey's ridiculous obsession.

"Batted zero. Never got a hit all season, but my coach played me in every game. Didn't make but two fielding errors all season."

"Only two errors? That's pretty impressive, but you say you never got a hit? That's not so good." Turning to Whitey, I offer a condescending smile and say, "You see. I was right. He can't hit squat. We got no place for a kid who can't hit."

"Never made an out either, Coach Mason."

"You never made an out, and you never got a hit. But you just told us you played in every game. That don't figure, son."

"I walked. I truly did, Coach. I got on base every single time I went to bat," young French informs me, trumping my allegation regarding his hitting ability.

A smug grin creeps onto Whitey's dark, suntanned face while he watches the boy's testament sink in on me. Wheels inside my brain whirl furiously, trying to calculate how many trips this young man could make to the plate in one hundred and forty-seven games, batting lead-off for our Trojans.

Now I understand what my assistant has in mind. Maybe, just maybe, we've found our jewel.

❖ ❖ ❖ ❖ ❖

"HEY, RICK. I'm leaving. I left the front door key laying on the desk in your office. Be sure and lock up. There's a lot of valuable equipment in here. Be mighty hard to replace."

"Sure thing, Whitey. I won't be long. Clyde is expecting me. Asked me to check in with him as soon as we finished. He's anxious about the tryouts."

"I've been bunking down at the Y. If you need a place to sleep tonight, they've got a vacancy. For a buck a night, it's the best deal in town. It ain't fancy, but it's clean."

"Thanks, Whitey. Lemme talk with Segars first. I wanna make certain he doesn't have something else in mind."

"Right. Maybe I'll see you later. Don't forget to lock up."

We cut the rookies loose shortly before one o'clock. Then Whitey and I lingered in the dugout, first catching up on each other's history, then talking about our prospects. When our conversation shifted to practice schedules and uniforms, we moved our discussion into the locker room. Whitey escorted me on a quick cook's tour of the facilities, proudly pointing out how he's sorted through the uniforms and every piece of equipment, cataloged each item, and stored them according to size and type.

Whitey was an assistant baseball coach and one of my favorite people when I played for John Tyler High. That was seven years ago. Neither of us has done much to improve our lot since.

Oh, I had plenty of opportunity, but I blew my chances for fame and fortune. Whitey's been less fortunate. Seems like he can't find his niche. He's been fired or demoted from most every secondary coaching job in the Tyler school system. Still, he won't leave. As far as I know he has no family. Perhaps that's why he hangs on. Maybe he has no other place to go.

My mind and body are totally exhausted. The early morning drive from Dallas and four hours of laborious baseball tryouts have done me in. I undress slowly and stumble into the showers. While the water streams over my fatigued body, my mind wanders, recalling happier times.

❖ ❖ ❖ ❖ ❖

MY FAMILY moved to Tyler when I was sixteen, the summer before my junior year at John Tyler High. From the day I was born until that summer, my parents were on the go, criss-crossing the country, always one step ahead of our debtors, never living in one town for more than a year, never living in the same house for more than a few months. My dad was a dreamer, always chasing some elusive opportunity that would put us on "easy street."

Although I never saw him back away from any man, my father was basically a gentle person and a hard worker. Possibly, if he'd stayed in one place and set his mind to it, he might have attained the prosperity he so desperately pursued, but he had visions of hitting the jackpot, making big money, being someone important. We'd no sooner get settled in one place than he'd begin talking about another job in another state where men were being paid double what he was making. Before long he and mom would commence packing our meager belongings and off we'd go.

Maybe it's his dream living inside me that drives me, the gnawing fear that urges me on—to be somebody special—to seek my pot of gold.

My father justified our moving in with my grandmother with grand stories about East Texas oil fortunes and the high paying jobs which were begging for workers with his kind of skills. According to my father, Tyler was loaded with rich people, people with money to burn. Nonetheless, I suspected we had run out of both money and options. Moving in with my grandmother was our only choice. We had no place else to go.

The promised high paying oil jobs never materialized. My father and I spent the summer toiling under a simmering hot sun, planting roses in the sandy fields of rural Smith County. Six days a week, on the job by six each morning and working until seven each night—it was the happiest summer of my life.

Two cousins living less than a half mile away instantly became my best friends. They introduced me to a life I'd never known. They had their own car, which not only provided transportation but also freed us from the shackles of childhood. On week nights we cruised Broadway. On Saturday nights we went to the drive-in movie. Sunday afternoons we swam at Fun Forest municipal pool. We camped out. We explored the wooded terrain inside Tyler State Park. We even shared our first cigarette together—getting choked and so sick that for weeks afterward the three of us would degenerate into laughing hysterics every time anyone so much as coughed. By midsummer I knew most every teenager in Tyler.

I fell in love with the countryside—the tall pine trees, the magnificent houses with brick exteriors and lush green, well-kept lawns. Many of my new Tyler friends lived in houses with a separate bedroom for every child. Texas people were warm and friendly, not like the cold, cliquish inhabitants up north. At sixteen I'd found my hometown.

My grandmother's house was north of Tyler, on the Lindale Highway, barely outside the highway sign which marked the city limits. Her house rested on a huge lot with more than an acre of prime sandy land, so rich and fertile plants would take root simply by sticking them in the sand and pouring a bucket of well water on the surrounding soil. A huge garden at the rear of her property produced more vegetables than we could eat. My mother and grandmother were both marvelous cooks. We may have been poor, but we ate like kings that summer.

By early fall dad began to get itchy feet. Work in the rose fields was beginning to tail off. Planting in the new fields was finished. Fewer men were needed to harvest the fall crop. I suspect he realized it was only a matter of time before he'd be laid off.

Despite the pitiful wages we earned planting the rose fields, dad had managed to save more than two hundred dollars—more than enough for a fresh start working in the copper mines he'd heard about in Montana.

❖ ❖ ❖ ❖ ❖

EVEN BEFORE I stepped off the school bus, I knew we were moving again. Our '38 Ford parked alongside the front porch was packed full with worn-out suitcases and cardboard boxes bound tightly with bailing twine. Pieces of loose clothing were stacked atop the boxes. It was a scene I'd witnessed many times before, but this time I intended to express my objections. This time I was gonna tell 'em how I felt. Hot flashes of anger raced through my body as I sprinted into the front yard.

"I'm not leaving. I've made up my mind, dad. This time I'm not going with you," I shouted to my father as he emerged through the front door carrying a cardboard box filled with jars of canned vegetables.

"Calm down, son. It's already been decided. Your mom and I agree. It's best you stay here with your grandmother until we get settled," he responded, sliding the box off his shoulder and shoving it into the back seat of the old Ford.

"You and mom don't mind?" Even though this was what I wanted, I was dumfounded. I was their only child. How could they leave me behind?

"No, you can stay. It's probably best. You're happy here. Where your mom and I are headed, life might be a little rugged. You'll be better off here with your grandma."

"You're headed for Montana, aren't you? Dad, you can't find work in Montana this time of year. The mines are closed during winter months. This is the wrong time of year. Why not wait and leave next spring?"

"It'll be okay. Me and your mom, we've seen plenty of rough times. We know how to survive. It'll be easier for us with you staying here."

"Then your mind's made up?" I asked cynically. For me, the prospect of spending an icy winter in Montana had absolutely no appeal. I was happy in Tyler. I suspected it wouldn't be long before they sent for me. If I'd known that would never happen, I'd never have let them leave without me.

"We can't hang around here all winter sponging off your grandma. I know a man up in Butte. He promised me a job at one of the logging camps. I'll work there until I can catch on with one of the mining companies next spring. We hear they're paying big bucks for men who can operate their digging machines."

❖ ❖ ❖ ❖ ❖

ACTUALLY, IT WAS my uncle's fault. He's the one who loaned me his worn-out fielder's glove. Otherwise, I'd have been cut the first day like my cousin. Otherwise, Coach Waters would've never taken a shine to me or helped me make the team.

My cousin Jimmy and I had signed up to tryout for the high school baseball squad. The head coach took one look at us and banished us to the outfield, to shag fly balls along with a dozen other have-nots. It was a time-killing drill the coach cooked up to remove us from the infield, so he could concentrate on players he intended to keep. Jimmy and I realized our lot had been decided, but nonetheless, we each were hoping to make some magnificent catch or do something special which might draw the attention of the coaches and change their mind.

"CRACK!" The sound of a wooden bat meeting a spherical shaped hunk of horsehide resounded across the practice field. A bright afternoon sun partially blocked my view of the baseball as it sailed high above the outfield and began its downward trek.

"I got it! I got it," I shouted with eager enthusiasm, along with three other hopefuls who raced alongside me chasing after the descending baseball.

Yielding to my stubborn insistence, the other players stepped back, allowing me to field the ball without interference. My mind was totally focused on making a fantastic catch which would change my destiny.

"POP! SNAP! THUD!" It all happened so fast. The glove webbing between the thumb and the index finger offered no resistance. It snapped and gave way. The baseball collided hard and full against my chest. A sharp, hot pain shot through me. I was out cold before I hit the ground.

❖ ❖ ❖ ❖ ❖

"WAKE UP. Wake up, son," someone called to me. Stars were circling in my head. Slowly regaining consciousness, I opened one eye. A wet towel stroked at my face. I struggled to sit up, but a dull pain in my chest restrained me.

Randall Waters was in his early sixties then, a third assistant coach assigned to baby sit the have-nots. As he stood over me, a gust of wind lifted his long white hair and sent it waving. My foggy mind cogitated whether I was dead, and if he was an angel of death.

"Don't try to get up. Just lay there a minute. What's your name, son?"

"Mason. Richard Mason. Don't kick me off the team, Coach. I coulda caught that ball. Honest I could. My glove busted. It wasn't my fault."

Coach Waters laughed loudly. "You're right, Mason. No question about it. You had your sights on it all the way. It was definitely the glove's fault. You ever play baseball before?"

"No sir. My folks move a lot. We never lived anywhere that had school baseball. Coach, I really wanna be on the team."

"Well, Mason, you have a lot to learn, but you darn sure got guts. Most fellows who took the kinda shot you took would turn in their cleats and call it quits. You sure you wanna stick this out? That ball won't get no softer. Next time you might get hurt real bad."

"Coach, I really wanna play baseball. I'll find someone to teach me. I have an uncle who plays church league softball. Maybe he'll teach me," I pleaded desperately, trying to give him a reason to keep me on the team.

"No, that won't work. Tell you what. I'll talk to the head coach so you don't get cut—at least not today. You meet me here on the practice field tomorrow morning at seven o'clock sharp. We'll find out whether you're a baseball player or just a green kid with a rotten glove."

❖ ❖ ❖ ❖ ❖

NEXT MORNING I was up early, hitching a ride with a neighbor who worked downtown, so I could be at the baseball field before seven. Even though I arrived early, Whitey was there waiting. Like an idiot, I forgot and showed up without a glove. Whitey should have chewed me up one side and down the other, but instead he just grinned and handed me one of his.

For the better part of an hour we worked on my fielding techniques. He patiently explained how to keep my body in front of the ball and to keep my head down, and how I should use my right hand to cover the baseball after it hit the glove pocket. It was almost eight before he was satisfied with my fielding. My legs were shaky. My back ached. Every muscle in my body shrieked with pain.

"We better call it quits, Richard. Don't want you to be late for class."

"But, Coach, what about my batting? What about fly balls? I need to learn that too. Otherwise what we've done this morning will all be wasted. If I don't learn fast, I'm gonna get cut for sure."

"Classes begin at eight. I'll catch hell from the principal's office if they find out I kept you out of class. Besides, book learning is more important than playing baseball."

"I'm not arguing with you, Coach Waters, but right now, ain't nothing in this world more important to me than learning how to play baseball. I gotta make the team. I just gotta."

We kept at it until classes let out for lunch, practicing under a boiling hot morning sun. When we finally quit, we were both exhausted. Neither Whitey nor I could lift a bat above our shoulders. During my afternoon classes, I was a total zombie.

Even though I only played occasionally my junior year, I made the team. That was an achievement which changed the course of my life.

Whitey Waters is the best man I ever played for, but sometimes I wonder if he did me a favor, teaching me baseball that morning instead of sending me to class.

❖ ❖ ❖ ❖ ❖

SEGARS' DESOTO MART is on West Erwin, only a few blocks from downtown and the courthouse square. The main sales building, the repair shops and the adjoining car lots cover an entire city block. A roof structure, which is supported by widely spaced concrete columns, extends out from the main building to the edge of the street. The enormous canopy provides convenient shelter for patrons. It also serves as a handy meeting place for teenage males and as a launching pad for Segars' oversized wreckers.

My father-in-law requested I check in with him the minute I arrived. Most likely he's anxious to see if I arrived sober. It's a few minutes before two when I wheel beneath the front canopy and park in a space reserved for visitors. While I stride across the pavement,

Larry Holmes spots me and waves from his sales post inside the showroom. He leaps to his feet and hurries across the sales floor toward the front door.

"Hey, Rick, how you been?" the young salesman inquires cordially, holding the door open and treating me like a valued prospect.

"Fine, Larry. How 'bout yourself?"

"Couldn't be better. I was top salesman last month. Already sold five cars this month. Got the rest of the sales crew whining and eating my dust."

The colonel pays his salespeople thirty dollars for each car they sell plus fifty cents an hour in straight wages. It's the seventh of April. A quick calculation of the teenager's potential earnings tells me he'll practically double my pathetic manager's salary.

"That's terrific, Larry. You keep going at that pace, and you'll own this place someday."

"I intend to do that, Rick. I'm gonna be filthy rich, just like Colonel Segars. Someday all these lazy bums will be answering to me. That's the day I'll fire every last one of 'em and hire me some go-getters who'll climb off their butts and sell cars."

Hopefully, Segars will understand when I explain about the nine o'clock tryout schedule and my after-practice meeting with Whitey. He might not understand why he was kept waiting while I shot the breeze with his top salesman.

"Larry, I need to check in with your boss. You know if he's in?"

"Yeah, he's here. Talked to him about a half hour ago after I racked up my last sale. He's in his office at the top of the stairs. You remember where it is."

"I remember. Listen, I really gotta go. See you later."

Inside the showroom three sparkling new DeSoto automobiles are seductively displayed, strategically angled to show off their distinctive profiles and draw the immediate attention of prospective buyers. Six tiny sales cubicles and a business department fill the length of the back wall. Repetitive clicking noises of typewriters pecking away articulate the busy hum of activity behind the glass enclosed offices.

A wide hallway at the left end of the showroom leads to the service area. Two salesmen engaged in idle chit-chat sit at a small table near the hallway entrance. A dozen or more half-empty paper coffee cups garnish the table top.

In spite of his ruthless reputation, Segars runs a seemingly disorganized, loose-knit operation. His employees are allowed complete freedom to come and go as they please. He also embraces a strict open door policy. No secretary is employed to protect him from unwanted visitors. You want to talk to Clyde—all you need do is appear at his office door.

My father-in-law's office is on the mezzanine floor. A full-height glass wall which encloses his office on the sales room side makes him visible to every employee down on the showroom floor. The glass encasement also allows him to observe every movement below. I scale the stairway and knock lightly on Segars' office door. I can see he's alone. A small pile of preprinted sales contracts occupy his attention. Nevertheless, I knock before I enter. It's a courtesy I learned at Texas University. Coach Falk had a strict rule—you knocked and waited to be invited before you entered his office. He had a wicked bite for those who forgot.

"You busy, Clyde?"

"Hello, Rick. I thought we agreed you'd check in with me when you arrived." Segars sounds aggravated. He glances at his wrist watch to check the time.

"Yes sir, we did. But the rookie tryouts began at nine. We didn't turn 'em loose until almost two. Then Whitey wanted to talk," I reply, fudging on the exact truth.

"Well, how did it go? Find any prospects worth keeping?"

"A few. We invited nine of the better ones to come back tomorrow morning. Whitey and I will give 'em a lot closer look then."

"When you decide which rookies you plan to keep, call me here at my office. I want the new players to come here and sign their contracts. I contacted the newspaper this morning. They've agreed to send over a reporter who'll interview the rookies and take some pictures. I'm fairly confident the story will appear on the front page."

"That's terrific, Clyde. The ball club can definitely use the publicity."

"Yes, we're off to a fine start. Now what we have to do is put together a winning team. That's your job. You locate a place to stay yet?"

"Not yet, but Whitey tells me there's a vacant room at the Y where he bunks. Thought I might sleep there tonight. Tomorrow, I'll buy a newspaper, check out the classifieds and look for a permanent place."

"I like that idea. The Y is a fine Christian organization. You should be okay there."

"Clyde, I told you. I've quit—no more drinking."

"You know, Rick, I'd be inclined to believe you if Kyle King hadn't called me this morning. He'd heard I purchased an interest in the Trojans and wanted to verify I'd hired you to manage the team. Kyle is one of my best customers—buys his wife a new DeSoto every Christmas. You remember Kyle. He's the county judge over in Canton."

❖ ❖ ❖ ❖ ❖

I BOUND DOWN the stairway, shaken by the unexpected encounter with my father-in-law. When I reach the showroom floor, I pause and glance back. Damn. How can he know everything about everyone? Then an insidious thought crosses my mind.

Canton's judge seemed like such a sincere, honest man, so devoted to his church. But somewhere among Segars' private files, the name of Kyle King is posted. I wonder what scandalous smut connects Judge King to the colonel's secret closet?

❖ ❖ ❖ ❖ ❖

AFTER WE CONCLUDE our second tryout session, Whitey and I convene inside the clubhouse office to compare notes. We decide to invite three rookies to join our Trojan squad—Hershel

Morgan and Matt Burns, two pitchers from Houston, and Henry French, the squatty second baseman from Van.

Using a pay phone beneath the grandstands, I telephone the colonel. He's waiting on my call. He instructs me to have the three rookies wait at the ballpark while he dispatches a limousine. Ten minutes later, a lengthy dark-blue Chrysler limo drives up alongside the front gate.

The three young men are overwhelmed. Giggling like schoolgirls and patting each other on the back, they run happily around the limousine inspecting the tires, the hood ornament, the headlights, even the door handles. Each time they circle the vehicle they pause to vigorously shake my hand and tell me how pleased they are to be selected. Eventually we persuade the youngsters to crawl into the back seat for the ride downtown.

Not wishing to distract from their moment of glory, Whitey and I elect to ride in my Pontiac and trail along behind the rookies' impressive automobile.

"Wouldn't it be wonderful to be that young again, Rick? No worries. No problems. Seems like that's when you have the most fun," Whitey laments, as we watch three grinning faces poke out the limo's back windows to wave and yell at every pedestrian within shouting distance.

"Yeah, I wish I could start over again. I'd do things different. I'd study harder and get me a better education."

"Hell, Rick, you're only twenty-six. You can still be whatever you want to be. It ain't too late."

"I know, but I feel like I'm seventy. My knees are bad. My bones sound like a popcorn popper when I climb out of bed in the morning. I've put a lot of hard miles on this body."

"Wait 'til you're my age, sonny boy. That's when you pay the real price. Some mornings I have to crawl to the toilet."

"I suppose every athlete pays for his success in one way or another. You have any regrets, Whitey? Anything you wish you'd done differently?"

"Only one."

"What's that?" I ask, thinking he'll divulge some deficiency regarding his love life.

"I never had my shot at making it big. You know—head coach at some high school, coaching in the majors. Came close a couple of times, but something always came along and squeezed me out."

"Whitey, I'm sorry. I never suspected you were interested in the Trojan manager's job. . . ."

"Naw, I never was. Nobody in their right mind would want either of our piss ant jobs, nobody except a couple of losers like you and me. Didn't Segars tell you? I was about to quit. It was only after he hired you that I decided to stay."

❖ ❖ ❖ ❖ ❖

LOUD CHEERS and enthusiastic applause greet our short procession when we pull beneath the shade of the DeSoto Mart's front canopy. A small, but zealous, reception party has gathered to congratulate our newest team members. Most of the assembled faces are familiar. Segars' employees make up a majority of the congregation.

Bright camera flashes reflect off the beaming faces of my three jubilant rookies as a photographer from the Tyler newspaper snaps picture after picture. Another reporter, clutching a miniature note pad, rushes feverishly among the crowd making a valiant attempt to obtain everyone's name and their reaction to the team's improved prospects.

Segars patiently allows the rookies a few minutes to bask in their new found popularity then hustles them up to his private office where his offer of a one year contract is immediately accepted by each player. Miraculously, in the short lapse between the time I called and the time we arrive in Segars' office, a secretary has prepared contracts for each of our rookies. Each young man is rewarded with a crisp, brand-new hundred dollar bill after he applies his signature.

A final round of pictures, taken down on the showroom floor with the three players huddled around the Trojan owner, wraps up the festivities. Holding their hundred dollar bills out toward the camera, the rookies happily display their bonus money. Naturally, a sleek new DeSoto is prominent in the background of every picture.

Segars is a shrewd businessman, a super salesman, and a genius at managing the local media. For a short limousine ride and three hundred dollars, he purchased these young men's undying loyalty and a thousand dollars worth of publicity.

❖ ❖ ❖ ❖ ❖

NORMALLY, it's the veterans who are the stragglers, the last to leave the dressing room, the last to drag themselves onto the practice field. They've seen the show before—the warm-up drills, the fielding routines, the lengthy waits for your turn in the batting cage. But this morning when I arrive, every veteran is suited out and on the practice field. Apparently two days of freedom, with no baseball, was all the regulars could handle.

Only Whitey and the three youngsters we signed yesterday remain in the locker room. The rookies are stationed, obediently and half-naked, on a long wooden bench facing the equipment counter while my assistant issues their team uniforms and equipment. Their youthful faces delineate their exasperation with Whitey's orderly efficiency.

For a moment I consider offering my help then decide against it. The equipment room is Whitey's domain. My presence would only compound the confusion.

Muffled laughter reverberates through the ventilation windows above the metal lockers. Outside on the baseball diamond, men are telling jokes and having fun. Hurriedly, I stride across the dressing room and out the door.

❖ ❖ ❖ ❖ ❖

FOR EVERY BALL PLAYER spring is the premier time of year. Like any actor or artist, an athlete is happiest doing what he does best. It's a rare baseball player who enjoys the off-season. Somehow, staying home with the wife, repainting the kid's bedrooms, and working out at the gym can't compare with meeting the guys at the ballpark, suiting up and winning a ball game. When a baseball player reports for spring training, it is always with enormous relief.

The practice field is a man's world—a world few women would comprehend. Even fewer would condone what goes on here. Being he-men, baseball players mask their affection for one another with noxious insults and boisterous ribbing. The lurid jokes, the vulgar language, the fierce competition for position and playing time—no mother would want her son here. Wives and sweethearts would be appalled at the crude speculation concerning their sexuality and the indecent references to their private body parts. But for men, it's a magical kind of ritual, a time to be a kid again, to whoop with laughter, to form friendships that last a lifetime.

Assembled in broad circles, my team is scattered about the diamond, limbering up their arms by throwing baseballs back and forth. On the open area fronting the first base dugout, one group is engaged in a heated game of pepper. With several minutes to spare before our practice session begins in earnest, I mingle among the veterans, making a point to speak to each man individually, shaking hands, introducing myself, talking small talk, hoping to dispel any reservations team members might harbor about playing for a new manager. A couple of the regulars seem surprised I know their name and where they played last season.

Many of the men I would have recognized anyway, but I've done my homework. Following yesterday's rookie celebration, I returned to the clubhouse, taking advantage of the free afternoon to study every man's file. Not only do I know every player's name and his hometown, I also know his baseball history—where he played last year, his batting average, and which positions he plays. I also discovered dark secrets these men would rather not discuss—like how many errors each man made last season and how many times he struck out with runners on base.

❖ ❖ ❖ ❖ ❖

WHEN WHITEY and his freshly dressed rookies emerge from the clubhouse, we assemble the players for a brief team meeting. Keeping my speech short and to the point, I tell the men how much I appreciate the opportunity to serve as their manager and ask them to give me a chance to prove my coaching ability. I vow that every position is up for grabs. No player, no matter his seniority, will receive preferential treatment. It's a long season and every man will be expected to give his best effort every day. When I announce that every practice will begin with a series of calisthenics and conditioning drills, the news is greeted with moans, groans, and long faces.

My first official act as head coach is to personally supervise stretching exercises and calisthenics. With a band of sour faces circled in a giant arc around me, I lead the squad through a brisk series of jumping jacks, sit-ups, leg lifts, squat thrusts, push-ups, and rocking horses. Each time we switch to a different exercise, indignant and vulgar grunts, intermixed with heavy breathing, rumble through the unhappy assembly.

"Alright, everybody on their feet," I command after we finish the rocking horse sequence.

"Anyone tired? Anyone wanna quit?" I ask the players as they slowly rise from their reclined positions.

"We're all wore out, Coach. When we signed on, we thought we'd be playing baseball. Nobody mentioned anything about conditioning. Hope you plan on paying us overweight wieners extra for getting in shape," a whimpering voice on the perimeter behind me complains.

The voice belongs to Jess Nelms who most likely will be my starting catcher. Nelms is the self-designated team comedian. Despite his piteous complaining, he is one of the few players who reported in excellent condition.

I spin around to face the whining voice. "I'll check with the owners, Jess. Meanwhile, why don't you take your pals for a couple of laps around the outfield? When you finish, we're gonna run the bleachers."

"Aw, Skipper, I was only joking. Ain't no reason you should take it personal."

"Nothing personal intended, Nelms. Two laps. Wanna try for three?"

"No sir. You got my full attention, Capt'n. No more back talk. You make us run another lap on my account, and my buddies here will slit my throat."

"Fine. Two laps and keep together. No stragglers. I wanna see you and your wiener teammates back here in ten minutes. Otherwise, you can figure on running two more," I threaten, holding my watchless wrist up as if I'm checking the time.

Whitey and I stand beside one another, watching our aggravated and sweaty players funnel up the baseline toward the right field fence.

"Don't take this as being critical, Rick. But ain't you being kinda rough on the guys? This being your first practice, you're not making yourself real popular."

"I've tried being popular. It don't win baseball games. I want this team in better shape. We have a long season ahead."

"But, Rick, opening day is less than a week away. You can't whip these fellows into shape in six days. Hell, it might take a year for an old guy like Peppy."

"We have to start sometime, Whitey. We do the best we can with what we have."

❖ ❖ ❖ ❖ ❖

AFTER THE BLEACHER RACES, we divide the team into two groups. Whitey ushers his group to the sliding pit to work on sliding techniques while I supervise batting practice.

Peppy Swanson is an aging first baseman who played with me at Cleveland in '48. Swanson's a power hitter, long past his prime, but still hanging on, hoping for one last shot in the big leagues. While he waits for his turn in the batting cage, Peppy has taken refuge inside the third base dugout. He sits slumped over on the dugout bench, coughing and spitting. A wet towel is draped across his neck. His face is flushed, his breathing labored. Seemingly, he's on the brink of passing out. This morning's strenuous conditioning session has been tough on everyone, but especially on Peppy.

Concerned for his well-being, I abandon my station behind the batting cage and trot over to check on him.

"Hey, Peppy. You all right?" I ask, laying an arm against the dugout roof and bending down to peek inside.

"Yeah, I'll survive. I ain't in the kinda shape I once was, Rick. Don't know if I can handle much more of this crash course in body building. Took me twenty years to put on this weight. Don't think it'll disappear in one day."

"You take it easy, old timer. Anytime you think you've had enough just stop. No one will say a word."

"Thanks, Rick. I've survived a lot of springs. Seen better players than me come and go. Be a shame if it was heat exhaustion that finally did me in."

"I was surprised to see your name on the roster. Thought you'd have hung up your cleats by now."

"Maybe I would, if I could land me a cushy coaching job like yours. But I can't afford to quit. I got me a wife and kids to support."

"How's your bat? This team's gonna need someone who can drive in runs."

"Had twenty-two homers while I was with Shreveport last year. Got bumped by a flashy college kid the Braves' organization sent down from Class Triple A. Spent the last month of the season here with the Trojans. We was twenty games outta first by the time I arrived, but I still smacked five more dingers just playing part time. I reckon you can count on me to carry my share of the load."

"Great. We'll be counting on you, big hoss. Looks like this team's gonna have a roster overstocked with young players. A seasoned vet like yourself can be a real plus. I may not play you every game, but I'll expect you to deliver when the chips are down."

"All I'm asking is you give me a chance. I ain't a spring chicken no more, but I can still hit with the big guys. If I have a good season, maybe one of the majors will call me up to help in their race for the pennant."

Walking back to the batting cage, I ponder the pathetic circumstance of my ex-teammate. He's pushing forty. That's equivalent to an eighty-year-old man competing in the business world. Even if Peppy hits thirty home runs and drives in a hundred runs here in Class B, no one's gonna care. He doesn't have a ghost of a chance of making it back to the big show.

Like me, he had his opportunity, and he blew it.

❖❖❖❖❖

WHEN A SHORT, but intense, thundershower interrupts our morning workout, I take advantage of the unexpected recess to search for new living quarters. One lively night at the Y, hanging out with Whitey and his odd collection of misfits, provided me with plenty of motivation to find a place of my own.

Fortunately, Tyler is blessed with wide streets and light traffic. Rush hour in the Rose Capital means more than one car stops for a traffic light. After struggling with congested traffic in Fort Worth and Dallas these past months, the easy moving Tyler traffic offers a refreshing change of pace.

In less than two hours I inspect two apartments and three houses, finally settling for a one bedroom pigeonhole duplex on Williams Court. Nestled in a cozy secluded neighborhood, the unit is only a short drive from Trojan Field.

Despite prolonged dialogue and haggling over rental terms, the landlady stands firm. She requires a thirty-dollar deposit, in cash, before she'll allow me to move in. However, she does agree to prorate my rent for the remainder of the month, making my first month of full rent due on the first of May. After Segars deducts his advance from my first paycheck, it's unlikely I'll be able to pay a full month in advance, but that's a battle I can fight later.

My Dallas debts, gas, a thirty-dollar deposit, and the prorated rent leaves me with less than fifty dollars. Still, in order to survive, I need food and a few basic necessities. In Tyler, grocery stores close at six. Hurriedly, I unload the Pontiac, dump my bags on the living room floor, and head for Brookshires Food Store on Rusk Street.

❖ ❖ ❖ ❖ ❖

THE HIGH-PITCHED SQUEAL of rubber tires straining against hot brick pavement stings my ears. A late-model, light-blue, two-door DeSoto swerves sharply off the street and screeches to a stop alongside my Pontiac. I recognize the driver instantly. Quickly, I shove my sack full of groceries into the front seat and turn back to face her.

The sleek automobile belongs to Kaye Mason, my estranged wife. An angry expression distorts her lovely face.

"I heard you were back in Tyler. Why haven't you called me?" she chides harshly through her open car window. Her flashing blue eyes reproach me for my thoughtless behavior.

A bright green ribbon tied in a loose bow secures thick, soft curls of long golden-blonde hair behind her head, highlighting the delicate lines of high cheek bones and meticulously painted ruby red lips. Watching the sunlight reflect off her hair, my heart skips a beat. My wife is truly an exquisite creature.

"I thought about calling. I really did. But I wanted to get settled in first," I stammer. Somehow I always wind up on the defensive side of our conversations.

"Vic tells me you attended Vickie's wedding. I don't understand you, Ricky. Why are you avoiding me? Just because I've filed for divorce shouldn't mean we can't be civil to one another."

"I'm sure this sounds like an alibi, Kaye, but I wanted to stick around. It was Vic and your father who insisted I not talk to you. They were worried we might get into another fight and spoil your sister's wedding."

"Well, if it was daddy's wish, I suppose I can forgive you. You're back home now. Maybe we can be friends again. Do I get a hello kiss?"

"Sure. You bet. You sure you're not mad?" I ask, approaching her car cautiously. How can I resist her? I've always been a sucker for those bedroom blue eyes and her soft red lips. Maybe she's ready to forget the past and drop the divorce suit—to kiss and make up. Perhaps it won't be necessary for her father to intervene after all.

"I've missed you, Ricky. Didn't you miss me too?" She whispers with exaggerated drama. Honey almost drips from her lips when she speaks.

"Yes, I really have. I've been crazy from thinking about you."

"How about a kiss then—for old times sake? Let's be friends again. Show me you're not mad any more."

"Okay," I say, kneeling down and leaning toward her open car window. I close my eyes, anticipating the thrill of pressing her sweet, warm lips against mine.

"WHACK!" The top of her car door bangs against the tip of my nose then slides by to crush my lips against my teeth. Reeling backwards, I fall to the pavement. Bloods gushes from my nose. My flattened lips shriek with excruciating agony.

"Oh, my. Did I hurt you, darling?" my wife coos softly.

"For Pete's sake, Kaye! What'd you do that for? I think you broke my nose," I wail, holding my right hand beneath my chin and rolling over on my side, so the streaming blood won't ruin my shirt.

"Good! It serves you right—you rat fink. I hope you bleed to death. Maybe you'll think twice before you ignore me again."

Her tires spin then scream loudly, filling the air with the pungent smell of burning rubber as she backs out into the street. When she stops to switch gears, she glances at me and smiles wickedly. Then she swerves the DeSoto sharply and propels down Rusk Street.

Wiping at the blood oozing from my nose and bruised lips, I can't help but smile. Her father was right. She does care. She really cares for me.

❖ ❖ ❖ ❖ ❖

"HOLD THE BOWL up under your chin, Rick. That way you won't drip blood all over my floor," Whitey advises while he stuffs wads of cotton up my nostrils.

"Sure, but take it easy. My nose hurts like the dickens. You think it's broken?"

"Yep, it's busted all right. The gristle is all soft and mushy—feels like a month old marshmallow. But don't worry. I can reset it. It'll be good as new in a couple of weeks. Now, tell me again how this happened. She hit you with the car door?" Whitey can barely hide his amusement while he works at repairing my damaged nose.

"Ouch! Dammit, Whitey. You sure you gotta do that?"

"Hold still. I gotta straighten the dang thang out before I tape it up. Otherwise, you'll look like a has-been prizefighter after it heals. We wouldn't want you scaring all the little kids, now would we?"

"No. I suppose not. Alright, do what you gotta do to make me handsome again. You know, for our female fans." A shooting pain rocks my senses as Whitey's huge finger pushes at the inner extremity of my nostril. I grasp the table top tightly and try not to flinch while he rotates his finger around inside my nose, snapping the broken cartilage back in place.

"Oh sure, wouldn't that be swell? You find one or two more ladies who'll love you like your wife does, and we'll have to hire a whole medical staff to keep you patched up."

CHAPTER FOUR

WITH OUR SEASON OPENER less than a week away, there's precious little time to evaluate players and set a lineup. We schedule practices for twice each day. To avoid the midday Texas heat, our morning session begins at seven. Our evening practice begins at eight. Since a majority of our regular season games will be night games, the evening sessions serve a dual purpose—we avoid the heat and acclimate the squad to playing beneath the stadium lights.

By Saturday morning it's as obvious as the swollen nose on my face. My baseball team is desperately short of players. My roster consists of fourteen men—three rookies and the eleven vets who reported Thursday morning—not even enough players for an intersquad scrimmage—darn sure not enough to charge into the grueling daily grind of a hundred and forty-seven game season. My pitching staff is a joke. How can any manager be expected to compete when his pitching stable consists of three starters and two relievers? And my two relievers are the recently signed, untested rookies.

So naturally I'm troubled. I desperately need quality professional ball players, and I haven't the faintest clue how to go about finding one. When I accepted this job, I expected I'd be faced with tough choices, but I assumed the decisions would involve which players to cut. In my wildest dreams I never imagined I'd be praying no one would quit.

When morning practice ends, I use the pay phone underneath the bleachers to call the colonel and voice my concerns.

"Clyde, we can't open the season with five pitchers. We need at least seven. And I'm short on infielders."

"Yes, I understand. I've been talking to an acquaintance of mine in New Orleans. He's lining up some prospects for us to look at. Promised to get back with me today."

"New Orleans? You sure about this guy? I didn't know they played professional baseball in southern Louisiana."

"Perhaps they have semi-pro teams, but my friend tells me the fellows he has in mind play an excellent brand of hardball. He's scouted out three Cajun youngsters he thinks can help. Says they're big and strong. Probably grew up in the bayous wrestling alligators for recreation," my father-in-law chuckles, amused by his witty analysis.

"Clyde, I don't need football players. I need baseball players with professional experience. I thought you wanted to field a winning team," I state emphatically, ignoring his foolish remark. He may find the situation amusing, but I fail to see the humor.

"A little joke, Rick. Hey, lighten up. Baseball is supposed to be fun."

"Sorry, Clyde, I'm not in the mood. Look, we're facing a deadline. League rules require my opening day roster be filed with the commissioner's office by midnight Monday. It's imperative we sign two or three more quality players right away."

"We will. We will. Trust me on this, Rick. There's no need to panic. Have a little faith in an old horse trader. You'll have plenty of players in camp by Monday—players you can win with."

"It's your team, Clyde. I hope you know what you're doing."

"You concentrate on managing the team. Let me arrange for players. I know people who can make things happen—people who don't make idle promises. If these folks tell me their prospects can play ball, you can count on it. They wouldn't dare let me down. They know better."

Our conversation ends with Segars assuring me he'll hear from his New Orleans connection in a few hours and with me agreeing to be patient. I hang up, not totally satisfied with the colonel's solution but having no choice other than to go along. Walking back to the dressing room, I can't help but speculate on how harsh the penalty might be for deceiving my father-in-law, for letting him down. A few missing teeth, a broken arm, a couple of fingers chopped off at the knuckles—the visual consequences cause me to shutter.

❖ ❖ ❖ ❖ ❖

A SINGLE MAN'S LIFE can be downright lonely, particularly when you're in your mid-twenties. You've been out of school a few years. Most of your close friends are married with families and regular jobs. Naturally, you'd prefer not to work, but even a single guy has bills to pay. So not wanting to be labeled a deadbeat, you accept a demanding job and succumb to the rigors of the working world. You leave home early and come home late. Gradually, you lose connections to your friends and to the fun days of your youth. Life becomes an endless string of uneventful days.

When you're dead broke, you have even fewer options. It's similar to serving a prison sentence. You're miserable. You want out. But you have no choice, except to serve out your time.

Conversation among our married veterans somehow always seems to revert to their families, either bragging about their children or complaining about some chore the wife wants done—mowing the lawn, fixing the plumbing. I envy the married men. They have someone who cares—someone to hug their neck and inquire how their day went when they arrive home.

Me, I come home to an empty house, and even worse, an empty refrigerator. Our morning practice ends at nine. Evening practice begins at eight. In between, there's a long stretch of time to kill. My solution is to sleep a lot. Sleeping passes the time, and it helps me forget my hunger.

A rapid knocking on my front door interrupts my late morning nap. Opening one eye, I check the clock on the table next to the couch. The time is 11:45 A.M. The knocking begins again, this time much louder than before.

"Okay. Okay. Hold your horses. I'm coming," I shout, rolling off the couch and trying to shake the fog from my sleep-dulled senses. Staggering to an upright position, I stumble across the living room floor, wondering who could be so anxious to see me. I open the door cautiously and peek out.

Victor LaBranch waits on my porch, his thick chest heaving with impatience. He shifts his weight from one foot to the other, nervously smacking a clenched fist into the palm of his opposite hand.

"Hello, Vic. What are you doing here?"

"Colonel Segars is waitin' at the airport. He sent me ta pick you up."

"The airport? I don't understand? What's he doing at the airport?"

"You and him are gonna fly to Louisiana and look at some baseball prospects. Get your pants on. We gotta go. The colonel, he don't like ta wait."

"But I have a practice session scheduled for eight this evening. I can't leave."

"The colonel already thought about that. You and me, we're gonna swing by the Y and tell Waters you're leaving town. He'll have ta handle practice by himself tonight. Come on. We gotta get going."

"Sure, Vic. Let me slip on my trousers. You think I'll need a change of clothes?"

"Naw, you'll be flying back tonight. But Colonel Segars said ta be sure and bring your baseball gear. You'll be playing catch with these guys he wants ta look at."

❖ ❖ ❖ ❖ ❖

WHEN WE REACH cruising altitude, the strained roar of the Cessna's twin engines diminishes, slowly changing into a steady hypnotic drone. My father-in-law's airplane seats six, with three individual cloth-covered seats on each side of a narrow, rubber-lined middle aisle. Except for the pilot up front, Segars and I are the only passengers. We occupy seats on opposite sides of the aisle, hardly an arm's length from one another, but we haven't spoken since the plane taxied up the runway prior to takeoff. The engine noise and our nervous anxiety during the prolonged acceleration made meaningful conversation impossible.

Without warning, the cockpit door swings open, and the pilot signals we can disengage our seat belts. Self-consciously I glance toward my traveling companion. When I see him fumbling with his seat belt buckle, I follow his lead.

Removal of the restrictive strap provides instant relief and freedom to survey the landscape below. Taking advantage of a rare viewpoint, I lean forward and press my face against the tiny window next to my seat. Thin clouds float by. In the distance behind us, the control tower at Pounds Field protrudes above the horizon.

"You ever fly before, Rick?" Segars inquires, noticing my curious surveillance.

"Not in a private plane. Flew to Cleveland once on a commercial flight for a tryout with the Indians. They paid for my ticket. Should have been the adventure of a lifetime, but I was too excited. About all I remember is the food was crummy."

"Well, relax and enjoy the flight. We're about three hours from New Orleans. There's some cold drinks and food in the galley refrigerator. Feel free to help yourself. I'm gonna ride up front with the pilot—help him with the navigating. Someday I'm gonna know how to fly this baby all by myself."

Segars slides out of his seat and disappears into the cockpit, leaving me alone in the passenger sector. My stomach growls, reminding me I haven't eaten since before practice early this morning. I decide to accept my father-in-law's offer and raid the galley refrigerator.

Halfway back to my seat, with one hand carrying a plate filled with food and an uncapped soft drink bottle in the other, the plane hits an air pocket. Suddenly the aircraft plummets downward. My feet leave the floor. My head bumps hard against the low ceiling. A second later I'm on my knees. My food and the soda bottle have gone cascading across the cabin floor.

The cockpit door rattles as someone on the other side jiggles with the latch. Finally the latch unlocks, and the door pops open. Segars' head appears in the doorway. "You all right back there, Rick?"

"Yes, I'm fine. At least I think so. What the heck happened? Are we gonna crash?" I respond, not bothering to hide my fear. Pushing myself up to balance on my knees, I gently investigate a swelling lump on the side of my head.

"No, we're okay. Just a summer storm. Looks like we might run into rough weather up ahead. Maybe you oughta buckle up."

"Sounds like a good idea. Let me clean up this mess first," I answer, surveying the food items scattered about the cabin floor and trying to quell a panic surging inside me. I thought this would be a pleasant afternoon flight. I hadn't counted on it being a test of courage.

Outside, the weather is changing from bad to mean and nasty. Dark, foreboding thunder clouds have replaced the bright sunshine and blue skies which welcomed us following our takeoff. Huge drops of rain streak across the cabin windows. Hastily, I scrape the scattered particles of my uneaten lunch into a cupped hand, retrieve the cold drink bottle, and deposit the refuse into a trash container beneath the galley sink. Then I scramble to my chair, belt myself in tightly, lean back and close my eyes. I force my mind to think about more pleasant times—the happy days, when success came easy—the days before my luck ran out.

❖ ❖ ❖ ❖ ❖

KAYE AND I were friends in high school. Well, not exactly friends—we knew each other. She was never what you would classify as snooty, but she wasn't necessarily the bubbly, friendly cheerleader type either. She was a rich society girl—always smartly dressed—always driving a nice car—slightly aloof and a little too good for the trivial nonsense of high school activities, and always involved in some civic function which I neither understood nor cared about.

We never dated—not that I would've stood a chance with a girl like her. She only dated one fellow all through high school. Ted Gooding was her steady. Ted and I were in the same class. Kaye was a year behind. Ted never participated in sports, but he was definitely a Big Man on Campus. He was elected class president for each of his three years in high school and student council president our senior year. Kaye was a lovely young girl, not yet fully developed, but decidedly attractive. Her good looks and long blonde hair were sufficiently provocative to make her the subject of a lot of locker room speculation.

Academics were never my strong suit. My mind was more focused on sports. My high school grades were mediocre, barely passing, but good enough not to annoy my coaches. A college degree was never high on my list of priorities, but during my senior year—my final hurrah at John Tyler High—I fell into an amazing hitting streak. I finished the baseball season with a batting average of better than four hundred—a feat which brought me considerable local attention and eventually a baseball scholarship from Texas University.

After I graduated and left for college, I lost track of Kaye, getting caught up in the excitement of college life and the drudgery of six months of constant baseball practice.

During the spring of my sophomore year, we were reacquainted. Oh sure, I was aware Kaye had enrolled at T.U., and that she'd pledged a sorority. One of the football guys asked me about her. She was in his history class. Because I was from Tyler, he was hoping I might possess inside information. He wanted to know if she would put out.

In spite of my curiosity, I neglected to follow up. What was the point? I had no time for girls. My schedule was brimful—almost equally divided between baseball practice, fifteen hours of class, and five tutors employed by the athletic department who were scrambling to keep me eligible for the spring baseball season.

We didn't cross paths until early April of the second semester. By then Kaye had blossomed into a very desirable woman.

❖ ❖ ❖ ❖ ❖

AT THE PEDESTRIAN CROSSING outside the student union building the shiny new convertible screeched to a halt, barely coming to a stop before it ran me down.

I jumped back and yelled at the driver, my heart pumping with fear, outraged by the driver's negligence. "Hey! Slow down, you stupid idiot. You're liable to kill someone."

"I'm sorry, sir. My books were sliding off the front seat. I was trying to catch them," she explained, pushing herself up so I could see her face above the windshield, offering an excuse for her demented conduct, but not actually apologizing.

"Kaye Segars. Aren't you Kaye Segars from Tyler?"

"Yes. Do I know you?"

"Rick Mason. We attended high school together, at Tyler High."

"I'm sorry, sir. I don't remember you. Now if you'll please step out of my way, I'm late for class," she answered snottily, acting like the rich, spoiled brat I remembered.

"Okay, I'll move, but you really do know me. I was in the class ahead of you. I played baseball."

"Oh, I see. You're one of the hired jocks. Well, I've never cared for contact sports. I can assure you I've never attended a baseball game in my entire life. Now please move. I'm late for class," she commanded, revving her engine to show her impatience.

"Sure. Sorry I got in your way. Maybe we'll see each other around campus."

"That's very unlikely," she replied nastily, beginning to ease the car forward. The second I was clear, she gunned the motor. Her tires squealed as she roared down the street. I stood at the street curb with my mouth agape, watching her speed away, thinking how, even though we attended the same school, we lived in separate worlds, and how a dumb clod like me could never hope to interest a beautiful rich girl like her.

❖ ❖ ❖ ❖ ❖

THREE WEEKS LATER Zeta Delta Pi Sorority hosted a get-acquainted reception for male students attending the university on athletic scholarship. My presence, and that of the entire baseball squad, was mandatory. To insure our proper behavior, our attendance was closely scrutinized by the man we feared most—Coach Bibb Falk.

In spite of our suspicion that not one of the sorority girls had ever attended one of our boring baseball games, we had little choice. Coach Bibb promised severe reprimands for any man who failed to attend. He was remarkably specific—either show up at the reception or watch the baseball season from the dugout bench.

By hosting their annual tea party, the sorority hoped to demonstrate their school spirit and support for the athletic program. Their party was an absolute flop—doomed to failure even before the first cup of lukewarm tea was served. The social gap between rich sorority girls and impoverished athletes was too wide to bridge.

The Zetas were dressed to the hilt, decked out in fashionable party dresses and high heels. Out of necessity as much as preference, we athletes dressed casually. We wore jeans and short-sleeved shirts. Without our scholarships, most of us would never have attended college. We barely survived on the ten dollars doled out to us each month under the guise of laundry money. I doubt if a single one of us jocks owned a decent suit or a tie.

To their credit the Zetas attempted to be friendly. They tried their best to be attentive hosts, but the girls were too rich, the finger food too fancy, and the music too highbrow for our taste. We athletes were accustomed to hamburgers, cokes and loud music. Sipping tea and making small talk against a background of chamber music was almost painful.

Coach Bibb lingered for about half an hour, chatting cheerfully with the housemother, snooping through the hors d'oeuvres for edible morsels and gingerly sipping the bitter tea. Then he sneaked out, apparently bored himself. His departure signaled we were on our own. We were free to leave any time we wanted.

Quickly I offered my thanks to the Zeta housemother and headed for the front door, grateful to be released from such pointless social shackles. That's when Kaye noticed me. Her face delineated her relieved elation. She waved and stepped across the room toward me.

"Hello. It's so nice to see you again, Mister Mason. We're so glad you could come."

Considering her attitude during our street encounter a few weeks earlier, her friendly greeting stunned me. I was surprised she remembered my name.

"Hello, Kaye. My first name's Rick. I didn't know you were a Zeta."

"Oh, yes. I've been looking forward to pledging Zeta since I was old enough to talk. My mother was a Zeta at Vassar back in the twenties."

"I'll bet your mother is very happy. I understand the Zeta's are very selective with their invitations."

"My mother died when I was thirteen. My father arranged for me to pledge Zeta," she stated coldly.

"Oh, I didn't know. I'm so sorry," I offered apologetically, silently cursing myself for being so insensitive and stupid. My amiable companion was not only a lovely female, she was also a lady, sophisticated and elegant—the kind of girl a fellow like me could only dream about. Here she was, affording me an opportunity to get better acquainted, and I responded by sticking my foot in my mouth.

"There's no need to apologize. My mother passed away a long time ago. Isn't this a dreadful party? My sorority sisters tell me we do this every spring semester. I can't imagine why. Everyone here is bored silly. You were about to leave. Would you mind if I tag along?"

"No, I'd like that, but I don't own a car. Maybe we could take a walk around campus. This spring weather is really terrific."

"We can take my car," she offered. "I know a spot out at Lake Austin where we can park right on the water. We'll put the top down and let the wind blow in our faces."

"Sure. I'd like that. But what about Ted? Aren't you two pinned or something?"

"I don't want to talk about Ted. Lately, all he's interested in is school and politics. I want to have some fun. You want to come with me, or not?"

During the drive to the lake, we smiled and laughed, but we hardly talked. With the convertible top down, any verbal communication other than abbreviated dialogue was impossible. Our primary conversation consisted of a brief discussion at the liquor store where I was forced to explain why I had no money. She pretended to be perturbed, telling me she'd never been out with a man who couldn't pay for the pleasure of her company. But eventually she went inside and used her own money to purchase the bottle of wine she insisted was necessary for our excursion.

Riding in the passenger's seat of the sleek convertible, I was impressed with myself. I leaned back in the leather seat and let the wind blow through my hair. What a fantastic day. I was in the company of a beautiful woman. And who could tell what might lay in store?

When we reached the lake, she turned off the pavement and parked beneath a tall oak tree. A titillating, tranquil breeze rippled the tree leaves. Sunlight sparkled off the tiny waves out on the velvet smooth blue lake.

"There's a blanket in the trunk. If you'll get it out, we can sit on the ground while we talk and drink our wine."

"You bet. We need a blanket. That's for sure," I responded stupidly. As I opened the door and hopped out, my imagination was running wild. A blanket—a bottle of wine—she was making this too easy. Shameful visions crowded my mind as I laid plans for my conquest on the blanket.

While I spread the blanket, she popped the cork from the wine bottle and poured us each a drink, using paper cups she had requisitioned at the liquor store. Obviously she'd done this before. I would never have remembered to bring cups.

Two cups of wine and I was feeling quite mellow, ready to make my move. I leaned toward her, reaching to take her in my arms when she leaped to her feet.

"I feel like swimming. Let's go for a swim."

"Are you insane? That lake's as cold as ice. Besides, we got no bathing suits."

"We'll go skinny dipping. Come on. It'll be fun."

I glanced around, checking if anyone could see us—searching for an excuse—some reason to convince her that swimming in an icy lake was a bad idea.

"Kaye, let's wait—until the water warms up, until summer."

Her offer was tempting. The prospect of swimming naked with a gorgeous young woman was more than appealing; it was my dream come true. But I knew the water would be like ice. As Coach Falk often laughingly proclaimed when he forced my team to practice outside in February, "It's colder than a salt miner's ass in Siberia." There was no way she could convince me to step into that freezing water.

"You're chicken, Ricky. A big strong athlete—afraid of a little cold water," she teased, strolling seductively toward the lake while she unzipped the back of her party dress.

"Kaye, you can swim if you want, but there's no way you're gonna catch me in that water. My team has a game scheduled tomorrow. Coach Falk will strangle me if I come down with a cold."

She shook her shoulders and let the expensive dress fall to the ground. She turned to face me, giving me an unobstructed view of her goddess-like physique while she removed the last of her underwear. Then she whirled and slipped into the lake. Her silky white skin contrasted starkly against the dark water.

"Come on, Ricky. Please come swim with me."

"Kaye, come out of there. You'll catch your death of cold."

"You wanted to touch me. I know you did. I'm so cold. Please come out here and hold me."

Her offer was too enticing to resist. My passion overruled my good sense. I unbuttoned my shirt, removed my shoes and stripped to my skivvies. My teeth chattered as I inched slowly into the ice cold water. When the water reached my knees, I inhaled deeply and plunged in. A few swift strokes and I was beside her. Her body yielded easily, so amazingly soft and warm. I pulled her close and kissed her for the first time. Her mouth had a fruity sweet taste from the wine.

My virginity had been recklessly discarded in a Matamoros tequila bar a year earlier, on a rare spring weekend when Coach Falk had neglected to schedule a ball game. But even for two bucks, the incident was a frustrating disappointment—far from the gratifying milestone I had expected. This would be my first time for sex with a willing, attractive woman.

My knees trembled. My hands were shaking. I wasn't sure whether it was from my anticipation or from the chilled water.

Wrapping her arms lovingly around my neck and pressing her breasts hard against my chest, she whispered in my ear, "Hold me close and touch me, Ricky, but that's as far as we can go. I hope you don't mind. I'm saving myself for after I'm married."

In a way I was disappointed, but in another way I was glad. I wouldn't have wanted her to be easy. I wanted her to be hard to get. I wanted her to be mine—the first time she made love and every time. She was beautiful and exciting. Her lips were divine. I'd never felt that way about a woman before. I've never felt that way about any other woman.

❖ ❖ ❖ ❖ ❖

I SPENT the next three days as a patient in the school infirmary. It took two more weeks to completely shake my cold. After missing baseball practice and four important conference games, I like to have never convinced Coach Falk to put me back in the starting lineup. He was mad as hell.

❖ ❖ ❖ ❖ ❖

MY EARS POP, interrupting my daydreams and informing me our aircraft has commenced its descent into the New Orleans airport. Up front, the pilot is talking to ground control. Outside, dark threatening clouds continue to dominate the sky, but the rain has stopped. As we fly overhead, trees and buildings on the ground below seem like miniature imitations.

Minutes later our wheels skid on the runway pavement. While we taxi toward the terminal, Segars emerges from the cockpit.

"Welcome to New Orleans, Rick. The weather fellow in the control tower tells us the cold front passed through Alexandria about twenty minutes ago. Be about an hour before it arrives here in New Orleans. Grab your stuff. We'll try and get this done before the rain hits."

"Clyde, I know we're here to check out some players, but I'm confused. Tell me where we're headed. How many players will I be looking at?"

"Sorry, Rick, I don't know much more than you. We'll have to play this by ear. But don't worry. There'll be a car at the terminal to take us where we're going. My contact has arranged everything."

The colonel hurries me off the airplane and through the terminal building. As promised, a long blue limousine sits waiting with the motor running alongside the curb outside the terminal entrance. When I hesitate, Segars pushes impatiently past me to open the rear door and shoves me inside.

A thin, dark-complected man, immaculately dressed in a solid black suit, starched blue shirt and multicolored purple tie, occupies the front seat beside the driver. The man's long black hair is slicked straight back over his head. Assuming he's a friend of my father-in-law, I lean forward to introduce myself, but Segars grabs my arm and puts a finger to his lips, imploring me to remain silent.

"Your fellows ready for us, C.J."

"Yep, they're ready. They're at the seminary ballfield next to Pontchartrain Park. That's about ten minutes driving time from here."

"Let's hit the road then. We need to get this done before it starts raining."

C.J. motions to the chauffeur who nods without speaking, shifts the car into gear, and stomps on the gas. Our rear wheels screech as they spin on the slick pavement.

Indisputably, the two men sitting up front are long time acquaintances of my father-in-law, yet their frigid behavior repudiates even a hint of familiarity. Once we're underway, Segars resigns himself to staring out the car window, seemingly preoccupied in his own thoughts. Evidently this trip is intended to be strictly business—no small talk allowed. Since no one is interested in conversation, I lean back to enjoy the scenery.

This is my first visit to deep Louisiana. Thick stands of magnificent oak trees adorned with draping strands of Spanish moss whiz by. Our limo crosses bayou after bayou.

In ten minutes, right on schedule, we turn off the main roadway into a small park. Slowly we wind down a sparsely traveled dirt roadway until we reach a small baseball diamond. A fifteen-foot-high chain-link backstop separates a U-shaped array of metal bleachers from the playing field. Three men dressed in baseball garb are playing catch in the infield. The men abandon their game of catch and turn to watch as our limousine rolls to a stop alongside the short wire fence bordering right field.

"We don't have much time, Rick. Take a quick look at these fellows and decide whether you can use 'em."

"Who are these guys, Clyde? You have any idea what positions they play or where they've been playing?"

"They're players off the Baptist seminary baseball squad. C.J. tells me they had one heck of a team this spring. Beat Tulane three times and L.S.U. twice. The seminary doesn't belong to an organized league, so their season ended early. If you decide you want 'em, we'll arrange it so they can complete their semester studies in Tyler."

"Preachers. Clyde, these people are preachers. You want me to manage a bunch of preacher boys."

"Just check 'em out, Rick. See if they can play. That's all I'm asking. You're not prejudiced against preachers, are you?"

"No. I suppose not. It's just. . . geez, Clyde. You're the last person I'd suspect of having inside connections with a Baptist seminary."

Segars grins broadly, somehow delighted because I'm impressed by his business genius. "Don't underestimate me, Rick. I have lots of connections. You'd be surprised at the people I know."

"I believe you, Clyde. And if these guys turn out to be ball players, I'll never question your judgement again. And that's a promise."

Grabbing my gear bag, I climb out of the limousine, nimbly vault the short fence and trot onto the infield. Except for facial hair, my three prospects could be duplicate clones of one another. The men are tall and muscular, each standing approximately six-foot tall and weighing in the neighborhood of 175 pounds. Their uniforms, which consist of a light gray, skin-tight jersey and coordinated dark green pants, are tattered and slightly faded. The words "Baseball Missionaries" are scrawled proudly across the front of their shirts. Two of the men are clean shaven. The other sports a neatly-trimmed mustache. All three have short-cropped dark brown hair.

"Hi, guys. My name's Mason. I'm the manager of the Tyler base-ball club. I'm here to oversee your tryout."

The mustached player grins and tosses me his scuffed-up base-ball. "Nice to meet ya, Coach Mason. My name's Johnson. Frank Johnson. This fellow on my right, his name is Philip. Philip Johnson. Philip's my brother. This fellow to my left, his name is Herb. Herbert Cates. Herbert's our cousin."

"Pleasure to meet you. Frank, Philip, Herb, I hear you guys had a pretty good season." The men are kin to one another. That explains why they look so much alike.

"We're ready anytime you are, Coach. Whatta you wanna do first?" Philip asks.

"Well, maybe you should tell me what positions you play. Then we can decide."

"We can play 'em all. Outfield, infield, pitcher, catcher."

"What I mean is—what positions do you generally play?"

"We play 'em all. We only have ten men on our baseball squad, so we have to know all the positions. You know, in case somebody gets sick or hurt. Tell us what you wanna see us do, Coach."

"How about pitching? I'm short on pitchers. Herb, why don't you go first? Step off about sixty feet and throw me a few pitches."

I crouch behind home plate and watch in awe while the quiet, clean-shaven young preacher goes into an extended, contorted full windup. Expertly, he hides the baseball and his glove behind his body. He kicks his leg high to enhance his delivery then steps straight toward home plate and fires his pitch. Pushing hard off the rubber, he squares himself into a crouched position, ready to field a hit ball.

The baseball zips on a straight line until it reaches a point about ten feet in front of the plate then begins to rise. I move my mitt upward quickly, barely getting it into position before it smacks hard into the leather pocket. The impact blisters the palm of my hand and almost topples me over backward.

Holy Smoke. This kid has the nastiest fastball I've ever seen. I grit my teeth, close my eyes, and try not to scream out. The painful sting reminds me why I've always preferred playing infield to working behind the plate.

"Hey, that's not bad," I shout to Cates, hoping my shaky voice won't reveal how badly I'm hurt. Pushing myself to a standing position, I loft the baseball back to him then remove my catcher's mitt and rub at the palm of my hand. "How about throwing me a curve."

The three players glance at one another, puzzled by my request. From the expression on their faces you might think their favorite professor has rewarded their best effort with a failing grade. Frank Johnson turns to explain.

"None of us ever throwed a curve before, Coach. All we've ever needed is a sinker and that riser Herb just throwed you. Philip's got a pretty good fastball, but he don't use it much."

❖ ❖ ❖ ❖ ❖

EACH BALL PLAYER takes a brief turn on the makeshift pitching mound. Then we move to the infield where I rotate each man through the infield positions and pepper him with hard hit baseballs. My ground balls are less than accurate, but I have a good excuse. The palm of my catching hand is beet red and swelling fast.

Regardless of my batting deficiencies, it's indisputable. Each of these players can handle every infield position quite capably.

Vowing never to crouch behind another home plate, I hike over to the first base fence line where Clyde has stationed himself to observe the workout. He smiles slyly when I get close.

"Whatta you think, Rick? Can these preacher boys play?"

"Yeah, they'll do. They'll do fine. Don't think I've ever seen anybody throw as hard as those three. If they have any kinfolk, we might want to sign them up too," I respond with a smile, but I'm not necessarily teasing about checking on the players' relatives.

"I'll check with C.J. Maybe they have some Cajun cousins," Segars replies, picking up on my humor.

"You suppose we could have these guys in Tyler by Monday afternoon? I'd like to have 'em work out with the rest of the team before the season starts."

"If you say they're okay, we'll have all three of 'em there for practice Monday morning. I had a premonition this would work out, so I had my secretary prepare their contracts before we left Tyler. These young fellows are hungry and anxious to play, not like some of the spoiled prima donnas already on our roster. I'll sign 'em up before we leave here. C.J. will arrange for their transportation."

CHAPTER FIVE

EVEN THOUGH our flight home was uneventful, I was dog tired when we arrived back in Tyler late Saturday night. Thankfully, a car was waiting for us at the terminal gate. Segars radioed ahead and persuaded the flight controller to contact Vic and have him pick us up. The colonel was tired too. We hardly spoke as Vic wheeled through the late night traffic and dropped me off at my duplex apartment. Two a day practices and the long recruiting trip caught up with me. I was asleep before my head hit the pillow.

Today is Sunday. Our season opens Tuesday night, two days from now. Still, we decided early last week not to hold practice this morning. For the men on our baseball squad, today is the last Sunday they'll be free to accompany their families to church services until the season ends in September. For me, it's also a welcome break, and I put the time to good use. I sleep in. It's past ten when I finally climb out of bed.

A twinge of guilt gnaws at my conscience. Yesterday, with an impatient Vic LaBranch prodding me and hustling me to the airport, I barely had time to tell Whitey I was leaving. There was no time for a lengthy explanation. I simply told Whitey I'd be absent and informed him he'd be in charge of evening practice. It wasn't my doing, but it was unfair. Hoping to find my assistant and offer an apology, I forego a late morning breakfast and drive straight to the ballpark.

A thin cluster of clouds moves across the sky to partially block out a blazing, bright April sun as I pull up alongside Whitey's ancient yellow Buick and park facing the entrance gate. Whitey is slumped lazily in the driver's seat, half-asleep. A baseball cap is slouched down over his eyes. His chin rests on his chest. The driver's side door is open.

"Hey, Whitey. You okay?"

My verbal intrusion has little effect. Whitey answers without moving or opening his eyes.

"I'm fine. Just resting my peepers. Been sittin' here listening to the radio, soaking up a few rays and reminiscing about the old days. They was playing a Jo Stafford record a few minutes ago. Boy, do I love to listen to that lady sing. She really turns me on."

"Yeah, you and about a million other horny old geezers. But why not listen inside where it's cooler? Out here you could get a heat stroke."

"The heat don't bother me, Rick. It's cold weather that gets me down. Seems like I hate cold weather more and more every year. Thought spring would never come this year."

"I hate cold weather too," I reply, recalling the hideous Cleveland weather when late spring snowstorms postponed our early season games. Sometimes snow was a blessing. A freezing April wind whipping off Lake Erie can chill you right down to the bone, make your fingers ache for hours afterward. Hot, sultry Texas weather is heaven compared to Cleveland's icy climate.

"We'll probably be praying for some cool air by the middle of July."

"Not me. The hotter it gets, the better I like it."

"How'd your practice go yesterday? I hated to leave you with no one to help, but Segars sprung his recruiting expedition on me without giving me a bit of notice. I was taking a nap when Vic came to fetch me. Barely had time to put on my pants."

"Practice went fine, Rick. We worked on our outfield relays then took some batting practice. Hope you and Clyde located some players. Right now we hardly have enough guys to field a team."

"We found three fellows who oughta help. Clyde signed all three of 'em right there on the spot. They promised to be here for our Monday morning workout."

Whitey pushes his cap back, rubs at his eyes, and reaches to turn down the radio. Grabbing the steering wheel, he pulls himself into an upright position and swivels around to face me. His sleepy disposition has vanished. An uneasy expression dominates his face. He starts to tell me something then changes his mind. His eyes wander across the parking lot. He has something on his mind, something he wants to say, but he's debating with himself about whether he should.

"What's on your mind, old timer? You have some kind of problem?"

"No, not really a problem—more like a situation. After the evening workout session yesterday I stayed late to bag up the practice outfits and get 'em ready for the laundry. This happened after all the players had showered and left for home."

"And?"

"You probably won't believe me, so I'm not sure I oughta tell you."

"Whatta you talking about? Do we have a problem, or not?"

"Well, not exactly a problem. I suppose you might say an avid fan has come to haunt us," Whitey snickers as if he finds his statement amusing.

"Whitey, will you quit beating around the bush. Spit it out. What the heck are you talking about?"

"Her name's Matilda. Rick, I know you're not gonna believe what I have to say. But it's true. I swear it's true." Now Whitey has doubled up in giggling hysterics. Tears of laughter stream down his cheeks.

"Matilda? Who the hell is Matilda?"

"Matilda is our resident ghost. I talked to her last night."

"Ghost? Come on. This is some kinda joke, isn't it?"

"Oh, no. Matilda ain't no joke. She's a big fan. Takes her baseball real serious," Whitey chuckles, wiping at his eyes. "It's the situation that strikes me as funny. You, me—busting our butts to coach the worst team in organized baseball, and our biggest fan is a female ghost."

"Whitey, surely you don't expect me to believe we have a walking, talking ghost living in our clubhouse?"

"She's for real all right, and she's anxious to meet you. But don't worry. She promised she won't cause no trouble, and she says she'll stick with us as long as we field a winning team."

❖ ❖ ❖ ❖ ❖

A BLISTERING HOT SUN beats down from a baby blue sky as we finish our Monday morning practice session. About ten min-utes ago Victor LaBranch appeared in the grandstands and took a seat in the shaded section. Now, eyeing me like a nervous banker, he stands and waves to draw my attention. While my sweat-soaked play-ers sprint for the locker room, I pause in the grassless area behind first base and yell up to him.

"Good morning, Vic. I didn't know you were a baseball fan."

"I ain't. Mister Segars sent me ta pick ya up. He wants ta talk with ya right away."

"Sure thing. Give me a couple of minutes to shower and change. I'll be ready to leave in a jiffy."

"Colonel Segars said right away. He didn't say nothin' about no jiffy."

"Cut me some slack here, Vic. I've been practicing baseball since seven this morning. I'm hot and sweaty, and I smell terrible. It'll only take a few minutes. I'll hurry."

"The colonel said right away." Vic frowns, obviously annoyed by my resistance. Hunching his back, he crouches low and moves deliberately down the stadium steps toward me. His wrestler's stance leaves little doubt about his intentions. If necessary, he's prepared to bodily pick me up and tote me to his car.

"Okay. Okay, Vic. Hey, there's no need to get physical. I can shower later. Where's your car parked?"

❖ ❖ ❖ ❖ ❖

I KNOCK LIGHTLY on the opened door and poke my head inside. My father-in-law is on the telephone. He lays a hand over the speaker and motions for me to come inside.

"Have a seat, Rick. I'll be with you shortly," he whispers, nodding toward a chair on the opposite side of his desk.

Like an obedient child, I slip silently into the chair and wait while he finishes his conversation. After a few minutes he excuses himself and hangs up.

"Good morning, Rick. I'm sorry you had to wait." Segars hesitates while he scrutinizes my sweaty attire. A wide grin consumes his face when he continues, "I see Vic wouldn't allow you time to shower."

"Vic insisted you wanted to see me right away. He takes your orders quite literally."

Segars leans back in his swivel chair and laughs loudly. "Rick, I'm truly sorry. I owe you an apology. I wanted to talk, but Vic should have given you time to shower and change clothes."

"Well, I'm here. Whatta you want to talk about?" My voice is razor sharp, but I don't care. I'm irritated. I'm hot and sweaty and in no mood for idle chit chat. The sooner this conversation is finished, the sooner I'll get my shower.

My belligerent manner erases his jovial smile. My father-in-law is unaccustomed to hostility, especially from the hired help. He glares at me then dismisses his indignation and continues. Only now he is strictly business. His voice is void of cheer.

"Rick, this baseball business is taking more of my time than I ever imagined. I'm being forced to neglect my other business interests."

Suddenly I'm ashamed. I wish I could take back my smart-ass response. This man has never treated me with anything but respect, no matter how poorly I have behaved.

"Gosh, Clyde, I'll be happy to pitch in and help any way I can," I offer sheepishly, hoping he'll notice my change in attitude.

"No, that's not what I have in mind. You have your hands full managing the team. What I need is help with the financial end—a business manager—someone who can devote their full time to ticket sales, concessions, travel arrangements, contracts, purchases. There's a lot of money involved. It's important we have someone we can trust."

"Maybe I can find someone who can help. Let me make a few calls. I know several baseball people who might be interested," I suggest, still confused about what role he wants me to play.

"I appreciate the offer, Rick, but that won't be necessary. I have someone in mind—someone who wants the job."

Segars pauses, watching his declaration sink in on me. Since I don't have the slightest clue where this is leading, I remain silent.

Segars continues, "I've talked with Ted. He has the time, and he's willing to take on the added responsibility."

"Ted. Oh, no. Clyde, he doesn't understand the first thing about baseball. Besides, he and I don't get along. We'd be at each other's throat the entire season."

"I understand there may be some harsh feelings to overcome, but I have the utmost faith in both of you. You two are like the sons I never had. This is family business, and a great deal of family money is involved. With some minor attitude adjustments, I believe you fellows can work together."

"Minor attitude adjustment? Clyde, the man despises me. I stole his girl. He's hell-bent on winning her back. He'll be trying to trip me up—stab me in the back—make me look bad every chance he gets. No way this is gonna work."

"I'm disappointed you feel so strongly about Ted coming aboard, Rick, but the matter is decided. I wanted to personally inform you, so there will be no misunderstanding about this being my idea. You and Ted will simply have to set your feelings aside and learn to work together—for the good of the team."

"Are we talking about the Trojan team, or do you mean the family team?"

"You already know the answer, Rick. Everything I do is for the family. You're a part of my family."

"Well, temporarily. Your daughter has the final say on that. I don't know, Clyde. This is a big pill you're asking me to swallow."

"I realize what I'm asking, but don't think I haven't given this a lot of thought. I have a plan. Remember what I told you Saturday. You should never underestimate me."

"Alright, Clyde. I'll go along, but only out of respect for you, not because I agree. Would you mind if I make a suggestion? I have an idea which might help."

"Certainly. Your input is always welcome."

"When I was with the Indians, we had two jokers who kept sniping at each other. Finally, Mister Greenberg divided up their duties. Each one was assigned a specific area of responsibility. The men never did get along, but the arrangement worked pretty well. At least it eliminated the constant back stabbing. You think maybe Ted and I could separate our duties so I make the baseball decisions and let him confine his talents to monetary matters?"

"That's essentially what I have in mind. Of course there'll be times when your responsibilities will overlap. When that happens, I'll expect you to behave professionally—get the job done, without argument."

"You can have my word on it. If Ted treats me fairly and respects my decisions on the playing field, I'll keep my nose out of his business."

"Thanks, Rick. This change will work out to benefit everyone. You'll see."

"If you're finished with me, I wonder if Vic could drive me back to the ballpark? I need to shower, and my car is there."

"There is one more thing. It's come to my attention that some of the local sportswriters refer to our baseball team as the 'rubber club.' You ever hear anyone call us that?"

I smile and lower my head, trying to think of a discreet response. What he's asking is common knowledge. *Trojan* is a popular brand of prophylactic—a birth control devise. Whoever named this baseball club must have been remarkably naive or dumb as a stump. It was inevitable the local teenage population would make the connection. After last season's disaster several local newspaper reporters joined in, using the nickname to amuse their readers.

"Yes. Uhh. You understand the connection?"

"Contrary to what you may think, Coach. I'm not that old. I know exactly what it means," Segars cackles.

"Whew. For a minute there I thought you wanted me to explain. I'm not sure I could find the right words," I reply with a grin. I'm extremely relieved to hear him laugh. The ill feelings of our earlier conversation have disappeared.

"Rick, I'm concerned this nickname could spill over into my car business. A thing like that could ruin the excellent reputation we've worked hard to achieve."

"I can see why you'd be worried, but I don't know what we can do about it," I say, trying not to smile. Fluttering through my mind are mental images of the humorous anecdotes clever Tyler teens might conjure up to connect Segars' sleek, sexy automobiles to his Trojan ball club.

"I've been thinking on it. I'm of the opinion we should change the team's name."

"Change the team's name? But our season begins tomorrow night. What about uniforms? What about our promotional material? Every piece of equipment in the clubhouse has 'Trojans' plastered all over it."

"The name change will cause some temporary confusion, but I think it's worth doing. Ted can straighten out the promotions and the printing. I'll handle the media."

"You have a name in mind?"

"East Texans. I plan to call the club the East Texans. Whatta you think?"

"Sounds fine to me. The East Texans. Yes, it has a nice familiar ring. It's a name our fans can associate with," I reply.

"The East Texans—Ugh, what a loser," I think to myself.

❖ ❖ ❖ ❖ ❖

THE BIG STATE LEAGUE is composed of clubs from eight cities—Austin, Gainesville, Sherman-Denison, Texarkana, Temple, Waco, Wichita Falls, and Tyler. Although the member cities are scattered throughout the central and eastern sections of Texas, all of the cities are within a five-hour bus ride of one another. Fortunately, Tyler is located near the midsection of the league cities. None of our out-of-town trips requires more than four hours riding time.

While Big State teams command only minor league status, the competition is fierce. Fans associate their baseball clubs with hometown pride, so winning is taken seriously. Fielding a competitive team is an absolute must. Last season was a disastrous year for both Tyler and the Trojans. The Trojan franchise finished in sixth place, twenty-six games out of first. Before the season ended, even our staunchest supporters abandoned the team. Whitey tells me attendance was so poor that several of the concessions were closed during the final home stand.

To the delight of avid Big State fans, occasionally a big name player on his way down will turn up on a team's roster. Such an occasion is, of course, the exception rather than the rule. Most men participating in this league will be in their early twenties, not good enough to be considered major league material, but nonetheless, hoping for one fantastic season where they'll catch the eye of some big league scout. Only a select few will ever move up even to Class A status. Most of the men will play here for two or three years, realize the futility, and find themselves a real job.

After practice Monday evening we hold a short meeting to talk about the upcoming season. Every player receives a travel schedule, and we go over the strict instructions regarding travel expectations.

More than half our team members are married. Several have children. Almost all the players' wives have jobs. Planning for transportation, baby sitters, and financial matters is vitally important to the men with families. Paydays will occasionally fall when the team is on the road. Even though players' traveling expenses will be the club's responsibility, back here in Tyler, household bills and mortgage payments will still need to be paid on time. We carefully explain how and where wives and relatives can pick up player paychecks.

Following the meeting, Whitey and I linger to address a bit of last minute paperwork. With the season opening tomorrow night, our final roster must be decided and telegraphed to the league office by midnight tonight. We're inside the manager's office applying finishing touches to the roster forms when a whining noise in the dressing room interrupts our homework.

"You hear that, Rick?" Whitey whispers. His hushed voice causes goose bumps to dance up my arms.

"Yeah, probably the wind," I answer, refusing to yield to his inane mannerism.

"No, I'll bet that's Matilda. She's anxious to meet you."

"Dammit, Whitey, you're scaring the hell out of me with this ghost business. Cut it out."

"She don't mean no harm, Rick. I thought I explained. She's just lonely and wants some company. Come on. I'll introduce you."

"Put a lid on it, Whitey. Now pay attention, and let's finish the roster. We don't have time for ghosts."

"Okay, if you say so. But she'll be disappointed."

❖ ❖ ❖ ❖ ❖

IT'S A QUARTER PAST ELEVEN when the Pontiac's front tires bump against the curb outside the telegraph office. The night clerk inside assures us his Austin office provides 24-hour service. There should be no problem having our transmittal delivered to the Big State offices before twelve.

With our late night assignment accomplished, I drop Whitey off at the Y and head for home. Our season begins in earnest at seven o'clock tomorrow evening. Our opponent will be Waco. The Pirates finished in sixth place last year, but only one game behind Temple who finished fourth. They were in a dead-heat for a playoff spot right up until their final series.

After considerable deliberation, I've decided to go with Nick Bounato as my starting pitcher. I'll delay making a decision on my other starters until after warm-up drills tomorrow evening. I want to take one more look before I finally decide.

As I drive along Front Street and pass the high school, a queasy premonition of doom overwhelms me. The significance of the upcoming season hits me with full force. My life is a disaster. I have no family, no close friends. My wife hates me. I'm lonely as hell. The decisions I make in the next twenty-four hours can turn my life around or sink me to the bottom. If I fail again, my baseball career is probably finished.

I swing the Pontiac right and brake to a stop parallel with the street curb. A car following behind swerves around me, honking loudly to demonstrate his annoyance. My uneasy feeling intensifies. My hands quiver. My entire body begins to shake. My mouth is bone dry. I need a drink.

❖ ❖ ❖ ❖ ❖

TAKING A LONG SWIG from the gin bottle, I wheel the Pontiac fearlessly into the stadium parking lot and slam to a stop at the entrance gate. I have carefully chosen the privacy of the Trojan clubhouse to get stinking drunk. It was an easy decision. The ballpark is at the edge of the fairgrounds, away from populated residential neighborhoods, and at this time of night, there's little chance anyone will notice me. The locker room is durable—constructed to take the brutal abuse of unruly baseball players. And I have the key.

Using my shoulder, I shove impatiently at the car door. The lock gives way, and it swings open. As I slide out, the door furiously oscillates outward, reaches it's limit then springs back to bang against my leg.

"What'd you do that for?" I chastise the Pontiac. "You mad at me too?"

When the car doesn't answer, I slam the door shut and stagger past the front gate into the concession area beneath the bleachers.

"Hey, Matilda Baby! Let's you and me have a party," I yell while I fumble with the key ring. My rubbery legs wobble and give way.

When I lurch forward to regain my balance, my head bumps hard against the door. Finally finding the right key, I shove it into the lock. A swift turn to the right and the door swings open. Rubbing at my head, I stumble inside.

"Hey, baby! Come on out. I won't hurt you. I'm nothing but a two-bit baseball player. I'm harmless. Hey, come out. Don't be afraid."

I've been sober for more than a week—since a week ago last Saturday. But being sober is such a drag. When I'm sober, I'm expected to live up to illogical standards—keep my nose to the grindstone—pull the plow—tend to business. That's all so boring. Besides, staying sober is so damn hard.

The world expects an athlete to be strong and wise. But I'm not strong, and I'm darn sure not smart. I'm just a man who once could hit a baseball. Now I can't do that. Life has treated me so unfairly.

Mumbling to myself, I reel recklessly across the room, tripping over a wooden bench which someone neglectfully left in my path. I reach out to break my fall, losing control of the gin bottle as I plummet headfirst over the bench. The bottle goes sailing, breaking into a hundred pieces as my body collides with the concrete floor. I lay there for a moment then roll over and try to push up. The effort required is too great. I slump back on the floor. My eyes fill with tears, and I begin to cry. My fear of failing and the gin take control of my mind.

Submersed in self pity, I lie on the floor, cursing at the bad luck which has hounded me—driven me to this humiliating manager's job. Once I was the fair-haired young man—the fellow everyone loved— the guy with nothing but fame and fortune ahead.

Where did I go wrong? How could I end up back where I started—with nothing to show for my hard work? In my drunken stupor I cry out for help.

"Somebody help me. I'm so damn lonely. I need someone to love me."

Suddenly, despite my inebriated condition, I sense another presence in the room. A gentle warmth ripples through my being, erasing my evil thoughts and filling my insides with an overpowering sensation of contentment.

"I know, my sweet. That's why I'm here," she whispers lovingly, cradling my head in her arms and pulling me close against her bosom.

CHAPTER SIX

A SLIVER OF SUNLIGHT peeks through a narrow ventilation window above the players' lockers, burning at my face and waking me from a deep sleep. Opening one eye, I curiously examine my surroundings. My face is pressed against a cool concrete surface. The right side of my body is void of feeling.

Without moving, I gaze across the concrete. I can see the underside of wooden benches and the bottom of metal lockers. My brain slowly becomes operable, and I realize I'm lying on the clubhouse floor. For a few seconds I remain still, unwilling to move until my mind articulates how I got here. Then I come fully awake. I sit up and glance around, my eyes searching the room. The dressing area is unoccupied. I'm here alone.

Grabbing the overturned wooden bench beside me, I set it upright and pull myself into a sitting position. I raise my hands above my head and rotate my shoulders and arms, trying to stimulate the blood circulation in my semi-paralyzed body. I slap at my face and try to remember the exact sequence of events which occurred before I passed out. A woman was here with me. I felt her touch. I smelled her fragrance.

A few feet away fragments of my broken gin bottle are scattered across the floor. My head must have hit the concrete, knocking me unconscious after I stumbled over the bench. Amazingly, I have no headache, and none of my normal hangover symptoms are present. My hands are steady. A curious feeling of contentment fills my being.

Mindlessly, I sit and stare at the players' lockers until all the machinery inside my head switches to on. Then I make a decision. I slide off the bench, crawl on all fours across the floor, and scoop up the bottle pieces. I survey the floor carefully, making certain all evidence of last night's drinking spree is eradicated. Satisfied I've done a thorough job, I rise to my feet and head for the shower. My handful of glass I deposit into a trash container next to the manager's office.

My stomach growls. I haven't eaten since yesterday afternoon. After I shower, I'll grab a quick breakfast at Mary's Diner. I have a thousand things to do before game time. I need to get moving. My team is ready. I can hardly wait. My Trojans have a baseball game to win tonight.

❖ ❖ ❖ ❖ ❖

IT'S ONLY FIVE-THIRTY when I pull the Pontiac into the parking area reserved for players and coaches, but already a circus-like atmosphere encompasses the ballpark. A clown on high stilts moves about the paved areas, greeting fans as they arrive. Another clown is stationed alongside the stadium entrance gate, passing out helium-filled balloons. Lively music resonating from loudspeakers mounted on the outside bleacher walls adds to a feeling of excited anticipation. Intertwined with the bold smells of mustard, relish and sizzling hamburgers is the aroma of freshly popped popcorn.

After he assumed the business manager's post, Ted's first item of business was to cancel the contract of every concessionaire who neglected to open for the final home stand last year. Now, with owner-friendly operators signed to ironclad contracts which require expanded menus and better service, our hungry fans will be well-fed, no matter how poorly the team performs.

Prominently displayed on the front page of this afternoon's *Courier-Times* was a photograph of last year's baseball squad. A huge caption beneath the picture predicted the drought is over—declaring that new owners, an experienced manager and plenty of brand-new talent are the solution to the woes which plagued this club last season. For the past week the newspapers' sports sections have been covered with pictures of our new players. Scorching commentaries have challenged Tyler fans to support their hometown club. Sunday's paper contained an interview with Dick Burnett, owner of the Gainesville Owls, wherein Burnett prophesied his Gainesville franchise would draw twice as many opening day fans as Tyler. Obviously, the statement was designed to infuriate Tyler backers. Segars and Burnett are longtime friends. I would lay even money a similar quote from Segars appeared in the Gainesville paper.

My father-in-law is not only a super salesman, he also understands how to stroke civic ego. Selling a second-rate, downtrodden baseball club to a public who hardly noticed last season hasn't been easy, but from all indications, tonight's attendance could be the largest in franchise history.

❖ ❖ ❖ ❖ ❖

WHILE I'M WRESTLING with last minute lineup decisions, I stroll to the end of the dugout and survey the enormous crowd. The bleachers are close to overflowing. A number of fans are roaming the grandstands searching for a seat. Generously sprinkled among the congregation are red and white, helium-filled balloons.

Ted Gooding and my father-in-law are sitting in the owner's box behind third base. They appear to be engaged in some important business discussion. This is no surprise. What does surprise me is seeing my wife there. Kaye hates baseball. I doubt if she came to watch me coach. She's certainly not interested in my ball team. No, most likely she's here to comply with a mandate from the colonel. Tonight's a big night for him. There's no telling what promises, or threats, it took to entice her here.

"Whitey, take care of things for a few minutes. I want to say hello to my wife."

"You sure, Rick? Last time you two said hello, you wound up with a busted nose."

"I remember, but if I don't say hello, she'll be furious. She's even more dangerous if you ignore her, and I have the swollen nose to prove it."

Even though my father-in-law promised to help patch up my disintegrating marriage, there's been no further mention of his offer. Not that it matters. With the demands of assembling my roster and preparing the baseball team, there's been zero time for personal business, not even time to pursue a beautiful, desirable woman. Kaye and I haven't spoken since our confrontation in the Brookshires' parking lot. Maybe now with the season underway, it's time I take the initial step to get back in her good graces. Sooner or later I'll play the fool for her anyway. It's bound to happen. I'm drawn to her like a moth to a flame. Lord knows I'm a sucker for those gorgeous blue eyes.

"Alright, but keep your guard up. Be a shame if our manager was our first casualty of the season," my assistant advises, showing me a wide, toothy grin. His gray eyes twinkle from beneath deep wrinkles of dark tanned skin.

"Don't worry. I'll keep my distance. Kaye and I have an understanding. I don't get too close, and she won't make me bleed."

Hurriedly, I climb the dugout steps and stride across the grassless stretch between the grandstands and the base lines, skirting behind home plate where the two game officials are huddled. When I pass, their conversation ceases. The plate umpire turns to frown at me, acting like he and the second umpire are exchanging secret information which I might overhear.

As I near the owner's box, I begin having second thoughts. Maybe this isn't such a red-hot idea. Since Ted assumed his role as business manager, he has avoided me like the plague. Kaye hates baseball. She's here to please her father, nothing more. Most likely, she'll be in a nasty mood.

Dismissing my reservations, I remove my cap and charge into the lion's den.

"Hello, Clyde, Ted. Good evening, Kaye. You folks ready for baseball season?"

"We can't wait, Rick. Who you planning to catch tonight?" Segars inquires. It's a dumb question. The batteries for both teams are plainly posted on the scoreboard behind the center field fence. Nonetheless, I'm delighted with the colonel's friendly reception. I answer like I've been struggling with my decision.

"Thought I'd give the nod to Jess Nelms. He works pretty good with Bounato."

"How about second base? You plan to go with our rookie?"

"Haven't made up my mind. French looks fine in practice, but he's never played a professional game before. If I do start him, I was thinking we'd use him as our lead-off batter. With the huge crowd and this being our season opener, I'm worried how he'll handle the pressure. It's a lot of responsibility to stick on a young kid."

"It's your call, Rick, but if it were me, I'd take the risk. From what you tell me he could be the key to our season. I have a deep down gut feeling about this youngster."

"You're the gambler with all the luck, Clyde. I reckon I oughta trust your instincts. Alright, you've helped me make up my mind. We'll start French at second. We'll find out right off the bat whether or not he can cut the mustard."

"Great. Well, good luck. It's gonna be a fun season."

Neither Ted nor Kaye responded to my good-natured greeting; each pretending to be preoccupied with the Pirates' infield drills. I could care less whether Ted responds. It's Kaye's attention that interests me.

"I appreciate your coming tonight, Kaye. It means a lot to both me and your father. You want to wish me luck?"

My well-meaning inquiry provokes an immediate reaction. Abandoning her aloof demeanor, my wife swivels in her chair to glare at me, her blue eyes flashing. "Why should I? You haven't called me. You don't care about my feelings. Why should I wish you luck?"

My spouse's angry outburst reverberates through the grandstands, interrupting casual conversations in nearby seats. My face burns with embarrassment as a hundred people shift their attention to the commotion in the owner's box—every person wondering why we would choose to argue in such a public arena.

My wife is a complicated and calculating female. She commands an arsenal of emotional weapons, and she has absolutely no hangups. If it means getting her way, she'll fire her barbed missiles anytime or anyplace, without hesitation. She also possesses a keen knack for choosing the exact time and place to position me on the defense and make me feel guilty.

After so many arguments and so many years, I should be wise to her tricks. Still, her tactless tantrum catches me off guard. Flabbergasted, I offer a stammering reply.

"I'm sorry, Kaye. I should have called. But I've been really busy, and I don't have a telephone yet. Can't we be civil to each other, just for tonight? It's your dad's team too. Surely, you want us to win?"

"You should have called me. I've been waiting and waiting for you to call, but you never called, not once. I don't care if this is daddy's team. I don't care who wins. You know how I hate baseball. It's a silly game you men play. I wouldn't have come if Ted hadn't been such a darling. He's promised to take me home anytime I get bored. Isn't that right, Teddy?"

Kay scoots up to the edge of her chair and leans forward. She wraps her arms around the back of Gooding's neck to demonstrate her loving appreciation then turns her head to flash me a bitchy smile.

"Sure thing, honey bunch. Anytime you wanna leave, I'll be happy to run you home." Ted tilts his head back to receive an affectionate peck on the lips then shifts in his chair to sneer at me.

Like a fat cat who's eaten the family's canary, he says, "Don't you worry, Rick. I'll see that Kaye's taken care of. You concentrate on winning the game tonight."

My inclination is to climb the railing and wale the daylights out of his pompous legal ass. But I contain my emotions, realizing violent action on my part would only worsen the situation. Instead, I endure the humiliation and excuse myself, using the calmest voice I can muster.

"I reckon I oughta mosey back to my dugout. Gotta turn in my lineup, so the umpires can start the game."

"Sure, Rick. Maybe you should take care of your baseball business. Perhaps we'll see you later," Ted concedes, a condescending smirk etched across his face.

Jogging back to the dugout, I make myself a solemn promise. The next time we meet privately I intend to wipe the grin off that arrogant schmuck's face — permanently.

❖ ❖ ❖ ❖ ❖

BUTTERFLIES NIBBLE furiously at the lining of my stomach as Bounato's final warm-up pitch pops hard into Nelms' mitt. Gracefully, and in one smooth, fluid motion, Nelms bounces up from his crouched position and fires the baseball to our second baseman Henry French.

This morning's euphoric feelings are gone now. Reality has set in. The hopes and dreams of 17 baseball players and two down-and-out coaches are directly linked to the successes or failures propagated here on this obscure Texas diamond. Not all of us will be allowed to watch the season close in September.

I study the players' faces, wondering which ones will survive. It's entirely possible I'll be among those who succumb to the grueling schedule ahead.

French fields the ball cleanly and whips it to third baseman Mel Neuendorff, beginning a pre-game, around-the-bases throwing ritual which will be repeated one hundred and forty-seven times before the regular season ends. A momentary hush falls over the stadium, then the noise intensifies as home fans shift their attention to the ballfield and yell to encourage the players.

"You nervous, Whitey?" I ask, my shaky knees on the verge of collapsing beneath me.

"Yep, I already chucked up my supper. If we don't get underway soon, I'm gonna puke up my lunch and breakfast."

"You think we're ready? There's so many things we should've worked on."

"Only time will tell, Rick. Five months from now, if the two of us last that long without gettin' fired, we'll either be heroes or goats."

"Whitey, I'm scared. I'm really scared. I've played a thousand baseball games, but I don't think I've ever felt like this before."

"That's 'cause you're the manager. Being scared comes with the job. You make the decisions and take the heat, but you're forced to depend on some green kid to make the plays. If the team wins, the players get the credit. If the team loses, it's 'cause the manager is a blithering idiot."

Whitey's been coaching baseball for a long, long time. Part of his analysis is correct. Every manager is at the mercy of his players. But in my case, there's even more at stake. If I blow this job, there's no where to go but down—to the slimy bottom. Baseball is all I know. I have no other skills to fall back on. The best I can hope for is a job selling cars—kissing peoples' asses—glad handing customers. My stomach will be plum full of ulcers before I'm forty.

From behind home base the umpire signals our players to remove practice baseballs from the playing field then turns his back to the infield and stoops down to sweep off home plate. Satisfied with his work, he shoves the small whisk broom into a rear pocket and dons his face mask. For a few seconds he glares at the boisterous spectators in the bleachers.

"Let's play ball!" he growls forcefully.

❖ ❖ ❖ ❖ ❖

THE HOME CROWD MOANS with dismay as the batter tosses his stick to Waco's bat boy and trots toward first base. Bounato walked Passineau, the Pirates' lead-off batter, on four straight balls.

Leaping from the dugout, I signal to the plate umpire, calling timeout. Apparently my starting pitcher has a bad case of opening game jitters. He needs stroking to calm him down. Slowly and deliberately, I stroll toward the pitching mound.

"Hey, Nick boy, you feeling okay?" I ask in a controlled voice, laying a fatherly hand on the lanky chunker's shoulder.

"I feel fine. Reckon I'm a little nervous. Never had anywhere near this many people watching when I pitched for Texas City last year."

"Forget about the fans and relax, big guy. Pretend you're pitching batting practice. Just fire the baseball across the plate. Make these jokers put the ball in play. Your teammates will do the rest."

"Alright, Coach. Maybe I'm trying too hard."

"Just concentrate on throwing strikes. Step straight at the plate and keep the ball down. This umpire has a low strike zone," I counsel wisely, hiding my anxiety behind a forced smile.

"Thanks for the advice. I'll be okay once we get somebody out."

"I know you will. Relax and let's have some fun. Every game counts the same, so tonight's game ain't no bigger deal than the one we play tomorrow," I lie in the calmest voice I can muster. I pat his shoulder gently and turn to trot back to our dugout.

"Nick gonna be all right, Rick?" Whitey inquires after I maneuver down the dugout steps. My throat is bone dry. I examine the metal cups hanging near the water cooler, hoping to find one not embellished with tobacco juice.

"He'll be okay. He's just anxious like the rest of his teammates. Don't think any of us expected to play in front of this many fans. Must be more than three thousand people here tonight."

"It's nice, but I don't expect this'll last. A majority of these fans got in for free. They've been handing out free tickets down at the DeSoto House all week. Most of these younguns came to see the clowns and get a free balloon."

"Let's hope the only clowns these fans see tonight are the ones out in the parking lot," I assert, reflecting on the pathetic play of the baseball club which represented Tyler last year.

My burning thirst compels me to abandon my search for a clean cup. I select the least objectionable, wipe the rim against my pants, and fill the cup to the brim. Placing my lips inside the rim, I close my eyes and swallow hard. The tobacco residue adds a bitter-sweet taste, but the cool water washes away the dryness.

"You can say that again, Rick. We didn't need to hire no clowns last season. We was the clowns."

❖ ❖ ❖ ❖ ❖

"HOLY CRAP!" I wail, slamming my scorebook to the floor after the baseball bounces in front of home plate and careens over our catcher's head. "I told him to keep the dad-gum ball down, not throw it in the dirt."

"Maybe we oughta switch pitchers. Don't look like Nick's got his stuff tonight. That's five straight balls. He ain't got one even close yet."

Taking advantage of the wild pitch, the Pirates' runner on first advanced to second. Tyler supporters vent their frustration with loud boos and obscenities, some directed at their pitcher, some directed at their manager. The crowd is irritated and restless. Our season is less than ten minutes old, and already the boo birds have emerged. Trojan fans remember last season all too well.

"No, let's stick with him for one more batter. But if he walks another man, we'll have to yank him."

"Ball two!" the umpire pronounces. After the pitch, Nelms swivels around to grimace at us. He nods positively and holds his hand a few inches away from his mitt, indicating Bounato's pitch was only a few inches outside the strike zone.

"That's better. He's getting closer. Maybe he's settling down," I whisper to Whitey, but without real conviction.

Exasperated home fans choose not to endorse my positive attitude. Abusive shouts urging us to, "get the bum outta there!" and loud catcalls burn our ears.

With a runner on base, Bounato has switched to pitching from a stretch delivery. As he lifts his leg to begin his off balance windup, the batter squares around to bunt.

"Bunt! Bunt! Look out for the bunt," Whitey screams, but his warning comes too late. Watching their pitcher throw six consecutive balls has lulled our infield into a lethargic stupor. They were expecting the hitter to take a strike before he swings, and with a Waco runner on second, our guys are playing deep.

Waco's batter lays down a perfect bunt. Bouncing softly in the infield dirt ten feet up the base line, the baseball gyrates in a zigzag pattern toward first base. Nelms and our first baseman Peppy Swanson scramble madly after the slow-moving ball. When the play ends, Peppy stands crouched midway between home and first, holding the baseball high above his shoulder, desperately searching for some place to throw. Waco has runners on first and third. Nobody out.

"Now ain't this a fine kettle of fish. We ain't even finished one inning, and we're already in trouble. Whatta you wanna do, Rick? You wanna change pitchers?"

Bounato's last pitch was a strike, right down the middle of the plate. I doubt if we could have thrown the batter out even if we'd been alert and expecting a bunt. Despite his inexperience, Bounato is my best arm. A ground ball to the infield will cost us a run, but with a runner on first, we have a decent chance for a double play. This is a hitter's league. A single run is never enough to win. With any luck we can still squirm out of the inning without serious damage.

I turn to Merv Connors, a multi-talented veteran who played first base for Tulsa in the Texas League last season. Connors is lazily lounging on the bench behind me. "Merv, you warm enough to play?" I ask.

"Yes sir. What position you want I should play?" the suddenly attentive veteran replies enthusiastically. Leaning forward, he begins searching beneath the bench for his glove.

"First base. You sub in and replace Swanson."

Whitey shoots me a concerned look, expressing his alarm. "Peppy? You sure about that, Rick? Peppy's our big gun. If they score, we're gonna need some runs to get back in the game."

"Peppy's left-handed, and he's too slow to handle a hot shot down the base line. Go with me on this, Whitey. I have a feeling."

"Okay, but getting jerked in the first inning before he has a turn at bat ain't gonna set too good with Peppy. He's counting on a big season to get him back to the majors."

"Yes, I know. How could I forget? He keeps reminding me—every day."

While Connors replaces Swanson at first base, I telephone the press box to report my player change to the scorekeeper. As our conversation ends, Peppy arrives at the dugout. Displaying his indignation, the pot-bellied slugger stomps down the wooden steps and dejectedly plops down on the dugout bench. For a few seconds he sits there silently, hunched over and sulking like a scolded child.

"Hey, Coach. Why'd you pull me out? You mad at me on account of that bunt play? Ain't nobody on this team could've got to that bunt."

"No, I'm not mad, Peppy. Don't take it personal. I simply made a defensive move. We've got a hundred and forty-six more games to play. You'll get plenty of chances."

"But I play good defense. First base is my best position."

"Look, Peppy, I'm going with a feeling. Get yourself a drink of water and pay attention to the game. You can coach first when we come to bat."

For a second I consider stepping over to explain my decision but decide against it. This is pro-ball. Every member of this team must accept my decisions, without complaint and without question. Otherwise we'd have no unity—no chain of command.

"CRACK!" The Pirate batter connects, sending the baseball whizzing down the first base line. Seeing the ball is hit hard, both base runners streak down the base paths.

"SMACK!" The flying baseball pops into Connors' outstretched glove as he dives to his left from his crouched position behind first base. Jumping to his feet, he tags first then rifles the ball to third where Neuendorff is waiting. The field umpire emphatically signals the base runner there is out.

An eerie silence ensues while the crowd digests the rapid chain of action. In an instant, one amazing play has altered the course of the game. The batter is out. Connors caught the baseball on the fly. Waco's runner on first is out. Connors tagged the base before he could run back. The runner on third is out. He was halfway home when Neuendorff snared Connors' throw and tagged third.

Tyler supporters leap from their seats, demonstrating their ecstatic approval. Every person in the stadium is on their feet—

clapping, cheering, screaming, stomping their feet, savoring the bliss of witnessing a triple play. Our reserve players jump from the dugout and run onto the playing field to congratulate Connors and Neuendorff and slap them on their backs. My East Texans have rallied, netting three outs with their first defensive play of the season.

"Well I'll be damned. How'd you know, Rick? What made you suspect their guy would blast a line drive down the first base line— that we needed a right-hander on first to snag it?"

"Don't know. Maybe I'm physic tonight. A weird premonition came over me, like somebody was whispering in my ear, telling me exactly what to expect."

"It was superb coaching. That's what it was. Substituting Connors for Swanson was an absolute stroke of genius," Whitey proclaims, his voice overflowing with admiration.

From the dugout I watch the spontaneous and joyous reaction generated in the owner's box. A number of excited Tylerites have dashed down to shake the colonel's hand, congratulating him for the excellent play. A satisfied smile brightens my father-in-law's face as he enthusiastically reciprocates. Ted and Kaye have also leaped to their feet, clapping and cheering our elated Tyler players as they jog off the ballfield.

"Maybe you're right, Whitey. Maybe it was a stroke of genius."

An insidious twinge of guilt suppresses my pompous self applause. I whirl around to glance behind me. My best hitter Peppy Swanson is sprawled out face up on the bench. Tears of disappointment fill his eyes. Without his big bat to carry us, this team won't be going far.

Okay, so maybe I'm not an absolute genius.

❖ ❖ ❖ ❖ ❖

"TIME OUT!" the home plate umpire bellows after Henry French fouls off another pitch. The official's decree temporarily suspends a magnificent battle which has evolved between our lead-off batter and Owen Maguire, the Pirate pitcher. The Waco right-hander's pitch count stands at fourteen. Each of his last eight offerings have been strikes—right over the plate. Methodically, Henry has fouled off each pitch. The umpire removes his facemask and motions for me to come talk.

"Where the hell did you come up with this kid, Coach? He can't hit worth a flip. Those last three pitches were fat and juicy—floated right across the middle of the plate. The pitcher's give up on striking your batter out. Now he's just trying to give him something he can hit."

"You're right, ump. The boy can't hit squat. But defensively, he plays one heckava second base."

"Listen, you nincompoop. You're supposed to bat your worst batter last. Every other manager in the league does it that way. Whatsa matter with you, fellow? Didn't you ever play this game?"

"Played for Cleveland back in '49, but it's been a while. Suppose I have a lot to learn. Are you sure about that? Sure, that makes sense—bat your worst batter last. Hey, thanks for the tip, ump."

Mortified by my response, the umpire glares after me, shaking his head while I turn and trot back to the dugout.

Behind home plate the helpful umpire and Peterson, the Pirate catcher, exchange a few words while French positions himself in the batter's box. Sharing the humor of the situation, they each turn to glance at our dugout and snicker before they don their facemasks.

Four fouled pitches later, Waco's hurler caves in, yielding to the perseverance of my stubby lead-off batter. Signaling to his catcher to stand out to one side of home plate, Maguire lobs in a called ball four.

Out on the pitching mound Maguire sneers and massages his throwing arm. Henry drops his bat and shuffles toward first base. When he passes our dugout, French pauses briefly to offer an imperfect salute.

❖ ❖ ❖ ❖ ❖

DESPITE HAVING RUNNERS on base in every inning, we are unable to score even a single run. The game becomes a duel between two excellent pitchers, each backed with sterling defensive play.

Nonetheless, eventually the momentum swings in our favor. Extended at-bats by our lead-off batter, each ending with French receiving a walk, leave the Pirates' pitcher frustrated and visibly tiring. On the other hand, Bounato, my starting pitcher, has settled down, finding a groove as he allows only one hit and a stranded runner in the fifth inning. In the top of the eighth, Bounato strikes out the side.

"Alright, we need base runners. You batters be patient. Look 'em over close and don't go swinging at the first pitch," I yell, clapping my hands to encourage my players. The nervous clamor of steel cleats scraping against a wooden floor echoes through the dugout as team members wander about searching for a seat.

"Connors, you're up first. Epps, you're on deck," Whitey bellows without looking up. His attention is focused on the scorebook in his lap.

"Listen up, Merv. Their pitcher's tired. He's not as sharp now. If he throws a strike, chances are he won't have much on it. Should be easy to hit. So be ready. Look for a fastball and try to meet it solid."

"Yes sir. Don't swing at the first pitch. Look for a big, fat strike. Don't swing too hard. Don't you worry, Coach Mason. I'll get on base. Then I'm gonna score our first run of the season."

"We're counting on you, big fellow. Bounato's pitched a heckava game. Let's don't go and waste it."

Connors takes two balls then lines Maguire's third pitch into left field. I issue identical instructions to Hal Epps. Again the Pirate pitcher gets behind in the count before he offers a sluggish, succulent strike. Epps' bat catches a piece and bloops a single into right center.

Two consecutive hits finish Waco's starter. Going to his bullpen, the Pirates' manager brings in a tall southpaw. Whitey and I discuss our options while the new pitcher takes the mound to toss his warm-up pitches.

"You ever see this guy pitch, Whitey? Looks like he's got pretty good velocity."

"Nope, never seen him before. He's probably one of the pitchers they picked up after the Texas League made their final cuts. If he can throw strikes, he'll be tough to hit."

"Maybe we oughta play the odds and bat a right-hander. Who's up next?"

"Akins. He bats right-handed. We only have three men who bat from the left side. That's Hal Epps, Peppy and Charlie Davis. We're saving Davis to pitch Thursday night, and Epps is on base. Guess we're in luck, huh?" Whitey advises, displaying a wide smile that exposes every tooth.

"Oh sure, lucky us. Whatta we gonna do against right-handed relievers?"

"Buck the odds, Rick. And pray a lot."

I can't help but laugh as I turn to watch the Pirates' left-handed fireballer throw his final warm-up pitch. The baseball zips in to the catcher, easily traveling more than ninety miles per hour. This guy makes Bounato's fastball look like a change up.

"You're right, Whitey, we'll be doing a lot of praying this season."

None of our batters have faced a pitcher with this kind of velocity. Hoping he'll be wild like many young fastball pitchers, I instruct Akins to watch a couple of pitches before he takes a cut. My instructions are a mistake. The southpaw's first two pitches are strikes, right down the pike. On his third offering, he delivers a high fastball which Akins swings at halfheartedly. Mel Neuendorff has a similar experience in his turn at bat.

With the Pirates' reliever nailing down two outs on six pitches, he seems unhittable, but he must have some weakness. Otherwise, with his stuff, he'd be pitching in the majors.

"Whitey, if this guy's as good as he looks, he wouldn't be in this league. You spot anything he's doing wrong?"

"No, don't see a thing. He's got a velvet smooth delivery. Haven't seen him throw a curve yet, but I doubt if he needs one. Nobody on our squad can hit his fastball."

"Maybe he can't field. I'll bet he's slow coming off the mound."

"Could be. With him throwing so hard, he comes off the mound in an awkward position. And being a southpaw, he might have trouble turning to throw to first after he fields the ball."

"That's gotta be it, Whitey. Bruzga, get over here. We need to talk."

Quickly I explain to John Bruzga why I want him to bunt the baseball up the first base line. This pitcher is left-handed. In order to make the throw to first after he fields the bunt, he'll be forced to rotate one-hundred-eighty degrees.

We signal our base runners to be off and running with the pitch.

Bruzga's been stuck in a batting slump during the preseason, and he's hitless tonight. Seems like he can't buy a hit, but he gets his job done by laying down a perfect bunt. With two men out, our tactics totally surprise the Waco defense. Their infield is playing deep, laying back, expecting a hard-hit ground ball.

The Pirates' southpaw stumbles and almost falls as he attempts to field the bunted baseball. Finally, he barehands the ball, looks at third, then second. Seeing he has no play at either base, he spins and flings the baseball toward first. His throw is high, sailing over the first baseman's head into the grassless wasteland beyond first. Our base runners on second and third shift into high gear, hightailing it around the bases to score.

When play ends, two runners have crossed home. Bruzga stands on second. Tyler fans leap to their feet—screaming, yelling and clapping.

"Nice call, Rick. It worked like a charm. How'd you know?"

"I didn't. But I'm on a heckava roll. These premonitions seem like they're coming from outta nowhere. Man, I truly love this game."

"Me too. And I don't care how you're doing it. Just don't stop. You hear?"

After his throwing error, Waco's fireballer completely loses his composure and makes another monumental mistake. He throws a hanging curve to Jess Nelms. Nelms promptly slams the baseball over the center field fence. Bounato grounds out to second to retire the side, but the damage is done.

106

In the top of the ninth, Bounato gets two out and runs out of gas. He gives up a single and walks two before I bring in Herb Cates. With the bases loaded, my hard-throwing Cajun fans Waco's hitter on five pitches for the final out.

Final Score: Tyler   4   Waco   0

CHAPTER SEVEN

"I'M FINISHED, Coach Mason. The problem was with your outside box. Darn thing was full of dirt dauber mud. Had to clean off the wires before I could get you a dial tone," the Southwestern Bell serviceman informs me.

"Thanks, Andy. We have a number assigned yet?"

"Sure do, Coach. Same number as last year—4646."

My reward for winning our season opener is a telephone in my manager's office. In the euphoria following our victory last evening, even tight-fisted Ted didn't object when I approached my father-in-law on the subject. The telephone man showed up early this morning to make the installation.

Having a private phone at my command produces an immediate sense of power, kind of like a prisoner who's been liberated from bondage. My first call is to the colonel at his office downtown. A female employee answers. She puts my call through immediately.

"Hello, Clyde. This is Rick. I'm here at the ballpark. Thought I'd call and personally thank you for the telephone."

"Good morning, Rick. I'm glad you called. Congratulations again on that exciting win last night. Even after I went to bed, my mind kept replaying that amazing triple play, and Bruzga's bunt. You're either the smartest manager in the league or the luckiest. I can't make up my mind. Which was it, Rick? Smarts or luck?"

108

"Nothing would please me more than to have you think I'm a smart manager, Clyde, but I can't lie to you. You know me too well. My coaching decisions may have helped us win, but the positive consequences were nothing more than pure luck. If anyone deserves a pat on the back, it's our players. Our guys played a heck of a game, not one fielding error. And once Bounato overcame his stage fright, he settled down and pitched like an old pro."

"Well, you deserve some luck, Rick, and I'm delighted with the job you're doing. Have you picked a starting pitcher for tonight's game?"

"Yes. I think I'll go with Jake Christie. He's looking better every day. Pitched for Hammond, Louisiana, last season. Don't know how tough the competition was, but I understand he chalked up 22 wins. If he, Bounato and Davis can stay healthy, I'd say we stand a good chance of playing five-hundred ball this season."

My ambitious prediction is met with silence. I'm certain we haven't been disconnected. I can hear Segars breathing on the other end. Fearing I may have said something to upset my benefactor, I endure the strained silence for a few seconds. Finally, I can no longer restrain my curiosity.

"Clyde? You still there?"

"Yes. I'm sorry, Rick. Didn't mean to be impolite. Listen, we need to talk. Can you come to my office?"

He must know about my drinking episode night before last. Damn. How does he know every mistake I make? Suddenly, my heart freezes. My tongue is thick and pasty.

"I'm trying to stay sober, Clyde. Honest I am. I helped your team win last night. I can turn this club around. Gimme a chance to show you," I plead, spouting out as many reasons as I can think of, hoping to convince him not to fire me. This man holds my future in his hands. A hard knot forms in the pit of my stomach while I wait for his response.

"Rick, this isn't about you. I'm quite satisfied with the job you're doing. But matters concerning the baseball club have changed recently. We need to talk in private. Can you come down to my office?"

"Sure, Clyde. You're the boss. I'll be there whenever you say," I answer eagerly, immensely relieved that he has something other than my transgressions to worry over.

"I'll expect you in half an hour. Don't linger in the sales room. Come straight to my office."

❖ ❖ ❖ ❖ ❖

MY PHONE RINGS while I sit behind the desk, frozen in subliminal meditation. Why should a man as rich as Clyde Segars be so concerned about winning a few baseball games? It makes no sense.

Before I can conclude my thoughts, the telephone rings again. I reach and grab the receiver.

"Hello. Uh, I mean East Texans' clubhouse," I stammer, making a mental note to powwow with Whitey and decide how we should answer our calls.

"Hello yourself, Coach Mason. I see in this morning's paper where you won a ball game last night. Congratulations."

The voice on the telephone belongs to Max Wagner, my college roommate. We haven't talked since last July when I was coaching for Fort Worth. The Cats were in Houston for a two-game series with the Buffaloes. Max heard I was in town and looked me up in the locker room after the second game. We visited for a few minutes, but at the time, I was in no mood for friendly chit chat. The Buffs had just whipped our butts, partially because of a dumb mistake I made coaching third base. Three weeks earlier the Indians had demoted me, reassigning me to Fort Worth as an assistant coach.

I'm both surprised and delighted by his call. I wonder how he got this number.

"Max, it's great to hear your voice. Where are you?"

"Right now I'm in Houston, but I plan to be in Tyler tomorrow. Been hired to find a pipeline leak. Thought maybe I'd come watch one of your games. If you can shake loose, maybe we could get together for a late meal afterward."

"That would be terrific, Max. I'd really like to see you. Hey, if you need a place to stay, I have an extra bed. You're welcome to bunk with me," I offer, hoping he'll accept. He's a good friend, a commodity which lately has been in short supply.

"Thanks, I'll take you up on that. This job I'm doing shouldn't take more than a couple of days. Gotta walk a few miles of pipeline and check some pump gages on the Amalgamated Oil Lease. That's out near Swinneytown. You ever been to Swinneytown?"

"Yes, I know about Swinneytown. Max, you watch yourself out there. That's some mighty rough terrain, full of underbrush, swamps, and snakes as big as your arm."

Swinneytown is not a tidy, prosperous community like Tyler. Downtown consists of two small grocery stores, a feed store, a dingy gas station, and a cafe which opens at five in the morning and closes an hour after lunch. The streets are unpaved. Houses are unpainted and dilapidated. Almost all the inhabitants are families of oil workers who perform the gritty oil field tasks—drillers, roughnecks, pipefitters, roustabouts.

The tiny settlement is located some eight miles southeast of Tyler. As you might suspect, the rugged citizenry fosters a reputation for violence. On a Saturday night in Swinneytown, a fellow looking for a fight is seldom disappointed. One winter when my cousins and I hunted ducks in the shallow marshes above Lake Tyler, we drove through Swinneytown several times. We only stopped once.

"Don't worry about me, Coach. I'm a survivor. A fellow who can play four years of football for Coach Dana Bible can survive just about anything."

"Okay, big guy, I know you're tough, but seriously, you be careful out there. And when you're done, if you still want to watch one of my games, I'll see you get in free."

"Man, what a deal. I'm really glad I called. Watching your team play, bunking in with you, should be great fun, like old times."

"When can we meet? You have any idea what time you'll be arriving in Tyler?"

"Can't say for sure. I'll leave Houston around nine tomorrow morning. Should take about five hours driving time and another couple of hours to do my preliminary investigation. Might be dark before I can wrap things up and drive into Tyler."

"I have to be at the ballpark by five-thirty. How about I leave you a ticket at the front gate?"

"That'll work fine. I'll catch the game and meet you afterward."

"See you Thursday night then."

"Sure 'nough, Rick. See you then."

❖ ❖ ❖ ❖ ❖

MY SECOND telephone call is a local call. I don't need a directory. The number is etched forever in my memory.

"Segars' residence," a voice answers. The person on the other end is Felix, the Segars' butler.

"Hello, Felix. Rick Mason here. I'd like to speak with Kaye. Is she in?"

"Good morning, Mister Rick. My, my, wasn't that a fine ball game last night? I had all my fingers crossed in that last inning when you had to go to the bullpen."

"Yes, I was plenty worried too. My heart was pumping like crazy when Cates got their batter to chase after one of his sinkers and end the game. All in all though, it was an exciting way to start the season. I never knew you were a baseball fan, Felix. Were you at the game last night?"

"No sir, I couldn't go. Colonel Segars would skin me alive if I left the house without his approval, but you better know I'm a baseball fan. I listened to the game on the radio. Matter of fact, I listened to every game last year, even when they were stuck in the middle of that awful losing streak. I love my Trojans."

"East Texans, Felix. The colonel changed our name. We're the East Texans now."

"Colonel Segars can call 'em whatever he likes. They'll always be the Trojans to me. Hold on, Mister Rick. Miss Kaye was in the garden earlier. I'll see if she's still there."

"Thanks, Felix. Hey, why don't you come to the ballpark some night and watch one of our games? If you're such a big fan, maybe you'd like to sit with the team in the dugout. I could introduce you to the players."

"Sit in the Trojan dugout? Oh, Mister Rick, that would be my dream come true. I'd be the envy of all my friends."

"How about tomorrow night? Isn't that your night off?"

"Yes sir. Thursday night would be fine."

"We have a deal then. The game starts at seven. I'll leave a ticket for you at the front gate. Be here around six before we take infield, and I'll introduce you to the team."

"I'll be there, Mister Rick. Thank you so much. Now let me run fetch Miss Kaye. You two need to talk. She's been acting mighty down lately."

"You really think she misses me. . . ?" I ask, but receive no reply. Felix has gone to find my wife.

In the background I hear high-pitched voices engaged in hasty debate. Apparently Kaye and her sister are deciding whether she should take my phone call. Their discussion ends, and Kaye comes on the line.

"Hello, this is Kaye Mason," she says, as if she hasn't been told who's calling.

"Hello, Kaye. This is Rick. Your dad arranged to have a telephone installed here in the clubhouse this morning. The telephone man just walked out the door. You're the first person I called." Surely she can't know I called her father first.

"That's so sweet of you. How've you been?" she inquires. She attended the game last night, but from her behavior, you'd think we haven't seen each other in ages.

"I'm okay. I looked for you after the game last night. I was hoping we could talk."

"I'm sorry, Ricky. Shortly after the game started, I developed a splitting headache. Ted drove me home. He's so considerate and such a gentleman. After he brought me home, he drove back to the ballpark, so daddy wouldn't have to sit alone."

"I'm disappointed you left so early. You missed a heckava ball game. Had to replace my starter Bounato in the ninth. Brought in Herb Cates to pitch relief. Cates is the Cajun rookie your dad and I signed last week when we flew to New Orleans. It was a risky move.

Everyone was sitting on the edge of their seats when Cates struck out the last Pirate batter."

"Yes, daddy was so talkative and happy at breakfast this morning. The baseball team is really important to him."

"Kaye, your father tells me you might consider canceling your divorce suit."

"That's right. Daddy has asked me to reconsider, but if that's why you called, you're wasting my time. I was hoping maybe you called because you missed me."

"I do. I do miss you. Kaye, we need to talk. Can we meet somewhere? Just the two of us—somewhere we can be alone."

A long stretch of silence follows while she considers my proposal.

"Kaye? Kaye, you still there?"

"I'm still here. Okay, I'll meet you. But only if you promise to behave yourself. No drinking and no sex. You understand me, Ricky—no sex."

"I only want to talk, Kaye. You and I have serious problems. Maybe if we talk, we can work things out. I've missed you so much. I want to be friends again."

"I'll need to get dressed. Can we meet at Fullers Drive In, at—say two o'clock?"

"Sure. That sounds fine."

"See you at two then. Don't be late."

"Nothing could make me miss this date. I'll be there waiting. Bye, now."

Placing the handset carefully back on the receiver, I close my eyes and breathe in deeply. I can almost smell her perfume. Visions of the many times I've wrapped my arms around her gorgeous, soft, warm body and pulled her close race through my mind.

Holy Moses. I ask if we can talk, and she leaps to conclusions. I wasn't even thinking about sex. But I don't suppose I'd object, not if she insists.

❖ ❖ ❖ ❖ ❖

IT'S A FEW MINUTES past twelve when I knock lightly on the office door and poke my head inside. Segars glances up from behind a huge stack of papers. A sea of pink telephone messages covers his desk.

"If you're busy, Clyde, I can come back."

"No, come in, Rick. These contracts can wait. We need to talk."

Segars shoves the contracts to one side, and I slip inside his office to take a seat in the leather chair on the opposite side of his desk. He removes his glasses, closes his eyes, and pinches at the bridge of his nose. He seems weary, like he's lost his energy. I've never seen him so vulnerable.

"You okay, Clyde?"

"It's been a hectic morning. My phone's been ringing off the wall with people calling to congratulate me on our win last night."

"It's nice to see people excited. That was a fantastic crowd last night. If we can win a few more, maybe more of our fans will come back."

"That's why I wanted to talk. We'll have to do better than field a winning team. A winning season won't be good enough. I'm committed to nothing less than making the league playoffs."

"The playoffs? Clyde, there's no way. I thought we agreed you'd be satisfied with a winning ball club. You never said we had to make the playoffs."

"I'm sorry, Rick, but since we purchased the team, the situation has changed. My New Orleans associates are insisting the franchise turn a profit. Making the playoffs is probably the only way we can accomplish that."

"A profit? Clyde, listen. Nobody expects to make money at this level. Less than half the major league teams wound up in the black last year. Minor league owners buy a franchise because they love the game, for the exposure and the publicity, not to turn a profit."

"The matter is not open for discussion. If our team does not make the playoffs, the consequences could be very grave. We're not dealing with people who accept excuses. They expect results."

"Who are these people? Don't tell me you've let those creepy underworld types we met in New Orleans sink their hooks into you?"

"I'm afraid so. I realize it was a mistake, but they're the ones who loaned me the money to purchase my share of the club. Now they want my assurance the franchise will show a profit."

"Clyde, what you bought is a poorly stocked team at the bottom rung of minor league baseball. Nobody expects a profit at this level," I reiterate.

"I'm afraid it's too late to back out. I'm in too deep. These are money people. We have little choice except to do things their way. Doing otherwise could be extremely hazardous to ourselves and to our families. Our only alternative is to deliver a profitable season. That means making the playoffs."

"You're not thinking straight, Clyde. Even if we win, that won't guarantee the franchise will make money."

"You take care of the winning, Rick. Ted and I will look after monetary matters."

"Does Ted know about your deal with these New Orleans characters?"

"Yes. Ted is usually informed about everything I do."

"Good Lord, you two are likely to get us all killed."

"Let's hope not. After watching the way you managed last night's game, I'm beginning to have faith in your baseball ability. I truly hope you can bail us out of this mess."

❖ ❖ ❖ ❖ ❖

FULLERS DRIVE-IN is a favorite hangout for Tyler young people. The food is excellent, and the soft drinks are ice-cold. Cute, perky waitresses dressed in green and white uniforms with tight-fitting short skirts courteously take your order then deliver it on a metal tray which attaches to your car window. The asphalt-paved spaces underneath the huge canvas canopy outside the service building are generally jam-packed during lunchtime and evening hours. Mid-afternoon is usually not so busy.

When I arrive, there's no sign of Kaye's blue DeSoto, so I select an empty space beneath the canopy and park. A waitress emerges from inside the building to take my order. She's seems irritated when I explain I'm waiting on someone, probably because I'm taking up a valuable parking space. Nevertheless, she leaves without argument.

Ten minutes pass before Kaye pulls alongside me. To my surprise she's driving a yellow Plymouth convertible. The top is pulled down.

I climb out of the Pontiac and stride over to her car, making a mental note to play this carefully. Close encounters with Kaye can be hazardous to your well being.

"Hi, hon. Thanks for coming. Hey, nice car. Is it yours?"

"No, my car's in the shop. This belongs to Vickie."

"You mind if I get in? I'd like to talk."

Kaye surveys my ten-year-old vehicle and smiles pitifully. "I see you're still driving the same old rattletrap. You should talk to daddy. I'm sure he can find you a better car. Ted drives a brand-new Chrysler with factory air conditioning. It's so comfortable. The upholstery inside is all leather."

"I didn't come to talk about Ted. I'm here to talk about us. Can I get in, or not?" My words are much too harsh. I'd hoped this might be a pleasant meeting of reconciliation, but I'm sick of hearing about wonderboy Ted. Why can't she see he's nothing but a butt-kissing, self-centered jerk?

"No, not if you insist on being hateful. We've hardly spoken to each other for months and right off you commence to acting hateful. You haven't even mentioned how nice I look."

"You look fantastic, sweetheart, but I don't appreciate being compared to Ted. Please let me in the car. We need to talk."

"Okay, get in on the other side. But you have to promise to be nice."

"I promise, Kaye. I promise to be nice."

She waits while I open the car door and slide across the cloth-covered front seat, then she cranks the motor.

"You mind if we cruise Broadway? Remember how much fun we used to have in high school? It's been ages since I've dragged South Broadway."

"That's fine with me. You wanna put the top up, so your hair won't blow?"

"No, it's such a nice day. Let's leave the top down. We can pretend we're still in high school. Won't that be fun?"

The convertible's tires squeal as they strain against the warm asphalt pavement. Kaye wheels the car in a wide circle, barely missing the column support at the end of the drive-under canopy. When she swings onto Front Street, an approaching car slams on it's brakes and swerves to miss us. My wife only knows two speeds—fast and suicidal.

Sailing up Broadway in a shiny new car with a beautiful woman beside me—this is a fantasy I frequently dreamed about during my high school days, but it never happened. The girls I fantasized about would have walked rather than accept a ride in my beat-up '37 Buick with it's faded exterior. The interior wasn't so hot either, stained and shabby, and no matter how often I doused the seats with scent killer, they persisted in emitting a stale, musty odor. My windshield wipers never worked. When it rained, I navigated by rolling down the driver's window and sticking my head out.

Touring the four-lane boulevard of South Broadway is a favorite pastime for Tyler residents. It's a pleasant, scenic trip. Historic old homes fronted by immaculately-groomed, thick green lawns line both sides of the wide street. Tall, majestic, old oak trees tower upward from the yards, their branches occasionally extending out to overhang the red brick pavement, blocking out the sky and providing a leafy parasol for the cars zooming underneath.

The easy route here would be to lean back and savor the fine weather—let the wind blow my hair and put off facing my problems. In the past that's how I solved my troubles. I'd buy a bottle and face my cares later. But I'm here on a mission, and my time is limited. Kaye and I need to talk. It's imperative we find a quiet place where we can calmly discuss our marriage situation.

"Kaye, can we go some place and talk, somewhere private where we won't be interrupted?" I say, gently probing for a positive response as we speed by the campus at Hogg Junior High.

"How about that place we used to visit in Kilgore? The Green Frog. Wasn't that the name?"

"Kaye, that's a beer joint. How about Bergfeld Park? We can find a shady spot and park. There's hardly ever anyone there this time of day."

"No. Let's go to the Green Frog. It's too hot to sit outside. You know how I hate to sweat."

"Alright, but no drinking. We'll stick to soft drinks."

"It's okay to drink beer, Ricky. That's not the same as drinking hard liquor."

"Kaye, I'm an alcoholic. We're both alcoholics. One drink of anything—even beer or wine, and I'll be back on the same meat grinder. I can't afford to fall off the wagon again. I'm trying to piece my life back together."

"Ricky, don't say that. You know it's not true. I'm not an alcoholic and neither are you. All I want is one measly little beer. Because it's so hot. What can that hurt?"

❖ ❖ ❖ ❖ ❖

"TWO BOTTLES OF JAX. Make sure they're cold," I tell the bartender, leaning across the counter.

"Coming right up. Nice and cold. You folks been here before? You look familiar," the man behind the bar replies with a smile.

"Yeah, but it's been awhile. Was a time when we came here almost every day," I reply, while the bartender retrieves two beers from the refrigerated cooler behind the bar.

"Well, I'm glad you came back. Business is kind of slow today. Nice to have some company. Here you go, mister. That'll be fifty cents. You want some music? It'll be on the house."

"Sure, that'd be nice. How about playing something by Jo Stafford?" I request, remembering Whitey's obsession for the female crooner.

"You got it. She's my favorite too."

My last dollar of folding money went to buy gas yesterday. Breakfast at Mary's Diner this morning cost thirty-five cents. I doubt if I can come up with fifty cents. Still, I go through the motions. A quick probe through my pockets confirms my suspicion.

"My wife will be out in a few minutes. Can I pay you then? Must have left my wallet in the car," I declare, giving up on my pocket search.

"Sure. No problem. If you two plan on staying awhile, I can run a tab."

"No, all we'll have is this one beer."

Using the bar as a backstop, I turn to survey the premises. Not much has changed. Four dark-green, vinyl-covered booths line the wall on the opposite side of the tiny dance floor. Situated next to the bar is the same juke box we often danced to. It's a cozy little bar—off the main highway—private enough to bring a woman you wouldn't want to be seen with—a place you could bring another man's wife and not get caught.

Explaining she wanted to freshen up, Kaye made a bee line for the ladies room the minute we arrived inside. She instructed me to order for her. While the bartender fiddles with the juke box, I grab the two beer bottles, stroll across the dance floor, and slide into our favorite booth. The juke box begins to play as Kaye emerges from the ladies room. She slips into the bench seat alongside me—the way she's done a hundred times before.

"Kaye, we can talk better if you'll sit in the other seat."

"I'd rather sit next to you. Aren't you glad we came here? We haven't been here in ages. Remember all the fun times we've had—just the two of us?"

"Sure, the two of us in love with a bottle of booze. But we can't live like that anymore. We've made a mess of our lives. We've gotta take more responsibility. And we gotta stop hurting each other."

"I'm sorry I hurt you, Ricky. Does your nose still hurt?"

"Yeah, a little. Especially when I breathe in too hard, but that's not what I mean. I love you, Kaye. I think you love me. We gotta stop fighting all the time—using our love to hurt each other and get our way. We gotta stop ripping at each other's heart."

"I do love you, Ricky. You know I do. I love you with all my heart. I hate it when we fight. But I'm so jealous. I want you to pay attention to me, be proud of me, tell me how beautiful I am, and how much you love me. But you're always going off to play baseball or scout some player. Other men don't go away. They stay home with their wives. Why can't you be like other husbands?"

"Baseball is a man's world, Kaye. That's what I do. I play baseball. It's the one thing I'm good at. If I don't play baseball, I'm just another strong back working for hourly wages. I doubt if I could make a decent living in the working world."

"Daddy will give you a job selling cars. We could live like normal people. You could be home every night. We could live in a nice house. We could have children. Oh, Ricky, I want to have children. I want you to be the father of my children."

"Yeah, children might be okay," I reply, yielding to her rationale only because I don't want to displease her. The last thing I need or want is the extra baggage of children, but now is not the time or place to resolve that issue. "But, can't you see? I'd wither and die in a job like that. I gotta be where the action is. I'm accustomed to bright lights."

"You could change. Maybe if we lived in a nice house with children of our own, you'd see things differently. If you truly love me, you should try and change."

"I do love you, Kaye, but I have all this ambition gnawing at my insides. I wanna be somebody. I want to do something special with my life. I can't settle for a job I hate and a mortgaged house. Don't drag me down, honey. Your dad understands. He's given me a brand new start. If I can turn his team around, maybe some big league outfit will notice. Everybody wants a winner on their team."

"Don't you remember how bad it was when you were playing in the majors? You were almost never home. Half the season you were on the road, living out of a suitcase. And you worried constantly about your hitting, whether you made the right fielding play, whether you'd be traded to another team, whether some younger player would come along and take your position. We've been through all that. It's a horrible way to live."

"I'm a manager now. A manager who can win will always be in demand. People respect a good baseball manager."

"Oh, darling, you're so naive. When things go wrong, a manager is the first one the owners fire. It's the manager who takes the blame for everything. He's the first one the fans boo, the one the press second-guesses, and the one the players blame when they play poorly. In Fort Worth, you despised your coaching job. You said coaching was for men who weren't good enough to play. Remember?"

"Yes, but that was different. Now I realize my playing days are finished. Now that I've accepted it, I see it's the best thing. Kaye, I'm a good manager. You saw my defensive move in the first inning last night. I wish you would've stayed to watch the ninth. I made exactly the right moves at exactly the right time. Another manager might have lost that game."

"But you've burned so many bridges. Not everyone is so forgiving as my father. You've made too many enemies—disappointed too many people. Even if your team wins, no one would dare take a chance on you, not with your reputation."

"You're wrong, Kaye. Winning can cure a lot of ill feelings. There'll always be some bigshot owner who wants to win—who wants to win so bad he'll take a chance and overlook a guy's past screwups. Give me some breathing room, baby. Lemme have this one last shot. If I don't make it this time, I'll quit baseball. I'll settle down and be a good husband."

"You promise? If things don't work out here, you promise you'll quit baseball and find a real job?"

"You have my word on it, hon. I promise. If I can't turn this Tyler club around, I swear I'll quit," I pledge, chugging down the last of my beer and setting it on the table. We've shared many similar conversations, but I never promised I'd quit before—at least not quite so emphatically. I've been living in a state of self-imposed celibacy for more than three months. With her so close, so soft, and smelling so good, I'd say anything to please her. The cold beer and the intoxicating fragrance of her perfume blend together to gently sweep away my convictions.

"You folks ready for another round?" the bartender asks from behind the bar.

"You have any money, Kaye? I'm broke. Didn't have enough change on me to pay for these beers. We owe the man fifty cents."

"I think so. Vickie and I went shopping yesterday. I cashed a check at Mayer Schmidt. I should have a few dollars in my purse." Curls of long blonde hair fall gently across my arm as she leans sideways and reaches to retrieve her purse from beneath the table. She rummages through her purse, fishes out a twenty, and hands it to me.

"Will this be enough?" she asks timidly. She seems unusually anxious to please me.

"Sure, that'll do fine. We could drink beer on that all afternoon."

"You sure you want another one? Don't you have a game tonight?"

"Our game's not 'til seven. We have plenty of time. Lets have another beer. Then what say you and me dance—just like old times."

"I'd like that. It's been such a long time since we danced." She snuggles up close, unbuttons my shirt front, and slips her warm hand inside to rub my chest. The touch of her hand sends a warm tingling sensation vibrating through my body. This woman always has the same effect on me. She sets me on fire. I could never love anyone the way I love her.

Leaning back, I wrap my arm around her waist and pull her close against me. She lifts her chin upward, anticipating my kiss. But before I accept her caress to seal our pact of reconciliation, I turn to our newfound friend behind the bar.

"Bring us two more, Mister Bartender! Make sure they're real cold!"

CHAPTER EIGHT

INTERMITTENT FLASHES from a neon sign outside the window interrupt my sleep. One eye clicks open. A shroud of drunken slumber urges me to lie still and resume my pleasant dream, but I fight back. Where am I? How did I get here? The bed is strange, but the warmth and the soft, breathing body cuddled against me seem familiar. I try to raise up, but give up on the idea. My head feels heavy, like I have a giant Texas watermelon affixed to my shoulders.

Suddenly it hits me. I know exactly where I am. It's pitch dark outside. I push myself into a sitting position and reach to shake the naked body sleeping beside me.

"Kaye, wake up. What time is it?"

"I don't know, darling. My wristwatch is on the night stand," she responds sleepily, rolling over to sling a loving arm across my waist.

Shoving her arm aside, I throw back the bed covers, leap to my feet and run to examine the night stand. Earrings, jewelry and my spouse's underthings cover the tabletop. Using both hands, I shuffle through the neatly stacked clothing until my fingers find the watch. I grab it and hold it up. In the blinking reflection of the flashing motel sign, the tiny numbers are hard to read. My heart sinks. It's a quarter past ten.

"I missed the game, Kaye. Dammit to hell. We slept through the game."

"Oh, I'm so sorry. Are you sure?"

"Yes, I'm sure. The game started at seven. By now it's over. Your dad's gonna string me up by my gonads," I groan in desperation. How could I be such a fool? One impetuous afternoon of indiscretion and my hopes of making a comeback are shot to blazes.

"Don't be so dramatic, darling. If you missed the baseball game, you missed it. It's not like it's life and death. They'll play another game tomorrow night. Come back to bed." Kaye lifts the bed sheet, enticing me with an unobstructed view of luscious white skin. Her invitation is tempting, but my anxiety negates my desire.

A thousand crazy thoughts gyrate through my brain. Christie was scheduled to pitch tonight. Did Whitey stick to our plan? When I didn't show, what did my players think? Did my absence affect their performance? What about Clyde Segars? What about the New Orleans people? If his team doesn't win, Kaye's father might end up lying face down in some mucky Louisiana swamp. Oh hell, they know me too. I might wind up alongside him.

Even before tonight, I was living on the edge. Now the suspicions have been confirmed. I can't be trusted.

"Don't you see, Kaye? If I missed the game, I'm finished. I've screwed up again. My last chance and I screwed it up." Tears fill my eyes as remorse for my imprudent behavior slowly sinks in. Dejected and tormented by guilt, I plop down on the bed and bury my face in my hands. I can't hold back heavy sobs of regret while I visualize the punishment which lies ahead.

Untangling herself from the bed cover, Kaye wiggles to her knees and crawls to me. "Please don't cry, Ricky. I love you so much. It breaks my heart to see you unhappy," she says sympathetically. She lays her head against my back and lovingly wraps her arms around my chest.

"Your dad had faith in me, and I've let him down. What's gonna become of me? I was getting my life back together. Why do I always screw things up?"

"Please don't cry, darling. So you missed one silly baseball game. I'll never understand why you and daddy make such a big thing out of baseball. No one else seems to care. More people will pay to see a B movie at the Tower Theater this Saturday than will come to the ballpark to watch a real live baseball game. Oh, Ricky, can't you see it's a losing battle? You and daddy can't win. Why won't you give it up?"

"I wish I could, Kaye. I wish I could be satisfied with a steady job and a family like normal men."

"You can. If you'll quit baseball, I'll love you so much you'll never miss it, not for a single minute. I'll have your children and make you the happiest man in Tyler, Texas." Affirming her declaration, she squeezes me tightly and kisses at the back of my neck.

Her argument makes sense. Why should a man want more than a loving woman who offers blissful happiness, a wife who's anxious to bear him children?

"Alright, Kaye, but let's leave it up to your dad. He gave me the job and the opportunity to manage his team. I owe him the courtesy of kicking my butt and showing me the door. After he fires me, I'll find a steady job."

"Do you promise? If daddy fires you, you'll quit?"

"It's a promise, Kaye."

Holding my face between her hands, she wraps her body around me to kiss my lips. Tears of joy stream down her face, giving her mouth a salty taste. "Oh, Ricky, I'm so happy," she whispers when our lips part. "Come back to bed. Let me show you how much I love you."

Under different circumstances her offer would be irresistible, but I'm hardly in the mood for more lovemaking.

"We oughta get back to Tyler, hon. People may be worried about us. I need to check in with Whitey and let him know I'm okay. They lock the doors at the Y at eleven-thirty."

"Alright, maybe some other time. You get dressed then take five dollars from my purse and run pay the motel bill. I'll slip on my clothes and meet you up front," Kaye coaxes, coolly issuing instructions for our departure. Her voice sounds casual, but her eyes

126

shine with the gleam of victory, like a coach whose team just nailed down a win over a hated rival.

❖ ❖ ❖ ❖ ❖

REGARDLESS OF MY DIRE CIRCUMSTANCES, I can't dismiss a gnawing curiosity. Our opening game victory last evening convinced me my East Texans are a team blessed with latent talent—awesome talent which a manager with the right touch might unleash to propel the club to a successful season. A second successive win tonight would help substantiate my theory. A burning desire to know whether my team won or lost demands satisfaction.

"Whitey! Hey, Whitey! You up there?" I shout to the window on the second floor. I pick up a small stone and fling it toward the window. The rock bangs hard against the glass pane.

"Whitey. It's Rick Mason. I know you're up there. We gotta talk."

A light flicks on inside the tiny bedroom above me. Seconds later the window moves upward, and a head, partially concealed beneath thick locks of unruly white hair, pops out.

"Who's out there? Whoever you are—go away. We're trying to sleep up here," Whitey sneers angrily.

"Whitey. It's me, Rick Mason. How'd the game go tonight?"

"Rick. Where the heck have you been? We had a game tonight."

"Yes, I know. How'd we do? Did we win?"

"Hang on. Let me slip on my trousers. I'll come down."

"All I wanna know is whether we won or not. No need to interrupt your sleep."

"Be patient. I'll come down."

During the trip back from Kilgore, Kaye chattered happily, dominating the conversation as she babbled on and on about finding a house near downtown, so I can walk to work and come home for lunch.

I listened without protest, but her trivial small talk only served to intensify my agony. A steady job, a mortgage payment due every month, a house full of kids, and no baseball—the horrifying implications made me nauseous. My befuddled mind began to search for reasons to blame her for my troubles.

In the past, that's the philosophy I've subscribed to—blame someone else for my problems. But why should I blame Kaye? Missing tonight's game was my fault. She forewarned me, declaring forcefully before she agreed to meet me that there would be "no sex."

No. There's no one to blame but myself. It was me who initiated the first move. If I'd done like she asked, we could've talked, drank one beer and been back in Tyler in plenty of time.

Kaye dropped me off at Fullers where my car was parked. After we kissed goodnight, she promised to talk to her father first thing tomorrow morning. She'll try and persuade him not to fire me. I doubt if she'll argue effectively. She's not terribly motivated.

Gunning the Pontiac, I headed straight for Trojan Park. The lights were out, and the gate was locked. For a short moment I contemplated whether I should drive straight to the Segars' mansion and have it out with my father-in-law, plead with him to give me another chance. Then I decided against it. He might be even more upset if I woke him in the middle of the night. I'll stop by the DeSoto House first thing tomorrow morning. Maybe I can convince him not to fire me. He's in a jam with the Louisiana people. That might work in my favor.

The back door rattles, and Whitey emerges, rubbing at his eyes. A wrinkled, unbelted pair of pants hang precariously about his waist. His fly is unzipped. A ragged undershirt covers his torso. A pair of tattered red house shoes adorn his unsocked feet. He yawns heavily, stretching two bent elbows above his shoulders as he ambles toward me.

"Rick, I was worried about you. Where were you tonight?"

"I'd rather not tell. It's too embarrassing. I apologize for interrupting your beauty rest, but I gotta know—who won tonight?"

"We did. I don't get it, Rick. You in some kinda trouble? Clyde knows a lot of people. We'll go see him first thing tomorrow morning. Surely you ain't done nothing so bad he can't help."

"No. No. It's nothing like that. I just can't tell where I've been. Tell me about the game. What was the score?"

"I don't understand what you could've done that's so bad you can't tell, not unless you've been shacked up with somebody's wife. Good Lord, I hope you're smarter than that."

"No, I haven't been sleeping with anyone's wife. I just can't tell. Whitey, tell me about the game. Did you pitch Christie? How'd he do?"

"Yeah, I pitched Jake—just like we planned. He went six innings. Only gave up two runs. It was a cake walk. We scored three runs in the first and two in the second.

"That's two wins in a row. Took six games to get two wins last year."

"Yes, we're off to a terrific start. Clyde came down on the playing field after the game looking for you. He was smiling and shaking everybody's hand. Never seen him so happy."

"You mean he wasn't upset about me missing the game? I thought he'd be spittin' fireballs. You know, he's taking a lot of heat on account of me. His partners were dead-set against hiring me to manage the team."

"Naw. He was happy as could be. I told him you came up sick right before game time, and I sent you home. He was so excited he forgot to ask what was wrong with you."

"You mean Clyde's not mad? Whitey, I love you. You're a real jewel," I yell, throwing my arms around his shoulders and hugging him.

"Yeah. Yeah. I love you too, you big lug. But take it easy. I'm an old man. These bones break easily."

"I owe you, Whitey. You saved my goose. I really owe you."

"Okay. Okay. So if you're so all-fired grateful, how about telling me where you've been."

"I can't. I wish I could say, but I really can't."

"Alright, if you don't trust me to keep my mouth shut, I reckon it's okay. Wasn't my idea anyway."

"What wasn't your idea? You mean about my being sick?"

"Yeah. I never woulda thought up such a cock and bull story. I can't take the credit. It was her idea."

"You can't mean Matilda? How would she know I'd be absent?"

"Danged if I know where she comes up with her information. But somehow she knew you'd be outta pocket tonight. She's the one who concocted the story I told Segars."

❖ ❖ ❖ ❖ ❖

IT WAS TOO LATE to call Kaye last night after I visited with Whitey, so I spent a fitful night pacing the floor. I hardly slept a wink. Occasionally I'd doze off. Then my mind would kick back in gear, and I'd be up walking the floor again, like a caged animal, worrying whether Kaye might speak to her father before I can talk to her and warn her to keep quiet.

It's six-thirty Thursday morning. I'm in the manager's office dialing Segars' home number. The telephone rings twice before Felix answers.

"Segars' residence."

"Felix, this is Rick Mason. I need to speak with Kaye. Can you roust her out of bed? It's important."

"Sure thing, Mister Rick. Say, I hope your invitation to sit with the baseball team tonight is still good?"

"You bet. My invitation stands. But if I don't talk to Kaye before she goes down for breakfast, you and I may find ourselves listening to tonight's game on the radio."

"Oh, my. I'll find her right away then. Hold on, Mister Rick."

In the background I can hear people talking. To my mild surprise, Felix's voice contains a sense of urgency. Sitting with the team is even more important to him than I realized. I make a mental note to leave tickets for him and my ex-roomie Max Wagner at the front gate tonight.

A strict morning ritual for the Segars family is to meet for breakfast and coffee at seven o'clock sharp. All family members are expected to make an appearance. Only death threatening illness or being out of town are acceptable excuses for absence. In the early days of our marriage, when Kaye and I sometimes partied into the wee morning hours and arrived home bleary-eyed and too intoxicated to walk straight, we clearly understood we were expected for breakfast. Many mornings we brought along hangovers as big as Texas, but somehow, we made an appearance.

Kaye's voice comes on the line. She sounds out of breath. "Hello, darling. Felix says you want to talk with me. He says it's urgent. I hope this is important. You know how dad feels about being on time for morning coffee."

"Yes, it is important, Kaye. It's very important. Listen, don't say a word to your dad about my missing last night's game, and don't tell him I was with you. Might be best if you don't mention either me or baseball."

"But, darling, you know daddy. He'll be mad as a hornet. I'll need to soothe things over. I was planning to tell him I'm dropping my divorce suit—that we're back together again."

"Listen, Kaye. There's no need to explain anything to your father. Whitey told him I was home sick last night, and your dad believed him. Our ball team won the game last night, so everything's okay. If you'll stick by me on this, it'll all blow over. I can keep my manager's job."

"But I want to tell daddy the good news. He'll be so pleased to hear we're together again. I was planning to ask if he could find you another job." Kaye's quivering voice divulges her disappointment.

"That's not necessary now. Hey, don't sound so sad. Be happy for me. My team won last night. I still have a chance to make good."

"I'm sorry, Ricky. I was hoping.... Oh, darn, I'm gonna be late for breakfast. Daddy will have my hide. I've gotta go."

"Come to the game tonight. After we get our stories straight, we can talk to your dad and tell him the divorce is off. And, Kaye, I want you to think about moving in with me."

"That may not be such a good idea, not if you'll be playing baseball all summer."

"Come to the game. Please say you'll come. It's important, for both of us."

"I don't know. Right now I'm so confused. I thought everything was settled. Maybe I'll be there. I just don't know."

❖ ❖ ❖ ❖ ❖

WHITEY GLANCES UP when I return from an early morning breakfast at Mary's Diner. He's half-hidden behind a heaping stack of grimy uniforms worn in last night's game. His grim face delineates his aversion to the gritty task of sorting the jerseys from the pants, getting them ready to launder.

"Rick, you heard anything about Peppy? He missed the game last night. Had to play Connors at first base. You think he might be sick?" Whitey questions me from behind the equipment table.

"No, not a word. Maybe he's hurt."

"He never mentioned anything about being hurt. He sure looked okay when he left here after our game Tuesday night."

"I think I know why he's staying home. Maybe I should go check on him."

❖ ❖ ❖ ❖ ❖

PEPPY SWANSON resides in a two-bedroom wood frame house on Dobbs Street, a half block west of Vine. His front yard is split into two levels. The lower level matches the street curb, but beginning at the inside edge of the sidewalk, the lawn slopes abruptly upward to a higher elevation. Steep concrete steps provide a pathway from the sidewalk up to the Swansons' front porch. A narrow gravel driveway near the edge of the lot angles sharply from the street to a detached garage and storage building.

A dozen or so toys lay scattered about the screened-in front porch. Apparently the enclosed porch serves as an outdoor playroom for Peppy's children. I step gingerly around the toys and knock on the front door. Sounds of movement in the back of the house testify that someone is home. I knock again.

I'm not here for a social visit. Actually I dread coming here. My veteran slugger is certain to be in a sour mood. Still, it's imperative I convince Peppy to put his damaged feelings aside and return to the team.

132

"Just a moment. I'm coming," a high-pitched voice responds from somewhere inside.

"It's Rick Mason. I want to speak with Peppy," I announce loudly.

The door rattles as locks unlock and latch handles are pulled back. Abruptly, the door swings open. A plump, middle-aged woman stands on the opposite side of the screen door. Strands of gray thread through her dark brown hair. Her brow is beaded with perspiration. I've interrupted her midmorning housecleaning.

"Good morning, Coach Mason. We've never been formally introduced, but Peppy's talked so much about you. I feel like we're old friends. I'm Virginia Swanson—Peppy's wife."

"Hi, Virginia. Nice to finally meet you. Is Peppy home? He and I need to talk."

"Yes, he's here. Been out in that so-called shop of his, sulking and drinking beer ever since I dragged him out of bed this morning. I can't do a thing with him. Maybe you can talk some sense into him." Her eyes fill with tears as she pauses then proclaims, "he swears he's through playing baseball."

❖ ❖ ❖ ❖ ❖

"PEPPY. PEPPY Swanson," I shout and knock repeatedly on the outbuilding door.

"He ain't here. Go away."

"Peppy, it's Rick Mason. Come on. Open up. We need to talk."

"You hard of hearing or something? I told ya. He ain't here. Now go away."

Realizing Peppy has no intention of answering the door, I reach for the doorknob, position my shoulder against the door and plant my feet. If necessary, I'm prepared to break the door down. To my surprise, the door is unlocked. Cautiously, I open the door and slip inside.

Peppy's so-called shop is actually a private hide-away. Three reclining chairs are arranged in a chatty semicircle to face a small television set which is encased in a crudely constructed, possibly

133

homemade, unpainted wooden cabinet. An aged white refrigerator is strategically situated within a few steps of the TV.

Peppy makes no move to acknowledge my entry. His eyes stare blankly at a late morning childrens' program.

"Peppy, can we talk? I want you to come back. The baseball team needs you."

"I told ya. Peppy ain't here. You come to the wrong house. The man you're looking for don't live here no more." Peppy speaks without moving. His glassy eyes remain glued to the television set.

This conversation is going nowhere. Electing not to compete with the TV for his attention, I walk across the room, reach down and jerk at the cord, disengaging the plug from the wall socket. A shrill gurgling noise precipitates a bright flash, then the picture fades from the screen.

"What'd you do that for? I was watching that."

"Well I'll be damned. If it ain't the real Peppy Swanson. There was a fellow here a minute ago, said you didn't live here anymore."

"Go to hell, Mason. I ain't playing for you no more."

"Hey, I thought you wanted another shot at the major leagues. I guess I was wrong about you. You sure as hell ain't gonna make it back to the big show sitting on your fat ass and drinking yourself blind."

"Can't you see? I'm washed up, over the hill. My best playing days are behind me. I ain't got a Chinaman's chance of making it back to the majors. I'm a has-been."

"Like hell you say. You're the best damn long ball hitter ever played in this league. Peppy, I made a dumb call taking you out so soon the other night, but I have a plan in mind. If you'll overlook a new manager's mistake this one time, I have an idea which might get you another shot."

"I don't know what you're talking about, Mason. You trying to pull something? Hell, you jerked me outta the game like I was some neophyte rookie. I deserve better than that. I paid my dues."

"You're absolutely right, and it won't happen again, not if you'll come back. Listen, I'm shooting straight with you. I really do have a plan. Gimme one minute, and I'll explain."

134

"You got the floor. I'm listening."

"How old are you, Peppy? Thirty-seven? Thirty-eight?"

"If you're gonna start in on that. I've heard it before—"

"Dammit, Peppy. Can't you listen for one minute without butting in? You wanna hear my plan, or not?"

"It ain't none of your business, but I'm thirty-eight," Peppy retorts, eyeing me warily.

"Fine. Now at your age no club would pick you up because you've got a good glove. So tell me. Why would any team want you?"

"Don't take no rocket scientist to know that. 'Cause I can hit the long ball, drive in runs."

"Exactly. And that's how we'll get you another shot at the big leagues."

"You got me confused, Rick. Hell, I've always been a good hitter."

"Sure. But you've had to take pot luck. How many times have you smacked a homer with the bases empty?"

"Oh, geez. Must've been more than a hundred."

"Well, I'm gonna fix that. From now on there'll be at least two men on base every time you come to bat."

"How you gonna do that? No way you can guarantee that."

"Yes, I can. I'm gonna make you my A-number-one pinch hitter. Every time you come to bat there'll be at least two men on base. If you don't have the best runs-batted-in average per at-bat by mid-season, I'll eat my hat. That's the kind of statistic that commands attention. Some upper level team that's making a run for their championship is sure to notice."

"You know, that might work. It just might work."

"Damn straight it'll work. Now climb your lazy ass outta that chair and have Virginia put on a pot of coffee. I want you showered, shaved, sober, and in uniform by seven o'clock sharp."

❖ ❖ ❖ ❖ ❖

"YOU FEELING better tonight, Rick?" Clyde inquires, flashing me a quick smile when I approach the owner's box.

"Sure am, and I'm raring to go. Sorry I missed last night's game. Musta been something I ate. When I woke up this morning, I felt fine."

"Well, we're delighted to have you back. The team got out in front early last night, so there was never much doubt about the outcome. But I still feel better with you at the helm."

"I appreciate your confidence, Clyde. I'll watch what I eat, so it won't happen again. Did Kaye come with you tonight?"

"No, she and Ted decided to take in a movie. Ted wanted to come. He's beginning to get attached to the team. Chances are he'll be a hard core fan by mid-season. But Kaye insisted he take her to a movie. Said the weather was too hot to be outdoors. Maybe I can convince her to come tomorrow night."

While I tramp back to the dugout, my disappointment hangs heavy. Yesterday, I would've sworn my wife and I had our problems ironed out. She came to me so willingly. Damn. Why must she be so stubborn? Why does she insist I choose between the two things I love most—baseball or her?

Felix meets me at the top of the dugout steps. A baseball cap, proudly displaying an oversized "T," crowns his short-cropped hair. A bright smile is tattooed across his face. He's literally beaming from ear to ear.

"Good evening, Coach Rick. I wanna thank you for the ticket and for inviting me to sit with the team. This is the happiest day of my life."

"I'm glad you could come, Felix. You meet the players yet?"

We shuffle through the dugout where Felix cheerfully greets each member of my team. Introductions are hardly necessary. Felix has memorized each player's number. He also knows each man's playing position and where he played last season. My heart warms as I watch Segars' butler heartily shake hands with the young men and inquire

136

about their families. Felix's happiness is contagious. In spite of my marital dilemma, I can't help but smile.

I understand precisely why Felix is so excited. Sharing a seat on the dugout bench is commensurate to receiving an invitation to join an exclusive private club. Here in this cozy cave, shielded from the prying eyes of paying spectators, education, wealth, and family background are immaterial. What matters here are sure hands, quick wrists, strong legs and a competitive heart. Inside his team's dugout a man's worth is measured only by what he contributes.

Possibly only a baseball player can truly appreciate the sanctity of a dugout or it's unique character, which is poignantly defined by the wear and tear of seasons long past—the pitted floor, scarred by the ravage bites of a thousand sharp steel cleats; the metal walls, tarnished by the disgusting stains of tobacco juice. For every baseball club their dugout is a special place, a sacred sanctuary where players and coaches can escape from the howls and accusations of fans outside, a place for physical and spiritual renewal. Players can dangle from the ceiling, use the roof structure to stretch tired, aching muscles, or lounge lazily on the narrow benches, or chew tobacco and spit on the floor. To a player his dugout is home, where tales of past games and past heroics are repeated over and over again. Usually the stories are told by the veterans. An unwritten law requires rookies to listen attentively to every story and laugh loudly or wince with revulsion at the appropriate time.

❖ ❖ ❖ ❖ ❖

SUDDENLY I'M FACED with a tough decision. After three warm-up pitches, Charlie Davis, my scheduled starter, walks off the mound holding his throwing arm. A hasty examination confirms Davis has strained a triceps muscle. Whitey hustles Davis to the locker room to ice down his arm while I ponder my options.

Bounato and Christie, my other two veteran pitchers, started our first two games. So I'm down to my rookies and Eric Felton, a new player who reported for duty this morning. Felton is a former Texas League hurler who Segars signed after he was released by Beaumont.

Problem is, the Roughnecks used Felton strictly for short relief. I doubt if he has the stamina to go the five innings I need from a starter. Herb Cates and Frank Johnson have looked sharp in relief, but because of this morning's deal with Peppy, I plan to start Frank at first base. I'd like to hold Cates and Philip Johnson in reserve, to relieve in the late innings. My choice is to start Felton or gamble on rookie Matt Burns.

Baseball is a game of skill and strategy. Frequently, it's also a game of nothing but dumb luck. If my luck holds, perhaps Matt can last five innings. That'll leave me with Philip Johnson and Felton to pitch middle relief and Cates to mop up if we get in trouble.

My unexpected decision unnerves the young rookie. Burns is on the mound taking his final pre-game warm-up pitches when Nelms calls time and jogs to the dugout.

"Coach Mason, you'd better talk to Burns. He's pretty rattled. If he don't settle down, these Waco hitters are gonna eat his lunch."

"Okay, Jess. Thanks for telling me. I'll see if I can calm him down."

Looking as confused and forlorn as a motherless calf, Burns turns to watch me spring from the dugout. His knees quiver, seemingly ready to buckle beneath him. A pained facial expression plainly reveals his anxiety.

Slowly and deliberately, I cross the infield, my mind searching for soothing words to boost his confidence. An idea strikes me as I reach the pitching mound.

"How's the arm, Matt? You feel okay?"

"I'm kinda nervous. Feel like I need to puke. . . ." Matt's weak voice trails off, like he's forgotten the answer to my question.

"So you have a few butterflies. That shouldn't bother you. Hell, Matt, we all get the jitters every now and then. As soon as you toss a few strikes, you'll be fine."

"I don't think so, Coach. I'm sick to my stomach, and my strength's all gone. I'm not sure I can throw the ball to the plate. I must've pitched more than fifty games in high school, but I was never scared like I am right now."

"What's bothering you happens to every rookie. It happened to me. It happened to every player on this ballfield the first time he played in a professional game." I pause to allow my words to sink in then change the subject. "Listen, Matt. I'm worried about their lead-off batter. I want you to walk him. Signal Nelms for a pitch out. Four pitches. Four balls. You understand?"

"Are you sure? You want me to intentionally walk their first batter? Holy cow, Coach Mason, I don't wanna start the game with a man on base."

"That's what I want. Can you follow instructions, or not?"

"But I don't get it. Nobody intentionally walks the first batter. No manager does that."

"You wanna manage this team, or are you gonna let me make the decisions?"

"No. I mean no sir. I got my hands full being the pitcher."

"Then walk the batter, like I tell you."

❖ ❖ ❖ ❖ ❖

"I HOPE THIS WORKS, Whitey. If it backfires, this crowd is likely to run us outta the ballpark."

"Where do you come up with these hair-brained ideas, Rick? You check with Matilda about this?"

"No, and don't start in with that ghost stuff. I saw Coach Falk use this strategy once. My Longhorn club was in the loser's bracket of the conference tournament. We were struggling to stay alive. Coach had run through all his experienced arms. Our bullpen consisted of one green, untested freshman pitcher. Coach Falk strolled to the mound and demanded the freshman walk Baylor's first batter. The young pitcher was so mortified he forgot how nervous he was. Ended up pitching the best game of his life."

Waco's lead-off batter takes ball four, flips his bat to the Pirates' batboy, and turns to face the grandstands. Illustrating his bewilderment, he raises his hands with palms up. His gesture ignites an angry eruption of cat calls and boos from unhappy home fans.

❖ ❖ ❖ ❖ ❖

"BALL THREE!" the umpire barks, hoarsely issuing judgement on Burn's anemic offering. The count is three and 0. One more ball and there'll be two Pirates on base with nobody out.

"Time out! Time out, ump," I shout. This isn't working like I planned.

Honoring my request, the home plate umpire removes his facemask and raises both his hands. I vault from the dugout and jog out to talk with my rookie pitcher.

"My instructions were to walk their lead-off batter. You handled that fine, but now I want some strikes. I'm not worried about this batter. I know him. He can't hit his weight."

"I'm trying, Coach Mason, but I ain't got it tonight. You better take me out."

Every fiber in my body bristles. I give the kid a silver-plated opportunity to make good, and he folds like a wounded dove. My inclination is to lash out, challenge his manhood, call him gutless, demand he suck it up and finish what he started. But instead, I affectionately pat his back and offer sympathy.

"Alright, Matt, if you're feeling bad, we'll bring in Felton. You check in with Whitey and hit the showers."

Burns hands me the baseball and ambles toward the dugout. I signal the bullpen I want Felton. That's when a loudmouth fan, unhappy with my game plan, bellows his displeasure.

"Hey, meathead! You're taking out the wrong guy! It's the nitwit manager who oughta get the hook! He's the one been taking stupid pills!"

❖ ❖ ❖ ❖ ❖

"BURNS IS SICK as a horse. I sent him to the locker room to shower. You might wanna look in on him," Whitey informs me after I return to the dugout. Eric Felton is on the mound taking his allotted warm-up pitches.

"Sure, but gimme a minute to watch Felton. Eric's in a tough spot here. Let's see how he handles himself."

After Felton tosses his fifth and final warm-up pitch, the umpire mutters something to Nelms. My catcher nods and bounces up to fire the ball back to his pitcher.

"Batter up," the umpire grunts. Waco's batter takes a couple of practice swings, stretches his arms, steps into the batter's box and digs in.

Felton winds and delivers. Sorrowful moans rumble through the grandstands as the home crowd watches Eric's pitch hit the ground four-feet short of home plate and bounce lamely into Nelms' mitt.

"Ball four!" the umpire declares, and I bury my face into cupped hands.

❖ ❖ ❖ ❖ ❖

CAPITALIZING ON my faulty judgement, the Pirates jump on Felton for three consecutive singles to score three runs. Only a diving stop by Bruzga and a spectacular outfield catch by Dub Akins to end the inning saves me from the wrath of our furious home fans.

"Damn. Damn. And holy damn. Man, when I make a bad call, I do it right," I tell my assistant while we watch our team run off the playing field.

"Don't worry, Rick. Everyone screws up occasionally. Hey, it's only the first inning. We'll score some runs and get back in the game."

"Maybe, but I'm afraid it's not our night. How could I be so dumb? I put us in a deep hole even before we have a turn at bat."

"You're too hard on yourself. That trick might work under different circumstances. You said it worked for your Texas coach."

"Sure, but I'm obviously no Bibb Falk. Listen, with our luck tonight, somebody's certain to get called out because he batted out of turn. You make sure everyone knows the batting order. I'll be back as soon as I check on our sick kid."

❖ ❖ ❖ ❖ ❖

I DISCOVER my young rookie sprawled out on the restroom floor. Both his arms are wrapped around a toilet stool. I step back, close my eyes and try to block out the indecent sounds of misery while he pukes his guts out.

Outside, I hear an angry crowd scream their disapproval as Henry French steps to the plate. My stomach churns. A wave of nausea sweeps over me, but I reject a strong desire to drop to my knees, crawl to an adjacent toilet bowl and join my sickly pitcher.

❖ ❖ ❖ ❖ ❖

AFTER A SHAKY START, Eric Felton finds the strike zone. Combining a sweeping curve with a sinking fastball, his geometric ballistics give Waco's batters fits. When the Pirates do put the ball in play, our alert defense sucks it up like a vacuum.

Methodically, we peck away at Waco's lead, scoring runs in the fourth and fifth innings. A double play relay from third baseman Neuendorff to French at second to Johnson on first crushes a Pirate rally in the top of the sixth.

As they lope to the dugout, the faces of my gladiators reveal their grim resolve. Regardless of their manager's stupidity, they intend to win this game.

The center field scoreboard tells the dismal tale:

HOME   2   VISITORS   3

❖ ❖ ❖ ❖ ❖

LARRY HOLMES appears at the top of the dugout steps while I parley with Felton. Eric has pitched six solid innings. He claims his arm feels fine, but I'm concerned. The last thing this team needs is another sore armed hurler.

"Hey, Rick. Garry Watkins is here. We need you and Henry French to pose for a few pictures."

142

"Watkins? I thought he was in Austin. Isn't the legislature in session?"

"Yep, that's right. Garry's in town to do some quick campaigning. Has to be back in Austin tomorrow morning. Can you and Henry come now?"

"Larry, we have a tight game in progress here. Whatever Watkins wants it'll have to wait."

"I'm sorry, Rick. This can't wait. Colonel's orders. The car is here. The girls are here. Watkins is here. We need you and French, pronto."

"Car? Girls? Larry, what the heck's going on?"

"Campaign pictures. Watkins is planning to run for Lieutenant Governor. The colonel wants you and French in the pictures. You get the connection—a winning baseball team and a winning candidate."

"But what about the car and girls?"

"The car's a brand-new DeSoto convertible. The girls are Apache Bells from the junior college drill team. You get the connection—beautiful girls, fabulous car."

"Sure, I see." What I see are pictures of pretty girls and a brand-spanking-new DeSoto which are certain to be plastered on billboards all across the state. Clyde Segars never misses a lick.

"This'll only take a few minutes. We'll have you two back in a jiffy."

❖ ❖ ❖ ❖ ❖

OUR PHOTOGRAPHY SESSION takes place at the front gate where Larry has blocked off an area to accommodate one of Segars' new convertibles. Henry and I are needed for only a few poses, but Watkins insists we remain until the last picture is snapped. He seems particularly obsessed with the two scantily-dressed young women, insisting they pose alongside him in every picture.

When French and I return to the dugout, I discover Whitey, Philip Johnson and Herb Cates huddled in conference. Peppy Swanson is at bat. John Bruzga is on third. Nick Gregory stands on second. The scoreboard indicates we have two out. The score remains unchanged:

HOME   2   VISITORS   3

"Hey there, Skipper. Glad you're back. Johnson here has an idea he wants to try. You ever hear of the sneaky possum play?"

"Not by that name, but I think I know what he's proposing. Looks like Gregory is limping. Maybe we oughta send in a sub to run for him."

"That's what we're thinking. Johnson tells me Bruzga knows all about his sneaky possum trick."

"Maybe we should wait. What's the count on Peppy?"

"0 and two. Not much chance of his walking. The Pirate catcher's real proud of his throwing arm, Rick. Been trying to pick off our base runners every time they get too big a lead."

"I assume you're planning to send in our speedster Cates to sub for Gregory."

"That's the idea. Whatta you think?"

"I like your plan. Let's go for it."

❖ ❖ ❖ ❖ ❖

WITH THE COUNT at no balls and two strikes, Waco's pitcher has room for play. His pitch is high and inside. Peppy is patient. He refuses to swing, opting to wait for a pitch he can hit. Cates, who we subbed in to run for Gregory, is off and running with the delivery. He's halfway to third when the umpire signals the pitch was a ball. Cates kicks at the dirt, starts back toward second then stoops to tie a loose shoelace.

The Pirate catcher takes the bait. Noticing Cates so far off base, he bounces up from his crouched position and rifles the ball toward second. A split second later our two base runners break for home and third.

Ten yards from home Bruzga leaves his feet, diving to belly slide across home plate. Cates kicks up a heavy cloud of dust as he slides

144

feet first into third. A confused Pirate shortstop, wearing a sheepish grin, stands on second, welding the baseball at head height, without the slightest idea where he should throw.

Since we fell behind in the first inning, Tyler supporters have been relatively quiet. Except for an occasional outstanding defensive play, there hasn't been much to cheer about. But after watching the amazing success of our sneaky possum play, the crowd is overcome with anticipation. Spectators jump to their feet, cheering and clapping. Suddenly our boosters sense victory is at hand. Players in our dugout yell encouragement to our batter, beseeching him to make contact, get a hit. Opposing players in the visiting dugout stand and shout to their pitcher, urging him to throw a strike, blow the bum away.

An electric-like excitement fills the air. Every person in the stadium is standing, screaming, stomping their feet, furiously pleading with our hefty slugger to drive in the go ahead run.

For a younger player the hectic situation and fanatic pandemonium might be distracting, but Peppy is a veteran, a seasoned gladiator who has fought and won many similar battles. Calmly blocking out the crowd noise, Peppy shifts his weight to his back foot. He holds his bat high, using a small circular motion to stabilize his batting stance.

"WOOMP!" Peppy's bat connects solidly with the pitcher's projectile. A hushed silence falls over the stadium. Fans, players, and impartial umpires stand quietly with mouths agape, watching the baseball soar high above the center fielder's head and clear the scoreboard by some twenty feet.

❖ ❖ ❖ ❖ ❖

WHILE THE TEAM showers and changes to their street clothes, I mingle among the players. Congratulating them on their fine play, slapping backs, shaking hands and swapping jokes, I hang around until the last player leaves.

I'm expecting my friend Max. It's unlike him to miss an appointment and not call. Max is an engineer, normally prompt and reliable. One of the few things we quarreled about when we roomed together was my being late. He has an obsession about being on time.

A noise in the equipment storeroom postpones my brooding.

"Whitey? That you?" I call nervously, recollecting my assistant left with Hal Epps. Whitey's old clunker is acting up. Epps gave him a lift home.

When no one answers, I call again. "Hey. Who's in there? Come on out." A tiny twinge of fear prompts a tightening inside my stomach. Whatever caused the noise, it certainly wasn't my assistant or one of my players.

A shadowy figure moves inside the darkened room.

"Matilda? Matilda, is that you?" I inquire fearfully, my mind rebuking my mouth for uttering such a dumb question. Despite Whitey's constant allusions, I'm positive there's no such thing as ghosts. Nonetheless, a cold chill races up my backbone.

"Don't be afraid, my love. I can't hurt you. I only want to talk. I'm lonely."

I slap at my face to make sure I'm not dreaming. Surely this is a dream.

"You're real. You're a real ghost. Like Whitey said."

"I would prefer you think of me as a spirit. We've met before— three nights ago. Surely you haven't forgotten. I held you in my arms. Don't you remember?"

"I remember. At least I think I do. I was rather inebriated at the time."

"We need to talk about your drinking. You'll have to stop. I can't tolerate a man who drinks."

"Hey, I'm trying to quit. It's not that easy. But why should you care?"

"I thought you wanted a winning season. Aren't you and your father-in-law in some kind of jam? If you fail to make the playoffs, people are likely to get hurt."

"That's true. But how did you know about that, and what's that got to do with my drinking?"

146

"Don't you understand? I'm here to help you. But I can't help a man who loves the bottle more than he loves baseball."

"Help me? How you gonna help me? What's a woman ghost know about baseball?"

"My father was a baseball player and a manager. If I told you his name, you would recognize it. He taught me a few things—like having your first baseman hug the line and pitching a right-handed batter on the outside of the plate and watching how a left-handed pitcher positions himself after his delivery."

"It was you. It's you who put those ideas in my head."

"Yes, and if you'll quit drinking, I'll stay for the season. I like you, Richard. You've been through some rough times. Perhaps I can help you have a winning season."

"Alright, we have a deal. You help me win, and I'll quit drinking." She may look and act like an angel, but I suspect I'm making a pact with the devil.

"Not so fast, my love. There's one more thing."

"What's that? You name it. You got it. As long as you'll assure me my team makes the playoffs, I'll agree to it."

"Your wife. You should treat her better."

"You mean, Kaye? Yeah, I know I should. I do love her. I love her more than anything, but we're always fighting. Mostly we fight about me and baseball. Now she's after me to quit. You know, settle down and get a steady job."

"Sometimes a woman can love a man too much—to his detriment and so much it poisons their relationship. That's the case with your wife. Except for her father, she has never loved another man before you. She yearns for your undivided attention. That's why she wants you to quit baseball. She wants you all to herself. She believes that will make her happy."

"Sure, but what about me? You think I'd be happy selling cars, working at a job I hate? No way. I'd smother and die."

"If you want my help, you must either give her up or give her more attention. You have no other choice."

Wheels inside my brain spin like a Las Vegas slot. There's no way I'll give up Kaye. The thought of never holding her again, never kissing her warm lips causes me pain.

"No, I can't give her up. I love her too much."

"Good. I'm glad that's settled. Starting tonight, you must change your ways. You must make her feel special and give her your undivided attention. Let her know she comes first, even before baseball. After the baby comes, I doubt if she'll be nearly so possessive. Another man in her life should make a huge difference in her attitude about you and baseball."

"Baby? What baby?"

"Your baby. Oh, didn't I tell you? You're going to be a father."

"But that can't be. I haven't touched Kaye in more than three months."

"Except for yesterday, my love."

"Oh yeah, I forgot about yesterday, but how did you know about yesterday?"

"I have my sources. You would be surprised by the things I know about you."

"And you're sure the baby's mine, not Ted's?"

"I'm surprised you would ask such a question."

"Yeah, me too. But are you sure?"

"Yes, I'm absolutely sure."

"We have a deal then. I'll quit drinking and start treating my wife like royalty. You help me manage this team to a winning season. That's the agreement?"

"That is the deal. It's late, Richard. You should go home."

"Right, I have a big day tomorrow. Doubt if I'll sleep a wink tonight though. I've got a lot to think about. You mentioned another man in Kaye's life. That mean the baby's a boy?"

"Yes, she's carrying your son. Be good to her."

Even though I haven't showered, I grab my clothes and head for the door. I'll bathe at home. Matilda might be embarrassed to have me undress in front of her.

"Oh, I'm sorry about your friend. I'm sure you'll miss him."

"My friend? You mean Max?"

"Yes. Wasn't he supposed to meet you tonight—after the game?"

"That was our plan. I suppose he got tied up."

"He won't be coming, Richard. Don't wait up for him."

CHAPTER NINE

WHEN I WAS a hotshot playing in the majors, I fell into the habit of sleeping late. It was an unhealthy routine which plagues many players long after their playing days are finished. Quite often, we played night games which didn't end until after ten. Our schedule frequently required night travel. Many nights we arrived at a strange hotel in a strange city in the wee hours. It became my custom to skip breakfast. In the days before I banged up my knee, I saved my breakfast allowance, sending it home to my grandmother. But after my grandmother's death, I quit saving. My breakfast allowance, and sometimes my lunch and dinner allowance, went to buy booze.

This manager's job is more demanding. My duties require an early presence at the ballfield each morning. Not that I mind. Early morning is my favorite time of day.

Mary's Diner is conveniently located on my way to the ballpark. The restaurant's major claim to food fame is a morning special. A plateful of breakfast consisting of two eggs, three strips of bacon, two pieces of toast, and all the coffee you can drink costs thirty-five cents. Being short of funds, I'm forced to forego breakfast. A cup of coffee is all I can afford this morning.

Mary also subscribes to the *Tyler Morning Telegraph*. Another of my favorite morning pastimes is scanning the newspaper over morning coffee.

Even though the colonel's imaginative promotions have more than doubled attendance compared to last year's first three games, local sportswriters have been slow to throw their full support behind the baseball club. Perhaps the reporters find difficulty adjusting to Segars' new name—"East Texans." Their reluctance is legitimized by the fact that, as yet, much of the signage at the ballpark still alludes to the team as the Trojans. And so does most everyone else in town. Even the announcers handling the nightly radio broadcasts occasionally get their tongues twisted and refer to the team as the Trojans.

Nonetheless, I suspect the main reason for the sportswriters lack of support is their fear our play will degenerate to last year's level, disillusioning the fans and embarrassing the city with another miserable losing season. That's why a large box enclosed inside a wide dark border on the front page of the morning paper is such a surprise.

A caption above the box reads:

FRENCH WALKS EAST TEXANS TO A RUNNING START

At Bats	Hits	Walks	Runs	Batting Avg.
14	0	14	8	.000

An accompanying story explains how the rookie French has scored half the runs manufactured by the offense, and how he is a major factor in the team's turnaround. At the bottom of the article is a mail-in coupon, offering two free tickets to the fan who can correctly predict the number of at-bats French will enjoy before he makes an out and another set of tickets to the fan who can predict which game Henry will get his first hit.

I can't help but laugh aloud. Having the advantage of an insider, there is very little risk on the part of the paper. It's very unlikely Henry will make an out the entire season, even less chance he'll get a hit. Nevertheless, it's a terrific promotional gimmick, and having the article appear on page one is quite a coop. Without a doubt the heavy hand of Clyde Segars is at work here.

I gulp down the last of my coffee and leave my last dime on the counter. On my way out, I stuff the morning paper back in the rack by the front door.

❖ ❖ ❖ ❖ ❖

A JUMBLE OF COTTON-LIKE CLOUDS floats lazily over the ballpark as I wheel into the stadium parking lot. Except for a shiny, bright-green Chrysler parked next to the front gate, the parking area is empty. Morning practice is scheduled for nine-thirty. My players won't begin filtering into the locker room until around nine.

The spiffy new automobile belongs to Ted Gooding. I may have married the boss's daughter, but Ted seems to be the one riding the gravy train.

Ted is not an early riser. No way he'd be here this early on account of business. No, he's here to confront me.

According to Clyde, Ted escorted my wife to the movies last evening. Maybe they went to the movies. Maybe they didn't. Wherever they went, I'm sure Kaye told him everything—probably even spilled the beans about my missing Wednesday night's game. Well, that information won't get me fired, not now. My East Texans have chalked up three consecutive victories. The colonel is delighted with my performance. Hell, everyone is happy, except Ted and Kaye.

Taking a deep breath, I muster my composure, repressing a burning inclination to charge the stadium, seek out my rival and bust up his handsome face. But remembering my promise to my father-in-law, I restrain my anger.

Still, I can't keep from clenching my fists. I slam the car door shut and march toward the ballfield. I intend to set things straight between us. I'm tired of Ted fooling around with my wife.

❖ ❖ ❖ ❖ ❖

SINCE HE ASSUMED his role as business manager, Ted and I have hardly spoken. He's looked after his business. I've confined my activities to managing the team. Tomorrow morning the team leaves for Wichita Falls on our first road trip. Ted and I need to discuss bus schedules, room accommodations, players' meal allowances, and a hundred other details pertaining to team travel.

Regardless of his arrogant personality, Ted is an excellent businessman, and he's extremely efficient. He is meticulously frugal with the colonel's money. That's why Segars trusts him. Ted will have negotiated every minor expenditure, systematically planned and organized every detail. Every penny spent will net maximum return.

I discover Ted sitting high in the stands where the bench seating is shaded from the morning sun by the overhanging canopy. His eyes are fixed on the infield. He appears to be in deep thought.

Ted is a particular dresser who takes great pride in his appearance. Normally, he wears a business suit. However, this morning he's dressed casually, wearing a bright plaid short-sleeved shirt and denim jeans.

"Good morning, Ted. You look worried. Anything I can do to help?"

"Oh. Hi, Rick. Didn't notice you walk up. No, I was sitting here thinking about baseball players. You know, Rick, athletes like yourself are so darn lucky. You fellows make a living playing a game you love while the rest of the world crawls out of bed every morning to work at jobs they hate. And women love you. Seems like there's always a hundred gorgeous females crazy to jump in bed with you. I wish I could have been good at sports. But I never was. You're a very lucky guy, Rick. Damn lucky."

Ted's unsolicited confession stuns me. Why should he envy me? He's the one with the brains, the law degree, the silky smooth manners—the perfect male—sensitive, reliable, attentive, without flaw, without weakness. But judging from his melancholy mood, you'd think he'd be willing to trade places with me.

153

"You make a ball player's life sound too glamorous, Ted. It's not like that. Athletes work hard at their jobs. It's not enough to compete well. You're expected to win. If you let up for even a minute, somebody will beat your brains out. If you get hurt, some other player will take your job."

"But when you win, you know you've won. When you win you can chalk it up and go on to the next game. It's not like the business world, or love, or real life. Hell, most of the time I'm out there knocking my butt off, without the slightest hint of whether I'm winning or losing."

"Are we talking about life, or love? Sounds like we might be talking about Kaye Mason," I question, my temper flaring. He and my wife were together last evening. Did they kiss goodnight? Did he wrap his arms around her and pull her close? Did her body melt against his, the way it does when she kisses me? My evil thoughts make my blood boil.

"Both. I owe you an apology, Rick. I've been a total ass. I thought if I could break up your marriage, I could win her back. I've loved Kaye since I was ten, from the first day we met. If I hadn't been such a stupid jerk in college, she'd never have married you. She'd be married to me. But last night she told me she loves you. I have no chance with her. In spite of everything I've done right, all I've done for her family, and everything you've done wrong—she loves you."

"Kaye loves me? Are you sure?" That's what Matilda told me, but still I'm surprised to hear Ted say it. When Kaye didn't attend last night's game, I was certain I'd lost her again.

"Yes. Kaye and I skipped the movie last night—drove out to Tyler State Park and had a long heart to heart discussion. Mostly we talked about you. Kaye says her heart belongs to you. She vows she'll never marry again—no matter how the divorce works out."

"I feel the same about her. I could never love anyone else the way I love Kaye. But seems like we can't say hello without getting into a fight."

"That's why I'm stepping out. Maybe with me out of the picture, you two can make a go of it. I want Kaye to be happy. She needs someone who'll love and appreciate her. I wish that person could be me, but I suppose it's not in the cards. I love her so much. I'd do anything to see she's happy. If that means giving her up and leaving town, then I'll leave."

"Leave town! Ted, no. You can't leave. The season's underway. It's important you stay."

"It would be better for everyone if I leave. I'm not sure I can handle watching you take my girl and become the old man's favorite. I have a job offer in Houston. If I climb off this Tyler merry-go-round, maybe I can get on with my life."

"Ted, it's important you stay. Clyde needs you. I need you. The baseball team needs you. Clyde's promised those New Orleans' big wigs he'll turn a profit. No way this franchise can show a profit without you watching the dollars."

"Yes, he's in pretty deep. Clyde's overzealous promises may have put all of us in jeopardy. I'd like to help, but with the animosity between you and me, I don't see how I can stay."

"What say we put past feelings behind us? No more back stabbing. You, me and Clyde—we'll see this thing through together. From now on we're a team. You take care of the business, and I'll field a winning team."

Ted mulls my offer thoughtfully, considering his options. Actually he has little choice. No way he can leave with so much trouble looming. Like myself, he owes Segars too much.

"Alright, Rick. We have a deal. I'll stay and see this thing through."

"I don't have many friends, Ted. But if you'd care to join a very elite group, I'd like to shake hands."

"Sure, I'll shake your hand, and I'll be your friend. But the day you mistreat Kaye, our friendship ends."

"Don't worry, Ted. That won't happen again, not ever again."

During our lengthy conversation, my team has arrived and dressed for morning practice. The appearance of several team members on the playing field prompts me to switch the discussion to team travel.

Ted explains he has arranged for a chartered bus to transport the squad to Wichita Falls. Mindful of every nickel, he has scheduled the bus to leave from Trojan Field at two o'clock Saturday afternoon, thereby avoiding the necessity of providing lunch for the players. Our bus should arrive in Wichita Falls sometime after five, barely giving us time to don our uniforms and take infield before the game. We'll lodge at a motel located in Jolly which is on the southern outskirts of Wichita Falls. Thinking I might object, Ted sternly informs me he's checked out every detail. The motel rooms are guaranteed to be clean, the beds comfortable. Still, he can't subdue a wry smile when he divulges the rooms are a dollar a night cheaper than at the Kent Hotel downtown where visiting clubs usually quarter.

Ted trails behind me as we traverse down the stadium steps. When we reach the breezeway next to the dressing room, we pause briefly to shake hands again. He promises to bring me money for players' food allowances before the bus departs tomorrow.

As I watch him walk away, leaving for his fancy office downtown, I feel much better about my coaching situation. Working with Ted, without the bitter animosity, will make my life much simpler.

Without Ted's interference, perhaps Kaye and I can patch up our marriage. Matilda told me Kaye loves me, and now Ted has confirmed it. A week ago I was alone in the world. Now it seems I'm in great demand. I have two women in my life—one who loves me so much she'd turn down a man like Ted, and another who promises the one thing every baseball player yearns for—a winning season.

❖ ❖ ❖ ❖ ❖

WITH MORNING PRACTICE, travel preparations, and tonight's game to worry over, time passes quickly. It's mid-afternoon. Whitey and I are sorting through equipment, deciding which items to pack when the telephone in the manager's office rings. Thinking it might be Kaye or my father-in-law with some urgent message, I hand a canvas tote bag to my assistant and hurry over to answer. On the third ring I pick up the phone.

"East Texans' field house," I answer, swearing under my breath. Surely I can come up with a more dignified way to answer. East Texans sounds so dumb.

A woman's voice comes on the line. "Hello. I'm trying to reach a Mister Richard Mason. I believe he manages the Tyler baseball team."

"You got him. This is Rick Mason."

"Hello, Mister Mason. We've never met, but I feel like we're friends. I'm Georgia Wagner—Max's wife."

"Hi, Georgia. Yes, I feel like I know you too. It's a shame we've never met. Max and I go back a long way. We were supposed to get together after last night's game, but he didn't show. Is he okay?"

"I'm not sure. That's why I called. I was hoping you may have seen him. He left Houston yesterday morning on his way to Tyler. No one's seen him since." The woman's voice quivers as she speaks. She sounds desperate. Most likely I'm not the first person she's called.

"He mentioned a job he'd been hired to do. Do you know who hired him? Perhaps they'll know where he is. Maybe he ran into something more complicated than he expected."

"I'm afraid I have no idea who he's working for. Max is frequently hired to investigate situations which involve corporate espionage, so he's generally secretive about his employers. But when he travels, he always calls me to check in. Last night he didn't call. Mister Mason, I'm worried about him."

"Georgia, could you call me Rick? Mister Mason sounds so formal. Look, it's been several years since Max and I hung out. He's married now, and he may have changed. But I have to ask. Does he still drink?" It's a subject I'd rather avoid, for obvious reasons. During our college days, Max was a prolific boozer. After college he became a dedicated alcoholic. He sometimes disappeared for days, usually emerging bleary-eyed and with some strange female he'd been shacked up with. Georgia Wagner doesn't impress me as a woman who would put up with that kind of behavior.

"No. He stopped drinking two years ago. Rick, do you know something? Oh, my God. You don't think he started drinking again?"

"No. No. I was only asking for information. Thought it might be important." I'm sorry I brought the subject up. The panic in her voice tells me she's been through some bad times. Loving a drunk can be worse than being the drunk.

"I don't think Max's disappearance is related to drinking, Rick. Max is sober now. He's been sober for a long time, and he knows I'll leave him if he so much as touches alcohol. I'm afraid he may be hurt or lost. Oh, I'm not sure what I'm afraid of, but I know he would call if he could." Her voice breaks. She's close to tears.

"When I talked to him Tuesday morning, he was planning to walk a couple miles of pipeline and check some pump gages. Didn't sound like he was taking on anything dangerous. You know how engineers are, Georgia. Sometimes they get so involved solving a problem they forget all about time and other people. Max has only been missing since yesterday. I'm sure he'll turn up."

"Perhaps you're right. Max can be very intense. I'm probably just being a silly woman, making a mountain out of a molehill."

"Listen, Georgia, my team's leaving on a four-day road trip. We'll be back in Tyler next Wednesday. If Max is still missing, we'll get the local authorities involved, and I'll personally run out to Swinneytown to search for him. Meantime you keep cool." Actually, I have no idea where I'd look, but I try to sound confident.

"Alright. Will you call me Wednesday morning?"

"Sure thing. The minute I get back."

Instead of immediately returning to assist Whitey, I sit on the desk and ponder for a moment. Last night Matilda advised me not to wait for Max. She said he wouldn't be coming. At the time I assumed she meant to be helpful, so I could avoid a fruitless postgame wait in the locker room. But was her message a warning? Surely she would have told me if Max was hurt or in some kind of danger.

My mind is full of unanswered questions, but I can't allow myself to be distracted by matters outside my control. My team has a game tonight. I haven't decided on a starting pitcher.

Forcing myself to dismiss further speculation about my friend's whereabouts, I hop off the desk. My mind shifts to the packing task at hand before I reach the equipment room.

❖ ❖ ❖ ❖ ❖

MY ASSISTANT AND I stuff four canvas bags with towels, medical supplies and miscellaneous gear. Early tomorrow morning we'll pack baseballs, bats, gloves, shoes, uniforms and the other equipment we can't pack today because of tonight's game. In less than an hour we make a huge dent in our packing chore, and we agree precisely on which items we'll take and which we'll leave behind. That'll make tomorrow morning's packing go much faster. While Whitey cleans up our mess and reorganizes his equipment domain, I muscle the heavy bags off the counter and line them against the wall.

"That ought to do it for now, Whitey. Reckon we've agreed on everything. Packing tomorrow morning should be a breeze."

My assistant gazes at me from behind a stack of cleated shoes. He tugs at his chin, like he's debating with himself.

"Well, there is one item we haven't discussed. Matilda wants to travel along with us. You have any objections?"

"No, I guess not. Matter of fact, I like the idea. She expecting to have a room for herself?" I quip, taking advantage of an opportunity to poke fun at my friend. There's no way tightwad Ted would ever agree to pay for an extra room.

"Naw, she can stay in the same room with me. Matilda won't be no trouble. She don't hardly take up no space at all," Whitey chuckles, picking up on my humor. Thoroughly amused at his clever response, he grins and happily returns to his work.

❖ ❖ ❖ ❖ ❖

ALL AFTERNOON my thoughts keep switching back and forth—thinking about Kaye and my conversation with Ted then worrying about Max. Matilda's announcement concerning my impending role as a father also weighs heavy on my mind. With a ball club to manage and so many personal problems, the last thing I need is a baby. I wonder if Kaye knows she's pregnant. No, probably not. But if she doesn't suspect, how could Matilda know?

My mind is an absolute mess as I sit alone in the dugout watching my team take infield. With me in outer space, Whitey offered to take charge of the pre-game warm-up drills.

Felix taps me on the shoulder, interrupting my garbled meditation.

"Felix? What are you doing here?" Segars' butler shared our dugout last evening. He had a fine time, and my players thoroughly enjoyed his company. Felix is a nice enough guy, but I never intended his presence be a regular occurrence. My brain grapples for a reason he should be here. If one of the players invited him back to sit with us again tonight, they never checked with me.

"Colonel Segars asked me to sit in his box tonight. He knew I sat in your dugout last night, so at breakfast this morning, he and I got to talking baseball. When he discovered what a big fan I am, he invited me to accompany him tonight. Can you believe my good fortune? Last night in the Trojan dugout. This evening I'm in the owner's box."

Last night, with Ted and Kaye supposedly off to the movies, Clyde was forced to sit alone in the owner's box, surrounded by a half-dozen empty seats. It never occurred to me sitting alone might embarrass my father-in-law. Despite his immense wealth, Segars is essentially a loner.

"Colonel Segars asked if you'd come visit his box before the game. Miss Kaye and Mister Gooding are also here this evening. They want to say hello."

"Say hello? I'm sorry, Felix. Tell Clyde I'm busy. Tell him I'm working on tonight's lineup," I say, which is not necessarily a lie. I'm semi-debating whether to start Bounato with three days rest or go with Philip Johnson. In my present confused state, I'm not up to a friendly chat with those three. No telling what they might lay on me.

"You better come, Mister Rick. The three of them have been talking all afternoon. It must be terribly important."

❖ ❖ ❖ ❖ ❖

"RICK, WE HATE to interrupt your pre-game routine, but Ted tells me the two of you had a most interesting conversation this morning."

"That's right. He and I agreed to quit stabbing each other in the back. Is that what this is about?" I answer, trying not to sound intimidated. In spite of Ted's pledge to cease interfering in my love life, I'm not completely convinced he can be trusted.

"Yes. Well, I understand the conversation went a great deal deeper. Ted says you resolved a number of issues—"

"I called my attorney today. I'm dropping my divorce suit," Kaye blurts out. A bright smile decorates her lovely face.

"You're not divorcing me?" I respond stupidly. I hope she's not expecting me to climb the railing and embrace her. This is hardly the time or place for a marriage reconciliation.

"Of course not, silly. I never wanted to divorce you. Last night, Ted convinced me to give our marriage another try. He, daddy and I have talked it over, and we all agree. Neither you nor I can be happy as long as we're separated."

"That's terrific. Look, I need to go. The game's about to get underway."

"Can we meet somewhere later? Ted and I came in my car. He can ride home with daddy. You and I need to talk."

"Yeah. Sure. I'll meet you in the parking lot after the game. Might take a few minutes before I can shake loose. The team's leaving on a road trip tomorrow, so I need to meet with the players before they leave. Our meeting shouldn't take long. Got some last minute details to go over."

"I don't mind waiting, darling. We have so much to talk about."

"Fine. See you after the game then."

I turn and hurriedly trot back to the dugout. Now my mind is really a total mess.

❖ ❖ ❖ ❖ ❖

BASEBALL IS A GAME with short spurts of dramatic action sandwiched in between long stretches of monotonous boredom. A home run, a nerve-racking duel between pitcher and batter with the score tied and runners on base, a diving catch, a double play—separated by repetitive innings with nothing but routine ground balls, fly outs, strike outs and pitching changes.

Unlike football or basketball, baseball is played at a slow pace. Fans can relax, visit with other fans, or simply enjoy the tranquil beauty of a pleasant summer evening. Spectators can visit the concession booths and purchase a hot dog and a soft drink, or make a quick trip to the rest room with little fear of missing some crucial play which might determine the outcome.

For Tyler boosters, tonight is an especially relaxing night. The game's outcome is never in doubt. We score runs in each of the first three innings. Bounato limits the Pirates to three hits and one run. He goes a full seven frames before I bring in Philip Johnson in relief.

Philip immediately discourages any fans who were planning to leave early by giving up two consecutive singles. A fielding error by Neuendorff loads the bases and puts our Cajun rookie in a deep hole before he settles down. Johnson gets his first out on a one-hopper back to the mound then strikes out Waco's third baseman Jim Rice and gets pinch hitter George Drury on a high fly to left field. In the top of the ninth Philip finds his groove and retires the side in order.

Adding to Tyler fans' delight is the continued success of Henry French. He walks in each of his four plate appearances and scores three runs. During French's fourth turn at bat, Pete Wilson, the Pirates' second relief pitcher, showing his frustration, throws an inside pitch which clips Henry's right arm. Our fans rise to give a standing ovation as Henry dusts himself off and trots down to first base.

Final Score: East Texans 6   Pirates 1

We win all four games in the home series with the Pirates.

❖ ❖ ❖ ❖ ❖

MY MEETING with the players lasts only a few minutes. I advise the men to be at the ballpark with bags packed no later than one-thirty. A hefty fine will be levied against any player who shows up after one-forty-five. Our bus will leave promptly at two. Goodbyes to children, wives, and girl friends are to be taken care of at home, not at the stadium.

❖ ❖ ❖ ❖ ❖

KAYE'S BLUE DeSoto is parked outside the front gate. I walk to the driver's side and crouch down to her open window.

"Hi, hon. Thanks for waiting."

She reaches to touch my hand on the car window. "Get in, Ricky. We need to talk."

"Sure. You want me to drive?"

"Yes, but I want you to kiss me first."

Kaye scoots over while I open the car door and slide in. She waits until I'm behind the wheel then reaches to gently touch my arm. A tingling sensation rushes through my body.

"Kiss me. Tell me you love me."

"I love you, Kaye. I never loved anyone. . ." Her lips interrupt me before I can complete my sentence.

"Oh, Ricky, can we go somewhere? I've missed you so much. Maybe we should go to your apartment," she says when our lips finally part. Sparkles of moonlight reflect through the windshield to softly illuminate her long blonde hair.

"Not tonight, hon. We'd only wind up in bed and with me oversleeping. I need to be at the ballpark bright and early tomorrow morning. Whitey and I have a gang of final packing to do before the bus arrives."

"Don't you want to be with me? Aren't you happy I dropped the divorce suit?"

"Sure, I'm ecstatic. But we'll have plenty of time for each other when I come back. What say we save consummating our reconciliation for another time. I've had a long day. I'm dog tired."

"Okay, if you're too tired, I can wait. But I've been thinking about what you said yesterday morning. I want to move in with you, so we can be together every day. Won't that be wonderful?"

"Move in with me? Oh, sure, that'll be great. Look, Kaye, it's been a long day. How about we say goodnight? I'm worn to a frazzle."

"Can I come to the ballpark tomorrow to see you off?"

"No, that's not a good idea. We told the players to say their goodbyes at home. Don't want a lot of hugging and crying while we're trying to load the bus. It's bad for team morale."

"Alright, I won't come, but I promise to miss you every single minute you're gone. Will you kiss me goodbye?"

"You bet, and I'll miss you too."

Even with my lips pressed against hers, my mind reels with questions. I love this woman. For so many months I've yearned to hold her, to kiss her, and now here she is, offering me her love, offering everything I've dreamed of.

So why should I have this eerie feeling, like I'm tied to a railroad track with a giant steam engine roaring down on me?

CHAPTER TEN

LEAVE IT TO TED and his penny pinching ways to squeeze the last dollar out of our travel budget. The tiny bus he chartered to transport the team to Wichita Falls barely contains enough seats. And as you might expect, the bus is not air-conditioned.

Nonetheless, our players cluster around the dilapidated old bus, anxious to leave. With the temperature hovering around ninety, our players are in no mood to complain. The humidity and the simmering heat make waiting outside unbearable. Already my clothes are soaked with perspiration. Even hot air blowing through the open windows, once the bus is underway, will make it seem cooler inside.

A scorching breeze whips up a cloud of dust in the parking lot as the men shove their bags into the storage compartment beneath the bus and pile inside. Equipment, medical supplies, uniforms and miscellaneous extra gear were loaded before team members arrived. Each player is responsible for his personal baggage.

I take a head count to confirm all players are accounted for while Whitey circles the bus, conducting a final inspection to make certain nothing has been left on the ground. When I'm satisfied no one is missing, I take a seat near the middle of the bus.

His inspection completed, Whitey grabs the handrail and pulls himself up the entrance steps. He taps the bus driver's shoulder and gives him a thumbs up then turns to face the players bunched closely together in the narrow seats.

"All aboard, you sinners! We're bound for glory," Whitey bellows. The old bus hisses and lurches forward.

❖ ❖ ❖ ❖ ❖

WICHITA FALLS IS LOCATED a few miles south of the Oklahoma border in Wichita County. Like Tyler, the city's economy is oil based. Last season the Spudders finished in third place, reaching the Big State playoffs for a second straight year.

Wichita Falls is affiliated with the Saint Louis Browns organization. Their agreement with the Browns provides the Spudders with a direct line to big league talent. Unfortunately, it also allows Saint Louis to pluck key players from the Spudder lineup at any time. The Wichita franchise is owned by local entrepreneurs who love their city and who love baseball even more.

Wichita Falls is renowned for its extreme temperatures. In winter, the city can be the coldest place in Texas. During the summer, it's quite often the hottest. For some perverted reason local citizens take pride in their intolerable climate. Residents claim their city is separated from the north pole only by a few barbed wire fences. When asked to define their summer weather, they smile broadly and proclaim proudly: "It's hotter 'n hell!"

When we reach the Wichita Falls city limits, the temperature is pushing at the mid-nineties. Our bus driver easily negotiates through the light traffic on Scott Avenue and turns right on Seventh. We cross the railroad tracks, drive a couple more blocks, and swing across a spacious gravel paved parking lot. The driver reduces his speed, swerves to avoid a huge chughole, and deposits us at the players' entrance gate behind the third base bleachers. Our arrival kindles little reaction among my squadron of young warriors. They rise sluggishly and stumble out of the bus, their energy sapped by the hot, boring ride.

166

❖ ❖ ❖ ❖ ❖

WITH CAPS HELD against their hearts, players from both teams stand like sentinels lined along their respective baselines. Having the crowd stand and sing the national anthem prior to a football game is standard practice, but it's a rarity in baseball. However, judging from their spirited singing, Spudder fans evidently think it's a splendid idea.

When the music ends, the two lines disperse quickly. Spudder players run to take their positions in the field. My East Texans hurry to our dugout. Whitey and I linger to argue over our batting lineup.

"Yes, it's a different lineup than we've been using, but that's what she suggested," I explain.

"But Cates and the two Johnsons are rookie reserves. I can think of three regulars who are gonna be mighty p.o.'d."

"That's what she wants. Because of her this ball club is four and 0. You wanna start betting against her?"

"Oh hell no. I ain't never bet against a woman's intuition."

Matilda's plan is to lead off with the two Johnsons and their cousin Herb Cates. Although the Louisiana players have proved to be reliable, up until now we've used them strictly as spot players—pinch hitters, late inning subs, and relief pitchers. Matilda believes our three Cajuns are due for a big night at the plate.

"Okay then, we're in agreement. Post the lineup while I make the changes with the scorekeeper."

❖ ❖ ❖ ❖ ❖

SPUDDER FANS heckle Philip Johnson as he swings two bats in the on-deck-circle, loosening up. Nasty jeers like, "Hey, rookie! What rock did they find you under?" and "Hey, farmboy! Bet you can shovel manure better than you can swing a bat!" originate from the grandstands.

Leading off with three untried rookies is a major gamble. First year players are often afflicted with "rabbit ears," which means they

167

hear every nasty remark by every demented fan. Spudder fans can be brutal, even to seasoned visiting players.

Because we're the visitors, we bat first. All sorts of scenarios flutter through my mind as I shout last minute advice to my anxious batter.

"Be patient, Philip. Make their pitcher throw you a strike before you swing. Don't get overanxious."

"I gotcha, Skipper. Yes sir, I'm gonna make him throw me a strike, then I'm gonna pop one over that center field fence. That's what I'm gonna do."

"No. No. Just meet the ball and get on base. We have good hitters coming to bat behind you. They'll bring you in."

Johnson stares at me blankly. His eyes are glazed. His mind is set on popping one over the fence in center field.

Frank Johnson grabs a bat and steps past me, taking his place in the on-deck-circle. His eyes have the exact same blank look as Philip's.

Damn. I give these guys a chance to start, and they've both gone plum loco.

On the mound for Wichita tonight is Grady Gardner, a right-handed veteran with a lively fastball and a mean curve. Normally you don't find a pitcher with Gardner's skills playing Class B, but Grady has control problems. He's often wild, particularly in the early innings. Frequently, a patient lead-off batter can work him for a free pass to first base.

Johnson digs in as the Spudders' veteran hurler toes the rubber. Gardner's first offering is an eye-level fastball, two feet above the strike zone. Philip swings at it anyway.

"Dammit. I told him to take a strike first. That pitch was a ball. Why can't he follow instructions?" I scream to no one in particular.

The next pitch is low, bouncing off home plate. Johnson tees up and swings away, missing the baseball by half a foot.

Two strikes and he hasn't come close. I should have known. Changing lineups was a mistake. Henry French, my regular lead-off man, hasn't made an out in four games. I had a winner. Why would I switch off a winner?

168

A third pitch is inside. Instinctively, Johnson swings, more to protect himself than to hit the ball. The baseball clips his bat and rolls foul.

"Holy Christmas. He's swinging at every pitch. I can't bear to watch this," Whitey exclaims, throwing a towel over his head and plopping down on the bench. I resist a strong inclination to join him.

"CRACK!" Johnson connects on a high fastball. Without making a move to run to first, Philip stands in the batter's box and watches the baseball sail high above the center fielder's head. When the ball clears the outfield fence, Johnson turns to the bench, tips his hat, and trots down the first base path.

Hearing the loud cheers from our bench, Whitey peeks out from beneath his sweat towel.

"What happened? Why's Johnson running to first?' Whitey asks, leaping to his feet.

"Maybe you oughta keep your head under the towel, old timer. Philip Johnson just hit our longest home run of the season."

Our bench empties as Tyler players charge out to greet our elated young preacher. Teammates slap his back and congratulate him as he slams his foot down on home plate, punctuating his lead-off home run and his first score of the season. The happy celebration continues until the umpire breaks it up by threatening to begin calling strikes on the next batter.

❖ ❖ ❖ ❖ ❖

"YOU KNOW, WHITEY, I have a sneaking suspicion we're not done yet," I surmise while we watch Frank Johnson take his final practice swings and position himself in the batter's box.

"You might be right, Rick. When Matilda has a hunch, it usually works out."

"CRACK!" The high-pitched sound of wood meeting in solid contact with a hard thrown baseball echoes through the ballpark. Standing on the pitcher's hill, Gardner swivels around to watch until the baseball clears the right field fence then removes his cap and throws it to the ground. Frank Johnson, mimicking his brother Philip, turns to our bench and tips his hat. His teammates rise to their feet and begin clapping, then as Frank rounds third, they leap from the dugout and rush toward home plate for another jubilant celebration.

❖ ❖ ❖ ❖ ❖

"NO. OH, NO. Not three in a row. If Cates hits another one, we're likely to get lynched. These Wichita Falls' people are gonna go bonkers."

"All I do is fill out the lineup card, Whitey. It's up to the players to play the game."

"CRACK!" Again the ringing sound of wood meeting horsehide echoes across the field. Spudder fans are infuriated. Loud boos emanate from the grandstands as Herb Cates begins his trek around the bases. In the dugout my players appear stunned by the surprising series of home runs. Team members glance at one another in disbelief then run to join another wild party at home plate.

❖ ❖ ❖ ❖ ❖

"PEPPY. PEPPY Swanson. Get up here," I yell, turning to face the bench.

"You want me, Coach?" Swanson answers, snapping to attention from a relaxed position at the end of the bench. His voice depicts his surprise at having his name called. He and I have an arrangement. When two men reach base, he automatically becomes my pinch hitter. That's not the case at hand, but I have an idea.

"Your name Peppy Swanson? If it is, get your butt up here."

"Yes sir. Sure," Peppy responds and awkwardly jumps to his feet. In his haste to obey my command, his feet get tangled. He almost falls, steadies himself and stumbles to stand beside me at the dugout steps.

"Peppy, what's the minor league record for consecutive home runs?"

"Don't have the foggiest. I ain't no encyclopedia."

"Three. Three consecutive home runs is the record. You wanna bat?"

"Sure. I never turn down a chance to bat. But what about our deal? There ain't nobody on base."

"Find yourself a bat. I want a home run, and I want a fellow named Peppy Swanson to hit it."

My demanding manner confuses the well-traveled slugger. Peppy stands frozen at the base of the steps while I send my assistant coach scurrying to notify the scorekeeper we're substituting Swanson for Epps in the cleanup slot. When I'm certain Whitey has completed his mission, I turn to prod my aging missile launcher.

"Whatta you waiting for, Peppy? If you're expecting an engraved invitation, we forgot to pack 'em. I told you. I want a home run. Now go get me one," I command forcefully.

"A home run? Sure, Rick, you're the boss."

Like an obedient puppy, Peppy climbs the steps, carefully selects a bat, and strolls toward the batter's box. While he swings the bat back and forth, loosening up the way he's done thousands of times before, he concentrates on the pitcher. He's halfway to home plate when he stops abruptly and swivels around to stare back at me. He drops his bat and comes loping back to the dugout.

"Hey, now I get it. You want me to break the record. You want me to break the home run record."

"That's about the size of it, hoss. A home run here might be your ticket back to the big show."

"Thanks, Rick. I mean, Coach. Thanks a lot."

Frustrated by his early bombardment, Gardner seems determined not to serve up another home run. He pitches Swanson carefully, throwing three consecutive inside pitches. Peppy refuses to swing. Years of experience have taught my seasoned fence buster to be patient, not to go fishing after bad pitches. The count is three and 0 when I climb the dugout steps and scream angrily.

"Swing at the dang ball, Peppy! I don't care if he rolls it to you on the ground. Take a cut at the next pitch," I shout. I want either a home run or a strikeout. I have zero interest in watching him walk.

Peppy steps out of the batter's box, spits into cupped hands, and rubs his palms together. He glances toward me and nods, indicating he understands.

The next pitch is a mile outside. Peppy swings vigorously, missing by more than a foot and spinning himself completely around. His comical batting antics prompt Spudder supporters into laughing hysteria. The umpire behind home plate fails to see the humor. He removes his mask and glares at me, like he's holding me responsible for my batter's unorthodox behavior.

"Chicken! Hey, pitch, you're a fat, yellow chicken. What's the matter, pitch? You afraid to throw the man a strike?" I challenge loudly.

My team picks up on my challenge. Players on our bench begin to squawk like chickens in a hen house. Jess Nelms and Hal Epps abandon their seats and stand behind the dugout railing to cluck and flap their arms. Then, seizing a rare opportunity for dugout buffoonery, they turn and hop toward one another, flailing their arms and bumping chests. The entire dugout erupts into hilarious laughter when the collision knocks Epps off his feet.

Despite the side-splitting sideshow inside our dugout, our taunting accomplishes the desired result. Our childish challenge to his manhood intimidates the pitcher. Gardner jerks his cap down low over his forehead. His jaw is squared, his eyes narrowed. He winds to make his delivery.

The pitch is low and outside, but Peppy leans forward, extending his arms full length as he takes a hefty cut.

"CRACK!" The sharp sound resounds across the diamond and through the grandstands. An eerie silence envelops the ballpark as Peppy drops his bat and sprints for first base. For what seems an eternity, the baseball hangs above right field, loses its momentum and begins a downward trajectory. The right fielder gives chase. He runs to the edge of the outfield, whirls around so his back is against the fence and waits to make the catch.

On the base path, Swanson stops between first and second and turns to watch the Spudders' right fielder leap high and snare the baseball in his glove, only to have the ball pop out and drop behind the fence.

Our bench unloads while Peppy gleefully circles the bases, dancing, hopping up and down like a giant kangaroo. The entire team meets him at home plate where we shake his hand and slap his back. Several minutes pass before the umpires issue their ultimatum for us to leave the field and resume play.

❖ ❖ ❖ ❖ ❖

AFTER OUR FIRST INNING FIREWORKS, the contest becomes a game of follow the leader. Wichita Falls scores a single run in the bottom of the first. We follow by pushing across a run in the top of the second. They score two runs in both the third and the fifth frames, which we match with dual tallies in the top of the fourth and top of the sixth.

But the outcome was decided in the first inning. After the fifth inning, my number two starter, Jake Christie, knuckles down and shuts out the Spudders, going the distance to notch his second win of the season.

Final Score: Spudders 5   East Texans 9

❖ ❖ ❖ ❖ ❖

ONLY A HANDFUL of fans remain in the grandstands while Whitey and I gather baseball gear strewed across the dugout floor. With the outcome decided early, many disillusioned Spudder boosters departed before the game ended. Out on the diamond a ground crew is dragging the infield. Yelps and wild screams originate from the visitor's quarters where our team is showering and changing into their street clothes.

"We're on a heckava roll, Rick. Five wins in a row. Took us almost a month to come up with our first five wins last year."

"Well, we have more working for us this season—good pitching, good hitting, plus a secret weapon named Matilda. Don't seem like we can do anything wrong."

"But that move with Peppy—giving him a chance to break the record. That had to be your idea. Matilda don't care much for Peppy. Thinks he's a fat slob who oughta pay more attention to his family."

"Yep, that was my idea all right. Worked out pretty good though, don't you think?"

"That was a nice gesture. Peppy is the happiest man on the squad tonight. How'd you know about the home run record? I didn't know you kept up with baseball statistics."

"I don't. For all I know, the record might be ten consecutive homers."

Whitey throws his bag to the ground and whirls to face me. His facial expression tells me he's appalled by my confession.

"You mean Peppy may not hold the record? Rick, that's mean and low down. Why would you pull such a dirty trick on an old guy like Peppy?"

"I didn't intend to be mean. I got nothing against Peppy."

"Why'd you do it then?"

"Peppy's been in the dumps lately. So I took a gamble. I thought maybe if he believed he set a new record, he might start hitting like his old self again. Looks like it may have worked."

"This could backfire on you, Rick. He's gonna be madder than an old hen when he finds out you tricked him."

"I don't plan on telling him. I'm hoping you won't."

"Hell, I ain't gonna tell. Peppy might break down and cry. Either that, or bust up his manager's lying face and make him cry. I hate to see grown men bawl."

"Yeah, me too, especially when it's me doing the crying. Let's make this our secret, Whitey. Right now Peppy's on top of the world. Somewhere down the stretch we're gonna need his bat to carry this team. When that time comes, I want him confident and up to the task."

"But what if somebody checks the official statistics and discovers you're wrong about the home run record?"

"Not much chance of that. You notice how many comic books the guys brought along to read on the bus? I'd lay odds not one member of our team even knows where to find a record book."

❖ ❖ ❖ ❖ ❖

IN ALL SPORTS winning breeds confidence. In baseball, confidence begets winning. We were riding high with four consecutive home wins under our belt when we arrived. But here in Wichita Falls, my players become a crowd-pleasing, acrobatic band of daredevils. Diving stops, breathtaking circus catches, and high leaps against the outfield fences to rob opposing batters of sure hits become the order of the day. Incredible defensive plays become routine. And our bats catch fire. In our first two games at Spudder Ballpark we score nineteen runs.

Instead of lodging the team in a downtown hotel, Ted leased an entire motel located on the outskirts of Wichita Falls. Actually, the quarters aren't bad, and boarding a long way from the central business district keeps our young men off downtown streets where they might be hassled by local police or maybe run into some other kind of trouble.

A truck stop near our motel immediately becomes the squad's favorite meeting place. The coffee is strong and hot. The food is better than average and served in generous quantities. And more importantly, the prices are reasonable. That's a vital necessity for a hungry group of males forced to survive on the miserly food allowances dispensed by our frugal business manager.

Sticking to a morning routine commenced in Tyler, I rise early, walk a half mile to kick-start my circulation then head for the truck stop.

When I push through the front door, the restaurant is bustling with morning breakfast activity. Every stool at the service counter and each of the six vinyl-covered booths are occupied. Three uniformed waitresses scurry back and forth taking orders and carrying trays filled with hot food.

John Bruzga waves to catch my attention. He, Jess Nelms and Hal Epps occupy a booth in the back corner. The large corner booth has become the team's social center. The table top is littered with coffee cups and newspapers, left there by early risers who lingered to join in the morning gossip then returned to their motel rooms.

"You seen the morning paper, Coach Mason? We're all alone in first place. Got the rest of the Big State League watching our backsides," Nelms reports when I walk up. He shoves the paper toward me while Epps and Bruzga shift sideways to make room for me.

"You don't say? How'd Texarkana do last night? They're next on our schedule."

"The Bears lost to Austin last night. Everybody, except us, has two losses now," Epps informs knowingly.

"Hey. Maybe we should have Colonel Segars contact the league office and have us declared the champs. Save everyone a lot of time and trouble. The way we're romping and stomping nobody else has a Chinaman's chance anyway," Bruzga chimes in, displaying a toothy smile to confirm he's joking.

"That's a hellava suggestion, John. I'm sure the colonel would be delighted to accept the league trophy and call it a season. He'd have what he wants, and save a ton of money by only paying you for playing six games," I josh back, challenging his humor. Actually, I like his suggestion. I'd have my winning season, and Segars would be off the hook with the New Orleans people.

"Well, maybe it's not such a red-hot idea. Maybe we oughta play the season out," Bruzga responds sheepishly then quizzes me seriously, "Hey, Rick, have you heard my good news? My wife and I are expecting a baby. We're gonna need the playoff money. How much extra you reckon we'll get paid if we make the playoffs?"

"Can't say for sure. Depends on how far we go. Might be as much as a couple hundred bucks apiece."

"Man oh man, that kinda money would go a long way toward paying our doctor bills."

"I imagine we each could use extra money from the playoffs. But don't start spending it just yet. With a hundred and forty-one games between us and the playoffs, we have a long row to hoe. A lot could happen between now and then."

"We were about to leave, Coach. John has a buddy stationed here at Sheppard Air Base. He's promised to show us through one of the B-16 bombers. You're welcome to come with us," Nelms intercedes when the conversation begins to lag. Nelms' offer is less than enthusiastic. He's hoping I'll turn down their invitation. I understand. My presence will cramp their style. We're separated in age by only a couple of years, but my authoritative position as team manager negates my being accepted as one of the guys.

"No thanks. My morning is already planned. You fellows go on and have a good time. But don't forget, our bus leaves for the ballpark at five."

"Sure, Coach. Hey, we gotta go. We'll see you later."

After the players leave, I chuckle to myself and rummage through the newspapers strewed about the table. I understand perfectly why the young men are so anxious to accept an invitation which they might turn down cold if they were back in Tyler. Their excursion will kill an otherwise boring afternoon—a lonely afternoon in a strange motel room.

No matter how glamorous the perception, life on the road can be an endless series of monotonous intervals between games. Maybe it's the pressure to win. Maybe it's because you're expected to give your best performance night after night. But with so much idle time on his hands, a man can get downright stupid—do wacky things he'd never dream of doing back home. Some men resort to chasing women. For a baseball player, women and the opportunity for infidelity are always present. Some men turn to drinking, hiding their fear of failure in a bottle. Very few men use the time wisely. Like the saying goes, "Idle hands are the devil's workshop."

Page six of the *Wichita Falls Record-News* contains the sports news and a synopsis of the latest standings. Because of local interest the Big State League is posted at the top of the column. Results of last night's games are listed below the standings:

BIG STATE LEAGUE
Class B

Team	W	L	Pct.	GB
Tyler	6	0	1.000	-----
Texarkana	4	2	0.667	2
Temple	4	2	0.667	2
Austin	3	3	0.500	3
Wichita Falls	2	4	0.333	4
Gainesville	2	4	0.333	4
Waco	2	4	0.333	4
Sherman-Denison	1	5	0.250	5

Sunday's Results

Tyler	10	Wichita Falls	3
Austin	4	Texarkana	3
Temple	6	Sherman-Denison	2
Waco	7	Gainesville	4

With a grueling schedule of one hundred forty-seven games, early season leaders seldom end up atop the standings. The real test will come during the dreary dog days of summer when the continuous grind of everyday play begins to wear down both managers and players. Injuries will have a big say in who wins and who loses. And there's the ever present possibility of a key player being called up by a team in a higher classification.

In minor league baseball there's an unwritten rule: *A manager must never deny a player the opportunity to move up, no matter how much it hurts his club's chances for winning.* By season's end we might see a dozen men come and go on our roster. In baseball, no matter whether it's major or minor league, a manager can't allow his team to become dependent on any one player. You never know when the ax might fall.

While I flip to the front page, a cute redhead arrives to fill my coffee cup. During our short stay, the perky waitress has become a primal object of my young men's attention. A skin-tight short skirt, terminating several inches above her knees, and a loose-fitting pullover top detail every seductive curve of her delightful female body.

"Good morning, Coach. You ready for breakfast? We have the special again this morning. Two eggs, sausage and toast for forty-nine cents."

178

"Good morning, Shirley. Yep, the special will be fine. Make the eggs over easy."

"The fellows said your team won again last night, and you're in first place. Congratulations."

"Thanks. You sound like a baseball fan. Ever make it out to watch a game?"

"Oh sure. My dad used to take me to all the Spudders' games. Haven't been to the ballpark in quite a while though. These days seems like all I do is work. My husband's a trucker—on the road most of the time."

"Why don't you come watch my team play tonight? I'll arrange for a couple of complimentary tickets. You can bring your husband."

"That might be fun, but my husband's out of town. Could I bring a girl friend?"

"Sure. You can sit behind our dugout. My guys will love that. Half of 'em are crazy in love with you."

"I'm not interested in any of your boys, but I am anxious to watch you coach. Your players tell me you make all the right moves."

"So far I've been pretty lucky. But it's a long season. We'll see if my luck holds out."

"Is it true what they say? Lucky in games, unlucky in love?" Shirley asks.

"I wouldn't know. I've never had much luck of any kind before this season. My love life sure hasn't been much to brag about lately," I lament, recalling the lonely months in Dallas before I moved to Tyler.

"Maybe we can change your luck in the love department. I'll come to the game tonight, and I'll bring my girl friend. She's a living doll."

"Terrific. I'll leave two tickets at the front gate, but don't make any promises to your friend. My wife and I are separated, but I'm still a married man."

"That's fine. She's married too. If you're not too tired, maybe we can go dancing after the game. I know a place where the music is slow, and the drinks are cheap. Patsy's a lotta fun. You'll like her."

"You mean just me, you and Patsy? How about me inviting one of the other guys to come along?"

"No, that won't work. We're nice girls. Two girls and one guy. That way Patsy and I can chaperone each other. You have a problem having two sexy women all to yourself, Coach?"

"Oh, no. No problem. Sounds like fun," I answer, my ego overloading my good sense. Her proposal is too enticing to resist. What she's offering is every man's dream.

A bell tinkles, interrupting our conversation.

"Oops. Gotta run, before the cook gets in an uproar. See you at the game tonight, Coach."

Stuffing her order book into the front pocket of her skirt, she twirls and bounces toward the kitchen. Her vibrant jaunt strains every thread of her tight skirt, lifting it high to expose two lean, shapely legs. Her prolific movements temporarily suspend friendly chatter in adjacent booths as truckers' heads turn to watch her pass.

The scene reminds me of a choice waitress observation manager Hank Greenberg frequently repeated when I traveled with the Indians: "The shorter the skirt, the bigger the tip."

Greenberg's adage definitely applies to Shirley. Second only to baseball, the attractive waitress has become the major topic of player conversation since we checked into our motel quarters two nights ago. Vying for her attention, my players occasionally leave tips which match their food bill. Until today though, she's played it cool—cordial and friendly of course, but showing no interest in after-hour games.

Although Shirley claims she's married, no ring adorns the ring finger on her left hand. I'd bet she's single, possibly divorced, and uses the marriage excuse to ward off unwanted suitors. If the right fellow comes along, I expect she could be coaxed into bed.

A few days ago the prospect of a night on the town with two desirable young women, and the possibilities which might unfold, would've had me drooling. Still, it might be fun. I'll have a few drinks, dance a few dances, show the girls a good time. What's the harm in that?

An article in the lower right-hand corner of the front page catches my eye. The heading reads:

HOUSTON MAN STILL MISSING

The column below explains the missing man is Max Wagner, a petroleum engineer who disappeared without a trace after he left Houston on Thursday of last week. Neither he nor his 1950 Willis Jeep have been seen since. The story ends with a plea from his wife— for anyone who may have seen him to contact her or the Texas Department of Public Safety.

The news is a shocker. With the unexpected reversal in my marriage situation and the distractions of preparing for this road trip, my telephone conversation with Georgia Wagner completely slipped my mind. I simply presumed Max would turn up. Apparently I was wrong. When my ball club returns to Tyler, I intend to make a visit to Swinneytown.

❖ ❖ ❖ ❖ ❖

OUR THIRD ENCOUNTER with Wichita Falls requires ten innings, but produces the same result, a seventh consecutive win for my East Texans.

After his stout performance against Waco, I've added Eric Felton to my starting rotation. With Bounato and Christie working the first two games and Davis still suffering from arm problems, Felton gets the nod. He performs admirably, setting the side down in order in the first and second frames.

In the bottom of the third, a walk and a fielding error allow the Spudders to open up a 2-0 lead, but we scramble back to knot the score in the top of the fourth.

The game remains deadlocked until the bottom of the fifth when Felton tires, giving up two consecutive singles and a walk to load the bases. Sending Felton off to an early shower, I call on Philip Johnson for long relief duty. Wichita Falls scores twice before Mainzer, the Spudders' shortstop, grounds into a double play to end the inning.

In the top of the seventh, back to back singles by Epps and Gregory and a two-bagger by Swanson pull us back into a tie.

The stalemate continues at 4-4 into extra innings, until the top of the tenth. That's when the wheels come off for the Spudders. With two out, a looping single to right by Epps, followed by walks to Gregory and Akins, load the bases. Then Merv Connors smashes a triple down the third base line. We score two more runs before Nelms pops up to right field to end the inning.

I move Herb Cates from third base to pitcher in the bottom of the tenth. He strikes out the side.

Final Score: Spudders 4   East Texans 9

❖ ❖ ❖ ❖ ❖

IT'S A QUARTER past ten when the final Wichita batter goes down swinging. Quickly, I explain to Whitey I have a date and ask him to tend to my post game duties. Ten minutes later I emerge from the visitor's dressing quarters, showered, shaved, and eager for a fun evening with two lovely ladies.

My two dates meet me on the concrete concourse outside our locker room. Shirley's description of her friend was right on target. Patsy *is* a living doll, every bit as attractive and shapely as her waitress girl friend. Both girls seem genuinely impressed by tonight's extra inning win.

As my players straggle off the playing field, word of my good fortune spreads like wild fire through our dressing room. A half-dozen, half-dressed teammates rush to stand at the locker room doorway and wistfully watch me stroll toward the front gate, sporting a ravishing woman on each arm. There's not a player on my squad who wouldn't give a month's salary to swap places with me.

"We're in Patsy's car, Coach. Why don't you drive?" Shirley says when we reach the front entrance.

"Sure, be glad to. But I don't know my way around Wichita Falls very well."

"You drive, and we'll show you the way. Shirley and I like a place out on the Jacksboro highway where we can dance. Sometimes they have a band, but probably not tonight," Patsy counsels, handing me the car key.

"Sounds like fun. They serve beer?" Like a debonair gentleman, I open the car door and hold it while the girls slip inside.

"Yes, but Patsy and I drink bourbon and seven. It's after ten. The liquor stores are all closed, but we know a local bootlegger where you can buy a bottle. You mind if we stop by his house?" Shirley asks, sticking her head out the window after I close the car door.

"No, not at all. I'm a bourbon man myself. Hey, there's three of us. Maybe we oughta buy two bottles," I offer while I step around to the driver's side, open the door, and slide behind the steering wheel. My entire bankroll consists of twenty dollars—team expense money carefully hidden inside my wallet. It's not my money, but who's to know. Opportunities like this don't come along every day.

"Shirley, your date is not only a looker, he's also a big spender. You sure know how to pick 'em, girl," Patsy declares admiringly, slipping her hand beneath my arm and scooting close against me.

"Hey, I'm both girls' date. This is a threesome. Remember?" I insert the key and crank the engine. The car fires on the first try and purrs like a kitten. "Okay, girls! Let's party! Now, how about telling me where we can find your bootlegger friend."

The tires squeal as I press down hard on the gas pedal. Both girls giggle excitedly as we surge forward. I steer the car around a disorderly string of parked cars and speed down the street.

This is gonna be a night to remember.

❖ ❖ ❖ ❖ ❖

MY IDEA to purchase two pints of bourbon from the bootlegger is a good one. Both girls are serious boozers, matching me drink for drink as they alternate from our table to the dance floor, taking turns dancing with me.

Less than half the second bottle remains when I return Shirley to the table, slug down a quick snort, and escort an anxious Patsy back onto the small dance area. She comes easily into my arms, snuggling her soft body close against me. As we dance, the sweet fragrance of Patsy's perfume fills me with warm desire. The fresh smell of her hair overwhelms my senses. Her lips gently brush against my cheek, and we glide in perfect unison to the familiar music of a Glenn Miller melody. Her hand squeezes mine, and she pulls me even closer when the music ends.

A stubby hand grabs my shoulder and whirls me around. The hand belongs to a burly, thick-chested bruiser of a man. Dark blotches of grease spot his arms and face. The man is obviously an oil field worker. He is badly in need of a bath.

"Hey, mister. You know that there's a married woman you're dancing with?" the man asks, weaving back and forth as he speaks.

"Yes, I suppose I do. The lady's name is Patsy. But what's it to you? She a friend of yours?" I answer coolly. The man is drunk and obviously looking for trouble. No sense in provoking him.

Patsy asserts herself into the strained conversation. "Don't pay him any attention, Coach. This spying low-life weasel is my good-for-nothing brother-in-law." She steps between us and shoves the man backward, away from me. Even though this man outweighs her by more than a hundred pounds, he yields easily to the force of her hands. He staggers backward, drunkenly trying to maintain his balance.

"Get off the dance floor, Bubba. You're making a fool of yourself. What I do when your brother's out of town is none of your business. Be a sport and leave us alone. You can tell big brother all about his cheating wife when he comes home. But we don't want any trouble tonight."

Ignoring Patsy's command, Bubba brushes her aside and glares at me. "This woman is married to my brother, fellow. When he finds out you've been dancing with his wife, he's gonna whip your ass all over town."

"Maybe. Maybe not. But I don't see how that's any of your business. This lady and the lady sitting at the table over there are friends of mine. We're here to dance and have a few drinks. You have a problem with that?"

"Yeah, I got a problem. I don't like your face. I might want a piece of your smart ass for myself. Save my brother the trouble of busting you up when he gets home," Bubba threatens boastfully. He turns to glance toward two men sitting at the bar. Bubba is apparently trying to impress his drinking buddies. Most likely his pals goaded him into this confrontation.

"Bubba, you're drunk, so watch you don't let your moron mouth overload your fat butt. Rick here is a baseball coach. You don't want to mess with him. He'd snuff you out like a cigarette. Now, why don't you slither back to the bar and join your sleazy friends," Patsy cautions, drastically overstating my fighting capabilities. Bubba may appear to be soft and flabby, but I suspect underneath the layers of fat and the beer gut is a man of enormous strength. Weak men don't survive in the oil fields. I have no intention of fighting Bubba. Heck, he outweighs me by fifty pounds.

"Listen, Bubba, I'm not looking for a fight. The girls and I are just out for a little fun. Dancing, having a few drinks, that's all that's happening here. How about we shake hands and let bygones be bygones?" I say, stepping forward and extending my hand.

"No way. I ain't shaking hands with no wife snatcher. You're gonna get yours, mister. You wait and see."

The juke box begins playing another song while I stand next to Patsy and watch her inebriated brother-in-law stagger back to the bar. She slips her hand into mine and raises up on her tip toes to kiss my cheek.

"You were absolutely wonderful, Coach. Bubba is a tough cookie. Some men wouldn't have the courage to stand up to him, but you didn't back down from him, not one inch."

"Well, maybe I had something worthwhile to stand up for," I profess, wrapping my arm around her waist and pulling her hard against me. We've been flirting and working up to this since the moment our eyes met. It's time I kiss her full on the lips. She accepts my advance willingly. She tilts her head to receive my caress. Our lips meet. Our tongues touch gently. The sweet taste of her mouth causes my head to spin and my knees to wobble.

"Maybe we should leave," she says when our lips finally part. "We can go to my place."

"Sounds good to me, but what about Shirley?"

"She'll want to come too. I have some new records. We'll roll up the living room rug and dance and have some real fun. Haven't you heard? Two girls can be twice as much fun as one," Patsy whispers, rubbing her body seductively against mine. Her soft red lips seem so inviting.

"One girl. Two girls. Who cares. But I'm about danced out. I'm ready for some serious action," I proclaim. I try for another kiss, but she turns her head away.

"Be patient, Coach. The night is young. Who knows how this will end. Shirley is even more infatuated with you than me. We might all wind up sharing the same bed."

Patsy's brother-in-law and two other unpleasant characters sitting beside him at the bar have been watching our open display of affection. Bubba seems particularly aggravated. While Patsy and I stroll toward our table, he nudges the man next to him. The man nods in agreement.

"We're leaving, Shirley. Grab your purse. Let's you and me run to the ladies room while Rick pays the bill," Patsy informs her friend when we reach our table.

"But I want to dance with coach. We've hardly had a chance to get acquainted." Shirley sounds jealous, perhaps envious because she wasn't a participant in the kissing scene on the dance floor.

"The party's not over, honey. We're merely changing locations. We'll go to my house. Rick says he's ready for some serious action."

"Alright then, let's get going." Shirley scoots her chair back, reaches for her purse, and accompanies Patsy as they head for the ladies room. Halfway there, she spins around and walks back to me.

"I didn't get kissed, and I'm jealous," she explains. She bends down to caress me softly on the lips. "There. That should hold me until we get to the car," she teases then turns and hurries to catch up with Patsy.

My prospects for the night ahead are even better than I ever dreamed possible. Leaning back in my chair, I try to envision what it will be like to share a bed with two luscious women, each vying for my attention.

Perhaps that's why I never see the beer bottle until it crashes over my head. Pieces of shattered glass cascade off my shoulders as I stagger and attempt to get to my feet. Then the sharp pain of something rock hard striking the side of my face sends me reeling. The last thing I remember is my limp body banging against a cold concrete floor.

"Ya want we should kill the sleazy polecat, Bubba? It'd be real easy," a voice overhead growls while I gradually regain consciousness. Flashing bright stars circle inside my head.

"That's what his sorry ass deserves, but the two women will know who done it. We can't take a chance," Bubba answers. Apparently this is his show.

"Then whatta ya think we should do? Don't seem right he should get off with just a knot on the head. Hey, didn't you say he was a baseball coach? How about we cut off a couple of his fingers? That oughta fix him good."

"Yeah, that'll work. Cut off his thumb, too. Ya can't throw a baseball when ya got no thumb."

"Which one? Whatta ya think? Is he right-handed or left-handed?"

"Hell's fire, how should I know? How 'bout we cut both his thumbs off? That way it won't matter which hand he throws with."

In my semi-conscious state, their intoxicated discussion seems like part of a bad dream. Mustering all my strength, I struggle to regain my senses, so I can argue in my defense.

"Bubba. Bubba, please don't cut my hands. Kill me, but don't cut off my hands," I hear myself plea.

"Hey look, Bubba. Our wife stealing coach has waked up. Hey, ya dumb baseball jock. We ain't gonna cut off your hands. Just a few of your fingers."

"Okay. So don't cut off my fingers. Please, Bubba."

"Screw you, lover boy. You've been fooling around with my brother's wife. We can't let ya get away with that. You understand? Ya gotta pay."

When I don't answer quickly enough to suit the man wielding the pocketknife, he kicks me in the ribs, taking my breath away.

"The man asked ya a simple question, smart guy. He asked if ya understand why ya gotta pay. Ya gonna answer or do ya want I should keep on kicking ya?"

"No, don't kick me again. I understand," I whisper hoarsely.

Another hard shoe strikes my face. Then total darkness.

❖ ❖ ❖ ❖ ❖

PATSY PULLS her car to a halt outside my motel while I remove the wet, bloody bar towel wrapped around my right hand. I wiggle the thumb gingerly and grit my teeth. A mass of raw flesh is exposed along the jagged open cut which encircles the base of my thumb, but by applying constant pressure, I've slowed the bleeding to a trickle.

Surprisingly, the thumb still works. Even though he sliced the skin right down to the bone, Bubba's drinking buddy isn't much of a surgeon. Who would've thought a West Texas oil worker would carry a pocketknife so dull it wouldn't saw through bone.

Whatever the reason, my right hand still hurts like the dickens.

"You sure you don't want a doctor to check your thumb, Coach? Looks to me like you might need a few stitches," Shirley ventures, breaking the silence inside the car. Since they discovered me lying unconscious on the bar room floor, revived me with a wet towel, and hustled me into Patsy's car, neither of the two women has said much. Possibly the sight of so much blood has thwarted their appetite for congenial chatter.

"No, it'll be fine. My assistant keeps a bag full of medical supplies in his room. I'll wake him and have him sew me up," I answer. I prefer to avoid a hospital emergency room where I'd be required to give my name and answer questions. Someone's certain to discover I'm the Tyler baseball manager. My late night escapades would make a juicy story for some local reporter. Might even be picked up by the news wire services.

"Oh, Rick. Shirley and I are so sorry this happened. I'm gonna murder that Bubba Jackson. I swear I will," Patsy cries. Tears stream down her cheeks, accentuating her proclamation.

"Yeah. I'd like a crack at him too. Well, maybe without his two pals. But you girls shouldn't worry about me. I'll be fine. Right now I'm thankful to have both hands intact. Any other time that fellow's pocket knife would've been razor sharp. I'm lucky he didn't cut off my thumb."

"Oooh. Don't talk like that, Coach. You give me heebie jeebies," Shirley exclaims. She grabs my shirt and buries her pretty face against my chest. Her tiny body quivers with sympathetic compassion.

A wave of nausea sweeps over me. The car begins to spin. I glance at the dashboard clock. It's past three o'clock.

"Shirley, Patsy, except for the way it ended, tonight has been great fun, but it's getting late. I'd better get this hand fixed."

I slither out of the car. My legs wobble like two rubber bands. My head reels. I seriously doubt if I can make it to Whitey's motel room without fainting dead away.

Patsy cranks the car engine, and Shirley sticks her head out the car window.

"Don't forget to leave tickets for us at the front gate tomorrow night, Coach. Patsy and I will see you then."

"Tomorrow night? You girls plan to come to the game tomorrow night?"

"Oh, sure. We love watching the way you coach. And if your feeling better, we'll go out again. Patsy knows this place over in Burkburnett. On Tuesday nights they have a country band."

"Sure, I'll leave two tickets at the gate," I say, shifting my weight from foot to foot. I doubt if I'll feel like dancing tomorrow night, but I'm not about to argue. If they don't leave soon, I may pass out.

"You sure you can make it, Coach? Maybe I should give you a hand," Shirley offers.

"No, I'll be fine. Goodnight girls."

"Goodnight, Coach. See you at the game tomorrow evening. You take care of that hand, you hear?"

"Yeah. Sure. I'll wake up Whitey and have him fix it right away."

189

Patsy's tires spin, sending chunks of gravel flying out from underneath the rear bumper, and the car lunges forward. Gingerly, I finger the lump on the back of my head and watch the two girls drive away. When the tail lights disappear behind the motel office building, I turn and stumble toward Whitey's motel room.

❖ ❖ ❖ ❖ ❖

"WHAT HAPPENED, RICK? Surely those two women didn't do this," Whitey curiously inquires while he scrapes a clump of dried blood from my injured thumb. When his cleansing operation strikes a sensitive spot, a sharp pain shoots up my arm. I want to scream, but instead I clench my lips and hunch my shoulders, determined not to jerk my hand back and reveal how much I hurt.

I don't want Matilda to think I'm a cry baby. She's perched on the end of the bed, articulating her sympathy by wincing every time I cry out. Her face bears a troubled expression. She listens apprehensively to my explanation.

"No. It was Patsy's brother-in-law and two of his hard case sidekicks. They slipped up behind me and hit me over the head with a beer bottle. Then the three of them proceeded to beat the living dookie outta me. I suppose they woulda cut both my thumbs off if that fellow's pocketknife hadn't been so dull."

Whitey temporarily suspends his medical alterations to stare into my eyes.

"Why would they cut off your thumbs? Good Lord, Rick. What did you do to deserve that kind of punishment?"

"Darned if I know what set 'em off. Said they wanted to teach me a lesson I wouldn't forget. Folks here in Wichita Falls seem to relish the sight of blood," I answer evasively. Matilda and Whitey don't necessarily need to know how close I came to sharing a night in bed with the two women.

"Rick, you ever stop to think how you get yourself in these situations?"

"Sure, Whitey, I got it figured out. Seems like every time I go near a woman lately, I end up with you patching me up."

190

Matilda huffs and turns away, noticeably annoyed by my answer.

❖ ❖ ❖ ❖ ❖

WHEN I DRAG MYSELF aboard the team bus, my banged-up, grisly appearance instigates a number of double takes, and inevitably, several carefully camouflaged snickers, but thankfully, none of my players approach me to specifically inquire about my bandaged thumb or my bruised, disfigured face.

❖ ❖ ❖ ❖ ❖

SOMEHOW, I MANAGE to overcome a splitting headache, a throbbing thumb, and a queasy stomach to endure pre-game festivities. I post the lineup, meet with the Spudders' manager and the two game officials behind home plate, and waddle back to collapse on our bench, hoping to lick my wounds and suffer silently. That's when our troubles begin.

Henry French strikes out. After twenty-three straight walks, my squatty lead-off batter registers his first out of the season. Then Bruzga and Akins dribble successive grounders to the Spudder second baseman for easy outs. Our side is retired with only twelve pitches.

In the bottom of the inning, rookie pitcher Matt Burns can't find the strike zone. He walks the first three Spudder batters, not getting a single man out before I'm forced to go to my bullpen.

My plan was to give Charlie Davis' sore arm another day to recuperate and have him start the initial game of our home series with Texarkana. But with Burns in trouble early, my options are limited. Davis barely has time to warm up before he's called to duty. Charlie throws plenty of strikes, but he doesn't have his best stuff, and our defense provides only minimal support. Spudder batters either blast the baseball through gaps in our outfield, or our infield makes an error.

By the top of the fourth, Wichita Falls has raced out to a nine run lead. Not one Tyler batter has reached first. My troops are thoroughly demoralized. My team seems determined to lose, and in my beleaguered state of agony, I have neither the strength nor energy to scold individuals for poor play or to plead with the players to pull together.

My right hand throbs. Every time I move, spells of dizziness inundate me. I can't think. I can't coach. Tonight my goal is to survive this game with a scrap of dignity, meaning—not having my teammates drag me to the visitor's locker room after I pass out on the dugout floor.

Adding to my anguish are hunger pains which regularly rumble through my intestines. I haven't eaten since yesterday afternoon. I'm seriously contemplating slipping out to the concession stand to grab a hamburger when Whitey ambles over to plop down beside me. Wanting to keep my troubles private, we've confined our dialogue to only essential conversation since we boarded the team bus.

"This is bad, Rick. Real bad."

"You're right about that, old timer. I've never seen a team play so poorly. But I thought you were coaching third this inning." Inside my lower intestines the hunger pangs begin again. I place the palm of my hand flat against my stomach and press gently, hoping the pressure will provide temporary relief.

"I gave the job to Peppy. It don't matter who coaches which base. We ain't had a man on base all night," Whitey complains. I can hardly disagree. His logic makes perfect sense.

"Maybe we oughta throw in the towel. Isn't that what they do when a boxer's on the ropes and unable to fight back?"

"I wish we could, but I reckon we'll have to tough it out and take our licking. This was bound to happen. We've been too lucky lately. I should have known when Matilda left."

This is news to me. Matter of fact, in my state of agony, I've forgotten all about Matilda.

"Matilda left? Why'd she leave? Was she mad about something?" I ask, but Whitey doesn't answer immediately, not until we watch John Bruzga fumble a ground ball, recover, and send it sailing past our first baseman into the grandstands. A Wichita Falls' base runner, occupying third, slaps his hands together to demonstrate his delight and turns to jog happily toward home.

My East Texans have trounced this Wichita Falls squad soundly for three nights in a row. No doubt every man in the opposing dugout is pleased to see us play so miserably.

"Danged if I know. Late this morning she simply packed up and left. She didn't say much, but you could tell she was upset. Kept muttering something about men being such ungrateful morons."

In spite of my misery, I can't help but chuckle at Whitey's analysis. Possibly it's just a figure of speech, but I can't imagine what baggage a ghost would pack before she left. Perhaps she brought along a few personal possessions. No, Matilda is a female, so that would be much too logical. Whatever she packed, it's unlikely a mortal man like myself would comprehend.

"Whitey, I'm ready to leave too. I've enjoyed about all this town I can handle. How about we talk to the bus driver? If he's willing, let's check out of the motel right after the game and leave for Tyler. Whatta you think?"

"That's fine with me. Don't think you'll get much argument from our players either. Some might've felt different a few hours ago, but after tonight's catastrophe, they'll be anxious to leave. This is worse than we ever got whipped last year."

Davis is getting shelled. No sense in leaving him in a game we have no chance of winning. Holding my right hand up and close against my chest, I climb the dugout steps, call timeout, and head for the pitcher's mound.

As I stride across the infield two attractive young women dressed in tight shorts and loose fitting halter tops leap to their feet and wave to me. My feminine admirers, whose company I shared last evening, have stationed themselves in seats directly behind our dugout, shouting words of encouragement every time I show my face. I lower my head and ignore their animated adoration. Some other time and in another situation, I might relish their attention, but at this moment, I have no stomach for romance. I doubt if either of the ladies is truly impressed with my shrewd moves tonight.

Out in center field the scoreboard indicates we're in the bottom of the fourth with one out. The scoreboard tells our sad tale:

HOME   10   VISITORS   0

How could I be so ignorant? Without Matilda this could be a long, long season.

❖ ❖ ❖ ❖ ❖

WHEN THE CONTEST evolved into a total rout, I reverted to stupidity. In an attempt to conserve my pitching staff, I used infielders to pitch the last three innings. The Spudders took full advantage, fattening their batting averages as every man in their lineup logged a hit. When the score became downright absurd, Wichita's manager took pity and instructed his batters to lay down bunts to our pitcher. Thoroughly humiliated, we accepted the outs gratefully, changed to our street clothes, and boarded the bus. On our way out of town we stopped at our motel to gather our belongings and check out. The motel stop took less than five minutes.

In the wee hours of Wednesday morning, nine hours ahead of schedule, our chartered bus drops us off at Trojan Park. The clubhouse immediately becomes a spectacle of frantic confusion as players unload their gear and stand in line to use the telephone, waking up sleepy wives and rousting relatives to come pick them up.

While the men leave, I linger to inspect the area outside the front gate where the bus unloaded. Whitey catches a ride with Bruzga who also offers to run me home, but I beg off, explaining I have crucial business to attend to.

When I'm certain every player has departed, I mosey back inside and lock the door behind me.

Turning to face the equipment room, I whisper, "Matilda. Matilda, you here?"

When no one answers, I try again.

"Come on, Matilda. I know you're here. Listen, about the waitress and her friend, I was only being sociable—showing them a

194

good time. Nothing happened. I promise. Matilda, please talk to me."

My appeal receives no response. The locker room is so quiet you could hear a pin drop.

Damn! Why must women be so dang unreasonable?

CHAPTER ELEVEN

SMALL, SCRAWNY pine trees intermingle amongst the towering oak trees which protrude from the undergrowth outside the fenced right-of-way. Much of Smith County's topsoil is sandy and fertile, valuable agricultural land which can match any other section of Texas for producing cash crops, but here, the dense red clay barely supports spotty patches of native grass. If it weren't for the oil discovered in the thirties, the real estate surrounding Swinneytown would be worthless.

An oil-paved roadway, almost too narrow for two cars to pass, winds aimlessly through the thinly populated countryside. The road is unmarked. It's like I entered the twilight zone when I crossed the bridge spanning an upper branch of Lake Tyler. There are no speed limit signs, no signs to indicate mileage to the next town, not even a sign to designate the road number.

An early morning rainstorm swept through Tyler just before dawn, providing much needed relief from an unusually dry spring, but now the lightly-graveled clay shoulder running alongside the pavement is slick and treacherous. Max must've driven down this road. It's possible he lost control of his vehicle and ran off the road, perhaps crashing into one of the numerous ravines which ravage the infertile landscape.

196

Searching for some sign of a car leaving the roadway, I navigate cautiously, making sure all four wheels stay on the pavement.

Some four miles east of Swinneytown, profiles of pumping oil wells begin to peek through the thick brush. The fence bordering the highway changes from four-foot-high barbed wire to an obtrusive, six-foot high, unpainted drill pipe fence. A heavy strand of barbed razor wire tops the pipe fence to discourage unwanted visitors.

An iron gate almost reels past without catching my eye. I slam on my brakes and skid to a stop. Affixed to the gate's top rail is a rusty sign which declares: "Amalgamated No. 1—No Trespassing."

Before I left Tyler, I stopped at the Gulf station on East Fifth to ask directions. The gate matches the gas attendant's description. Apparently this is the entrance to the Amalgamated Oil Lease.

The driveway leading to the entrance gate is unpaved, but there's nowhere else to park. I can't leave the Pontiac on the highway. Disregarding my better judgement, I decide to chance it. I make a bad decision. My tires sink in mud up to the hubcaps the second my rear wheels clear the pavement.

Realizing my error, I shift into reverse and try to back up. The tires spin in the soft slush and sling slimy globs of red mud back onto the main roadway. A sudden panic grips me. I'm miles from the nearest town. I haven't seen a car since I passed Swinneytown. It could be hours before I can flag someone down to pull me out.

Using my bandaged right hand, I shift the car into low gear. By moving forward then shifting quickly back into reverse, maybe I can create a rocking motion which will allow me to escape my frightful predicament. My wheels spin, and the Pontiac begins to inch forward toward the iron gate.

❖ ❖ ❖ ❖ ❖

A BLAZING SUN bursts through the blanket of clouds over-head as I trudge along the muddy trail. I'm following a pair of fresh tire tracks and cursing myself for my stupidity. Most likely, the furrowed ruts were left by some oil worker employed to maintain the oil wells. Probably he was driving a vehicle equipped with four-wheel drive. Otherwise he'd be stuck like me. With any luck the man is still here. My plan is to find him and have him shove my car back onto the highway.

My shoes are caked with mud. Perspiration fills my eyelashes and trickles down my face. Streaks of sweat spot my thin short-sleeved shirt. My right hand aches. I hold it against my chest. Even slight movement causes a painful throbbing sensation to erupt at the base of my thumb.

Up ahead I hear sounds of activity. The repetitious drone of pump motors resonates down the pathway, raising my hopes and encouraging me to walk faster.

A break appears in the underbrush, and I spy a pipeline pump station. Enclosed inside a six-foot-high chain-link fence are two metal buildings and a tall circular storage tank. An odd conglomeration of silver painted pipes generously adorned with numerous valves and gauges is crowded tightly inside the fenced yard. In oil patch language unusual piping arrangements such as these are referred to as Christmas trees. And rightly so—few gifts could equal the riches found beneath this kind of tree.

Engine sounds emit from the smallest building inside the fence. Discovering the entrance gate is unlocked, I slip inside and call out, "Hello. Hello. Is anyone here?"

When no one answers, I try the front door. Finding it locked, I walk around the building to a side window, rub at the thick scale of oily dirt and look inside. Inside the building are four huge motors mounted side by side, each connected to a large diameter pipe. I surmise the motors are in some way responsible for transporting oil pumped from local wells to some distant Gulf Coast refinery.

A second larger building appears to be designated for storage. It's nearly the same width, but much longer, and equipped with double-wide, garage-type, wooden swing doors on each end. The door is cracked open, so I step inside.

Two vehicles fill the space inside the building—a faded red pickup and a newer model Willis Jeep. Almost certainly the jeep is equipped with four-wheel drive. My spirits soar at my good fortune.

Two thick, hairy legs connected to huge loose-fitting work boots protrude from beneath the pickup.

"Hello. Hello under there. Hey, could you come out for a minute? I need some help."

"What tha hell. Hey, you ought not ta sneak up on a fellow like that. You scared the peewaddly outta me."

"I'm sorry, mister. Didn't see you underneath the pickup until I was already inside. Can you come out? I really need some help."

"Sure, be glad ta help. Gimme a minute ta tighten up this oil pan."

"No problem. Listen, I apologize for bothering you, but my car's stuck in the mud down at the front gate. I need some help to get back on the pavement."

Irate grunts emanate from beneath the pickup while I wait for the man to finish his repairs.

"Whatcha doing out this way, fellow. You get yourself lost or somethin'?"

"No, I'm looking for a friend of mine. His name's Max Wagner. Last time I talked to him he was headed out here to check some oil gauges. He's an engineer from Houston. Don't suppose you've seen him? His wife tells me he was driving a green and white Willis Jeep."

My words leave my mouth before I can stop them. The man begins to scramble out from under the pickup while I stride over to inspect the jeep. The interior matches Georgia Wagner's description precisely. A set of calibration tools in the rear cargo space confirms my diagnosis. This is no coincidence. This vehicle belongs to Max. But why is it here? Where is Max?

"Hey, keep away from that automobile! That there's private property," the man yells as he shoves his roller cart to one side and pushes himself upright. The mechanic is short and overweight. His attire consists of a ragged pair of greasy overalls. He wears no shirt.

"You're darn right it is! This vehicle belongs to the man I'm looking for. How'd you get this car? Where's the man it belongs to?"

"You must be loco, mister. I bought that car in Kilgore three months ago."

"You got papers to prove that? If you do, I wanna see 'em, and I wanna see 'em right now."

"I left my papers at home. Hey, how 'bout you and me go pull your car outta the ditch. Then I'll go get my bill of sale." The man's voice changes quickly from panic to a more friendly tone.

"Alright, but if you can't come up with proof you own this car, you and I are gonna visit the sheriff."

"Don't worry, mister, I got plenty of proof. Let's go get your car. I'll drive. You wanna hop in on the other side?"

Even before my hand touches the car door handle I realize I've made a dreadful mistake. His steel wrench clips my ear, knocking me to my knees. Shooting stars blur my vision. I fight to stay conscious. A big shoe strikes me hard in the ribs, lifting me up and sending me sprawling across the dirt floor. The hefty mechanic chases after me, continuing to swing the deadly bludgeon. I roll over on my back, using my arms to block his flurry of blows while I desperately search for a place of refuge.

His big wrench finds its mark, cutting an ugly gash on my upper arm. A split second later I roll over and scramble underneath the pickup, barely avoiding another lethal blow.

"Come out from under there and take your lickin', fellow. You ain't got a snowball's chance in hell of leaving here alive. You're dead meat. You hear me—dead meat, like the buddy you're looking for." The man is breathing hard, obviously out of condition and unaccustomed to strenuous physical exertion.

Trying to buy time so I can figure a way out of my perilous situation, I ask questions, hoping to temporarily distract the man's attention away from his intended goal—which is to murder me.

"What makes you so anxious to kill me? Is that what you did to my friend?"

"Your friend was too damn curious. He ain't so curious no more."

"Then you killed him? But why would you kill him? He was an engineer—came out here to do a job. He wasn't here to harm you."

"Let's just say he knew too much. Now come on out before I get my gun and shoot you under the pickup."

A small pan filled with thick black oil rests next to my shoulder. Apparently, my adversary drained the pickup's motor before he tightened the oil pan. A solution to my precarious predicament is right beside me.

"Alright, I'm coming out. Gimme some room to slide out. Don't hit me."

Half expecting to be kicked or stomped when I emerge, I inch out feet first from beneath the pickup.

"Can you give me a hand? I think you broke my arm," I whimper, striving to make him think I'm badly injured. Very little acting is required. My entire body is racked with pain.

"Screw you, wise guy. Now crawl your scrawny ass out here. If I have ta get my gun, you'll be singing with the angels a few minutes from now. You won't be feeling nothing at all."

"I really do need some help. I think I'm stuck. How about giving me a hand?" I say, pulling my upper body partially out from beneath the vehicle. Gripped tightly in my bandaged right hand is the oil pan. Considering the circumstances, somehow the excruciating pain pulsating up my wrist seems inconsequential.

"Okay, but don't try nothing funny. Otherwise I'll have to kill you right here," the shirtless man warns. Taking pity on me, he bends down to grab me by my left arm.

The warm oil splashes full against his face. He screams and rubs at his eyes while I scramble to my feet. An exhilarating rush of adrenaline washes away all feeling of pain. I slam my clenched right fist viciously against his left temple, and his head snaps sideways. A half-second later my left fist crushes the bony gristle of his nose. Blood spurts from his nostrils. His knees buckle, and he falls to the floor.

Two knockout blows should have finished him, but my opponent is a stubborn hombre. He doesn't quit easily. Shaking his head, he rolls over and pushes up onto one knee, struggling to stand.

His semi-conscious condition and his kneeling position make my adversary an easy target. Grabbing the back of his head, I smash my right knee against his oil-covered face. Streams of bright red blood flow from the corners of his mouth and mix with the dark oil. A loose tooth drops from his open bleeding mouth. He's out cold even before he collapses and falls forward.

"There. Now that we've finished our conversation, how about we take a trip to see the sheriff? I tell you what. You just lay there and take it easy while I get the door," I tell the unconscious carcass lying on the floor, swaggering with the euphoric exuberance of meeting and conquering my enemy.

When I whirl around to start for the garage door, a rifle butt strikes me square in the face. Flashes of bright light precede acute, intense pain, then darkness.

❖ ❖ ❖ ❖ ❖

"DAMMIT, ALVIN. I told ya we shouldn't bring that jeep out here. I told ya somebody would recognize it. I knew it was a mistake," a husky voice chides from somewhere above.

Slowly I open one eye. My face is a mass of throbbing hurt.

"It rained this morning. We had to use the jeep. We sure as hell couldn't drive in here in no pickup. We'd a got stuck for sure."

"But now we gotta whack this new fellow. You know who he is?"

"Naw, we never got around to formal introductions. He said he was a friend of that engineer we caught snooping around the valves last week. Don't make no difference who he is. He knows too much now."

"Yeah, but we gotta slow down. If we're gonna have ta kill somebody every week, I'm gonna ask for a pay raise."

"Heck, I won't need no extra money to whack this dude. I'd do this one for free. This miserable skunk hit me when I wasn't ready and broke my nose. Look, Oscar, his eyes are open. Ya ready to meet your maker, mister smart guy? We know just the spot to dump wisenheimers like you who know too much."

My swollen nose is resting in a warm pool of wetness, making it difficult to breathe. Fearing I might drown in my own blood, I roll over on my side, my foggy mind struggling to compose some sort of argument which might alter my captors' decision to kill me.

"Hey, I don't know anything. Honest, I'm just a baseball coach," I whisper hoarsely.

A heavy shoe batters my cheek, putting an end to the one-sided discussion.

❖ ❖ ❖ ❖ ❖

THE JEEP BOUNCES up and down, rousing me from a fitful half-sleep. The rear tires bump against the end of a bridge and climb onto the wooden deck. Bridge timbers rumble thunderously as the vehicle rolls out onto the span and brakes to a stop.

Outside the car window, light from a half-full moon hanging low on the horizon is partially blocked by huge pecan trees which overhang the river. Chirping night creatures and the sound of gently flowing water kindle memories of times long past. I'm not lost. I know exactly where I am. We're parked on Deep Eddy Bridge. So this is where they intend to kill me. It's a fitting place for murder. People have died here before.

Deep Eddy Bridge crosses the Neches River about four miles west of Noonday and some ninety yards upstream from a sharp bend in the river channel. When I was a teenager still in high school, the mystique of this place lured me and my cousins here on several occasions. Once, when I was seventeen, my cousins and I camped overnight on the river bank. We didn't select the location for its beauty. Our outing was strictly a male thing—an exhibition of bravery—to prove to the world we could thumb our nose at danger.

Except for this particular spot, the Neches is normally a peaceful, slow-moving body of water. The headwaters originate forty miles northwest over in southeast Van Zandt County, so the river seldom ever fills its banks even following the heaviest rains. This place is named Deep Eddy because of the hazardous circular currents generated as the river waters gyrate around an abrupt right angle bend.

Some speculate the river depth at Deep Eddy measures more than sixty feet during normal flow. More than a few believe the river here is bottomless. In either case, no one swims here. It's too dangerous. The swirling current acts like a gigantic whirlpool, sucking everything toward its center. Local Negroes who frequently fish this river avoid the riverbend like it bears an incurable plague. They truly believe Deep Eddy is the doorway to hell.

The summer after our senior year my cousin Tommy tried to float through Deep Eddy riding an inner tube. We tied a long rope around his waist and followed him along the bank. The current flipped him over, and he went straight down. Took three of us to reel him in. You should have seen the expression on his face after we finally pulled him to the bank. His face was whiter than a sun-bleached sheet. Having survived a near death experience, you'd think he'd have been anxious to brag to our friends—how he'd run the river and lived to tell about it. But Tommy could hardly talk about the episode without getting the shakes. He acted like he'd come face to face with Satan himself.

Car doors squeak, and the vehicle sways from side to side as the two men riding up front crawl out. My feet are bound together. My hands are tied tightly behind my back. But by rolling over on my side and using a kicking motion, I'm able to scoot myself around so my back is braced against the back seat. My feet extend toward the tailgate door. There's little chance I can avoid my intended fate, but I won't die without putting up a fight.

"You drag our buddy outta the back, Oscar, while I rig up the anchor. Let's get this done and beat it outta here before someone sees us."

In the twilight darkness outside I can barely distinguish one man from the other. Shuffling sounds of footsteps tramping on the wooden bridge deck warn me that one of them is coming for me. I coil up like a snake. When the tail gate swings open, I lash out, jabbing at my captor with both feet.

My ambush misses its mark. Oscar jumps back out of reach, avoiding a second strike.

"Hey, Alvin. Gimme a hand. Our partner back here wants to put up a fight."

"Okay. Okay. Lemme get the rope tied to this piece of rail. Then we'll jerk his contrary butt outta there."

Oscar stoops down so I can see his face but keeps his distance so not to invoke another foot attack.

"You might as well come peaceful, mister. It'll go a lot easier on ya. If ya git Alvin riled, he's likely to break ya in ta little pieces before we dump ya in the drink." Oscar sounds like he's concerned about my health, giving me fatherly advice.

"Come out peaceful? You think I'm stupid? You cold-blooded creeps plan to kill me. If you want me, you'll have to come in and get me," I respond defiantly, gathering myself into a tight knot alongside the seat behind me.

"Have it your way. Anyway we do this, you're gonna wind up dead. You can have it easy, or ya can have it rough. I'm trying to save ya some useless pain."

Alvin's face appears next to Oscar. Apparently he's finished with the anchor. "Whatsa matter, Oscar? Mister wisenheimer giving ya trouble?"

"Yeah, he wants to play it tough. Says we'll have ta drag him out. Ya wanna kill him now? Be a lot less trouble."

"Naw. That'd mess up the cargo bed. And besides, the lousy bastard busted my nose. I can hardly breathe. I want him to die real slow—let him feel the life ooze out while he gasps for air down at the bottom of the river. I'll climb in and grab his feet. We'll pull him out feet first."

"Right, but watch out. He kicks like a mule."

Alvin leaps inside and crawls toward me on all fours. When he's halfway inside, I kick out. He takes the blow full on his shoulder then grabs my legs, slams my knees together and uses his thick hairy arms to apply a full leg-lock. Having me under control, he grins and begins to back out, pulling me along while I twist and turn trying to escape his vice-like grip.

"Grab hold of his feet, Oscar, and pull his ass outta here," Alvin barks.

My back slides along the car bed floor until I'm three-quarters outside. My shirt catches on the door handle and rips the sleeve when I fall. Big shoes begin kicking me the instant I hit the bridge deck. I kick back and roll sideways. I scream for help. Then a gun butt crashes against the side of my head. Shooting stars and bright flashes of light oscillate through my brain, but I don't pass out. I enter a dream world. I can see the two men moving. I can hear them talking, but I can't move.

❖ ❖ ❖ ❖ ❖

WATER SPLASHES on my face, bringing me back from my semi-conscious state. A voice from somewhere high above calls to me.

"Wake up. Hey, fellow, wake up. Me and Oscar wanna say goodbye."

As the fog dissipates from my mind, I realize where I am. I try to raise up, but a big shoe shoves me back against the bridge floor. I kick, but my feet won't move. A short rope attached to a heavy piece of railroad track renders them useless for defense.

"You sadistic ghouls. If you're gonna kill me, why don't you shoot me and get it over with? Why keep torturing me?"

"Well, normally we woulda shot ya already, but you're kinda special. Alvin is taking killing ya real personal. Nobody ever broke his nose before."

"Yeah. I wanna see the expression on your face when ya slide off the bridge, knowing you're taking your last breath of fresh air," Alvin sneers.

I turn my head, glancing from side to side. There's no point in calling for help. No one will hear me. Up until this very minute I've hoped for a miracle—some unexpected turn of events which might change the outcome of this ungodly nightmare and save me. Now, for the first time, I actually believe I am about to die. There's no way to avoid my fate. I never expected I'd die so young. I am poorly prepared.

"This won't work, you know. You're doing everything all wrong. You're both gonna get caught," I argue, trying to buy some time. Neither of these two seem overly endowed with smarts. Maybe I can convince them their plan for killing me is flawed.

"What won't work? Whatta you talking about?" Oscar responds, obviously annoyed I would question his tactics.

"The rope. Don't you two ever go to the movies? You're supposed to use a steel chain. Ropes expand and come loose underwater. My body will float up and wash downstream. Somebody's sure to find me. Then you two will be in big trouble."

The men glance at each other and consider my argument. Alvin grins and laughs loudly. Then his face hardens, and he lowers himself to glare directly into my eyes.

"Nice try, mister smart guy. But me and Oscar done this too many times. We don't need your dumb ass advice. We're like experts. Besides, me and Oscar gotta hit the road. You'd better stop talking and start praying. Bye now."

"No! No! Listen to me. . . ," I scream, but Alvin sneers wickedly, unveiling a mouthful of big, dirty teeth. Cackling gleefully, he uses his foot to shove the section of railroad track off the side of the bridge. My knees pop as the force of the falling steel jerks me toward the edge. A loose nail slashes at my shoulder, and I slip over the edge.

Air rushes past my body as I spiral downward. All sorts of questions rush through my mind while I wait for the collision which will mark my impact with the dark river below. Should I hold my breath to prolong my dying, or should I inhale the water and hope for a quick end? If my body is recovered, I wonder how many will take time to attend my funeral? I don't have many friends. Paul, Whitey, Clyde—surely they'll be there, along with a few members of my baseball team. Kaye will probably come. I'm not sure about Ted. No, I doubt if he'll come.

"SPLASH!" The sound of the railroad track and my bound feet smacking against the water's surface echoes off the river banks. Even before my body is fully submerged, the swift current begins to tug at me.

Black swirling water envelopes me, twisting and contorting my body as I sink downward. In muted horror I decide to hang onto life as long as possible. I hold my breath and close my eyes. My ears pop, and I sink deeper and deeper beneath the surface.

My anchor strikes the river bottom, but the ever deadly whirling current drags me along, circling slowly toward the center of the whirlpool. Finally, I can hold my breath no longer. I exhale and open my eyes. My body bumps against something moving alongside me.

Even in the deep semi-darkness, I recognize the object beside me. It is the lifeless torso of my friend Max. My tormentors must have tossed him in here too. How unimaginative. They claim to be experts killers, but those two have absolutely no imagination—no imagination at all.

I've often heard your life flashes before you in the seconds before you die. It's not true. Instead, while my lungs fill with water, my mind struggles to recall which movie had the scene where the crooks got caught because they stupidly used ropes to secure their victims' bodies to cement blocks, but I can't remember. Nevertheless, I'm certain I'm right. Alvin and Oscar are bound to get caught. Knowing their fate makes me the victor. Those two galoots are so ignorant. I can't help but giggle as life expires from my body.

❖ ❖ ❖ ❖ ❖

DYING DOESN'T HURT like I imagined, not if you don't struggle. Your spirit simply separates from your physical body, and you float upward.

Down below me at the bottom of Deep Eddy, I can see my lifeless carcass swaying in the swift current alongside Max Wagner's body. What happens next? Is there such a thing as Heaven and hell? Will I get a chance to plead my case? Where will I end up?

In some ways my dying will solve a lot of problems, so it may not be all bad. Everything that was ever right in my life I've managed to screw up. My baseball career is in shambles. Marrying Kaye was definitely a mistake. We truly love each other, but our love only makes us unhappy. Except for Paul and Whitey, I have no real friends. What little family I have left won't speak to me. A week after my death there won't be ten people who will care or even remember I'm gone.

Damn. If I had my life to live over, I'd do things differently. I swear I would.

208

❖ ❖ ❖ ❖ ❖

A SMALL HAND slips into mine, sending a warm sensation radiating through my being, eliminating all my negative thoughts and filling me with a feeling of incredible love.

"Come with me, Richard. I'm so glad you're finally here. I've been waiting and waiting."

"Matilda? I wasn't expecting to find you here. Am I dead?"

"You're in the in-between zone, my love. Don't be frightened."

"Hey, about the girls in Wichita Falls. I'm sorry. Are you still mad at me?"

"Harsh feelings are not allowed here, Richard. But no, I'm not mad anymore. Come with me. We have to go."

"Go? Where to? You mean like to Heaven?"

"To the Judgement Hall. That's where they'll decide about you."

"You mean whether I go to Heaven, or to hell?"

"Something like that. Hold my hand tightly now. It's not far, but I don't want to lose you."

Matilda whisks me away, and we glide high above the earth. For a short time white, pillow-like clouds whiz by, then we reach the stratosphere where the sky is amazingly clear. Gigantic stars, brighter than I have ever seen, twinkle down from above and light our way.

From as far back as I can remember, I've been taught there was a Heaven and a hell. If you were good and believed in God, you'd go to Heaven. If you were bad, you'd go to hell. But no one ever mentioned a Judgement Hall. I expected the decision whether you were sent to Heaven or condemned to hell would be automatic—decided before you died.

Neither Heaven nor hell holds much appeal for me. Secretly, I've always hoped that when you died that would be it. Life would be over and done—kaput. I'm not so sure I want to live forever, for darn sure not in hell—maybe not even in Heaven. Heaven sounds terribly dull—gliding around the stratosphere with everybody loving every-body—no problems, no cares, and most likely, no sex.

And what if they don't play baseball?

Heaven is supposed to be up in the sky somewhere. Hell is supposed to be down beneath the earth's surface. If you wind up in hell, your soul will burn forever in fiery hot lava. I really hope they don't send me there. I have a very low tolerance for pain.

"We're here," Matilda informs me, squeezing my hand and steering me toward what appears to be an enormous asteroid. The celestial body is round and flat with a glassy smooth rock surface. An inauspicious domed shell is centered in the mass of rock.

"Is that Judgement Hall? It seems awfully small." I'm disappointed. I had expected a more majestic structure—something more stately and appropriate for deciding a person's final fate.

"Yes. Spirits don't need much space. Once you're inside, you'll be impressed. The judges are very fair. You'll be given every chance to change their minds about sending you to hell."

"Sending me to hell? You mean they've already decided? That doesn't sound right. What about my rights? What about being innocent until I'm proven guilty?" I have no idea what rights I might have here, but convicting me and then giving me a chance to try and change their minds doesn't seem fair. That's not democratic.

"They know everything, darling—your every move, your every thought from the minute you were born until the very second you died. But inside the Hall, you'll be allowed an opportunity to explain your behavior. Occasionally, there are extenuating circumstances which will cause them to reverse their verdict."

"Extenuating circumstances? You mean like I was temporarily insane—like my mother breast fed me too long—like the devil made me do bad things? What kind of arguments can I use?"

"That'll be strictly up to you. But do your best. If you can change their minds, we can spend eternity together. We need to go inside. They're waiting."

While I'm certain Matilda's offer is made with the best of intentions, somehow the thought of sharing eternity with her, or any other woman for that matter, seems dreadfully boring. Thousands of years, eons of time, all with one woman. Good grief. What would we talk about?

"Alright, but I have one more question. No matter how this turns out, it's something I gotta know."

"Yes?"

"Do they play baseball in Heaven?"

❖ ❖ ❖ ❖ ❖

RICHARD C. MASON. Mister Richard Carl Mason. If you're here, please come forward," the court bailiff heralds gruffly.

Matilda squeezes my hand and tries to smile. She's visibly concerned for my welfare. "Do your best, my love. I'll be praying for you," she whispers.

"I'm back here. I'm Richard Mason, and I'm ready to testify," I respond bravely. I slip out of my pew-like seat and glide courageously down the aisle.

The courtroom arena inside Judgement Hall is small and unpretentious. Spectator seating is limited to three rows. Except for the long magistrate bench, the front of the room is void of furniture. Three men wearing long black robes and solemn expressions sit silently behind the bench. The bench is elevated so the judges can peer down on their defendants. To my left is a juror box with maybe twenty fixed seats, but there are no jurors here today. Perhaps I can request a jury trial if I don't agree with the judges' decision.

"Sirs. Uh, I mean Your Honors. My name is Richard Mason. I'm here to answer any questions you may have. Don't I have to swear to tell the truth or something?"

"That won't be necessary here, Mister Mason. We'll know whether you're telling the truth or not," the judge to my left advises.

"Oh, yeah. Sure, I suppose you would."

"Mister Mason, we understand you are a baseball manager."

"Yes sir. At least I was for a few games. My team was doing pretty good until Matilda got mad and left. I guess you know why. I broke my promise to stop drinking and carousing around with other women. Will that count against me?"

"Yes. We consider breaking a promise to be very serious."

"I reckon I'm done for then. I've been breaking promises ever since I left college early to play with the pros."

The middle judge who has been silent up until now breaks in. His hands hold some sort of scrolled document. He holds it up for the other judges to inspect.

"Your record indicates you were exceptionally reliable until a few months before you turned twenty. Anything happen along about that time that caused you to change."

"That's about the time I started drinking. I reckon you know about my drinking, but I've been trying to quit. Honest to God. . . . Uh, excuse me. I was trying to quit. Honest I was."

"Anything cause you to start drinking? You have family problems, or a health problem?"

"No. It was nobody else's fault. Except, well, I fell in love with this girl. She liked to drink, so I started drinking too. But you shouldn't blame her. She didn't have a drinking problem until she met me."

"Mister Mason, your record looks very bad. Right now the court has you condemned to burn in hell. Can you give us any reason we should change our minds?"

"No. I really wish I could, 'cause maybe then you could send me back like you did with Matilda. I left things back there in a heck of a mess. Colonel Segars is up to his neck with those New Orleans people. If his baseball team doesn't make the playoffs, you'll probably be here judging him before long. Those two guys, Alvin and Oscar, are out there, running around loose, killing everybody in sight. And with me gone, my wife's gonna wind up married to Ted Gooding. He's such a pompous ass."

"Watch your language, Mister Mason. We're very close to Heaven here. That kind of talk is totally inappropriate."

"I'm sorry, Your Honor, but surely you understand what I mean."

"Yes, things back there certainly aren't good, but that's life. It goes on. Anything else?"

"Is it true about hell? Do you really burn? And does it hurt a lot? I don't stand pain very well."

"Yes, Mister Mason, you really do burn. Of course none of us here can say for sure, but we've heard it hurts like the devil." The judge cuts his eyes left then back to the right, seeking some kind of support from his peers. When none is offered, he lowers his voice and mutters, "Uh, in a matter of speaking. You understand."

"Gee, I was afraid you'd say that. Listen, Your Honors. I'm really not such a bad guy—not nearly bad enough to be sentenced to burn in hell. I honored my parents, up until that time they struck out for Montana. I never cheated on my wife. Okay, maybe I came close, but I never actually did anything. Check your record. You'll see," I implore, racking my brain, trying to remember the other eight commandments. I'm fairly certain I never broke more than three or four out of the ten.

I hold my breath and cross my fingers while the middle judge studies his scroll. Apparently the scroll contains a list of every single thing I've done wrong.

"This looks bad. It says here you murdered a woman—an Ethyl Mason. I'm sorry, Mister Mason. Murder is the one thing we can't forgive."

My heart sinks. I was hoping they wouldn't know about my grandmother, but I've always suspected I'd have to pay for what I did.

"Yes, she was my grandmother. I didn't actually kill her. I only helped her die. She was suffering and in so much pain. Her body was eaten up with cancer. She had absolutely no chance of recovering. She was ready to die, and she begged me to help. No one else in the family had the courage. Not one of my gutless relatives loved her enough to do what I did."

"So this was a mercy killing. I'm afraid we can't condone taking another person's life, no matter what the circumstances."

"But surely there must be some cases where killing is justified, like when soldiers go to war. Situations like that."

"Well, yes. I suppose there are certain occasions where we're allowed some leeway. Maybe if you tell us how Mrs. Mason expired we can find a loophole."

"I'd rather not. Are you sure it's not explained on my scroll?"

"No. I'm afraid you'll have to tell us your story."

❖ ❖ ❖ ❖ ❖

IT WAS SATURDAY NIGHT when my cousin Jimmy called. I could barely hear his voice. Many of my half-naked teammates were out in the hotel hallway, screaming and hollering—celebrating the end of spring training. Two hours earlier we had defeated the White Sox in our final contest of the exhibition season. We were scheduled to open our regular season in Cleveland the following Tuesday.

Jimmy's news about grandmother's condition struck me like a bolt of lightning. My grandmother was my anchor, my source of strength. If she hadn't been there to love me and console me after my parents were killed in the car accident, I'd never have survived my sorrow. She was my biggest fan and my best friend.

I packed a bag and caught a bus out of Tampa. Three bus changes and thirty-three hours later I arrived in Dallas. Jimmy met me at the downtown bus station. During the trip to Tyler he tried to explain how seriously ill our grandmother was. He left out a lot.

The moment I saw her I realized Jimmy hadn't told me everything. Grandmother's face was white and drawn, like the life had been sucked out of her. I couldn't believe she had aged so quickly. When I left for spring training two months earlier, she seemed so happy and full of life.

From the instant our eyes met, as she clasped my hand tightly and held it lovingly against her cheek, I knew she would never get well.

Late that night when we were alone, my grandmother asked me to help her die. Her stomach cancer had spread to her intestines. Her doctor told her she had a month, maybe two, to live. She was facing a long, drawn-out and painful death.

I watched her lie in bed, moaning, suffering and quivering in agony for two days before I agreed. Actually, the part I played wasn't difficult. We decided she should die at dawn before any relatives who might object showed up.

Grandmother had lots of pills. Pills for pain. Pills to make her sleep. We waited to watch one last sunrise together, holding hands and talking about my mom and dad and how glad she would be to see them again. Then I helped her swallow a dozen or so pills. It took maybe fifteen minutes for the pills to take effect. Once she was asleep, I followed our plan. I slipped a plastic dry-cleaning bag over her head and bound it tightly to her neck with a cotton scarf she often wore while she tended her garden.

Then I waited.

When her hands started to move, to reach for the bag, I gently placed them back at her side. In a few minutes it was all over.

My Aunt Martha arrived around nine that morning. By that time I had removed the evidence. I'd placed the plastic bag back over a dress in the closet, folded the scarf and put it back in a dresser drawer, washed the glass and set it inside the kitchen cabinet.

Maybe I looked guilty. Maybe my grandmother had begged my aunt to help before she asked me. But somehow Aunt Martha suspected what I'd done. Without saying a word, she darted for the front door.

We buried my grandmother the next afternoon. None of the family has had much use for me since.

❖ ❖ ❖ ❖ ❖

THE HELPFUL MIDDLE JUDGE fidgets with his chin and glances to each side, checking his two comrades for their reaction. He nods and they scoot closer together to discuss my situation. A few seconds later they slide back to assume their stately positions behind the magistrate bench.

"We find your story heart rendering, Mister Mason. The other judges and I remember your grandmother. She passed through here about three years ago. She was a good woman, almost a saint already. We had absolutely no reservations about sending her straight to Heaven. Now that we understand the facts, perhaps we can render a more appropriate decision in your case."

"Then there's a chance you might not send me to hell? You might send me to Heaven?"

"No, there's no way you'll qualify for Heaven. The way you were living, you were headed straight down the pathway to hell. The

215

problem as we see it is—you simply died too soon. Our charts have you projected to commit every sin in the book before you arrive."

"Then what's to become of me? Surely you don't intend to leave me in limbo, stuck here somewhere between Heaven and hell?"

"No, we won't do that. Your early arrival seems to have caused a flaw in our evaluation system. We need to study your case further. If you'll wait outside, we will notify you of our decision."

❖ ❖ ❖ ❖ ❖

TIME CREEPS BY while I wait in the corridor outside the courtroom. Other spirits pass by, gawking curiously as if they know my every sin and why I've been ordered to wait here. My fear of the pending verdict makes me want to bolt for the front doorway, but it's too late to run. I made my bed. Now I must face the consequences.

Without notice, the courtroom door swings open, and Matilda emerges. Her face bears a grieved expression. My insides churn while my hopes vanish. Matilda obviously will not be bringing good news.

"I'm sorry, darling. You put up a very convincing argument. For a moment there, I thought you might have a chance."

"Oh, no. They're sending me to hell?"

"No. Oh, Richard, I'm so sorry. They're sending you back— back to life."

Chapter Twelve

"HEY, MISTER. ARE YOU OKAY?" a voice shouts in my ear. An icy chill grips my body. My teeth begin to chatter. I pull my knees against my chest, squeezing my body into a tight knot. The bitter cold, the wetness combine to articulate my discomfort.

But if I'm dead, how could I feel cold and wet?

My eyes blink open. A huge muscular Negro man is crouched over me. Lines of worry wrinkle his face.

"I don't know. Where am I? Are you an angel?"

"Nope, I sure ain't no angel. My name's Luke. Say, don't I know you? Yeah, we was cellmates in the Canton jailhouse."

A steady rush of cold liquid pushes at my legs. My left ear is clogged with sand. I roll over to discover I'm lying on the edge of a river. The lower portion of my body protrudes out into the water.

"That's right. Big Luke. Yeah, I remember you too. How about giving me a hand? I need to sit up and collect my wits."

"Be glad to. But I wanna know how you wound up here alongside the river. Man, you musta been on one heckava drunk," Luke says, shoving a big hand beneath my shoulders and gently raising me to a sitting position.

"No, I wasn't drinking. Last thing I recall was sinking to the bottom of the river. My feet were tied to a piece of railroad track.

Look, I got rope burns to prove it," I explain, pulling at my pant legs to expose a section of raw skin above my ankles. My gesture causes me to notice my right hand. Strangely, the knife cut around the base of my thumb is completely healed.

"A piece of railroad track. Good Lord, man. Was you trying to commit suicide?" Luke jerks away, disengaging his hand which supports my back. Big Luke apparently garners some deep superstition about suicide. I almost topple backward before I can regain my balance.

"No, it was these two hooligans who tied me to the rail section. They beat me up and tried to kill me. I'm not quite sure how I wound up here."

"Looks like their rope come loose from that piece of iron you was tied to. You're a mighty lucky man. Somebody up there must be watching after you."

"You're right about that, Luke. I have a guardian angel, and from now on, I'm gonna listen to what she says."

"If I was you, I'd do more than listen. I'd drop down on my knees and kiss her feet. Come on, Mister Lucky. My pickup's parked up the river a piece. I'll give you a ride home."

❖ ❖ ❖ ❖ ❖

LUKE'S PICKUP SPUTTERS and spits out a puff of black smoke when he slows to turn onto Williams Court. We coast for several yards, and he pops the clutch. The engine coughs, shakes violently then starts up again.

"It's the third house on your left," I say, pointing out my duplex and exhaling a silent sigh of relief. Our trip back to Tyler has been an experience I won't soon forget. Luke's battered old vehicle is years past replacement. How he keeps it running is a marvel to behold. But now, a half block more and I'm safely home. I never imagined my rented duplex would look so good. I plan to soak my weary body in a tub of hot water, slip on some dry clothes and grab a bite to eat. Then maybe I'll contact the police and file a complaint against Alvin and Oscar.

"Yep, the one with the blue Pontiac parked out front. That your car?"

Parked alongside the curb directly in front of my duplex sits my automobile. How did it get here? Last time I saw the Pontiac it was stuck in the mud facing the oil lease entrance gate.

"That's my car all right. But I don't understand what it's doing here. It's supposed to be out near Swinneytown."

"Come on, Rick. Cars don't drive themselves. You sure you wasn't drinking?" Luke asks, surveying my Pontiac and slowing to a stop.

"There's something mighty weird going on here, Luke. I don't know what it is yet, but I'm gonna get to the bottom of this. Hey, thanks for the ride. I don't know how or when, but I'll make this up to you. If I had some cash on me, I'd offer to pay for your gas, but I'm broke as a skunk."

Luke waves me off. "No problem. Next time it might be me who's sleeping off a drunk and needs help. You take care now, you hear."

"I wasn't drinking, and I wasn't drunk. Really, I wasn't."

"Well, it don't matter how you got down there on that river. Fact is, you're home safe now. Look, Rick, I gotta be getting on home. My old lady will be worried."

"Sure, Luke. Hey, thanks. If you ever wanna take in a baseball game, call me. I'll see you get the best seat in the house."

"I might just take you up on that. I listen to them Trojan games on the radio all the time. Sure would like to see 'em play."

After Luke's pickup rounds the circular drive and disappears from sight, I run to inspect the Pontiac. Someone has washed it thoroughly, meticulously removing every trace of mud from the body, the tires, even beneath the fenders. Inside, nothing has been touched. Trash, scorebooks, discarded lineups and notebook paper with diagrams and sketches for baseball strategy litter the back seat. My keys are in the ignition. It's as if I my visit to Swinneytown never happened.

❖ ❖ ❖ ❖ ❖

"TAKE A SEAT, MISTER. I'll see if I can locate someone who's got time to take your statement," a surly desk sergeant tells me, shoving a half-eaten sandwich back inside a brown paper bag and pushing the bag to one side. He makes no effort to conceal his indignation at having his lunch interrupted.

"Got time. Listen, two men tried to kill me. I'm lucky to be alive. You need to issue an arrest warrant and put out an all points bulletin, right away."

"Well, maybe we'll do that. Maybe we won't. But someone's gotta take your statement first. Now what's your name again?"

"Richard Mason. I'm the victim."

"Alright, Mister Mason. Please take a seat. Detective Stone should be with you in a few minutes. When he finishes with the person he's working with, I'll tell him about your case. I'm sure he'll be fascinated with your story."

"My story? Hey, what kind of place is this? You people are hired to protect innocent citizens like me. Doesn't anyone care? These two goons tried to kill me. And my friend Max Wagner—they did kill him."

"Sure. Sure. Now take a seat, Mister Mason, or I'll have to call in the duty sergeant."

❖ ❖ ❖ ❖ ❖

MOMENTS PASS SLOWLY while I wait impatiently, occasionally shifting my hip weight so my butt won't go numb. The wooden bench I've been assigned to is rock hard.

A winding stairway directly behind the reception desk leads to a second floor. The section to my left contains three private offices. The offices are separated from the public lobby by an eight-foot-high partition covered with dingy wood paneling. Opaque glass windows are framed at intervals designed to furnish each room with two closely spaced windows. Entry to each office is provided by a glass paneled door. On the glass of each door, the word "Private" is painted in gold with black trim. Muffled voices come from inside.

The door to the middle office swings open. Two men emerge. One man wears a dark business suit. Evidently, he is a police officer. The other man is dressed casually, wearing slacks and a short-sleeved shirt. The men seem in exceptionally good spirits. They smile and laugh and make exaggerated hand gestures as they stroll across the lobby floor. At the front door the men linger to exchange a few final pleasantries.

Several minutes pass before the two men shake hands and wave goodbye. The man in the business suit stands at the front door until his friend disappears from sight then turns and leisurely ambles to the reception desk. He picks up the clip board where I signed in and begins scanning the list of names. The desk sergeant whispers something to the man and points toward me.

The man nods affirmatively, places the clipboard back on the desk, and walks over to speak to me.

"Mister Mason, our desk sergeant tells me someone tried to kill you." The man speaks curtly, sounding like I'm the one who's committed a crime.

"Yes sir, that's right. These two goons named Alvin and Oscar tied me to a section of railroad track and pitched me in the Neches River."

I wonder if Detective Stone has a home. He's dressed like an unmade bed. Judging from his appearance, you'd think he's been sleeping in his clothes. His double-breasted suit coat is badly wrinkled. The sleeve ends are tattered from wear. His white shirt, with collar unbuttoned, is spotted with coffee stains. A too-wide tie printed with large yellow and purple roses is a perfect accessory to his pathetic attire. Compared to the way this fellow dresses, I could be a window model at Joyner Fry Men's Store.

"My, what an unusual story. You wanna come inside my office and tell me all about your experience."

"Experience? Hey, you think I'm making this up?"

"Oh no, Mister Mason. I believe every word, and I want to hear all about how you swam out of the Neches River with a section of railroad track tied to your feet and wound up here at the police station in dry clothes and with your hair combed."

❖ ❖ ❖ ❖ ❖

BEFORE HE'LL TAKE my statement, the poorly dressed detective insists I write down my full name and home address. He's extremely disappointed when he discovers I don't have a home phone. I can't imagine why he'd need the name of my nearest of kin, but he insists. He's unimpressed when I tell him I manage the Tyler baseball club, but when he learns I'm Clyde Segars' son-in-law, he perks up, scribbles something in the note pad on his desk, and tenders his full attention, hanging on every word. When I finish my story, he leans back in his chair and clasps his hands loosely against his chest.

"That's quite a tale, Mister Mason. Anyone who can collaborate your allegations?"

"No, not really. There's this Negro man who found me lying on the river bank and drove me home. He didn't actually see Alvin and Oscar drop me in the Neches, but he can verify I had a rope tied to my ankles. The rope burns are still there. Wanna see 'em?"

"No, that won't be necessary. What about this Negro fellow? He have a name?"

"Luke. He calls himself Big Luke."

"He have a last name?"

"I'm afraid I didn't ask. I was pretty shook up when he found me."

"You ever see this Big Luke fellow before? Maybe we can trace him someway."

I consider relating how Luke and I met inside the Van Zandt County jail, but decide against it. It's obvious the detective already has reservations about my story. Telling him Luke and I were introduced earlier, while we were serving jail time for public intoxication, would only add to his doubt.

"No, never saw him before."

"Okay then, I guess we're finished. I'll type up a report and assign a file number to your case. Can you come by tomorrow morning? I'll need you to look it over and sign it."

"Is that all you're gonna do—file a report?"

"Well, under the circumstances, I don't know what else we can do. As you can see, my department is rather shorthanded. Besides, you don't have a witness to back up your story, and you don't know the last names of the two men who tried to do you in."

"What about my friend Max? He's still out there at the bottom of the Neches River with a section of railroad track tied to his feet."

"Yes, I think we have a missing report on him. Perhaps we can dispatch a search party to see if he's there."

"He's there all right. I saw him myself."

"You say he's at the bottom of the river? You think you could find him again?"

"Yes. I know the exact spot. He's dead center in the middle of the Deep Eddy whirlpool."

"Deep Eddy. Good Lord, man. Surely, you don't expect the Tyler Police Department to send someone out there?"

"Isn't that your job—to recover the dead body and find the killers?"

"Yes, but we have a problem here. Deep Eddy is outside the city limits. That's the county sheriff's jurisdiction. When I finish my report, I'll see that a copy is delivered to his office."

❖ ❖ ❖ ❖ ❖

IN SPITE OF MY OBJECTIONS Detective Stone courteously maneuvers me out of his office and ushers me to the front door. He promises he'll contact the sheriff and have him call me. He advises me to be patient, explaining that because my information is so sketchy, I shouldn't expect a quick arrest.

When I reach the Pontiac, I'm steaming mad. No one wants to believe my story. Big Luke thought I was drunk. The Tyler police don't seem eager to get involved. Why can't I get anyone's attention?

I slip into the driver's seat and press my head against the steering wheel, dejectedly pondering my next move.

The colonel. Sure. Why didn't I go straight to him? He'll know how to handle this.

With renewed enthusiasm, I turn the key and start the engine. Why did I waste my time talking to the police? Clyde Segars has connections. The colonel knows how to get things done.

❖ ❖ ❖ ❖ ❖

SUMMONING MY RESOLVE, I knock lightly on the door and boldly stick my head inside.

"Clyde, you got a minute?"

Segars glances up from a stack of papers piled high on his desk. Uncharacteristically, he wears no jacket. His shirt sleeves are rolled up. His collar is unbuttoned, his tie loosened. When he sees me, a terrified expression engulfs his face. He gasps for breath. The fountain pen he's holding drops and falls to the floor. Obviously, my unannounced entrance caught him by surprise.

"Sorry, Clyde. Didn't mean to startle you."

"Rick. What are you doing here? You're supposed to be. . . what I mean is, I'm surprised to see you."

"Listen, Clyde. I know you're busy, but I have a serious problem. Thought maybe you. . ."

Segars leaps from his chair, steps around his desk and rushes to shake my hand, pumping it up and down like I'm an old friend he hasn't seen in ages.

"I'm so glad you're here, Rick. How've you been? You feeling all right?"

"I'm fine. A little bit worse for the wear. Listen, I ran into some trouble, and I could use your help. If you can spare a minute, I'd like to tell you about it."

Segars returns to his chair while I settle into the chair on the opposite side of his desk. He listens intently, traumatized by my tale of the events which led to my being dumped in the river. Not wanting to complicate the story, I decide to leave out the part about my reincarnation.

"So the Tyler police don't seem interested? And who was this person who took your statement?"

"A Detective Stone. Told me he'd file a report, but he wasn't much help. Claimed Wagner's body is outside his jurisdiction. Said I should contact the sheriff's office. That's when I decided to come see you."

"You did the right thing, Rick. The sheriff is a personal friend of mine. Invited me to share the podium when he made his acceptance speech after the election last fall."

"You think you can convince him to investigate? My friend Max is still there in the river. Maybe if we show the sheriff a body, we can get some action."

Segars reaches for his telephone and places the receiver to his ear. He grins at me while he waits for the operator.

"Hello, operator. Get me the Smith County sheriff's office.

"No, I don't know the number. You think I call the sheriff every day?

"Fine. Can you ring for me please?"

Watching the anxious look on my face, Segars holds his hand over the mouthpiece and whispers, "Don't worry, Rick. We'll get to the bottom of this.

"Hello, this is Clyde Segars. Can you get Sheriff Grimes on the line please? Tell him it's urgent."

While he waits to be connected, Segars spies the fountain pen he dropped earlier and leans forward to retrieve it. He lays the pen on his desk then picks it up and removes the cap, apparently with the intention of applying his signature to one of the sales contracts. He never completes the task.

"Good afternoon, Bob. Yes, it's good to talk to you too.

"Yes, the girls are fine. Vickie and her new husband are back from their honeymoon. They plan to live in Tyler. I'm hoping they'll make me a grandfather before long.

"Listen, Bob. There's a young man in my office. You may remember him. He's my other son-in-law.

"Right. The one who drinks too much. But these days he's straight. I have all the confidence in the world in him. Got him managing my baseball team.

"Yep, you're right there. He's doing a fine job. The team's playing excellent baseball. We're in first place. Listen, Bob, Rick here has a problem. Tells me two men killed a friend of his and dumped the body in the Neches River. Tried to do the same with Rick."

At the colonel's insistence, Sheriff Grimes agrees to assemble a search party and meet us at the riverbend below Deep Eddy Bridge. Reluctantly, he also promises to bring along a diver and equipment to drag the river for Wagner's body. Always the diplomat, Segars offers to furnish a wrecker to assist in the operation.

Following his telephone conversation with the sheriff, Segars dials downstairs and arranges to have the wrecker follow us. I try to object, but he waves me off. He insists on accompanying me to the river site.

Clyde hustles me down the stairs and into his car. A huge wrecker is ready and waiting beneath the front canopy, with lights flashing. Segars signals the wrecker to proceed then turns to me, smiles happily, and reaches to affectionately pat my shoulder.

❖ ❖ ❖ ❖ ❖

SHERIFF GRIMES and three of his deputies stand beside Clyde and myself as we wait on the bank, anxiously eyeing the whirling waters of Deep Eddy. The river is lower now, having receded by more than a foot since early this morning. The effect of yesterday's showers has quickly dissipated.

Two steel cables connected to a double winch behind Segars' giant wrecker extend down the river bank and disappear into the muddy water. Somewhere out there, deep in the deadly swirling waters, is a professional diver hired by the sheriff. He's searching for Max's body.

A hard tug on the tow cable pulls out all the slack. Another solid tug snaps the cable into full tension.

226

Sheriff Grimes frowns and nods to the wrecker driver. "Looks like Dave's found something. Give him a minute to tie on. He'll signal when he's ready to tow it in."

Noticing my anxiety, Segars lays a fatherly hand on my shoulder. "I know this is tough on you, son. But hang on. We should know something in a few minutes."

"This may sound crazy, Clyde, especially after all the trouble I've caused you and the sheriff. But I hope I'm wrong. I truly do."

Sheriff Grimes overhears my compromising admission and whirls to reprimand me. An angry scowl is scrawled across his face.

"You better not be wrong, Mason. This operation is costing Smith County one hell of a lotta time and money. That diver out there made me promise to pay him double wages before he'd set foot in the river. Even after I agreed, he almost changed his mind. You see these three deputies I pulled off other duty? They don't come cheap. And that wrecker goes for about twenty bucks an hour. No, you damn sure better not be wrong, or I'm gonna own a large chunk of your ass."

"Don't worry about the wrecker, Bob. I wouldn't think of charging your office for using it, not after you've been so helpful."

"Well thanks, Clyde. I appreciate that. Sometimes I wonder how you can be so generous and still eke a profit outta your car operation."

"Oh, I get along, but making a profit is secondary to my civic duty."

The two men's mutual admiration is interrupted rudely by a sudden tension in the diver's cable. The line begins to gyrate wildly, like a heavy fishing line with a giant fish twisting and turning at the other end.

"Good Lord Almighty! Our diver's in trouble! Winch him in. Get that man outta there. Mike, you and Ronnie wade out in the water and help bring him in," Sheriff Grimes screams.

Two deputies hurriedly bound down the river bank. When they reach the water's edge each man grabs a cable and uses it as a lifeline. The men pull themselves slowly out until they stand waist deep in the river and wait maybe thirty seconds before the moving cable drags the diver into view. Simultaneously, the deputies grab the diver's arms and hoist him to the shoreline. Sheriff Grimes, the colonel and I scramble down the embankment. The sheriff reaches the diver first. He grabs the diver's face mask and jerks it off.

"You okay, Dave?" the sheriff inquires, breathing hard.

Groggily, the diver responds, "I guess I am now. Lucky we had that cable tied right. Thought I was a goner for sure."

"What was it? The current too swift?"

"No, something grabbed at me and tried to pull me down. Felt like two giant hands. I ain't going back in there. I don't care if you pay me triple. You hear me? I ain't going back."

"Sure, Dave, and no one's asking you to. Now calm down and tell me exactly what you found."

"I'm not really sure. It was awful dark and really deep. I musta been about sixty foot down when the thing first touched me."

"Did you see a body? That's what we're interested in."

"There's a body down there all right. I hooked the carcass to the tow line just before the hands grabbed me. It oughta still be connected."

"Hey, Mac! Get your other winch rigged up and reel in the tow cable! Dave here says we've found us a body," the sheriff yells, grinning like an old fox. Now he has a real case to investigate. Now he can call the newspaper. A juicy murder case and all the publicity that comes with it will do wonders for his stature with county voters.

With head lowered, the colonel uses his foot to dig at the river sand. For some reason he's not nearly as delighted with the situation as the sheriff. He seems more interested in his shoes than in the murder.

❖ ❖ ❖ ❖ ❖

"YES, THAT'S MAX," I confirm regretfully, then look away. The sight of my friend's body sickens me. Max's waterlogged face is puffed and distorted, bloated with sallow skin the texture of day-old pancake batter. His mouth is cracked open like he's trying to cry out. His eyes resemble two oysters on the half-shell, both wide open. No doubt he died suffering and in a terrible state of fright.

"Looks like you were right on target, Mason. Somebody tied his feet to that piece of railroad track and dumped him in the river. From the expression on his face, I'd say he was still alive. The murdering scoundrels—that's a hellava way to kill a man, making him spend his last minutes here on earth gasping for air," the sheriff hisses.

"Depends on your attitude, sheriff. If you don't fight too hard, dying can be rather peaceful."

Sheriff Grimes shakes his head back and forth and turns to Segars. "Clyde, you need to talk to your son-in-law. Except for the grace of God, this could be him we dragged out of that river."

"Yes, Rick is a very lucky fellow. It's a miracle he's here to finger the killers."

"Mason, we need to find the sorry S.O.B.s who done this. You think you could identify them?" the sheriff inquires grimly.

"Yes, and I know exactly where you can find 'em."

"You want to come, Clyde? Not every day a prominent citizen gets a chance to participate in a homicide arrest."

"No, I can't. I have urgent business back in town. My desk is littered with a dozen contracts needing my attention. Surely you fellows can solve this murder case without me."

"Of course we can. Just wanted you to feel welcome. You know, invited to the party," Sheriff Grimes laughs. Since we retrieved Wagner's body, the sheriff's disposition has improved dramatically.

"Thanks, Bob. I'll pass on your invitation and follow my wrecker back to the shop. But I want to know how this comes out. Will you call me if you find the killers?"

"You bet, Clyde. I'll call you the minute we slap handcuffs on them two dudes."

With a murder to investigate, the sheriff moves quickly into action. Instructing one deputy to stay behind and guard the body, he shoves me into the back seat of his squad car. He and Mike Harris leap into the front. A second squad car driven by Deputy Ronnie Dobbs follows as we burn rubber in the direction of Swinneytown. With sirens wailing, our two speeding vehicles squeal onto the black asphalt of State Highway 155.

Using his car radio, the sheriff contacts the coroner's office and arranges for an ambulance to pick up the body. He tells the coroner he's on his way to make an arrest and wants a preliminary analysis on the cause of death before the body is removed from the crime scene.

❖ ❖ ❖ ❖ ❖

WHEN WE PASS Swinneytown, the deputy leans forward to flip off the siren switch. The sheriff turns and nods to me in the back seat.

"Don't want 'em to hear us coming," he explains. "You say this place is about a mile past the Affiliated Oil reservoir?"

"Yes, should be around that next curve. There's an iron pipe gate. That's where my car got stuck." While we ease along, my eyes search for the dirt road and the entrance gate. Deputy Mike glances back at me. He's driving with one hand. His free hand rubs at the handle of the pistol strapped to his waist. Arresting a real live murderer is a rare opportunity for a sheriff's deputy. Mike appears anxious, obviously anticipating some sort of shootout.

"There it is. That's it. The pump station I told you about is right up that road."

"Mike, you catch the gate. If it has a lock on it, bust it open. We'll drive right up to their hideout. I wanna catch these guys by surprise," the sheriff commands. His tense voice confirms he is also ready for action.

❖ ❖ ❖ ❖ ❖

WHEELS SCREECH loudly as the two patrol cars roar into the pump station compound. Sheriff Grimes and his two deputies leap out, their guns drawn, like army commandos. In less than a minute they search the entire area, but find nothing. The tools, the old tires, even the pickup inside the storage building have been removed, swept away clean as a whistle. Not a single piece of evidence remains to confirm my story.

"Sorry, Rick, looks like our chickens have flown the coop. You got any idea where they might be hiding?"

"No, not a clue."

"Let's run back to my office. I want you to look through my mug sheets. Maybe we'll get lucky. If you can identify either of the men, I'll issue an arrest warrant."

❖ ❖ ❖ ❖ ❖

WHILE I SCAN the county's mug sheets, Sheriff Grimes telephones the coroner's office. Their heated conversation filters through the paper thin walls.

"Whatta you mean you can't say for sure? You're the coroner in this county. If you can't tell me, then who can?

"Okay. Okay. I'll contact Wagner's family and get their approval. But I need an answer quick, before the press gets wind of this. I don't intend to be made the fool because your people can't do their job.

"Sure, I'll contact his family as soon as we hang up. The deceased is a close acquaintance of Clyde Segars' son-in-law. You know, the one who manages the Trojans. Got him here in my office.

"Yeah, I heard. They're in first place. Maybe we oughta get the wives together and go out there some night. I'll talk to Clyde. See about some tickets.

"Fine, I'll get back to you. Soon as I have the family's approval."

Grumbling some inaudible grievance to himself, the sheriff slams the receiver down hard, ruthlessly demonstrating his frustration. His chair scrapes harshly against the concrete floor as he scoots himself back from his desk. Heavy footsteps forewarn me he's in an unpleasant mood.

"You finished with that mug book, Mason?"

"Sure am. But I can't find either of the killers in here. You think maybe the Tyler Police might have some different pictures? I'd sure like to identify those guys."

"No, their book is an exact duplicate of ours."

"You got any other ideas?"

"Not really. You hear me talking to the coroner?"

"Yes. Sorry, but I couldn't help but hear. These walls don't allow for much privacy."

"Then you know what I want?"

"Yes sir. You want Wagner's family to approve an autopsy."

"You wanna handle it? Might make it easier on the wife and kids if a friend delivers the bad news, instead of a stranger."

❖ ❖ ❖ ❖ ❖

GEORGIA WAGNER bursts into tears at the sound of my voice. She's obviously been expecting the worst. It takes several seconds for her to regain her composure and speak coherently. Even then her voice is strained. Our conversation is interrupted by occasional spells of sobbing.

"Rick, please forgive me. We've all been so worried. Have you heard anything?"

"I'm afraid so, Georgia. I'm sorry, but I don't have good news. You might want to gather your family about you. This is gonna be rugged."

"Oh, no. He's been hurt. How bad is he?"

"Georgia, he's gone. I hate to be so blunt, but you need to know. Max is dead."

Wails of anguish reverberate across the phone line. I wait a few seconds before I continue.

"Get hold of yourself, Georgia. If you truly love Max, you have to calm down. We have some hard decisions to make. I need your help."

"I'm sorry," she sobs. "I knew something was wrong. But this is so final. I'm not prepared to deal with it. How can I help?"

"Georgia, Max was murdered."

"Oh, no. But who would want to murder Max? He was kind and gentle. Why would anyone want to kill him?"

"We don't know. The sheriff wants to perform an autopsy to determine the exact cause of death. He needs your permission."

Explaining the details as best I can, I tell her about discovering her husband's body in the river and how anxious the sheriff is to bring his killers to justice. I leave out how close I came to joining Max in his watery grave. She has enough problems dealing with her husband's death. No sense confusing her with facts she doesn't need to know. Before I hang up, Georgia agrees to allow the autopsy. We also decide that I should accompany the body to Houston after the autopsy is finished. She explains she wants to bury Max in Richmond alongside her parents.

❖ ❖ ❖ ❖ ❖

AS EXPECTED the coroner's autopsy finds the cause of death to be asphyxiation by drowning. Despite two bullet wounds, one in his left shoulder and one in his abdomen, Wagner's lungs were full of water, verifying the sheriff's conjecture that he died gasping for a last breath of air. With his work finished, the coroner furnishes me with a death certificate and releases the body for transportation to Houston.

❖ ❖ ❖ ❖ ❖

THE SECOND PLACE Texarkana Bears arrived in Tyler on Thursday for a four-game shootout. For both teams it's a key series. Up until now we've been playing the dogs of the league. Texarkana will be much tougher. Last season the Bears walked away with the Big State championship, finishing eleven games ahead of second place Gainesville. Our home stand against the Bears could be the turning point in our season. We're either as good as we seem, or we've been winning because of the caliber of teams we've faced.

Nevertheless, I keep my promise to escort my friend's body back home. With the colonel's permission, I turn the team over to Whitey and ride inside the ambulance alongside Max's final remains. The long trip to Houston is both monotonous and tiring.

Funeral services on Saturday include only family members and a few close friends. In spite of the sparse attendance, many tears are

233

shed as Max is laid to rest during a quiet graveside service in a tiny cemetery near Georgia's hometown of Richmond. Standing sorrowfully next to my friend's coffin and listening while the pastor reads Max's last rites, my mind keeps repeating a single question over and over. If this were my funeral, would anyone cry?

Explaining my team is in the midst of a crucial series, I catch a bus back to Tyler immediately after the funeral.

❖ ❖ ❖ ❖ ❖

SINCE THERE'S no direct bus route between Houston and Tyler, I'm forced to change buses twice. I arrive in Tyler Sunday morning, shortly after midnight, ten exhausting hours after I board in Houston. Fortunately, my Pontiac is parked near downtown in the funeral home parking lot, saving me a long walk home.

Despite several inquiries at the bus station, I'm unable to obtain an answer for my burning question—who's winning in our series with Texarkana? My curiosity demands to be satisfied. I drive straight to Trojan Ballpark.

❖ ❖ ❖ ❖ ❖

"MATILDA. MATILDA, are you here?" I call in a loud whisper. When I get no response, I call out again. "Matilda. Listen, if you're here, we need to talk."

A faint rumble among the equipment boxes, a wisp of steamy mist, and the fragrance of perfume announce her arrival.

"Matilda, is that you?"

"Yes, I'm here. Sorry, but I wanted to make certain you were alone," she explains apologetically, suddenly appearing in the equipment room doorway.

"How's the team doing? I've been in Houston. Couldn't find a single word about our East Texans in the Houston papers."

"We're winning, of course. Unlike yourself, Whitey allows me to participate in every decision. Tonight he let me decide the batting order. I penciled in Philip Johnson to bat cleanup. He went three for four. Drove in three runs."

"So we're still in first place?"

"Oh yes. Well, we did lose on Thursday night. Peppy dropped an easy fly that would have gotten us out of the inning. The Bears went on to score four runs before we brought in Paul Walker and shut them down. Occasionally those things happen. I suppose we shouldn't win them all. That might spoil our fans."

"I hope you didn't jerk Peppy outta the game after he made the error. He's a sensitive guy. We have to treat him with kid gloves."

"Sensitive? He's a has-been, with a beer gut. I don't know what you see in that man, Rick. If it were up to me, I'd have shown him the door long ago."

"Trust me on this, Matilda. I have a feeling. It's a long season. We're gonna need Peppy before it's over. Somewhere along the way we'll be glad we stuck with him."

"It's your baseball club, Richard. You can run it any way you please, but the day you start losing, I'm out of here."

"No, you can't leave, not until you get me straightened out and earn your wings. Isn't that the way it goes? Aren't you my guardian angel?"

"I don't know where you're getting your information, darling, but you're dead wrong. I hang around strictly because I love baseball. Didn't Whitey explain?"

"Yes, but what about the trial—to determine whether I should go to Heaven or hell. You remember. When I was dead. What about that?"

"You've been hallucinating, dear. I don't know anything about a trial, and I'm much too busy to be anyone's guardian angel."

CHAPTER THIRTEEN

ON SUNDAY AFTERNOON we wrap up our home stand with Texarkana, taking advantage of a Henry French walk and back to back singles by Akins and Neuendorff in the bottom of the ninth to down the Bears 4 to 3. After the final game fiasco in Wichita Falls, winning three out of four in this crucial series against Texarkana allows us to regain momentum and maintain our grip on first place. Our victory surge couldn't come at a better time. A long road trip to Austin, Temple and Waco, playing eleven games in eleven days, lies ahead.

Begging out at the last moment, Matilda has decided not to make the trip. Whitey's convinced she's still fuming over my romantic transgressions. He's pleading with me to talk to her and apologize again when the telephone rings. Grateful for the interruption, I grab the phone and answer.

"East Texas Baseball Club. This is Rick Mason," I answer enthusiastically, elated that Whitey and I have finally agreed how we should greet incoming calls.

"Ricky, are you okay? Daddy says someone tried to kill you." The voice on the other end belongs to Kaye.

"Hi, honey. Yes, I'm fine. Been meaning to call you and tell you the whole story, but I didn't get back from Houston until late Saturday night. Then yesterday morning I slept in. Seems like time just slipped away—"

Not waiting to hear me finish my flimsy excuse, Kaye interrupts, "You should've called me. The Tyler newspapers have been full of stories about your friend's murder. I've been so worried about you."

"Hey, I had a close call, but I'm all right. Guess you could say I'm lucky to be alive though. Could've been me they buried Saturday."

"Oh, Ricky. Don't say that. You scare me. I don't know what I'd do if something happened to you."

"Marry Ted. That's what you'd do. Might be the best thing could happen for all of us. At least Ted would be happy."

"You're being tacky. Here I am worried sick, and you're being mean. I would never marry Ted, not even if something happened to you. Don't you know? It's you I love, Ricky. I could never love anyone else."

"I'm sorry, Kaye. I don't know what made me say that. It just came out. Listen, I'm really glad you called. It's nice to know somebody cares about me," I apologize, recalling how concerned I was about no one crying at my funeral.

"I love you, Ricky. I love you so much, but sometimes you can be so cruel."

"All that's going to change, Kaye. I promise. Those two goons who tried to kill me actually did me a favor. Coming so close to death made me realize what a fool I've been—about you, about baseball, about everything that's important in my life."

"We've both been such silly fools, darling—fighting and acting like two spoiled brats. Can you come to the house? I want to see you."

"I wish I could, but there just isn't time. Our bus leaves for Austin at one. That gives me and Whitey less than two hours to pack. But listen, we'll be back from this road trip in two weeks. When I come back, I want you and me to put our past differences behind us and start all over, live together in the same house like normal married couples do. I have to hang up now, Kaye. Whitey and I have a thousand things to pack."

237

"I really want to see you. I'll get dressed and come to the baseball field."

"I want to see you too, hon. We have so much to talk about, but honest, right now I'm busier than a barefoot boy in a red ant bed. I really don't have time. I promise I'll call you the minute our bus rolls back into Tyler. I need to go. Whitey's acting nervous."

"Alright, I suppose I can wait, but before we hang up, tell me you love me."

"For Pete's sake, Kaye," I stammer, lowering my voice to a whisper. "Whitey's sitting right across my desk, listening to every word I say."

"Tell me you love me, or I'm not hanging up. I want to hear you say it." Her loving voice drools into the receiver.

I place my hand over the mouthpiece and glance around. Fortunately, Whitey and I are alone in the manager's office. I grit my teeth and close my eyes while I say the words, "I love you, Kaye."

"Will you call me the minute you come home? Please say you'll call me."

"Sure, I'll call you as soon as I get back in town. I already promised I would."

"I just wanted to hear you say it one more time. So long, darling. Have a safe trip and take care of yourself. I love you so much."

Whitey grins profusely as I hang up the phone, obviously amused at my embarrassing dilemma. Crossing his arms, he leans back in his chair and clears his throat to gain my undivided attention. "Rick, you know what your problem is?"

"What's that, Whitey?"

"You got too many dern women in your life."

"You're right about that, old timer. And you know what your problem is?"

"No. I didn't know I had a problem."

"You don't have nearly enough."

"That's for sure, Rick my boy. That's for dern sure."

❖ ❖ ❖ ❖ ❖

PARKED ALONGSIDE the entrance gate is a sleek, air-conditioned silver bus which proudly displays a banner reading: "Tyler East Texans." Our bus is chartered from Chaparral Bus Lines, but it represents a substantial improvement over the embarrassing bargain basement transportation provided for our road trip to Wichita Falls. This newer bus is tangible proof that winning can loosen even the tightest pocketbook.

Despite my suggestion to say their goodbyes at home, many of the players' wives and sweethearts ignore my advice and come to the ballpark to see their warriors off to battle. The women's presence substantiates my prophesy. When it's time to leave, the farewell scene at the entrance gate deteriorates into a prolonged crying session with many tearful goodbye kisses and hugs exchanged. A passing stranger might think these young men were soldiers departing for a war zone.

Eventually the passionate farewells yield to a blistering sun and a temperature pushing at ninety degrees. Team members stumble listlessly into the bus and take a seat while Whitey takes a final turn around our fancy coach to make sure nothing has been left behind.

Since Whitey is familiar with the highway route we'll take to Austin, he'll occupy the seat behind the driver where he can assist with directions. I'll take a seat somewhere near the middle of the bus. Most likely, I'll sit alone the entire trip. No player wants to be accused of sucking up to the manager.

Grabbing the handrail next to the door, Whitey bounds up the narrow steps, wipes at the perspiration streaming down his brow and gives the driver a thumbs-up. The driver nods, and pulls the lever to close the door. Our bus hisses loudly and lurches forward. Wives and girl friends run alongside the bus until we reach the street, waving excitedly and affectionately throwing kisses to their loved ones.

Frowning, as if he's displeased with the young men's behavior, Whitey hitches his trousers, squares his jaw and sternly surveys the rows of seats packed with players. In a fairly good John Wayne imitation he bellows, "Saddle up, Pilgrims! We're bound for Canaan land!" A huge smile creeps across his face before he swings into his seat behind the driver.

For several seconds the bus is unusually silent. Whitey's bizarre impersonation surprises everyone, including me. Then, sounding like a devoted disciple, Frank Johnson shouts a positive response.

"Hallelujah, brother!"

Our bus rocks with hilarious laughter.

❖ ❖ ❖ ❖ ❖

AUSTIN WILL BE our first stop on this extended road trip. We're scheduled to play a four-game series. The Pioneers are off to a rough start, losing eight of their first twelve. Nonetheless, Austin usually fields a solid ball club. Six of their eight losses have come on the road. Playing on their home field in front of friendly fans, they'll be much tougher than their early season record indicates.

Austin boasts a population near ninety thousand, more than three times the size of Tyler. Last season their franchise finished in eighth place, but unlike our Trojan supporters, Pioneer fans never gave up on their baseball team. Almost three thousand fans watched Austin drop their final game to Temple. Now, after signing a whole slew of seasoned players during the off-season, the team's owners and fans foster high expectations, regardless of their team's poor start.

To everyone's delight, our business manager has arranged to quarter our squad in the Alamo Hotel on West Sixth Street only a few blocks from the Capital. Exploring downtown Austin with its history and historic old buildings is a marvelous and inexpensive way to while away the monotonous hours between games. Also within walking distance of our hotel are a number of excellent cafes. The Piccadilly Cafeteria, one of my favorite eating places, is less than three blocks away.

Our bus trip from Tyler to Austin will take approximately four hours. Tonight's game with the Pioneers begins at seven, so we're on a tight schedule. Our plan is to drive straight to Disch Field where we'll unload, don our uniforms, and take the field for warm-up drills.

After the game we'll climb back aboard, and the bus will deliver us to our hotel.

❖ ❖ ❖ ❖ ❖

FRENCH DIVES backward, barely avoiding a wayward baseball which screams directly across the batter's box. In the grandstand, rowdy home fans squeal with delight, seemingly amused at my lead-off batter's acrobatics.

"Hey, ump!" I yell from the dugout, "You can't let their pitcher get away with that. You gotta give him a warning."

The umpire swivels to sneer in my direction, but makes no move to discipline Austin's pitcher. The Pioneers' catcher grins, fires the baseball back to the pitcher's mound and stoops down to say something to French who lies stretched out alongside the batter's box.

Henry rolls himself to a sitting position. For a few seconds he sits there without moving, perhaps contemplating the catcher's comment. Then he slowly climbs to his feet, dusts himself off and calls timeout. His troubled young face reveals his anxiety while he trots toward our dugout.

"Coach Mason, their catcher says they plan to put me on first base—feet first."

"He can't get away with that kinda talk. Did the umpire hear what he said?"

"The ump was standing right there, listening to every word. Coach, I'm scared. Their pitcher throws awful hard."

Rubbing at his chin, Whitey saunters up to join in our conversation.

"Austin pulled this same crap in their home opener against Waco last year. I suspect the pitcher will knock Henry down again with another inside rocket. Their strategy is to shake him up with a couple of wild pitches, get him thinking about bailing out, then throw him three strikes right down the pike."

"Surely the umpires won't allow that kind of demented behavior," I argue, turning to question my assistant coach. "Isn't there a league rule against dusting off batters?"

"Don't mean nothing. It'll be the same every time we play here. These game officials let the home club get away with murder. Must be some kind of political thing. Maybe the governor owns a piece of the franchise."

"We'll play it their way then. Henry, next pitch, you be on your toes. Be ready to bail outta there. Let's see what they're up to. Maybe we can get you on base with all your brains intact."

While we watch French trudge back to the batter's box, I offer an observation. "You know, Whitey. If we were managing for Cleveland, I'd have my batter hang tight and take the lick."

"Well, this ain't Cleveland. Most of these players are kids, still wet behind the ears. They don't get paid like big leaguers."

"I'm just thinking out loud—how managing here is so different than in the majors. You know I'd never intentionally put one of our guys at risk."

"Your manager ever ask you to take one for the team when you was in the big leagues, Rick?"

"You're dern tootin'. Too many times. Some of those places still ache."

"I got a few spots like that myself. Hurts worse in cold weather though, don't you think?"

French stutter steps then lunges forward, doing a belly flop as another lightning fast baseball soars overhead. In desperation he glances in my direction, perhaps expecting me to somehow end his barrage. I have no choice but to oblige. A manager's primary obligation is to protect his players.

"Time out! Hey, ump! Time out," I shout and spring onto the playing field. Distorting my face into an angry scowl, I stomp toward home plate.

The umpire signals timeout, whirls and steps out to meet me. "You got some kind of problem?" he barks gruffly.

"You darn right I do! How about you put a stop to these beanballs before the situation gets out of hand, before someone gets hurt?" I yell, waving my hands wildly.

"Watch your language, mister. Otherwise, you're liable to find yourself in the parking lot listening to the game on the radio."

"Hey, there's no need for you to take things personal, ump. I'm worried about my player. All I'm asking is for you to tell that lunatic on the pitching mound to stop throwing at my batter's head," I say, lowering my voice and backing off a bit. I want to make my point, but it makes little sense to get myself thrown out in the first inning.

"You mean ole Ed boy? He's always a little wild early in the game. Nothing to be concerned about. He'll settle down. Besides, the count is two and 0 in your favor. Don't see as how you got much to complain about."

"League rules require you eject a pitcher if he intentionally throws at a batter. I want the rule enforced," I argue, raising my voice again.

"You trying to tell me how to call my game? You think I don't know the rules?" Showing his authority, the umpire moves closer so we're nose to nose. In the bleachers behind me, the boisterous, sellout crowd endorses the official's forceful stance with screeching howls of approval.

"Are you gonna warn him, or not?" I bellow, not budging from my position.

"No. He stays. Now get back to your dugout, before I pitch you out," the umpire threatens, raising his volume to match mine. Our noses are only inches apart.

Seeing I've lost the argument, I step back. But to make certain my aggravation is duly registered, I continue to glower at the official.

"If you're not gonna enforce the rules, how about giving me a minute to talk with Austin's manager? Maybe he and I can agree to stop this brain splattering contest, before the game evolves into a bloody riot."

"Alright. You got two minutes to talk. Then I'm gonna start calling strikes on your batter." To illustrate his impatience, the umpire glances at a watch strapped to his left wrist.

Vicious boos and catcalls burn my ears as I hike over to the Pioneers' dugout. Tom Jordan is Austin's manager. He's a crusty old bird. We met behind home plate when we exchanged lineups prior to taking pre-game infield. Jordan and an assistant coach meet me at the dugout steps.

"Coach Jordan, the umpire says your pitcher is always this wild in the first inning."

"That's right—wild as a hoot owl. You over here to complain? If you are, you're wasting your breath. Santulli is my best pitcher. I ain't planning on replacing him."

"As a manager, I can understand why you'd want to stick with him. But I thought I'd better warn you. These fellows on my squad are short-fused and hot-tempered. I'll try to persuade them not to retaliate, but I doubt if they'll take this beanball business lying down. If your pitcher keeps throwing at my batters, this game is likely to get real ugly."

"You making a threat, Mason?"

"No sir. Merely trying to avoid a nasty situation. My team came here to play baseball, not compete in a head bashing tournament."

"You Tyler people are new to this league. I hope you ain't gonna be over here whining and complaining ever' time things don't go your way. Hell, my pitcher ain't throwed but two stinkin' pitches."

"Yes, but both those pitches were aimed at my batter's head."

"Get used to it, mister, 'cause it ain't gonna stop, and we're gonna be kicking your sorry, cry baby butts all summer long."

❖ ❖ ❖ ❖ ❖

DESPITE HAVING two runners reach base, my East Texans are unable to score. Hard-flung baseballs sailing wildly past their thinly-clad, flailing bodies unnerve my hitters. Intermixed between the wild pitches are perfect strikes, thrown straight across the middle of the plate.

Paul Walker is a right-hander Segars signed on option from the Harlingen Capitols of the Gulf Coast League while I was in Houston. He pitched two innings in relief against Texarkana last Thursday. Both Matilda and Whitey were impressed, so we've decided to start him tonight. Before he takes the mound, I collar Walker and issue an order which I hope will end the beanball competition.

"I can't do that. I might hurt somebody."

"You'll be coming to bat next inning, Paul. You want that maniac throwing at your head?"

"Well, no. But isn't there some other way? If I do what you want, the ump's liable to throw me outta the game."

"If you get pitched, Davis is ready to go. I'll start you again tomorrow night."

"Alright, Skipper, I'll do like you say. Man, I sure hope nobody gets hurt."

"Me too, Paul. Me too."

❖ ❖ ❖ ❖ ❖

WALKER PAWS at the pitching mound, leans forward to take the sign from Nelms then glances toward our bench and nods his head affirmatively. He toes the rubber, pumps his arms and begins an extended, contorted windup. Kicking his left leg high, he moves his glove behind his waist to expertly hide the baseball from the batter's view before he proceeds to the final phase of his delivery—which is to step directly toward the third base line and hurl a hard fastball directly into the Pioneers' dugout.

Bats, water cups and caps go flying as coaches and players scatter to avoid the ricocheting baseball. Yelps, screams and irate curses commence from inside the home side dugout as the men climb off the floor, dust themselves off and check each other for injuries.

A split second later Tom Jordan leaps from the Austin dugout and comes charging toward our bench, pointing an accusing finger in my direction and yelling loudly.

"You two-faced, slimy snake-in-the-grass! You had your pitcher do that on purpose! That baseball could've killed someone!"

"Hey, Tom, I'm truly sorry, but ole Paul boy is always kinda wild in the first inning. He'll settle down though—after a few innings."

"A few innings? Like hell! That madman has thrown his last pitch in this ballpark. He almost killed me. That ball didn't miss my head more than a few inches."

"Won't do a bit of good to send ole Paul to the showers. My bullpen is chock full of pitchers just like him. I'm afraid they're all gonna be just as wild, that is unless we can reach some sort of agreement."

"You're crazy. I ain't agreeing to nothing. You tell your pitcher to stop bombarding my dugout."

"Tell you what, Coach. I'd hate to see you fellows waste your energy dodging baseballs all night. Lemme check with my pitcher. Maybe we can do something about his control problem. Perhaps you could talk to your pitcher. Whatta you say? How about we call a truce? No more beanballs."

Jordan frowns, lowers his head and fiddles with the bill of his cap while he considers my proposition. I can almost hear his brain churning.

"Alright. Now I ain't saying my pitcher was intentionally throwing at your batters, but I'll talk to him. If we keep throwing at each other, someone's likely to get killed, and it might be me."

"Good. I'm glad we're finally able to see eye to eye on this."

"You understand—we're only agreeing to a cease fire. That don't mean we're scared."

"Of course, Tom. No one's making any insinuations here. We're both looking out for our players—that's all."

"Right. And my club's still planning to kick your lily-white asses, tonight and all season long."

"And we'll be trying our best to whip your skinny butts. Coach Jordan, I wouldn't want it any other way."

❖ ❖ ❖ ❖ ❖

REGARDLESS of my agreement with Austin's manager, the game officials rule Walker's cannonball into the Pioneers' dugout was intentional and eject him from the game. Only by giving my solemn promise the incident won't be repeated do I convince them not to report the episode to the league president for punishment.

With Walker making an early exit, I bring in Davis. Whitey started Charlie on Friday night, but only worked him five innings. We were six runs ahead, and with a tough road trip coming up, he and Matilda elected to save Charlie's arm for more meaningful duty.

❖ ❖ ❖ ❖ ❖

AFTER THE HEAD HUNTING subterfuge of the first inning neither team is able to mount any kind of offense. The game evolves into a classic battle between two stubborn, unyielding pitchers. Working with only three days rest, Davis delivers a superb performance, shutting out the Pioneers and allowing only two hits through eight innings. Unfortunately, our sticks are as cold as the Pioneers'.

Austin's pitcher is first to falter; the first to succumb to the heat, the humidity and the pressure of an energy-sapping pitchers' duel. In the top of the ninth, a walk, an infield error, and a wild pitch allow Bruzga and French to advance to second and third. With two outs, I sub Swanson in to pinch-hit for Gregory. Like an old workhorse, Peppy gets the job done, driving in the two base runners by chopping a looping single into left field. Akins strikes out to end the inning, but the demise of the pitching duel ends the unstable truce. Our meager scoring spurt sets off a clamor of furious insults from unhappy Pioneer fans. This home crowd was expecting a win tonight.

During the preseason, local sportswriters optimistically apprised their readers of the big bucks Austin's owners were forking out to sign experienced players. Their zealous predictions that the Pioneers would be strong contenders for the Big State Championship gained wide acceptance in the state's capital. Now, in only their second home stand of the season, the Pioneers are losing to Tyler, a club that finished dead last in the Class C East Texas League last year.

Surly Austin boosters display their frustration with loud abusive language and by throwing debris onto the playing field. Between innings, paper cups, wads of paper and miscellaneous pieces of concession trash come flying out of the grandstand. Even though the hateful jeers seem more directed toward the home team than at my East Texans, we caution our players to stay inside the dugout and not to wander within throwing distance of the grandstands when they're on the field.

In the bottom of the ninth, Davis also shows signs of tiring. He walks Austin's first batter then nails their second hitter square in the mid-section with an errant inside pitch. Our pitcher's inaccuracy infuriates the home crowd and sets off another round of derogatory howls and jeers. Dissident spectators leap to their feet, booing, screaming obscenities and showering the playing field with flying objects. A green coke bottle sails out of the bleachers, landing less than five feet from the entrance to our dugout.

Perhaps hoping to appease his hysterical fans and direct their wrath away from the home team, the Pioneers' skipper charges out onto the playing field, calls timeout and strides briskly toward the umpire working behind home plate.

"Whitey, signal the bullpen to start throwing. Davis has probably had it," I say while we watch Austin's manager commence a frenzied, arm-waving temper-tantrum. I vault over the dugout wall, shove my hands into my rear pant pockets, and casually saunter over to join the heated parley.

Out in center field, the scoreboard visually documents the game's history:

	1	2	3	4	5	6	7	8	9	R	H	E
Visitors	0	0	0	0	0	0	0	0	2	2	4	0
Austin	0	0	0	0	0	0	0	0		0	2	0

"He's deliberately throwing at my hitters. You gotta boot him out. If he hits another batter, this crowd's likely to riot. You want that on your head?" Jordan shrieks to the umpire.

"Hey, hold on. Give my guy some slack. Nobody's throwing at your batters. My man out there is a little tired, that's all," I shout, wading in and asserting myself into the one-sided argument.

The umpire turns to me. "It don't make no difference whether it's intentional or not, Coach Mason. This crowd is in an ugly mood. If your pitcher hits another batter, all hell could break loose. Might be best if you sub in another pitcher."

"But Davis has a two-hit shutout working. Be a shame for him to lose it because of these loony Austin fans."

"The subject's no longer up for debate, Coach. Get him outta there."

Throwing up my hands and huffing indignantly, I tramp out to the pitcher's hill, imitating antics I've watched Bibb Falk use many times to make the game officials feel they've treated you unfairly. A good performance will occasionally influence their decision on the next close play. I was planning to remove Davis, even before the umpire issued his ultimatum.

While I approach the pitcher's mound, Davis grimaces and rubs at his throwing arm.

"I'm sorry, Charlie. We gotta take you out. Umpire's orders."

"It's okay, Coach Mason. My arm feels like a dead log. I should've asked you to relieve me after last inning. But when we scored those two runs, I was hoping to go one more inning and maybe get credit for a win and a shutout," Davis explains, handing me the baseball.

"We'll let the bullpen take charge from here, tough guy. You pitched one heckava game. You won't get your shutout, but we darn sure intend to get you a 'W' tonight."

While Davis trots to the dugout, I turn to face the bullpen in right field and tap my left arm, signaling I want Hershel Morgan, our left-handed rookie. My options are limited. Bounato pitched eight innings on Sunday. Felton started last night's game with both Herb Cates and Philip Johnson pitching in relief roles.

Morgan seems surprised to be selected. That's understandable because he hasn't pitched in a game since our regular season began. Taking a step toward me, he points a finger at his chest as if to ask, "You mean me?" My positive response causes a flurry of activity inside the bullpen as teammates help locate his cap and check his uniform, making sure shoes laces are tied and shirt buttons buttoned. A moment later Morgan emerges from the bullpen. He glances back and says something to the other men in the bullpen then turns and hightails it toward the pitching mound, running the entire distance at full speed.

"You sure you want me?" Morgan asks, arriving panting and short of breath. His youthful face is flushed with excitement.

"Yes, I'm pretty sure you're the one. Aren't you my ace reliever?" I jest, thinking a humorous reply might ease the pressure-packed situation. It doesn't seem to work. Hershel is in no mood for witty conversation.

"Don't tease with me, Coach Mason. You know I've never pitched in a real professional game. All you keep me for is to pitch batting practice."

"Well, you're my ace tonight. How's your arm? You warm enough to pitch?"

"My arm feels fine. I guess I'm as ready as I'll ever be," Morgan replies, his voice trembling. Attempting to compensate for unsteady legs, he shifts his weight from one foot to the other

"Great. Now, this next fellow coming to bat is their first baseman Ankoviak. He bats from the left side. We want him to hit the ball on the ground, so keep your pitches low and outside. If the baseball comes back to you, don't go for the double play, not unless you're certain."

"I understand, Skipper. We get the batter out first—before we worry about base runners."

"You got it, wise guy. Now let's see if you can cut the mustard in the pros."

❖ ❖ ❖ ❖ ❖

MORGAN'S FIRST PITCH sails high and outside. Nelms leaps to his left, barely spearing it with his mitt to avoid a past ball.

"Dammit. I told him to keep the ball low. What's wrong with that kid? Don't he know high from low?" I bellow, slamming my cap to the ground and throwing my arms up.

"Cut the youngster some slack, Rick. That was Morgan's first pitch in the pros. We're probably lucky he didn't throw it over the backstop. You remember your first game? You were so doggone nervous, none of your teammates would sit next to you for fear you might puke on them," Whitey chuckles.

"You darn right I remember. Made three errors the first inning. Coach Davidson was madder than hell. When the inning was over, I thought he was gonna strangle me right there at the third base coach's box. Don't think he ever forgave me. Even during my senior season when I was on that hot streak, I worried about making some dumb mistake which would give him a reason to jerk me out of the game. He woulda done it too."

Morgan's second offering is lower but right across the plate. Ankoviak swings hard and sends the baseball screaming down the third base line. Austin's third base coach hops backward to dodge the hard-hit missile when it flies past.

"Foul Ball!" the umpire behind home plate signals, pumping his left fist in and out.

"We're skating on thin ice here, Whitey. Ankoviak's likely to get hold of the next one. If he does, it's two runs for sure. Maybe we oughta take Morgan out. Charlie pitched a great game. I'd hate to see his effort wasted on account of a dumb move by the manager."

"Give the boy a chance. It's a long season. We need to know who we can depend on. If Morgan can't handle the job, let's find out now."

"CRACK!" The lightning-like clap of Ankoviak's bat meeting in solid contact with Morgan's fastball reverberates across the diamond. Ankoviak smacks the ball hard, but directly at our shortstop. Bruzga fields the baseball on one hop and flips it to French who is dashing toward second. French gloves the ball, touches second, spins and rifles it to Connors on first.

Double Play.

Every man on the team is pulling for our rookie pitcher. Players on our bench leap to their feet and run to the edge of the dugout, jumping up and down, screaming at the top of their lungs, cheering the terrific play.

For several brief seconds the bleachers remain silent. Then the malicious booing and catcalls commence again, chastising the home team for blowing another opportunity. Affirming that Austin supporters aren't affected by prejudice, many Pioneer fans abandon their seats to roam the bleachers and yell irate obscenities, venting their anger equally toward both players and game officials.

The double play helped, but this game is far from over. Austin's lead runner advanced to third on the ground ball to shortstop. The meat of their batting order is coming up. I call timeout and trot to the mound to talk with Morgan. He begins apologizing even before I reach the infield.

"Sorry about those first two pitches, Coach Mason. My hands were shaking so bad, I could hardly hold on to the ball."

"You okay now?"

"My knees are still knocking, but I'm feeling a heck of a lot better."

"You're doing fine, Hershel. One more out and you can chalk up your first save in the pros. We'll head outta here and grab a hot shower. Listen up now. Here's how I want you to pitch to Lawrence. The Pioneers have Lawrence in the cleanup slot because he's a long ball hitter, likes to swing for the fences. . ."

❖ ❖ ❖ ❖ ❖

MORGAN WORKS the batter perfectly, jamming him with the first pitch then keeping the ball low and outside on the next two. The count is two and one when Lawrence catches a hanging curve and drives a long foul into the left field bleachers.

"Two and two," the umpire declares, raising both arms above his head and displaying two fingers on each hand to indicate the count. He straightens his face mask and crouches down behind Nelms, ready to judge the next pitch.

On the pitching mound, Morgan steps on the rubber, bringing both hands to rest at his waist line. With a runner on third he's pitching from a stretch delivery. The rookie checks the Austin base runner and glances at me to verify our strategy. I nod my head, touching my wrist then my nose to confirm I haven't had second thoughts.

Morgan rears back and steps toward the batter, sending the baseball sailing slowly on a high arc toward home plate. The Pioneers' fence buster can't believe his eyes. He was expecting something low and outside, not a big, fat slow ball that's begging to be clobbered. He steps forward in zealous anticipation.

Lawrence spins, dancing on one foot as he struggles to regain his balance. His open mouth and widened eyes reveal his shocked surprise. In his eagerness, he swung too early and missed the baseball completely. Finally, yielding to the centrifugal force of his mighty swing, he crumples to the ground.

"Strike Three!" the umpire bawls and shakes his head in pity.

❖ ❖ ❖ ❖ ❖

MORGAN LEAPS from the mound, throws his glove in the air and runs toward first base where his East Texas teammates mob the rookie, excitedly grabbing at his cap and slapping his back. Ear piercing whoops of joy echo through the stadium as players crowd around their young hero.

For a few moments Morgan basks in the adoration of his colleagues, laughing and swapping handshakes, then he spots me and plows through the jubilant celebration toward me. He grabs my hand and commences to pump it up and down. An enormous grin is tattooed across his face.

I grin back and shout, "Congratulations, Hershel. Fine job. You got yourself your first save and your first strikeout in the pros."

"Thanks, Coach Mason. But I couldn't have done it without you. How'd you know that pitch would work?"

"Just a lucky hunch. Saw it done once in the Texas League."

"Coach, I was really scared out there."

"Yeah, I know, and I was scared for you, but you didn't let me down. You came through like a real pro. Tomorrow morning the league office will log your name in their record book and mark down a save. You keep pitching the way you did tonight, and there'll be plenty more. A good relief pitcher is always in demand."

"Yes sir, and I'm gonna be the best relief pitcher who ever pitched in the Big State League."

"I hope you're right, Hershel. This team could sure use another good arm."

"Coach Mason, you know what I was thinking right before I threw that last pitch?"

"No, I don't have the faintest notion. What were you thinking?"

"Well, my head was pounding and my knees were wobbling so bad I could hardly keep from falling down. I was trying to calm myself and concentrate, so I kept trying to remember how you spell relief. You know, in high school I never was much of a speller. Then I figured it out. You wanna know how I spell relief?"

"How's that, Hershel?"

"O. V. E. R."

❖ ❖ ❖ ❖ ❖

EIGHTEEN EXHAUSTED baseball players and two dog tired managers stagger into the lobby of the Alamo Hotel. A long afternoon bus ride followed by a down-to-the-wire game has zapped our energy. There'll be no after-hours horseplay tonight. Foremost among everyone's thoughts is a hot shower and a good night's sleep.

From his position behind the check-in counter, a nervous hotel night clerk seems overwhelmed by our sudden appearance. He performs a headcount of my team members and shakes his head.

"Mister Mason, could I please speak to you? Seems we have a slight snafu with your reservations," the high-strung night clerk whispers politely. His eyes shift nervously from side to side as if he's worried someone will overhear.

"Sure. What's the problem?"

"Your home office wired us to reserve ten rooms. We thought that was a little strange. Seems you have twenty men in your party."

"Right, two men to a room. No problem with two guys bunking together, is there?"

"Well, no. But it may cause some inconvenience. Mister Mason, the rooms your home office reserved are singles—only one double bed."

"I'm afraid that won't work. These guys are baseball players— extra large fellows. You'll have to find us some more rooms."

"I'm sorry, Mister Mason. The governor called the legislature back into special session on Monday. With so many delegates and lobbyists back in town, there's not another vacant room in the city."

❖ ❖ ❖ ❖ ❖

"HELLO," a sleepy voice answers.

"Ted, this is Rick. You asleep already?"

"Yeah, had a long day. While the team is on the road, Clyde has me going over the dealership books. Wants to know if I can figure out where all his money is going."

"We have a problem here, Ted. Our hotel tells me the rooms you reserved were singles. The rooms come with only one double bed."

"So what's the problem?"

"You only reserved ten rooms."

A long silence develops on the opposite end while Ted's groggy mind diagnoses the problem.

"Yes, I can see where that might be inconvenient for your people. Alright, get with the hotel manager and have him make whatever changes are necessary. I'll call tomorrow and take care of the financial issues."

"You don't understand. The hotel doesn't have any more rooms. The legislature is in special session. There's not another room in Austin."

Another long pause. "Listen, Rick, I'm sorry about the screw-up, but there's nothing I can do about it tonight. If there are no more rooms, there are no more rooms. You and your players will have to make the best of it. I'll get on the horn first thing tomorrow and see if I can remedy the situation."

"That's the best you can do? You expect my players to bunk together in the same bed?"

"I'm sorry, Rick. That's the best I can do for now. Look, it's late. Tomorrow morning I'll get things straightened out. By the way, how'd our team do tonight?"

❖ ❖ ❖ ❖ ❖

AMIDST ANGRY HOWLS, I explain about the room mix-up. Several players voice their objections, but with no alternative available, they eventually accept the situation, mostly because they're too tired to argue.

❖ ❖ ❖ ❖ ❖

"WHICH SIDE you want, Rick? Right side or left?" Whitey asks. He and I have elected to share a room.

Neither side has much appeal. I'm not exactly excited about sharing a bed with another oversized male.

"Right side. I prefer the right side, Whitey."

"You got it then, partner. Don't make one bit of difference to me. I'm so tired I'll be asleep by the time my head hits the pillow."

"You wanna use the bathroom first? I usually shower and brush my teeth before I hit the sack."

"No, I'm fine. I'm half asleep now."

❖ ❖ ❖ ❖ ❖

A HOT BATH improves my attitude, but it's been a long day. I emerge from the bathroom with heavy eyes and my body begging for slumber. Whitey is already asleep, so I quietly shuffle across the darkened room, sling my bathrobe over a chair and slip into my side of the bed.

"HRRR! HRRRRR! HRRRRRRR!" a startling torrent of sonorous vibration promulgates from the opposite side of the bed. I roll over on my side, trying to ignore the obnoxious brays.

For a few seconds the snoring ceases, then it begins again. This time the snores are even louder. "HRRR! ACHOOOO! HRRRR! ACHOOOO! HRRRRR! ACHOOOO!"

Pictures rattle against walls, window shades quiver, the bed quakes as Whitey's noisy bellows reverberate through the room. No wonder he never married. What woman would sleep with a man who snores like a freight train? I wonder if Whitey's snoring isn't the real reason Matilda decided not to accompany us on the road trip.

No way I can endure this clamorous racket all night. I roll over and shake Whitey's shoulder.

"Whitey, you're snoring. Wake up and roll over."

When I get no response, I try again. "Whitey, roll over. You're keeping me awake."

Still no response, only another aggravating whistling sound followed by a deafening silence. Suddenly I'm concerned for Whitey's well being. How would I ever explain if my assistant manager expired while we were sleeping in the same bed?

I reach out and grapple for the lamp beside the bed. My fingers find the switch. I flick on the light and turn back to check on my bed partner.

❖ ❖ ❖ ❖ ❖

"OPERATOR, I want to place a collect call to a Mister Ted Gooding in Tyler, Texas. Make it person to person. The number is 7868. My name is Rick Mason."

"Please wait, while I ring," the operator politely requests.

A high-pitched clicking noise echoes over the telephone line, followed by a dull buzz as the phone on the other end rings.

"Hello," a sleep-dazed voice answers on the other end.

"I have a collect call for a Mister Ted Gooding."

"I'm Ted Gooding," the voice attests.

"A Mister Rick Mason is calling from Austin. Will you accept the charges?"

"Yes, I suppose so. Is there some kind of an emergency?"

"You may speak to your party now," the operator advises.

"Hello, Ted. You in bed?"

"Rick, it's two in the morning. Where else would I be?"

"Just checking. Got something to tell you."

"What's this about, Rick? You still having trouble with the room thing?"

"No. I'm bunking with Whitey. He and I are sharing the same bed."

"So?"

"Ted, I can't get to sleep. Whitey snores like a bear."

"You called me in the middle of the night to tell me that?"

257

"Oh, no. There's something else—something you oughta know."

"And what's that?"

"Whitey sleeps with his eyes open. Just thought you should know. Goodnight, Ted. Don't let the bed bugs bite."

Loud, inaudible cursing erupts from the receiver before I can hang up.

❖ ❖ ❖ ❖ ❖

"MISTER MASON, please wake up. Mister Mason, you're wanted on the telephone," a far away voice beseeches me. Rather than return to the thunderous snoring inside my hotel room, I decided to sleep on a leather chair in the hotel lobby. It was a poor choice. Every time I'd doze off, someone would walk through the lobby and interrupt my sleep. I'm truly amazed by the number of night people who seem to flourish in a city the size of Austin.

"What? What'd you say?" I ask groggily, waking from my fitful sleep. Hovering over me is the distraught night clerk who informed me of the bed shortage last evening.

"A Mister Ted Gooding is on the telephone. He wants to speak with you."

"Ted Gooding? Oh yeah, he's my business manager. He wants to speak with me?"

"Yes, it appears he's moving your baseball team to another hotel. Mister Mason, I'm so sorry." The sensitive night manager seems truly grieved we'd consider moving to another hotel.

"Yeah, me too. Where's the telephone?"

Ted explains he's been on the telephone since seven this morning, checking with every hotel in the phone book. He's located new quarters for the team at the Rainbow Motor Courts. He sounds like he's also had a bad night.

"But, Ted, that place is way out on South Lamar. It's on the wrong side of the river, almost a mile from downtown. There's not a decent restaurant anywhere within walking distance. Where will we eat?"

Evidently his telephone quest has concentrated on finding a facility with a sufficient number of rooms. After a long pause, he offers his solution, "Some of the units are kitchenettes. Perhaps some of the fellows can pitch in and cook your meals."

"Ted, this is a baseball club, not the ladies' auxiliary. We came to Austin to play baseball. Surely you don't expect us to do our own cooking?"

"I'm sorry, Rick. This is the best I can do. Look, it's only for three more nights. It's either the Rainbow Motor Courts or bunking double at the Alamo. You make the choice."

"We'll move. I suppose we can survive the inconvenience for three nights." Given a choice of starving at the Rainbow Motor Courts or sharing a room with Whitey, I'd choose starving every time.

❖ ❖ ❖ ❖ ❖

TO MY SURPRISE, the players accept Ted's relocation program without complaint. In fact they actually cotton to the idea, especially when I mention the kitchenettes and timidly inquire if anyone is interested in cooking a few meals for the team.

Nick Gregory and Dub Akins volunteer to serve as cooks, boastfully professing their culinary proficiencies. By the time our bus delivers us to the motel's front office, my two outfielders have planned a menu and sketched out a preliminary list of kitchen duties. When the motel clerk tells them about a small grocery store nearby, they excitedly requisition forty dollars from the meal kitty and hurry out the front door. A half-hour later Akins and Gregory return to the motel carrying six paper bags filled to the brim with groceries.

❖ ❖ ❖ ❖ ❖

LUNCH IS SERVED in three shifts, six to a sitting, on a picnic table located in a small courtyard within the confines of the motel. The food is excellent and bountiful, but finding a place to sit becomes more and more difficult with each passing shift as players who have finished eating linger to talk baseball and swap war stories.

Many of the veterans' stories are more fiction than fact, but it makes little difference to the younger players as they listen with starry-eyes to the older guys tell about players who have passed through Tyler on their way to the majors.

"Hey, Peppy. You ever play against Roy McMillan? Didn't he get his start with Tyler?"

"Sure did. He's from Bonham. Never played a lick of baseball before he signed on with the Trojans, but he's one heck of a ball player. Covers the territory between second and third like a wet blanket."

"Come on, Peppy. McMillan plays shortstop for the Reds. You never played in the National League."

"Yes I did. I swear I did. Played against Roy in the Grapefruit League back in forty-nine, during preseason. That was the first year the Reds called him up for spring training. That guy can hop like a kangaroo; robbed me of two sure hits in that game."

"How 'bout Monty Stratton? He played for the Trojans. You ever see him pitch?"

"Yeah, I batted against him a bunch of times. When he was in his prime, he had a fastball that would make your head swim. But after he lost his leg, he went to throwing mostly curves and junk stuff. Didn't make no difference, I never could buy a hit off him, no matter what he throwed. Man, that guy could flat pitch."

"What about George Sisler? Wasn't he. . ."

Maybe it's the camaraderie. Maybe it's the reminiscing. Maybe it's every player being accepted, made to feel he's an integral part of this team. Whatever the reason, my East Texans discover they have a purpose here on the south side of Austin. A kind of close friendship evolves among players and coaches, a collective chemistry, and an overwhelming premonition that this is a team of destiny, bound for greatness. Each man begins to sense that this is a team blessed, not only with exceptional talent, but also with a heroic reason for being, which renders it unstoppable and unbeatable.

❖ ❖ ❖ ❖ ❖

ON TUESDAY NIGHT Walker returns from his brief exile with a vengeance, allowing only eight scattered hits and pitching magnificently as we wallop the Pioneers for a second night in a row by a score of 10-4.

Wednesday evening we jump out to an early lead, but Bounato never quite has his stuff. Austin keeps hacking away, never allowing us to stretch our lead. Finally in the sixth, Bounato wilts, allowing four Austin runs before he heads for the shower. Even though we score in both the seventh and eighth innings, the Pioneers hang on to squeeze out a 9-7 victory.

Thursday night we come roaring back. A pre-game show featuring nationally famous baseball clown Johnny Price leaves the partisan crowd in hysterics, but that's their last laugh of the evening. In a game featuring four Pioneer errors, our hitters pound Austin's rotation for eleven hits and twelve runs. Final score 12-1.

The Pioneers are delighted to see us leave town.

❖ ❖ ❖ ❖ ❖

FRIDAY MORNING, we bus seventy miles north to face the Temple Eagles. The Eagle squad has been on the road too. Their bus arrives in Temple almost simultaneously with ours. Their road trip was a disaster. In Texarkana, the Eagles lost three in a row to the Bears, dropping Temple into last place to share the cellar with Waco.

Temple is poorly prepared to face the momentum of a chopping, whirling baseball machine. We add to the Eagles' woes, scoring twenty-two runs in three games to take two out of three on their home field.

❖ ❖ ❖ ❖ ❖

BY THE TIME we arrive to play at Waco's Katy Ballpark, team confidence is at a peak, but pitching is thin. Playing seven road games in seven days takes its toll. Our bats stay hot, but hot sticks can't make up for tired limbs. We drop the opening game to the Pirates by a score of 7-6.

Tuesday evening I shuffle the lineup, giving my regulars a much needed night off and my reserves some well-deserved playing time. Philip Johnson starts the fireworks with a blazing triple. Brother Frank follows by banging a double off the left field fence, and the outcome is never in doubt. Peppy climaxes the scoring by belting his ninth homer of the season with two on in the eighth. Final score: 11-5.

Wednesday night Jake Christie handcuffs the Pirates with a nifty five-hitter. We go hitless ourselves until the top of the fifth when Gregory breaks the ice by beating out a slow roller to third. Then Merv Connors sparks a brief power surge by smashing a scorching single past Skinner, the Pirates' first sacker. A bouncing fielder's choice grounder by Swanson drives in Gregory and advances Connors to second. Hal Epps completes the job by lacing a line drive into left center to give us a two run lead. A bases empty home run by Nelms in the ninth provides an insurance run we never need. When Christie falters, I bring in Matt Burns to relieve. Using only three pitches, Burns nips the Pirates' rally by forcing Drury, Waco's cleanup batter, to hit into a double play. We thump the Pirates again 3-0.

We close out our road trip Thursday night by burying the Pirates deeper in the league cellar. Every man on our club fattens his batting average as we chase one Waco pitcher after another to an early shower. Home runs by Epps, Akins, Gregory and Connors leave the Pirate bullpen in shambles. Except for French, not a man on my squad leaves the game without a hit. Final score: 15-6.

❖ ❖ ❖ ❖ ❖

REGARDLESS of our road wins, no matter that we're in first place, riding high atop the Big State League standings, my battle-weary gladiators are in no mood to celebrate. These men have been separated from their families for almost two weeks. They're homesick and anxious to leave for Tyler. After the game ends Thursday night, it takes less than thirty minutes for the team to shower, change to their street clothes and board the bus. Our bus speeds past Waco's eastern city limits shortly after ten-thirty.

❖ ❖ ❖ ❖ ❖

A DARK BLUE DESOTO maneuvers cautiously into the stadium parking area, finds a parking space near the entrance gate, and parks. The parking lot is jam-packed with players' families who have come to welcome their triumphant warriors home. I recognize the automobile. It belongs to my wife. Something must be wrong. I've never seen her drive so slow.

"Whitey, can you handle unloading these bags without me? That's my wife who just drove up."

"Sure, but watch yourself, Rick. You know how hazardous women are to your health," Whitey snickers.

"I remember, but thanks for reminding me."

Grabbing a canvas bag and pitching it at my assistant, I head straight for Kaye's automobile, strolling casually, but cautiously watching for some hint she might mean me harm. When I reach the driver's side window, I stoop down to look inside.

"Hello, Kaye. You looking for me?" I ask. After that I'm speechless. My wife wears a strapless sundress, shrewdly designed to expose an abundance of silky-smooth skin. Moonlight shimmering through the windshield lends a soft glow to her blonde hair, in contrast to the lightly tanned skin of her neck and shoulders. Two, long shapely legs protrude from beneath the skirt raised slightly above her knees.

"Yes. I came to welcome you home."

"Thanks. I'm sure glad to be back. It's been a long eleven days," I say, thankful I'm able to speak without stuttering.

"You remember what we talked about before you left, Ricky?"

"Yes, I've been thinking about you a lot. I hope you haven't changed your mind?"

"I haven't. I'm ready to move in with you tonight, if you still want me."

"Want you? That's what I've been praying for. Of course I want you."

"Good. I packed a bag. It's there in the back seat. I'll move in with you tonight if that's okay."

I raise up to examine a tiny suitcase lying on the backseat of her DeSoto. I'm confused. My wife is an immaculate dresser and terribly fussy about her clothes. No way she could cram her belongings into one small bag.

"Is that all you packed? Your bag seems awfully small. Where are the rest of your clothes?"

"All I brought is a nightgown and a toothbrush, darling. I was hoping I wouldn't need anything else," she sighs seductively.

"No. No. You won't. That sounds great," I stammer and turn to shout to the bus. "Hey, Whitey, I'm leaving. See you tomorrow."

"Sure, Rick, but I need some help with the laundry. What time you wanna meet?"

"Can't say for sure. Not sure I can make it at all. Maybe you better get one of the players to help."

❖ ❖ ❖ ❖ ❖

OPENING ONE EYE, I examine the clock next to the bed. The time is ten-forty-two. Ted usually breaks for lunch sometime around eleven-thirty. If I hurry, I can still catch him in his office. I need his help. He's a lawyer. He oughta know his way around the courthouse.

Kaye lies sleepily beside me. Our clothes are strewn across the bedroom floor, discarded there as we hastily undressed in heated desire. Kaye's tiny suitcase rests next to the wall inside the front door. The nightgown inside was never unpacked.

"I need to leave for awhile, hon. I have to talk with Ted."

"Can't it wait? You've been gone for so long. There's so many things we need to discuss, and I wanted to fix you breakfast."

"Kaye Mason, you've never cooked breakfast in your life. When did you become so domestic?" I say, rolling out of bed and searching for my underwear. My shorts and one shoe are on the floor next to the bed. I find my other shoe in the hallway.

"I have many talents you haven't discovered. Would you stay if I model my new nightie while I cook? It's very naughty—made with peek-a-boo black lace."

"I really need to see Ted. It's important."

"Suit yourself. You can eat downtown with Ted for all I care," she pouts playfully.

I bend over and kiss her softly on the lips. I love the smell of her. The idea of her bouncing around my kitchen wearing see-through lingerie is almost too enticing. If I don't leave now, I won't be able to go.

"Kaye, I love you, but this is important."

"Alright, sweetheart, but hurry back. I miss you already."

❖ ❖ ❖ ❖ ❖

TED OFFICES downtown on the seventh floor of the Peoples Bank Building. When I emerge from the elevator, he is locking his office door, preparing to leave for lunch. His startled expression tells me he's surprised to see me.

"Hi, Rick. How you doing? I heard the team arrived back in Tyler last night."

"Yep, our bus arrived back at the ballpark a little after midnight. Listen, Ted, I need your help."

"Sure, but can you come back later? I was on my way to lunch," Ted replies obstinately, acting like lunch is the most important event of his day.

"This shouldn't take long. I want to look up some information over at the courthouse, and I need your help."

Reluctantly, Ted agrees to accompany me. We ride the elevator down to the first floor, cross College Avenue, and stride side by side along the sidewalk leading to the Smith County courthouse steps. Once inside, Ted leads me down a wide corridor to the county clerk's office.

"Now, what is it you want to locate? An oil lease?"

"Well, either the property owner or who owns the oil lease. Preferably both."

"And you say the property is out near Swinneytown?"

"Yes. About four miles east of Swinneytown."

Ted motions for me to follow, and I trail behind him as we amble down a long aisle of tall shelves filled with huge cloth-bound books. Evidently these books contain the names of oil leases filed with the county clerk. Finding the book we're searching for, Ted pulls it down from the shelf and carries it to a wooden table. He opens the book for me to inspect.

"This has something to do with your friend's death, doesn't it Rick? Didn't those men who tried to murder you hang out somewhere near Swinneytown?"

"Yeah, that's right. I can't understand why Sheriff Grimes didn't check to see who owns the property. You'd think that's the first thing he'd do. There's the property I want to know about. Tract 36G, George Maxwell Survey, Abstract A-14. What's that mean? I hope you understand all this legal mumbo jumbo."

Ted laughs. "It's not nearly as complicated as it seems, Rick. When the legislature divided the State into counties, they broke the land up into parcels called surveys and named the surveys after whoever owned the property at that time. As pieces of the surveys were sold off, the county assigned tract numbers, for tax purposes."

"To a lawyer that may seem simple, but for me it's complicated," I counter, examining the long rows of shelves filled with the oversized books. "How do we look up who owns the property?"

"Now that we know the Survey and the Tract Number, that's no problem. The information you want will be in the Tax Records. Wait here, and I'll have the clerk look it up."

I'm stunned. To think the information to trace down the two killers is recorded right here in the courthouse. It's beyond comprehension.

Nervously, I watch Ted walk to a long, waist-high counter which separates the public waiting area from the clerks' work zone. Leaning over the counter, he says something to one of the women behind the counter and engages her in conversation. A moment later the woman clerk invites him behind the counter and leads him to another row of shelves filled with oversized books. Always the perfect gentleman, Ted moves quickly to help the woman remove a heavy book from the rack and place it on a table near the book shelves.

Ted turns the pages cautiously. When he finds the data he's after, he glances at me, seemingly horrified by what he's discovered.

Not bothering to write down the information, he slams the book shut and accompanies the woman to another row of shelves. There, they pull out another huge book, and Ted begins frantically flipping through the pages. He stops when he finds the one he's searching for. His finger moves slowly across the page.

Without a word, Ted hands the record book to the helpful clerk and walks swiftly across the work zone. He heads straight down the hallway, ignoring me as he passes.

"Wait up, Ted. Tell me what you found out," I say, catching up to him and walking fast to keep up.

"You don't want to know, Rick. We'd best leave this alone."

"No. I want to know what you found. You have to tell me."

"There's some things you're better off not knowing. This is one of those things. Go home, Rick. Hug your wife and forget this ever happened," Ted says, continuing to set a fast pace.

I grab his arm and spin him around to face me.

"Dammit, Ted! I have to know! Tell me what you found. If you won't tell me who owns that property, I'll find someone else who can look it up. Either way I'm gonna get to the bottom of this. There's no way you can keep me from finding out who controls that property."

"Rick, please. Leave it alone. What I discovered could ruin your life—maybe both our lives."

"No, I have to know. Tell me. Who owns the oil lease?"

"Marathon Oil Company, out of New Orleans. Rick, listen to me. You're better off not knowing any thing more."

"Marathon Oil Company? Never heard of them. Who owns the property?"

"Rick, you know too much. And dammit, now I know too much," Ted pleads. He is close to tears.

"Somebody associated with that property hired those two thugs who tried to kill me. I have a right to know who that is. Now tell me. Who owns the property?" I demand emphatically.

"C. S. Enterprises," Ted divulges, yielding to my emotional outburst.

"I don't understand. Who the hell is C. S. Enterprises? What does C. S. stand for?"

"C. S. stands for Clyde Segars, you stupid hick! Now you satisfied?"

I can't believe my ears. He must be wrong, but Ted's pale face assures me it's true. Slowly, the implications sink in on me. Now we've both lost our appetite.

❖ ❖ ❖ ❖ ❖

DRIVING ALONG, barely keeping pace with the sluggish midday traffic on Broadway, my mind is inundated with a thousand questions. How is Clyde Segars involved in Max Wagner's murder? Is the sheriff somehow in cahoots with my father-in-law? Surely his people checked to see who owned the property. Is there anyone in this city I can trust?

Can I trust Ted?

Damn, how did I get myself involved in this mess?

I try to erase my gloomy thoughts by thinking of Kaye. She promised to cook me breakfast. Kaye was raised in a house with butlers and cooks, where people are hired to do the household chores, so she's not exactly a world-class cook. Nonetheless, I'll eat whatever she cooks—make her feel she's appreciated.

When I pull up alongside my front curb, I remember there's no food in my house. I've been on the road for two weeks. Reaching down to fish around inside my pant pocket, I find only three small coins.

Maybe Kaye will have a few dollars. We can run down to Mary's diner for a quick bite.

If she doesn't change her mind about moving in with me, I'm gonna have to hit on her father for a pay raise. I darn sure can't afford to feed two mouths on my pitiful manager's salary.

Man, life was a heck of a lot less complicated when I was an out of work drunk.

CHAPTER FOURTEEN

TONIGHT WE begin a four-game home and home series with the Gainesville Owls. The first two games will be played in Tyler. Then we'll switch locations and play the second two in Gainesville.

Despite their owner's boastful talk during preseason, the Owls are stuck in sixth place. But no matter the standings, this is an important series, especially for Clyde Segars. This will be an ego series—played for bragging rights. Segars and oilman Dick Burnett, who controls the Gainesville franchise, are longtime friends. They are also fierce competitors. Both men attained their wealth by investing in the East Texas oil fields, a roll-the-dice vocation which requires a strong stomach, nerves of steel and a competitive heart. Perhaps their willingness to gamble everything on a hunch has something to do with their business success. Certainly their combative nature is rooted in the dog-eat-dog oil world.

❖ ❖ ❖ ❖ ❖

DARKNESS CLOSES IN as we complete our pre-game infield warm-up. A once dazzling amber sun, which is now barely visible on the horizon beyond the right field fence, is sinking fast. While Nelms fields my bunt and rifles the baseball to first, the stadium flood lights flick on.

A ground crew rushes out even before my infielders can trot off the diamond. Our ground keepers have special instructions—to rake the infield and water down the base paths. This Gainesville club may be stationed in sixth place, but they lead the league in stolen bases. Matilda suggested we over-water the base paths to slow down Owl base runners. We've also moved both of the batter's boxes six inches forward, a minor modification which will allow our catcher to set up closer behind home plate and which we hope neither the umpires nor the visiting team will notice. Occasionally a few inches will make the difference whether a runner stealing second is out or safe.

For the first time since the season kicked off, the owner's box is jam-packed, with every seat occupied. Segars' guests include not only Ted and my wife Kaye, but also Sheriff Grimes, Fred Varner, the county coroner, and their wives. Dick Burnett and his wife also share Segars' choice box seats.

An unprecedented late afternoon phone call from Clyde to inquire about the health of our pitching staff substantiated my belief that, to my father-in-law, this is not just another baseball game. So, yielding to his anxiety, I've decided to open the series with Nick Bounato instead of Paul Walker who under more normal circumstances would start tonight.

❖ ❖ ❖ ❖ ❖

"CRACK!" GAINESVILLE'S lead-off batter lines Bounato's first pitch into right field and hustles up the first base line. The Owl runner rounds first and fakes a try for an extra base. Hal Epps retrieves the baseball and hurriedly hurls it in the direction of second base. Epps' hasty throw soars high over Henry French's head, allowing the base runner to easily trot down to second while our third baseman chases after the errant missile.

"Jiminy Christmas. Epps ain't made an error all season. How come he overthrows second all of a sudden?" Whitey wails, throwing up his hands to illustrate his frustration. Not waiting for my response, he whirls and stomps angrily down the cleat scarred pathway fronting our dugout bench.

"Darned if I know. Maybe the ball was wet. Maybe the ground crew put too much water on the outfield, but there's no reason to get yourself in an uproar. This isn't the first time we've allowed a man to reach second with nobody out. Keep your hat on. We'll be fine."

"I ain't so sure, Rick. I got an uneasy feeling. Been eating at me all day. You know, like our luck has run out."

"Don't be so paranoid, old timer. Think positive. Bounato's our ace, and he's on a roll. Won three of his four starts. And this club's clobbering the baseball. According to this morning's paper six men on our team are batting over .300. I've been thinking about maybe letting French take his cuts," I boast to show my unwavering confidence.

"Baseball is a funny game, Rick. You'd best leave well enough alone. One day you're cruising along with everything going your way, then all of a sudden—blam. Your darn wheels come off, and nothing works right."

"I've seen that happen, but I'm not the least bit worried. The way this team's playing we could spot half the clubs in the league five runs and still beat their socks off," I chuckle, finding humor in my assistant's dismal mood.

"CRACK!" Another sharp report rocks the stadium. Bounato's second pitch of the evening propels on a swift trajectory into the outfield gap between Akins our center fielder and Epps in right. On the crack of the bat, the base runner occupying second is off and running. The runner rounds third and digs for home.

Akins and Epps converge on the baseball. Our center fielder reaches the ball first. Snaring the baseball with his bare hand, Akins spins and flings it toward second base, hoping to cut off the hitter who has taken the turn at first. Problem is no one is covering second. Expecting a relay throw to try and cut down the lead runner at home plate, both French and Bruzga have run out onto the outfield grass.

Bounato and third baseman Mel Neuendorff scramble madly in pursuit of the overthrown baseball. Meanwhile, Gainesville's second runner reaches second base and keeps on going. He slides safely into third as Neuendorff catches up with the baseball, grabbing it just in time to prevent it from rolling into the visiting team's dugout.

"Holy crap. These guys act like they never played this game before. We've worked on that relay play a thousand times," I groan, baffled by our neophyte behavior. Like a father who's shamed by his wayward child's wrong doing, I lower my head and stare mournfully at my shoelaces.

"It's something in the air. I had a feeling all day today that something was wrong. Ever since I rolled out of bed this morning, my bones had this tingling sensation."

"Whitey, will you cut out the superstitious hogwash. So they scored one stinking run on us. It's not the end of the world. We'll get it back in the bottom of the inning."

My dogmatic attitude has no effect. Whitey's convinced some sort of evil spell is responsible for our poor play. His lowered voice contains a disturbing hint of morbid anxiety when he moves up close and whispers, "Maybe I oughta check with Matilda. I'll bet she'll know what the problem is."

"Put a lid on it, Whitey. Before you psyche me out. Before you psyche out the whole team with your superstitious nonsense."

"Okay, but sometimes you can nip these things in the bud. Carrying a rabbit's foot, a lucky coin," Whitey counsels, keeping his voice low.

"Knock it off, Whitey! I'm not listening!"

❖ ❖ ❖ ❖ ❖

"A SQUEEZE! Pull in! Pull in! It's a suicide squeeze," I yell to my infield when Gainesville's hitter squares around to bunt. With nobody out, our infield is playing deep.

"PLUNK!" The batter bunts the baseball softly up the first base line. Our infielders scamper forward, trying to recover. Surprised and off balance, Bounato stumbles off the pitching mound and staggers after the slow-moving baseball. In desperation, he grabs the ball with a bare hand and backhands it to Nelms standing on home plate. Bounato's aim is way off target. The baseball flies high above Nelms'

273

outstretched mitt, eventually bouncing against the backstop at the edge of the grandstands.

The runner from third slides unchallenged across home to score. The batter, obeying frantic signals from his first base coach, rounds first base and digs for second. Nelms hurriedly retrieves the baseball and rockets it toward second. When the ball catapults past Bruzga into center field, the Owls' base runner dances happily on to third.

"Good Lord Almighty. Can't we do anything right? The way we're playing tonight, we may never get their side out," I howl, grabbing my cap and throwing it to the ground.

"Maybe I oughta check with Matilda. Whatta you think, Rick? Can't do no harm," Whitey mumbles quietly, stubbornly refusing to abandon his zany bad luck theory.

I reach down, pick up my cap and dust it off. My brain searches for some rebuttal to refute Whitey's superstitious intuition, but no logical explanation comes to mind. Out on the baseball diamond my players, like myself, seem totally baffled by our inept performance.

If questioned, many members of my team would deny they believe in luck. Me, I believe luck comes in direct proportion to your commitment—how hard you practice, the mental and physical effort you devote to improving your game.

Once, after my Longhorn team rallied in the ninth to beat a talent-laden A&M squad, I made the mistake of telling Coach Falk we were lucky to win. Obviously perturbed by my comment, he frowned and reprimanded me angrily. His response was, "Teams that practice hard are always lucky."

At this particular moment though, I'm wavering. For the past few days my father-in-law has been bragging to his friend Dick Burnett—how he's taken a losing baseball franchise and turned it into a winner, and how much of his Tyler club's success can be attributed to his son-in-law's superior managing ability. Clyde has looked forward to this contest between Tyler and Gainesville with great anticipation. He was expecting to show out tonight. Now, he's been thoroughly embarrassed by my team's disgraceful performance, and the colonel don't take kindly to people who let him down.

"Okay, Whitey. Run check with Matilda. But let's keep this strictly between ourselves. We don't want to spook our players," I say, keeping my voice low so the players won't hear.

"Oh, sure. Strictly between us chickens," Whitey grins, apparently delighted I've caved in to his arcane persuasion.

❖ ❖ ❖ ❖ ❖

GAINESVILLE SCORES five runs in the top of the first before Bounato gets the final out on a high fly ball to left field, which Gregory bobbles and almost drops before he finds the handle.

With heads hung low, my troops come running off the playing field. I clap my hands and yell words of encouragement, hoping a positive attitude will improve their disposition.

"Alright, men, it's only five runs. We'll get 'em back. This game's not over yet. Whatta you say? Anyone wanna quit?" Not one player responds. My challenge is answered with blank expressions—like how can anyone be so positive in the midst of an unmitigated disaster.

For a second I consider chewing ass, humiliating my team, pointing out their mistakes, but I know that's not the answer. My players' dismal faces chronicle their apprehension. In one disgraceful inning this baseball club has switched personalities. These players arrived here tonight thinking they were invincible. Now they're losing shamefully—to a team that's floundering in sixth place. Their air of confidence has abruptly changed to fear. Criticizing these demoralized men would be akin to beating a dead horse.

When no solution comes to mind, I plop down on the bench alongside a column of long, sorrowful faces. It's gonna be a long night, and Clyde Segars is gonna be madder than hell tomorrow morning.

"Psst. Rick. Hey, Rick, up here," Whitey's voice beckons me. His face is barely visible as he squats down to peer into the dugout.

"Whatta you want, Whitey?" I ask despondently.

Putting a finger to his lips, Whitey motions for me to follow him. Reluctantly, I abandon my seat and meet with him alongside the bleacher wall outside the dugout.

"It's not the players, and it's not you or me. It's the colonel. He's the one," Whitey mysteriously informs me. He seems immensely pleased with his information.

"You mean Clyde? Whitey, what the heck are you talking about?"

"It's the colonel who's responsible for our bad luck. Matilda checked it out. Clyde was born in July. That makes him a Cancer, and now his sun moved into some sort of double moon, or something like that. Anyway, it's real bad. Matilda keeps charts on all that celestial stuff."

"Astrology. It's called astrology, but I've never known anyone who takes it serious. Most people who believe in that gibberish are considered wackos."

"Matilda believes in it, and we both know she's seldom wrong about anything."

"Well, she's wrong this time. There's absolutely nothing wrong with this team a few runs won't cure. Come on, Whitey. Let's get back inside the dugout before French comes to bat."

❖ ❖ ❖ ❖ ❖

"STRIKE THREE!" the umpire bellows, after French swings listlessly at a third consecutive pitch.

"What the hell's wrong with us tonight?" I wail, slamming my bare knuckles against the concrete dugout wall. The impact results in immediate, excruciating pain. I spin around to face my players, trying not to reveal how badly I've hurt myself.

"Doesn't anyone on this team remember how to play baseball?" I scream.

Stuffing my hands into my pockets, I stomp along the wooden deck in front of the bench, huffing, snorting, showing my indignation, all the time praying the pain in my hand will subside.

Players sitting on the bench keep their heads down, fearful they might become the object of my wrath.

When I reach the opposite end of the dugout, I pivot on one foot and tramp back to my original position next to Whitey. We stand there for a few seconds watching Bruzga take his final swings with the leaded bat in the on-deck-circle. Then I lean sideways and whisper in my assistant's ear.

"Did Matilda say how long the colonel's sun will be lined up with those dadgum cotton-picking moons?"

❖ ❖ ❖ ❖ ❖

IN SPITE of our errors and lethargic play, Gainesville is unable to salt the game away. Inept hitting, poor base running, and a half-dozen fielding mistakes explain why they're relegated to their lowly position near the league's cellar. Finally in the top of the eighth, the Owls prove pitiful play will always beat bad luck, scoring four runs to stretch their lead to eleven runs. My East Texans persist in continuing along their fruitless path, going scoreless in the bottoms of both the eighth and ninth.

The score board in center field tells the gloomy story:

	1	2	3	4	5	6	7	8	9	R	H	E
Visitors	5	1	1	3	2	0	0	4	0	16	15	6
Tyler	0	0	1	0	1	2	1	0	0	5	4	7

❖ ❖ ❖ ❖ ❖

IGNORING OUR usual postgame cleanup chores, Whitey and I sit side by side on the dugout bench, dejectedly watching the ground crew drag the base paths and lightly sprinkle the infield.

"How long she say this would last, Whitey?" I say, repeating a question I've asked numerous times during the course of the game.

"About forty days. Has something to do with Clyde's birthday. We can check with her again as soon as the guys clear out of the locker room."

"Let's do that. There's another situation that's bothering me. Maybe I can talk to her about that too," I divulge, referring to my dilemma over the information Ted and I uncovered at the county courthouse.

"Anything I can help with? You know I'm a good listener."

"No, it's kind of personal," I reply without thinking. Then seeing the hurt puppy look on Whitey's face, I tell a lie. "I need some feminine advice concerning my love life."

"Yeah, you're right, Rick. I wouldn't be much help there."

Without warning, Clyde Segars appears at the top of the dugout steps. He bends down to glance inside.

"Hey, Rick, Whitey. You coaches come up here. Got some people I'd like you to meet."

Like two schoolboys caught playing hooky, Whitey and I scramble through the dugout, slicking back our hair, grabbing our caps, bumping into one another as we scramble up the steps. Segars has ushered his entire entourage down onto the playing field to meet us. Even though I recognize most of his guests, this is the colonel's party. I wait to be introduced.

"These are the two men who have turned our Tyler franchise around. We're very proud of the excellent job they've done," Segars expounds, his face beaming with adoration. "Rick Mason, my son-in-law, is the team manager, and Whitey Waters, my long time friend, is our assistant manager. Rick, Whitey, you two know Sheriff Grimes and Mister Varner, but I want you to meet their wives, and my good friend Dick Burnett and his lovely wife Dale."

Everyone shakes hands, and for a minute or so, Whitey and I engage in small talk, telling the wives we're delighted they came to watch our team play and promising them a Tyler victory next time they come. Segars' friend Dick Burnett I like immediately. He has a firm handshake and a charismatic smile. When he jokingly offers me a job if I ever get tired of working for my father-in-law, everyone laughs, but I make a mental note to remember his proposition.

As the party breaks up, I kiss Kaye and tell her not to wait up, explaining I have some baseball business to attend to. She accepts my advisory without argument, but pouts playfully to let everyone know she's truly disappointed.

Segars lags behind to inquire about the team's sorry performance.

"I don't know the reason, Clyde. Maybe we should chalk it up as a bad night."

"But seven errors, Rick. Have you ever seen a team make seven errors in one game?"

"No, I've never seen any team play as poorly as we did tonight. I'll hold a special practice tomorrow morning. Work on our basics. Maybe that will help."

"I hope so. Our play tonight was embarrassing, especially with Dick and his wife sitting in my box. I've been bragging to him all week."

"I realize how important this series is to you, Clyde. I'll see what I can do."

"Fine. I'll expect you to fix whatever is broke. And tomorrow night let's kick some Gainesville butt. Okay?"

"You bet. Say, Clyde, don't you have a birthday coming up soon?"

"Sure do, but how'd you know? I gave up celebrating birthdays after my wife passed away."

"Just a lucky guess. You mind telling me the date? Thought Kaye and I might buy you a gift."

"No. No, that's not necessary. I have everything I need. Use your money to buy something for Kaye. She's the one in the family who appreciates presents."

"I'd still like to know the date, for future reference."

"July 4th, but I'd appreciate your not telling anyone else. Don't want everyone in town buying me a gift."

"Sure, Clyde. I promise. I won't tell another soul," I lie. I know of two souls I intend to tell right away—Matilda and Whitey.

Good grief. The fourth of July. That's more than a month away. Surely we'll win another game before then.

❖ ❖ ❖ ❖ ❖

PROBABLY CURIOUS ABOUT my love life, my assistant coach lingers inside the manager's office until almost eleven. Finally, I remind him the Y bolts their doors shut at eleven-thirty and insist he leave or be forced to sleep on the locker room floor.

After Whitey departs, I lock the front door and call out to Matilda. A rumble in the equipment room suggests she's near. I drag up a chair and wait for her arrival.

"I'm so glad you stayed, Richard. We need to talk. Your team is in big trouble."

"I know. Whitey told me all about your charts. You really expect me to believe all that hooey about the colonel's sun being linked with the wrong moons?"

"It's much more complicated than that, but yes, until his sun moves out of its present course, your club will be plagued with bad luck."

"Baloney. How could the colonel's birth sign affect an entire baseball team? No way you'll ever make me believe in your stupid astrological mumbo jumbo," I state emphatically. Actually, after watching my team's pathetic performance, I'm pretty much convinced she's right.

"You're free to believe what you choose, Richard, but I assure you my charts are accurate and very scientific. This kind of bad luck only occurs once in a blue moon. Well, perhaps that's a poor choice of words," Matilda giggles, like she's messed up the punch line to a funny joke. Somehow I fail to see the humor.

"Charts or no charts, I believe baseball teams make their own luck. I don't believe in things I can't see."

"You never believed in ghosts before you met me, did you?"

"No, but that's different...," I say defensively. I try to formulate a more intelligent response, but my mind refuses to cooperate.

"How about the lucky shorts you wear before every game? And the way you avoid stepping on concrete cracks outside the dressing room? And how about—"

"Okay. Okay, Matilda, I get the picture. You win. Maybe I am a little superstitious."

"Good. You're a very stubborn man, Richard Mason."

"So I've been told. So, assuming I accept your bad luck theory, what can we do to change the situation? We can't go on losing until after the fourth of July."

"The fourth of July? How did you know the exact date?"

"I asked the colonel. That's his birthday."

"Then why have we been arguing? Richard, sometimes you can be very exasperating."

"Maybe I wanted you to convince me. So what's the answer? Isn't there some way we can change our luck?"

"Oh yes. The answer is ridiculously obvious."

Matilda stares at me while my mind searches desperately for the answer she apparently thinks I know. Her face cracks a knowing smile when the answer hits me, like an avalanche of bricks falling on my head.

"Get rid of Segars? Surely you don't mean what I think you mean?"

"Isn't he responsible for your friend's death? Except for my intervention, he would also be responsible for your demise."

Matilda's revelation stuns me. Perhaps it's a slip of her tongue. Perhaps she intended to tell me, but now I know for sure. My trial, the judges, and their decision to send me back weren't simply a hallucination. The implications are baffling, but I'm still not convinced she's an angel. She frequently seems more like a devil.

"I'm not so sure Clyde had anything to do with Max's murder. Those fellows, Alvin and Oscar, are two mean hombres. I doubt if they work directly for the colonel. I think they answer to the New Orleans oil outfit, the one that operates the oil lease."

"Makes no difference. If you expect to turn your luck around, you'll have to get rid of the colonel. I've warned you before. If your team starts losing, I'm leaving."

"Surely you don't expect me to kill my father-in-law," I argue. Now I'm absolutely convinced. Listening to her advice is a sure route to hell. No way she's mine or anyone else's guardian angel. This is the devil's messenger I'm dealing with.

"No one mentioned murder, although that is one solution. Your father-in-law is an evil man, so killing him could possibly be justified. But I'm not allowed to participate in those kinds of decisions. I'll leave getting rid of him strictly up to you."

"That's it? You issue an ultimatum and then leave it up to me."

"That's the way it works, my love. I can help you with baseball decisions, but I'm not allowed to meddle with decisions involving morals."

"Let me think on it. Maybe I can come up with a better solution—one that will solve our problem, without me ending up in a jail cell."

"Good, I'm glad that's settled. Anything else we need to talk about?"

"There's one more thing. You seem to know about the ownership documents Ted and I discovered at the courthouse. What's going on out there? How is Clyde Segars involved? Why was Max Wagner killed?"

"My, my, that's an awful lot of questions. Maybe that's the reason our baseball team is playing so poorly. Maybe it's not all bad luck. Maybe the manager's distracted. Maybe he's overworked his tiny little brain."

"Stop stalling, Matilda. You know the answers. Tell me."

"If I tell, that would spoil all the fun. But I'll give you a hint. Call your friend Paul."

"Paul? How can he help?"

"He's an engineer. Engineers can see things the rest of us overlook."

"So you recommend I contact Paul and have him check out the oil lease?"

"Oh, Richard, you're so perceptive. Solving the mystery is going to be such fun."

"Cut out the crap, Matilda. This is serious. Last time I went snooping around that property, I almost got myself killed."

"Forgive me, darling. Sometimes I get caught up in my emotions. That's why they keep sending me back. Are we finished? I really need to go, and Kaye's waiting up for you."

"I reckon you've given me plenty to think about for one night, but I do have one more question."

"And what's that, Richard? What's your question?"

"I can't figure you out, and it's eating me up. Are you my guardian angel, or are you a devil who's after my soul?"

Tilting her head back, Matilda laughs gleefully. Then pursing her lips to suppress her amusement, she wags a finger at me. "You have such a keen sense of humor, darling. Maybe that's why I care so much what happens to you."

❖ ❖ ❖ ❖ ❖

IT'S ALMOST NOON when the last player finishes dressing and departs from the locker room. At my insistence we practiced long past our customary two hour morning session. After a snappy infield warm-up and a short, but crisp, batting session, Whitey was ready to send the squad to the showers. That's when I interceded. Remembering my promise to Segars, I sent the squad back onto the playing field to work on outfield relays, insisting that each player carry out his assignment perfectly.

The extra practice didn't help. My dogged persistence only made the men irritable and more lethargic. After practice, Whitey was anxious to leave, probably perturbed with my incessant tenacity. I stayed to lock up, and acceding to Matilda's suggestion, take advantage of the rare privacy to telephone Paul.

Realizing the probability of catching Paul in his office is comparable to filling an inside straight, I decide to call person-to-person. A secretary answers. After a brief discussion between my operator and the secretary, the phone rings through. A man's voice answers.

"Hello. Estimating department."

"I have a call from Tyler—for a Mister Paul Matlock," the operator explains.

"This is Paul Matlock. Can you tell me who's calling?"

"Your party is on the line, Mister Mason," the operator informs me, disregarding Paul's curious inquiry.

"Hello, Paul. Rick Mason here. How you doing?"

"Rick. It's nice to hear your voice. I'm doing fine. How about yourself? You staying sober?"

"I'm doing fantastic. Actually I'm doing better than that. Kaye and I have reconciled our marital differences, and we're living together again. My baseball team's in first place, and I haven't had a drink in almost a month. Paul, for the first time in a long time, I've got my life squared away," I proclaim proudly, surprising myself with my account of how well I'm doing. Somehow amongst all the mental anguish and baseball battles, my life has improved dramatically.

"I'm glad for you. You attending the AA meetings in Tyler?"

"No, I've been too busy. I know I should. Maybe after baseball season I can get started again."

"I don't mean to preach, Rick, but you're an alcoholic. Somewhere down the road you're gonna need support. Right now, when everything's going so good, that may not seem important, but the time will come when you'll need the group. Now's the time to make the connection, so they'll be there for you when you need them."

"You're right, Paul. I know it's important. Somehow I'll make time," I say, hoping if I agree he'll be satisfied. My strategy doesn't work.

"I hope you will. I've seen too many men who thought they had their problem licked fall off the wagon and go back to drinking. Every time you slide back, it's tougher to quit the next time."

"Paul, there's another reason I called. I need your help," I state abruptly, interrupting what has the makings of a lengthy sermon. Briefly I describe the situation, telling him about my confrontation with Alvin and Oscar at the oil lease, about recovering Max Wagner's body from the Neches River, and about my suspicion that the valves and gages at the pump station are somehow connected to Max's death. I skirt around the question of ownership, but Paul's keen mind immediately hones in on that missing piece of the puzzle. After a little prodding, I capitulate and tell him everything.

"You say your father-in-law owns the property? Good Lord, Rick, that implicates him in the murder."

"Yes, at least that's the way it looks. And not knowing whether he's responsible or why Max was killed—my questions are driving me nuts. Paul, this situation is horribly complicated. I have to get to the bottom of this thing."

"Are you sure? Seems like everything that's going right in your life you owe to your father-in-law. The wrong answers could royally screw you up. Might even put your life in danger."

"I understand that, and maybe I'm crazy for wanting to know. But I can't leave it alone. Will you help me, Paul?"

A long pause of silence follows while my friend considers my request.

"Alright, but can you wait a few days? We're bidding a big job next Monday. Until I get that behind me, I'm up to my ears in specifications, subcontractors and bid documents."

"Sure. My team has an off day scheduled on Tuesday. That'll be perfect."

"Fine. Tuesday it is then. I'll meet you at the Tyler ballpark. Let's say around ten o'clock. If we finish our snooping in time, maybe we can drop by an AA meeting that evening."

"Sure, that'll be great. Give me an opportunity to meet some of the members," I reluctantly agree. That Paul, he has a one track mind.

❖ ❖ ❖ ❖ ❖

TO THE COLONEL'S chagrin, we drop four straight games to Gainesville, allowing the Owls to sweep their first series of the season. Last night, with two outs in the bottom of the ninth and the bases loaded, Herb Cates walked in the winning run on four consecutive balls, which Jess Nelms swears should have been called strikes. Even the umpires seem dead set on extending our shameful losing streak.

285

Meanwhile, the Temple Eagles have shrugged off the pounding we handed them two weeks ago, finding a soft spot in their schedule and winning six in a row to overtake us in the Big State standings.

"Good morning, Coach. You want the breakfast special?" Bea, the stout, pear-bottomed waitress who minds the quick service counter at Mary's Diner asks while I straddle a bar stool. She fishes for an order book stuffed inside her apron pocket.

"No, just coffee. My wife's cooking breakfast for me these days."

"Been wondering why we haven't seen you. Thought maybe the baseball team was playing out of town."

"We have, but we've been playing Gainesville. We've been commuting back to Tyler after the games. It's a three-hour bus ride each way, but we don't mind. Lets us sleep in our own beds for a change."

"Coffee with cream. You wanna see the morning newspaper?"

"Probably make me sick to my stomach, but I reckon I oughta take a look at the sports section."

"Yes, I suppose you're sad about losing your job."

"Losing my job? Bea, who told you I was losing my job? Okay, so my ball club's lost four in a row, but Tyler's still in second place," I object strongly, wondering what nincompoop could've invented such a cockeyed story.

"That's not what the *Morning Telegraph* says. Haven't you read Charlie Eskew's column?"

"No, but whatever he says, he's wrong—dead wrong."

"You better read his column, Coach. Charlie Eskew is never wrong."

Unwilling to wait for Bea to deliver the paper, I slide off my stool and rush to the magazine rack near the front door, snatching the last newspaper out from under the nose of a slower, less impetuous, late morning patron. Hurriedly, I flip through the pages, hardly noticing when I bump against another customer at the checkout counter. I locate the sports section at the same time I reach my stool. A steaming cup of coffee waits on the counter.

Charles Eskew is a popular local sportswriter with an uncanny nose for news. His daily column is cleverly labeled *The Morning After.* Today the title is particularly appropriate.

Eskew's article explains how, during the current losing streak, a riff has developed between the East Texan owners and their bull-headed manager. According to Eskew's sources, the disagreement originated over a difference in philosophy for the baseball franchise. The owners demand a playoff contender for Tyler this year and are willing to open their wallets to purchase whatever players may be necessary to achieve that lofty goal. I, on the other hand, am ardently opposed to making wholesale roster changes, resisting the owners' win now, no matter what the cost, tactics. The writer's source believes the differences are irreconcilable. He expects a managerial change to be announced any day.

"What a load of crap. Like I even have a coaching philosophy," I pronounce, laughing loudly. Then sensing my impassioned outburst has drawn the attention of every person in the restaurant, I lift the opened newspaper higher and bury my face between the pages.

❖ ❖ ❖ ❖ ❖

REGARDLESS how erroneous the article, predictions of a manager's removal and player personnel changes can pluck the heart and soul from a baseball team. So much of baseball depends on mental attitude. No ball club can compete effectively with a cloud of impending doom hanging over the locker room. Speculation over who will be replaced can torpedo a team's confidence. Players become testy and blame each other for every minor miscue, spawning harsh feelings which linger even after the personnel purge ends.

It's nine-thirty. Paul promised to meet me at ten. If I hurry, I can talk with Clyde and still make it back to the ballfield in time to catch Paul. This rumor needs to be nipped in the bud before it affects my team.

I switch on the ignition and stomp at the foot starter. The engine fires on the first try. The Pontiac roars eagerly, impatient to get underway.

❖ ❖ ❖ ❖ ❖

I KNOCK lightly on the office door and stick my head inside.

"Clyde, you busy?" I inquire cautiously.

"I'm always busy. What's on your mind?" Clyde sounds cranky this morning, no doubt the residue of last night's bitter loss to the Owls.

"You see the morning paper?"

"No, didn't have time. With both the girls out of the house, I've been skipping breakfast, coming straight to the office."

"There's an article in the *Morning Telegraph*. Says I'm about to get canned. Thought we should get together and issue some kind of contradicting statement. You know, a show of confidence to boost team morale."

"I'm afraid I can't do that. There's a chance we may make a managerial change. I'm sorry you had to find out by reading the newspaper."

"But we're in second place. We're almost a lock to make the playoffs. What the hell does it take to make you happy? I thought we agreed you'd be satisfied if the team made the playoffs," I spout angrily. This man is impossible to comprehend. First he gives, then he takes away.

"Calm down, Rick. This isn't necessarily my idea. You know my partners have never particularly relished the idea of your managing the ball club. This losing streak has provided them with ammunition to demand you be replaced."

"But some of it is your idea. Admit it, Clyde, or tell me it's not true."

"I'll admit I'm a little miffed. These last four games have been an embarrassment."

"Clyde, not one of those losses had a darn thing to do with my managing ability. You saw how Gainesville scored their winning run last night. Every one of Cates' pitches were in the strike zone. There's nothing wrong with my judgement or my coaching. The reason we're losing is we've run into a streak of bad luck."

"I don't believe in bad luck. A man makes his own luck."

"That's what I've always believed, until recently. But this argument isn't about luck. What you're hacked about is losing four straight to your friend Burnett."

"Alright, so I don't like losing, especially to Dick Burnett. So what's the crime in that?"

"Clyde, don't you see? You own a ball club that's picked itself off the deck, shrugged off the losing stigma of last season, and fought its way into the first division. But that's not good enough to suit you. No. Now you want to mess with the formula that got you here."

"Sometimes it's necessary to shake things up. Get things moving in the right direction again. That's the strategy my partners want to try."

"If you want my resignation, all you have to do is ask. I'll be delighted to oblige. After watching me turn this baseball franchise around, there'll be a dozen teams begging for my services," I boast, pausing to watch Segars' facial expression while he considers whether I've overstated my value. Before he can reach a conclusion, I quickly continue, "but if you make one roster change without my approval, you won't have to ask. My resignation will be automatic. Then you and your so-called business partners can take your money-sucking, bush league baseball franchise and stick it where the sun don't shine."

When I finish, my heart is pounding. I'm breathing hard. I stand there, staring eye to eye with my father-in-law. I didn't come here expecting a confrontation. I've said things I never intended to say. I want to apologize, but the words won't come. If I don't leave now, our conversation will only deteriorate into finger pointing and name calling, which could spoil our relationship forever. I whirl around and stride swiftly out of the office.

"Nobody's asked for your resignation, Rick, at least not yet. . . ." I hear Segars argue, but I'm already out the door.

❖ ❖ ❖ ❖ ❖

MY BLOOD boils as I traverse down the stairway from Segars' office. Matilda insists it's necessary we get rid of the colonel. But now it's possible I may get fired before I can figure out what to do about him.

One of us is gonna go. That's for darn sure.

❖ ❖ ❖ ❖ ❖

AT A QUARTER past ten the telephone rings, startling me and causing me to almost fall out of my chair. My feet are propped up on top of the manager's desk. My eyes are half closed. I'm still simmering over the heated discussion in Clyde Segars' office.

"Hello. I mean East Texas Baseball Club."

"Rick. Where've you been? I've been trying to call you since before nine." The voice on the other end belongs to Paul.

"Oh," I answer, somewhat confused. Paul is supposed to meet me at ten o'clock. I glance at the wall clock. He's obviously late. "Sorry, Paul. I went out to grab a cup of coffee. Took longer than I expected."

"Listen, Rick, it looks like we're the low bidder on that big job I've been working on."

"That's wonderful. Congratulations," I say stupidly, still confused, wondering how his company's good fortune affects me.

"Yes, but we're still negotiating on several items. Could mean the difference whether we get the job or not. Looks like I'm stuck here until late afternoon."

"But you were gonna help me check out the oil lease. Does this mean you can't help?"

"No, not at all. I'm perfectly willing to help. But I need to reschedule my visit. How about tomorrow morning?"

"No, that won't work. My team's leaving for Sherman tomorrow afternoon. We're scheduled to play a three game series. We'll be traveling back and forth every day."

Having reached an impasse in our time negotiations, a quiet pause ensues while we each search our minds for a plan which will suit the other.

"What about this evening, Rick? I'm sure I can wrap up things here by three o'clock. That would put me in Tyler around six. That'll give us a couple hours of daylight to do what we need to do."

"Sure, but what if we find something? I don't want to be out there in the dark," I shudder, recalling my after-dark skirmish with Alvin and Oscar on the Deep Eddy Bridge.

"You're not afraid of the dark, are you, Rick?" Paul laughs. If he knew Alvin and Oscar the way I do, he wouldn't think my reservations were so humorous.

"I'll meet you here at six. I want to get this done," I reply, avoiding the embarrassment of answering his question.

"Fine. See you then. I suppose this means we'll have to skip the AA meeting."

"Yeah, too bad. Maybe we can attend some other time. Hey, Paul, one more thing."

"What's that, Rick?"

"You own a gun, like a handgun?"

"Sure, a forty-four revolver. Got a holster and a belt that holds my bullets, just like in the western movies. Haven't fired it in a long time."

"Bring the gun, Paul. We may need it."

❖ ❖ ❖ ❖ ❖

"RICKY, WHAT ARE you doing home? I thought you were packing for your trip to Sherman," Kaye questions, running to meet me at the front door and reminding me of the lie I told her earlier this morning.

I reach to take her hand and pull her close. She responds willingly, wrapping her arms around my neck.

"Got tired. Thought I'd come home for a quick nap and some female companionship," I explain, nuzzling my face against the soft skin at the base of her neck.

"If you wouldn't run off to the ballfield so early, you might get a lot more companionship. You know I'm a late morning person," she whispers alluringly, brushing her lips gently against my cheek. Her lips are soft and warm. Her smell is intoxicating. I pull her closer.

She grabs my exploring hands and pushes me away. In an instant her romantic mood has vanished.

"Don't muss me, sweetheart. Vickie's coming by in a few minutes. We're going shopping."

"But our closet's full of your clothes now. I can barely find a place to hang my trousers. What could you possibly need that you don't own already?" I protest, doing a poor job of hiding my disappointment. With the rendezvous with Paul postponed, I was planning to spend a lazy afternoon in bed with my wife.

"We don't plan to buy anything, silly. We're only going shopping."

"I don't get it. You're going shopping, but you don't plan to buy anything. Kaye, that's absolute lunacy."

"It's a girl thing. Men love sports. Girls love to shop. Besides, it's important we know where to find the best bargains."

"Why is that?" I ask, knowing her answer won't enlighten my confusion. I've never understood what motivates women. Females play by a different set of rules.

"It gives us something to talk about when we're with other women."

"Oh, I see. You and Vickie scout out the shops where your women friends can shop, and not buy anything either."

"You're so clever, Ricky, and I love you so much. If Vickie wasn't on her way—"

"What? What would you do, Kaye?" I inquire hopefully. Maybe there's a chance she'll change her mind and stay home.

"I'll show you when I come back. Vickie and I should finish our shopping by five. Then we plan to stop and have coffee with daddy. I should be home by six-thirty at the latest."

"I won't be here. I have to meet a fellow at the ballpark," I tell her despondently. A car honks out front, piercing the tranquility of our quiet neighborhood.

"That's Vickie. I need to go," Kaye says excitedly, grabbing her purse. "Can I borrow a dollar? I'm completely out of spending money."

"I'm sorry, Kaye. I'm broke too. Spent my last dime on coffee at Mary's this morning."

"Darn. I hate to shop without money. Well, maybe I can borrow a few dollars from Vickie. Oh, I meant to tell you. The landlady came by this morning. She claims you haven't paid the rent this month."

"I've been meaning to take care of that," I stammer. Actually, I haven't forgotten to pay the rent, but it's an issue I've tried to avoid. I simply have no money. Since Kaye moved in, my food bills have skyrocketed. My slender wife eats like a horse.

Possibly my despair shows on my face. Ignoring another loud blast from the car horn outside, Kaye lays down her purse and comes to comfort me.

"Are we that broke, darling? We can't even pay the rent?"

"Yes, and payday's almost three weeks away. But don't you worry, hon. We'll be okay. You may have to eat at your dad's place next week while I'm out of town."

"Didn't you ask daddy for a pay raise? I thought that was settled."

"Never got around to asking. With us in the middle of a losing streak, didn't seem like it was a good time to bring up money."

"Ricky, sometimes I think you're schizophrenic. How can a man, who will stand nose to nose with a mean, nasty umpire and argue whether a pitch was a ball or a strike, be such a wimp when it comes to financial matters. You need to stand up to daddy. Listen, I need to go. We'll talk about this tonight."

"Sure, hon. You and Vickie have a good time. We'll get everything settled tonight."

As Kaye scurries down the front walk, I step out on the porch and wave to Vickie. I smile bravely while the two sisters happily greet one another and drive away.

Brooding thoughts fill my mind while I watch Vickie's car disappear from sight. Paying the rent is the least of my worries. My team is in the midst of a four-game losing streak. Most likely Segars and his partners will fire me before the week's out. And a few hours from now, I'll be with Paul searching for evidence which could land my father-in-law in jail.

I close the door, step slowly across the room, and collapse on the living room couch. Man, talk about having a bad day.

CHAPTER FIFTEEN

A LIGHT MIST sprinkles my windshield. When we left the ballpark, there was hardly a cloud in the sky. Now the sky is dark and overcast. East Texas weather can be so unpredictable. This soft drizzle may escalate into a torrential downpour, or the clouds may blow over. In ten minutes the sun may be shining again.

"It's along here somewhere," I tell Paul, leaning forward and straining to see through the water specked glass. "There's an iron pipe gate."

"Be nice if this rain would hold off. I'd like to get this done and drive back to Dallas tonight. My boss is nervous about my numbers. Wants me to double check all my figures before he signs the contract."

"I don't expect this'll take more than an hour, Paul. Maybe not that long. There's four big pumps in one building and a bunch of valves. . . . Look! There's the entrance," I announce excitedly and let up on the foot feed. A sudden rush of adrenaline titillates the hair at the back of my neck.

I swerve left into the narrow driveway. When my rear tires clear the pavement, I brake to a stop and turn to my companion. "You wanna catch the gate, Paul?"

"Sure, I got it," he responds. Paul grabs the door handle and uses a shoulder to force the door open. Globs of wet clay stick to his shoes as he hikes awkwardly toward the iron gate.

"It's locked. You got the key?" Paul yells, turning back to look at me.

"No. Guess we'll have to break the lock. I brought a hammer. It's in the trunk," I advise, leaning sideways and poking my head out the car window. I was hoping we could do this without leaving a tell-tale trail.

Paul shakes his head to disagree and tramps back across the mud to the open window on the passenger side.

"Don't see why we should ruin a good lock. Hand me that tool kit in the seat beside you."

"You think you can pick that padlock?"

"No thinking about it, Rick. I plan to live my next life as a cat burglar. Gotta be more fun than crunching numbers for a living."

In two twists and a prick the lock unlatches, and Paul pushes the gate open. He waits for me to drive through then closes the gate and snaps the padlock back on the sliding steel lever. With any luck we'll be in and out of here without anyone knowing.

❖ ❖ ❖ ❖ ❖

IT'S EASY to understand why Paul's boss values his judgement. Paul is thorough, not necessarily efficient, but decidedly thorough. After he easily picks the lock on the door of the pump building, he carefully sketches the piping layout and meticulously records the reading on each pump gage. Then we move outside where he repeats the same procedure, recording the make and measuring the dimensions of each valve. My occasional attempts at small talk are met with aggravated disdain. Paul waves me off, shaking his head impatiently to rebuke me for interrupting his concentration, and returns to his figures. When he finishes, we march back inside the pump house where he rechecks his sketches and re-records the exact information he wrote down previously.

After following Paul around the compound for almost an hour, I'm soaking wet from the humidity, bored stiff, and without a clue as to what we may have discovered.

"You about done, Paul?" I ask, inspecting the sky. The dark clouds, which earlier threatened rain, have dissipated, but the sun never reappeared. A fading bright light on the horizon indicates it's past sunset. "It'll be getting dark before long."

"Almost. Let's hike down the pipeline a piece. There's one more thing I'd like to check."

Despite my reservations, I follow Paul along the raised earthen berm which marks the course of the underground pipeline. Even though rain never materialized, a lingering residual humidity leaves the air heavy and muggy. Before we've traveled a thousand yards, perspiration fills my eyelashes and streams down my face. Hidden among the high weeds are cactus-like bushes with sharp needles which prick through my britches and sting my legs. If Paul weren't so dogmatic, I'd turn back. I haven't the faintest idea of what we're looking for.

I'm on the verge of suggesting we abandon our investigation when Paul suddenly stops. At a right angle to the berm we're tracking is the grassless scar of a recently installed pipeline. The humped mound leads off into the thick woods bordering the right-of-way.

"You find something, Paul?" I ask foolishly.

"I think so. We may have solved the mystery," Paul divulges with a self-satisfied grin.

"That's great. What did we find?" I inquire, but my single-minded sleuth has charged ahead, following the pipeline excavation into the dense thicket. I lower my shoulders and follow, plunging through the high weeds and disregarding a strong premonition of impending danger.

A hundred yards beyond the edge of the cleared pipeline right-of-way, we break through the thick brush and discover a small clearing. Near the center of the open space is a circular reservoir tank and an oil well. The monotonous hum of a gas fueled motor echoes across the opening. Paul stoops to inspect the valves which control the reservoir tank piping then walks to examine the oil well.

"What is it? Did we find what we're looking for?"

"We sure have. Rick, you and I have solved the riddle. This is why they killed your friend. He must've traced the pipeline down to this spot. The gages tell the whole story."

"Tell me, Paul. What did we find?"

"A very elaborate skimming operation. Whoever designed this gizmo is an absolute genius. If it weren't illegal, he could make a fortune."

"I don't get it. How do you steal oil from a pipeline with an oil well?"

"No. No. Don't you see? This is a bogus well. There's no oil here. Look, I'll show you."

Paul walks to the oil well, shuts down the pump motor, and returns to the reservoir tank where he grabs a valve and wrestles it into an open position. Oil begins to flow from the pipe out onto the ground.

"You see, Rick? Oil. Oil, where there should be no oil."

While Paul twists the valve to shut off the flow, I scratch my head and try to figure it out. I still don't understand.

"I'm just an ignorant baseball coach, Paul. You're gonna have to spell it out for me."

"It's so simple and so ingenious. Supposedly, this pipe is the supply line from the oil well. At least, that's what they want people to think. Not supposed to be pressure in that line, not when the well's not pumping, and you saw me turn off the well motor. The actual oil supply comes from the main pipeline. The whole story's right there in the gages back at the pump station. These folks have tapped into the oil company's pipe line right below the pump station. They pipe the oil down here to this bogus oil well and resell it to the same outfit they stole it from. It's a brilliant scheme and a marvelous piece of engineering."

"I still don't understand how it works, but I'll take your word for it, Paul. It's getting dark. Have we got all the information we need?"

"Yep, I reckon we're done. When I get back to Dallas, I'll put together some drawings and compile everything we've found in the form of a report. Then we'll need to decide what we want to do with our little discovery."

"I already know what to do with it. We'll give it to the Smith County sheriff."

"Uh, uh, Rick. That might get us both killed. This is much too big for the local sheriff to handle. Besides, didn't you tell me the sheriff is a close friend of your father-in-law?"

❖ ❖ ❖ ❖ ❖

DARKNESS CLOSES IN while Paul and I lethargically plod back toward the pump station. In spite of our weary outward appearance, inside we're both elated over our discovery. When we reach the Pontiac, we pause to scrape off the mud caked to our shoes and brush off the prickly weeds and burrs snagged in our trousers.

Minutes later we crawl in. I'm reaching for the ignition to start the engine when Paul lays his hand on mine.

"Don't turn on your lights. Someone's coming," Paul warns.

In the distance two moving headlights meander up the same dirt pathway which led us here. My hands tighten on the steering wheel. Suddenly my mouth is dry. I try to breathe, but my breath lodges in my throat.

"You think it's someone you know, Rick?"

"No. No one knows we're here. I didn't tell a soul. But I have an idea who it might be. Check your gun, Paul. Make sure it's loaded."

Quickly I start the engine and pull the Pontiac into a grove of young pine trees and out of sight. Paul and I quietly climb out of the car. Crouching low, we dash back to the edge of the trees. We drop to our knees and wait there silently, hiding in the tall weeds as we watch the car lights approach.

Straining every piston, a faded red pickup roars into the pump station compound and brakes to a stop. I recognize the vehicle immediately. I lay my hand on Paul's shoulder and motion for him to keep down.

A pickup door slams shut, sending a thunderous clamor across the clearing.

"Hey. Hold it down. We don't want the whole world to know we're here."

"Hell's bells, what you worried about? Ain't nobody gonna hear us this far off the road."

"Maybe not, but there's no sense in gittin' reckless. Let's get this job done and hightail it outta here. This place gives me the willies."

"Yeah, me too, especially after dark. Hand me that tool box in the truck bed. Then pull the truck around and point the lights inside the fence, so we can see what we're working on."

The two men unload their tool box along with several sections of steel pipe and tote the items to the pump building. While one man unlocks the door, the other returns to the pickup, backs it up and pulls the front end close against the chain-link fence. The bright glare from the headlights illuminates the conglomeration of valves and gages inside the complex.

Paul moves close to me and whispers, "Those the fellows who killed your buddy?"

"Yes. That's Alvin and Oscar. Don't know their last names, but it was those two who killed Max. Whatta you think they're up too?"

"My guess is they're here to disconnect the piping apparatus that skims off the oil."

"Get out your gun, Paul. We gotta stop 'em, before they remove the evidence," I declare, raising up.

"No, now's not the right time," Paul commands, grabbing my arm and pulling me down. "We gotta stay calm. If these fellows are as mean as you say, we're overmatched even with my handgun. No telling what kind of firepower they have stashed in that pickup. We make the wrong move, and we might wind up dead like your friend Max."

"But we gotta do something. We can't just lay here and do nothing."

"Yes we can. Now keep quiet. Maybe they'll split up. If they separate, maybe we can get the jump on one of 'em."

For what seems an eternity, we wait and watch Alvin and Oscar scurry back and forth between the pump building and the tree of valves inside the fence. Seeing the two murderers still roaming the countryside, free to reek havoc wherever they please, ignites my temper, but regardless of my strong emotions, I know Paul is right. If we confront the killers in the dark, they might get away, or worse yet, Paul and I might not get away.

"Hurry up, Oscar. We ain't got all night," Alvin growls.

"I'm hurryin' as fast as I can. You want this done right, or wrong? Why you so jumpy anyway? We ain't going nowhere, not until tomorrow morning," Oscar grumbles, obviously annoyed with Alvin's impatience.

"Don't know why. Got an eerie feeling, like someone's watching us."

"You're not going soft on me are you, Alvin, not after all we been through."

"Hell no. But I can't say I ain't glad we're leaving. That Smith County sheriff's got a bead on you and me. We keep hanging around his territory, and sooner or later, someone's bound to see us and tip him off."

"We don't have to worry about the Smith County sheriff. He's nothing but a lightweight. Segars has him in his shirt pocket."

"You think so? You think the sheriff is on Segars' payroll?"

"Sure. I'll bet the sheriff rakes in more payoff money in a month than we make sweating our balls off for the company all year."

"That ain't right. That just ain't right. Oscar, we gotta ask for a raise."

"You're damn right. And that's the first thing we're gonna do when we get to New Orleans. We're gonna march right into the boss's office and tell him straight out. We ain't gonna whack no more guys until we get us a pay raise. How about giving me a hand here. This blasted valve don't wanna come off."

Grunts of strong powerful men exerting maximum effort permeate the darkness as Alvin and Oscar struggle with the difficult valve. A moment later the valve yields to their strength.

"There. That's the last one. Let's load up and git."

"Suits me. I've seen enough of this place to last me a lifetime. Whatta ya say we head for New Orleans tonight? I hear there's a street fulla whiskey that runs right through downtown. I'd sure like to see that."

"That's Bourbon Street, you ignorant galoot, and it runs through the French Quarter, not downtown."

"I don't care where it runs as long as it's fulla whiskey. Whatta ya say, Oscar? How about we leave tonight?"

"No, we was told to leave tomorrow morning. That's when we'll leave. We'll never get us a raise if we don't follow orders."

"Okay, I suppose I can wait. But I'll still be glad to go. Maybe if we had some beer the time would pass faster. You reckon we could stop and pick up some beer on the way home?"

"Sure, don't see why not. We been working hard tonight. We'll stop and pick us up a couple of six-packs."

Apparently the decision to reward themselves with beer motivates the two men to hurry. They load their tools, gather the disconnected valves and extra sections of pipe, and pitch the items into the bed of their pickup. While Oscar polices the area, scouring the grounds to retrieve any piece of evidence which might indicate they've been here, Alvin turns the pickup around and backs up alongside the pump building. Oscar slams the door shut, locks it and skirts around the pickup to jump in on the passenger side.

Alvin is anxious for his beer. The pickup tires spin, slinging chunks of rock and damp clay out from behind the truck as their vehicle digs out toward the front gate.

Without speaking, Paul and I lie motionless until the red tail lights disappear behind the high grass bordering the dirt roadway.

"Let's follow them. Before they get away," I say, pushing myself up to a standing position.

"I don't know, Rick. Let's not go off half-cocked here. Might be better if we contact the authorities and let them handle this."

"Paul, you heard what they said. The county sheriff is on the take. And they're leaving the state tomorrow. This might be our last chance to nail these low down skunks. Come on. We gotta at least find out where they're hiding."

❖ ❖ ❖ ❖ ❖

MY SPEEDOMETER is pushing ninety when we spot the pickup's tail lights. By the time we reached the highway, Alvin and Oscar were out of sight. Then in the dark, Paul had trouble unlocking the front gate padlock. We were forced to make a choice— whether our culprits turned left or right. Luckily, we made a good guess. Knowing the nearest beer joint is located at the Kilgore city limits helped.

We trail behind the ancient pickup, keeping plenty of distance, so the killers won't suspect they're being followed. When they stop at a Kilgore bar, I continue past and pull into a driveway several hundred yards further down the road. From our observation point Paul and I command a panoramic view of the parking lot and the red pickup parked out front.

"What time you have, Paul?" I ask. The Pontiac's dashboard clock quit working several days ago. I never bothered to have it repaired.

Paul checks his wristwatch. "Ten-twenty-two. You think they'll stay in there until closing time? If so, this could take awhile. Texas bars don't close until twelve on weekdays. But I reckon you know that."

"Not long ago that was the second most important hour of the day."

"You don't have to remind me, Rick. I know what the most important hour was—ten o'clock in the morning, the hour the bars open."

"I'm glad those days are behind me, Paul. Since I stopped drinking, my life has changed for the better."

"They're never behind you, Rick. People like you and me, we stay sober one day at a time. We're one drink away from lying dead drunk in some dark alley."

Our redundant conversation is rudely interrupted by the appearance of Alvin and Oscar outside the bar's front entrance. We watch while they walk to their pickup and crawl in.

Grimly, I reach to flip on the ignition and start the engine.

❖ ❖ ❖ ❖ ❖

AN UNPAINTED picket fence separates the unmarked graveled roadway from an overgrown and neglected yard which fronts the small house where Alvin and Oscar reside. A covered porch extends across the front width of the house. The porch serves little purpose since it is partially hidden behind a high swooping hedge whose thick branches push at the underside of the roof. Exterior walls faced with a faded white asbestos siding add to the dilapidated impression.

With our lights off, Paul and I coasted to a stop here less than a hundred yards from the house. A few minutes earlier we watched the killers swerve into the narrow driveway and park their pickup inside a separate garage building at the rear of the lot. Lights flick on as Alvin and Oscar occupy the house.

"Now we know where they live. Let's go get the police," Paul urges impatiently. He glances at his watch. Evidently he's tired of playing cops and robbers.

"You stay here, Paul. I'm still not certain we can make a murder charge stick. There's a piece of evidence missing. Check your watch and slide over here behind the wheel, in case you need to leave in a hurry. If I'm not back in ten minutes get the hell out of here because you'll know something's gone wrong."

❖ ❖ ❖ ❖ ❖

CROUCHING LOW, I dart swiftly through the wooded area surrounding Alvin and Oscar's property, occasionally using a tree to take cover. Perhaps it's the excitement, perhaps a rush of adrenaline, but I'm breathing hard when I reach a waist-high wire fence which encompasses the small lot. I scale the fence, drop down on all fours and steal slowly across the yard.

When I reach the house, I stay close to the wall, creeping quietly along until I'm directly beneath a window. I raise up slowly and look inside to discover a kitchen area.

On the wall to my left a large white refrigerator provides a bookend for a linoleum-covered counter. The other end of the counter contains a badly stained, white enamel sink. On the opposite wall is a gas range which at an earlier time was white. Now the smoke and grease of a thousand cooked meals tarnish the old stove.

Two six-packs of beer rest atop a small table next to the gas range. Alvin and Oscar live very austere lives. Three metal chairs with ragged vinyl-covered seats make up the remainder of furniture in the room.

Wiping at his arms with a thin dirty towel, Oscar appears in the doorway at the opposite end of the kitchen. His sudden appearance reminds me I have a purpose. I lower my body and sneak across the driveway toward the garage. Glancing back over my shoulder to make sure I haven't been discovered, I quietly pull the garage door open.

Once inside, not wanting to bump into some unseen object or make a noise which might announce my presence, I remain perfectly still while my eyes adjust to the darkness. The pungent odor of oil intermixed with gasoline saturates the stagnant air. Dry limestone gravel which covers the floor adds a musty, dry smell.

The garage is narrow, only wide enough to accommodate one vehicle, but it's deep enough to hold two. My hands grapple for the pickup. I find it and shuffle sideways toward the rear section of the building. A slight gap separates the front end of the pickup from the rear bumper of another car parked in front. In the darkness I grope along the second vehicle, trying to identify the make.

Damn. Why didn't I think to borrow Paul's lighter? Like most alcoholics, he smokes like a fiend. Still, I have to be certain. There's only one solution. I grasp the door handle, push down and jerk the door open. The dome light flashes on.

Yes. Alvin and Oscar are so stupid. Just like I hoped, Max's green and white Willis Jeep is parked inside their garage. Right here is all the evidence we'll need for a murder conviction.

❖ ❖ ❖ ❖ ❖

LOCAL EAST TEXAS POLICE seem to operate under the illusion that crooks work an eight-to-five shift. When Paul and I finally locate the Kilgore police station, it is closed. A sign posted on the front door informs us the station will open tomorrow morning at 7:00 A.M.

Longview, the Gregg County Seat, is less than twenty miles away, but neither of us know the sheriff's name and the Longview police will probably give us the same runaround as the Tyler police, claiming Kilgore is outside their jurisdiction. Frustrated, and with our choices limited, we decide to take our chances with Sheriff Grimes back in Tyler.

❖ ❖ ❖ ❖ ❖

"WHERE'S THE SHERIFF? I've located the men who murdered Max Wagner," I state emphatically to a half-asleep deputy when I barge into the Smith County sheriff's office.

My impassioned announcement startles the young officer whose legs are propped up on the desk in front of his chair. The chair titters backward, but the deputy recovers and lurches forward, his hands searching for a notebook, something to write on so he'll appear professional.

"Sheriff Grimes is in Dallas, but maybe I can help. You say you found these men? And they murdered somebody?"

"Yes, Sheriff Grimes knows all about the murder. He and his deputies fished the victim's body out of the Neches River back in April. You should have a file here somewhere."

"But the sheriff, he's in Dallas attending a law officers' seminar. He won't be back until tomorrow afternoon," the young man advises and stares at me with a blank expression. Not knowing how to handle the situation, he expects me to make a decision.

"That'll be too late. What about Deputy Harris? Can you get in touch with him?"

"Yeah, sure. Mike lives over on Mahon Avenue. You want me to call him?"

During my fevered discussion with the night deputy, Paul has assumed the role of interested observer, allowing me to take charge. While the flustered lawman dials Mike Harris, my friend moves up alongside me.

306

"Rick, I hate to be a party pooper, but it's after eleven. No telling how long it'll take to get a warrant issued and mobilize the deputies. My boss will skin me alive if I show up late tomorrow morning."

"You don't want to stay? We're about to nail those two thugs, Paul."

"I'd like to, but you don't need me to make the arrest. You and the sheriff's deputies can handle things from here."

"Sure, but all this is happening on account of you. Please stay. You deserve the credit."

"Wish I could, but I gotta leave. Maybe someone can run me out to the ballpark before you head back to Kilgore."

"I'll do better than that. Here take my keys. Leave the Pontiac in the parking lot. I'll pick it up later after we have those two in jail."

"Thanks, Rick. And good hunting. Wish I could be in on the kill."

"I'll call you first thing tomorrow morning and give you all the gory details."

"Great. Talk to you then," Paul says, turning to start for the door.

I watch him walk away, thinking how lucky I am to have such a reliable friend. Suddenly I remember something.

"Paul. Wait up. I need one more favor," I shout, calling down the hallway and trotting after him.

"Sure, Rick. Name it. You got it."

"Can you leave the pistol? Oh, and your bullet belt. I may need a gun before we're done tonight."

❖ ❖ ❖ ❖ ❖

DESPITE BEING in bed asleep when we call, Mike Harris springs into action. In less than an hour he has rousted a judge, obtained a search warrant and enlisted two other deputies to accompany us. Shortly after midnight the four of us pile into a patrol car. The trip to Kilgore takes thirty minutes.

"You know how to use that pistol, Mason?" the deputy asks, referring to the holstered forty-four strapped to my waist.

"I think so," I say, removing the forty-four from its holster. "You put the bullets in here—"

"Hey. Leave it in the holster. That thing's liable to go off and kill someone."

"It's not loaded. I wouldn't carry a loaded gun, not in a car full of people."

"Looks loaded to me. Lemme see," the deputy observes, reaching to take the handgun from my lap. He releases a tiny lever, and the firing cylinder snaps open. The cylinder contains six bullets, one in each chamber.

"Thought you said it wasn't loaded. You sure you know about guns, Mason?"

"It's my friend's pistol. I guess I assumed it wasn't loaded," I explain lamely.

"Well, your assuming could get someone killed. Maybe you'd better wait in the car. This'll be tough enough for me and my deputies. We don't wanna be worrying about a civilian running around with a loaded gun."

"But, Mike, these hoodlums tried to kill me. I wanna be in on their arrest."

"I'm sorry, Mason. I understand how important this is to you, but I'm ordering you to stay in the car."

❖ ❖ ❖ ❖ ❖

A SHOT RINGS OUT! In the darkness I hear men yelling. Then another shot. Something's gone wrong. The deputy's plan was to break down the front door and catch Alvin and Oscar off guard, while they were in bed.

A shadowy figure appears on the roadway some thirty yards in front of the patrol car. Not knowing whether it's one of the deputies or one of the crooks, I crouch down in the front seat. Only my eyes are visible above the dashboard. The dark figure is walking fast. He glances back over his shoulder like he's being chased.

My heart beats fast. A cold sweat slickens my palms as I deduce the approaching figure is one of the killers. He's slipped through the dragnet of the law officers. My hand searches for the pistol on the seat beside me. I unsnap the handle strap and withdraw the gun. My unsteady hand nervously searches for the switch on the dashboard, and I flick on the headlights.

Alvin wears only a pair of boxer shorts. His massive, hair-covered body makes him seem even more imposing than I remembered. He's barefooted. Perhaps that's why he chose to make his escape over the gravel roadway rather than though the burr infested woods behind the house. Blinded by the sudden bright glare, he stops in his tracks, raising his arm to shield off the brightness. I grip the pistol tightly and shove open the car door.

"Hold it right there, Alvin. You're under arrest. I have a gun, and I have you covered," I command, sounding like the town marshal in a western movie.

"Don't shoot, mister. I'll come peaceable," Alvin answers, lowering his arm and stepping toward me.

"Drop your gun and put your hands over your head," I say forcefully, referring to a handgun he was carrying when I bathed him in car light. His pistol is now held in a hand hidden behind his back.

"I ain't got no gun. Hey, you got the drop on me. I'm giving myself up." Alvin continues to walk toward me as he speaks. He is less than twenty yards away when I realize what he's up to. I'm fumbling with the safety of Paul's forty-four when Alvin drops to his knees and jerks the gun out from behind his back.

"KABOOM!" Gunfire rings my ears. The car window shatters.

"KABOOM!" A second bullet whistles by my ear, and I locate the safety. Without thinking, I flick it to the off position and pull the trigger. A dull click reminds me Deputy Harris removed the bullet from the firing chamber, after he scolded me for carrying a pistol with the firing pin on a loaded chamber.

"KABOOM!" Alvin's third shot rips through the metal at the top of the car door less than an inch above my head. I cock the forty-four and try again, closing my eyes and squeezing the trigger with all my strength.

"CRACK!" The sudden deafening explosion surprises me. The recoil almost rips the pistol from my hand. I regain control, cock and aim to fire again. Then I see Alvin's gun drop from his hand. For a second he kneels there, his wide eyes gazing at me in disbelief. He topples sideways, his half-naked body crumpling to the gravel pavement.

Mike Harris appears in the ring of illumination provided by the car lights. He pauses to look at me before he strides over to check the body sprawled on the roadway. He kicks Alvin's gun to one side and bends down to check the burly man's pulse.

"You all right, Mason?"

"I think so. How about Alvin there? Is he dead?"

"Not yet, but I'd say his chances of surviving are pretty slim. You hit him right above the heart. Oughta let the slimy snake bleed to death, but I suppose we should get him to a hospital."

"How about Oscar? He get away?"

"No, Glenn and I caught him slithering out a side window. Put up a heck of a fight. Like to broke my jaw, but we finally got him handcuffed. He's on the ground in the front yard. Glenn's guarding him."

"Then we caught 'em both. Mike, you'll probably get a medal for rounding up these two characters."

"Well, maybe. When the sheriff finds out I'm responsible for one of his deputies getting shot, he may not agree."

"Shot? Someone got shot?"

"Yeah, Ronnie's in pretty bad shape. Your friend Alvin gunned him down when he and Ronnie locked horns at the back door. That Alvin's a crack shot. Lucky for you he didn't get off a shot before you nailed him."

"But he did. My safety jammed. Alvin shot at me three times before I got off my first shot."

"Then you oughta thank your lucky stars, Coach. You're a mighty lucky man. That should be you lying on the road instead of Alvin."

❖ ❖ ❖ ❖ ❖

POOR PLANNING presents us with an unexpected dilemma. Our patrol car had plenty of room for four men, but we neglected to

310

consider the possibilities after our raid. With Oscar in handcuffs and Alvin's practically lifeless carcass in need of immediate medical attention, our party includes too many bodies. After a brief discussion we decide to load Oscar into the back seat of the patrol car, with Glenn and me riding up front. Alvin and a wounded Ronnie Dobbs ride with Mike in Max Wagner's Jeep. Our short caravan steers straight for the Kilgore Hospital emergency entrance.

❖ ❖ ❖ ❖ ❖

SOMEWHERE CLOSE to six o'clock Wednesday morning, Glenn and I deliver Oscar to the Smith County sheriff's office. With both Ronnie Dobbs and Alvin undergoing emergency surgery, Mike Harris stays behind at the Kilgore Hospital. We wait around only long enough to see Oscar booked, escorted to a jail cell and safely locked inside. Then Glenn taxis me to the ballpark, drops me off and heads back to Kilgore.

❖ ❖ ❖ ❖ ❖

"RICKY, WHERE have you been?" Kaye moans sleepily, as I wiggle into bed beside her.

"I'm sorry, hon. My meeting took longer than I expected. Go back to sleep. I'll explain everything later."

"I waited and waited. I thought we had a date."

"We did, but something came up. I'll tell you about it later," I mumble, trying to stay awake, but my eyelids are so heavy. I'm asleep the second my head touches my pillow.

❖ ❖ ❖ ❖ ❖

"WHACK!" Something smacks hard against my cheek, interrupting my sound sleep.

"WHACK!" The object strikes me in the face again. Severe pain replaces a peaceful dream as I struggle to come fully awake.

311

"You were with another woman. Get out of my house, Richard Mason. You hear me? I want you out." Kaye stands over me, my shoe in her hand.

"Kaye, what's got into you?" I complain groggily. Evidently she has no intention of explaining. She draws back to clobber me again.

"I won't live with a man who cheats on me. I want you out of my bed and out of my house."

My infuriated wife wields the shoe menacingly, waiting to hear my alibi but ready to hit me again if she's not satisfied. I have a legitimate excuse, but nevertheless, I keep my hand up to protect my face from another shoe attack.

"Please don't hit me, Kaye. That shoe really hurts. Besides, I'm innocent. I haven't been with another woman. I promise. You're the only woman I care about."

"Then where were you? Why did you stay out all night?" She drops the shoe and begins to cry. Huge tears roll down her cheeks. "I was so worried. I waited and waited, but you didn't come home. I thought maybe those awful men had killed you."

"Kaye, a lot of strange things have happened to me lately. If you'll slip on a robe and put on a pot of coffee, I'll tell you everything."

❖ ❖ ❖ ❖ ❖

BLEARY-EYED and sipping at a hot cup of black coffee, I tell Kaye the entire story—about Max Wagner's disappearance and about my initial confrontation with Alvin and Oscar. When I tell the part about being dumped in the river, she reaches to touch my hand but does not interrupt. She gasps in disbelief as I describe how I died and appeared before the judges who couldn't make up their minds and decided to send me back. She seems relieved when I explain that segment may have been a hallucination and possibly the reason I escaped was because the wet ropes came loose. I complete the story by telling her how Paul and I visited the oil lease, discovered the oil skimming, and ran into the two killers.

"So you were out with the sheriff all night. Ricky, why didn't you tell me?"

"I wasn't with the sheriff, Kaye. I was with the sheriff's deputies. It's rather complicated."

"So you helped catch the men who murdered your friend. What's so complicated about that? Why didn't you tell me you'd be with Paul? I would have understood."

"Well, it was where we were going that caused the problem. The oil lease is out near Swinneytown."

"So?"

"So, the oil lease is located on property belonging to your father. These two thugs, Alvin and Oscar, evidently they work for him."

Kaye stares at me, her lovely face stricken with anxiety. Sharing this knowledge with my wife could spell the end of our marriage, but there is a redeeming aspect. This is the first time I've been completely honest with this woman I love—since the day I stepped into that ice cold lake and took her in my arms.

CHAPTER SIXTEEN

ONSIDERING THE ANIMOSITY between the two
cities, it's amazing that Sherman and Denison have agreed to
be represented by one baseball club. Their ill feelings are
long simmering. Way back in 1870, Sherman flat-out refused to
bestow their blessing on a proposal by the Missouri-Kansas-Texas
Railroad to sell investment bonds which would bring the railroad
through Sherman and make that city the Katy's North Texas railhead.
Sherman's rejection forced the railroad to seek another location for
their terminal. The M.K.T. selected a site ten miles north and named
the new town after George Denison, the railroad's vice-president. So
actually, Denison was built to spite Sherman's uppity citizenry.

What's even more astounding is the team name they've chosen.
Even though the two cities are only ten miles apart, no one could
possibly mistake the two for *Twin* cities. Sherman is the county seat
of Grayson County, a center of wealth, full of bankers, prosperous
merchants, government employees and politicians—a civilized city.
Denison is a blue collar railroad town with a wild and wooly
reputation. Up until the mid-forties, Denison's Main Street was lined
with saloons and brothels. Bootlegging was one of the major sources
of employment.

Last season was the Twins' first year to compete in the Big State
League. They finished seventh, forty games behind the league leading

314

Texarkana Bears. Glancing over the Twins' lineup, it's evident they don't have many top notch players. The Twins' ballpark is one of the worst in the league. And even by combining their populations, Sherman and Denison have the second smallest fan base. But despite all the negatives, their grandstands are jam-packed night after night with enthusiastic, excited baseball fans.

Heck, maybe baseball can soothe over even the harshest of feelings.

❖ ❖ ❖ ❖ ❖

EXCEPT FOR ITS NAME, Sherman is no different than a hundred other small town county seats. The courthouse square is bordered with parking meters and cars angled neatly between painted diagonal stripes. Two and three-story brick buildings, which house numerous downtown owner-operated retail shops and other local businesses, line the outer periphery of the square. Each building faces the majestic old courthouse, perhaps paying homage for its role as the city's predominate rainmaker.

Turning right off Highway 82, our driver maneuvers the bus along the dark brick pavement of Travis Avenue. As we pass, people on the sidewalks stop and stare at our bus and at the curious young men with their noses pressed against the windows.

When Travis dead ends into Highway 75, we turn right, and the bus accelerates. A few minutes later, midway between Sherman and Denison, we catch our first glimpse of towering floodlights protruding above the Twins' baseball stadium. Our driver reduces speed and swings onto a wide gravel-paved parking area. Swerving to avoid a large chughole filled with muddy water, he cuts diagonally across the parking lot and brakes to a halt at the front gate.

Grasshoppers, crickets, and dead June bugs blanket the area around the entrance gate. Creating a repugnant spectacle similar to a biblical story told in the book of Exodus, swarms of insects have literally invaded the Twins' ballpark. Grimly, my beleaguered warriors shoulder their gear and tramp across the asphalt paved expanse inside the fence. We step gingerly, but it's impossible to ignore the appalling popping sounds of bugs being squashed beneath our shoes.

Inside the dressing quarters the situation is almost as bad. Before they can store their gear, players are forced to sweep dead and dying crickets from their locker compartments.

❖ ❖ ❖ ❖ ❖

"IT'S A BAD OMEN. That's what it is, Rick. A bad omen," Whitey moans, waving his hands to swat at the host of flying insects fluttering through our dugout. After the stadium floodlights were turned on, a myriad of gigantic mayflies flooded the air. Now, a few minutes before game time, the lights are practically obliterated by huge swarms of the pesky flying critters.

"Nonsense, Whitey. I talked to Billy Capps, Sherman's manager. He says the bugs migrated in here from Oklahoma late yesterday afternoon. Has something to do with a cold front which stalled out up near McAlester. Caused some kind of temperature inversion. Cold air on bottom. Hot air on top. That's what brought in all the bugs."

"Temperature inversion. Well kiss my Aunt Sally. And here I was thinking it was something bad. Like one of our infielders might inhale a bug when he stoops down to field a grounder, or one of our outfielders might lose sight of a high fly ball up there in the insect maze and catch one square between the eyeballs."

"There's no need for dramatics. I get the picture," I say chuckling at Whitey's colorful assessment of our situation. "Surely, you're not suggesting we cancel the game? If we insist the game be called on account of bugs, we'll be the brunt of every baseball joke for the rest of the season."

"You darn right I am. Playing with all these nasty little critters swarming around is worse than playing in a rainstorm. It ain't natural to play baseball and dodge bugs at the same time. The way our luck's running something real bad is bound to happen."

❖ ❖ ❖ ❖ ❖

CHOKING, COUGHING and occasionally half-swallowing one of the annoying flying creatures, French works Garza, the Twins' pitcher, for a lead-off walk. Akins follows with a sharp single to left field, advancing French to second. Gregory runs the count to three and two then check swings on a high hanging curve for a called ball four. Bases loaded. Nobody out.

"Peppy, you warmed up?" I ask, twisting around to glance at the disorderly string of players lounging on our bench.

"You bet, Skipper. I'm always ready."

"Then grab a bat and get your butt on the ballfield. We've got ducks on the pond," I scold harshly and turn back to wink at my assistant. Bugs or no bugs, there's reason to smile. We haven't seen the bases loaded in a long, long time.

"Whitey, call the press box. Tell 'em we're substituting Swanson for Connors at first base."

Swinging his bat vigorously, Peppy steps to the plate. His jaw is squared. Tiny beads of perspiration trickle down his face. Like an enraged bull, his feet paw at the loose dirt inside the batter's box.

Pitching from a stretch position, Sherman's hurler checks the runners on first and third, winds and fires.

"CRACK!" Resembling the sharp report of a high-powered rifle, the sound of wood impacting in solid contact with a rock hard baseball jolts the stadium. Sherman infielders rise from crouched positions to turn and watch the baseball soar high above their teammate stationed deep in center field, bisect the thick cloud of swarming mayflies and disappear into the darkness above the lighted arena.

For a few brief seconds the bleachers remain silent. Then oohs and aahs ripple though the grandstands as the significance of the mighty blow sinks in. Several fans stand and begin clapping. Following their lead, the entire congregation rises, clapping and cheering, showing appreciation. Even these hostile home fans are impressed by such a colossal grand slam homer.

Grinning from ear to ear like a happy six-year-old, Peppy tips his hat ever so slightly as he makes the turn at third and heads for home where French, Akins and Gregory are waiting to congratulate him.

"Holy Toledo. What a hit," Whitey exclaims, slapping me on the back and hopping up and down as our players pour out of the dugout to join the festivities at home plate.

"Don't think I've ever seen a baseball hit so far. Man, that was worth the price of admission all by itself. Come on. Lets go shake Peppy's hand," I howl, happy for Peppy, but also tremendously pleased with myself. What these Sherman-Denison spectators have witnessed is the exact scenario I imagined when I promised Peppy I'd get him another shot at the big leagues.

❖ ❖ ❖ ❖ ❖

FAILING TO FOLLOW the example of Peppy's impressive home run rocket, our bats fizzle. Epps taps a slow roller to second. Neuendorff pops up to short, and Bruzga strikes out to end the inning. Nevertheless, when Charlie Davis takes the mound in the bottom of the first, we enjoy a commanding 4-0 lead. Using only twelve pitches, our fireballing southpaw sets the top of the Twins' batting lineup down in order.

Davis holds Sherman's potent offense scoreless until the bottom of the fourth. With the count at 2 and 2, Taylor, the Twins' second baseman, dribbles a weak grounder to Bruzga at short for the first out. Frustrated by the easy put-out, Sherman's manager goes to his bench, subbing in Bo Dyer, a speedy outfielder the Twins optioned in from the Sooner State League only yesterday. Dyer immediately demonstrates why the Twins were anxious to recruit him. He nails Davis' first pitch, sending it screaming down the third base line past Mel Neuendorff. Only good hustle by Gregory in left field and an excellent throw to second keeps Dyer from stretching his hit into a double.

Possibly hoping success will breed success, Capps goes to his bench again, bringing in Dean Stafford to hit in place of Parker, the Twins' right fielder.

"What's the skinny on this fellow Stafford?" I ask Whitey, as we watch Sherman's pinch hitter take his warm-up swings and stroll to the plate. "We got anything on him?"

Whitey thumbs through a stack of scouting notes, finds the batter's name, and uses his index finger to trace through the statistics he and Matilda compiled prior to our road trip.

"Says here he's a long ball hitter and a sucker for an inside pitch. Stafford's a big swinger. Strikes out a lot. Hardly ever walks."

"Let's pitch him low and inside then. Signal Nelms. Nothing but fastballs, low and inside."

Davis' first delivery is eyeball high and about six inches inside. In anxious anticipation Stafford steps forward, sees the ball is way inside, and barely bails out in time to keep his brains from being splattered across the infield.

"No! No!" I scream angrily in the direction of the pitching mound. "Low. Low and over the inside corner."

I know it's a mistake to verbally telegraph my pitching strategy. Prudent managers silently and secretly signal their instructions to players, but we've lost four in a row. I want no mistakes in relaying my message. Matilda says Stafford can't hit an inside pitch, and she's never wrong. Davis nods, indicating he understands.

Checking the runner on first, Davis winds, rears way back and catapults a picture perfect fastball, low and inside. I can't help but smile as I watch Sherman's hitter take the bait. An overanxious Stafford shifts his weight forward and swings his bat mightily.

"CRACK!" A sharp pop explodes across the playing field. At third base Mel Neuendorff raises his glove, but all he can do is wave goodbye. The hard hit baseball sails high above his head.

"How did that happen? That pitch was perfect," I say, turning to Whitey after we watch the baseball clear the left field fence. "Didn't she say he couldn't hit an inside pitch?"

"Yep, that's what's on the stat sheet, but what say we pitch Stafford high and inside next time he comes up?"

❖ ❖ ❖ ❖ ❖

IN THE TOP of the sixth Hal Epps smashes a line drive through the gap in left center for a stand-up two-bagger. Neuendorff follows with a looping single into right, driving in Epps and stretching our lead to three runs.

The Twins come right back. After Davis strikes out their lead-off batter, Sherman validates why they lead the league in hitting. A triple and back to back singles score one run and leave runners at the corners. A sizzling line drive double which bounces against the center field fence brings in another. A flawless relay from Akins to Bruzga to Nelms cuts down the Twins' runner trying to score from first and keeps Sherman from tying the game.

With two out and a man on second, Davis seems rattled. He paws at the mound, toes the rubber, checks the runner on second, glances toward home plate and steps back.

"Charlie looks tired, Rick. Maybe you better check on him," Whitey advises.

"Damn. I was hoping he could go seven innings. Signal the bullpen to warm up. We'll bring in Burns. He hasn't pitched since Saturday," I say, despondently laying my scorebook on the bench behind me. My battle-weary bullpen resembles a war zone, shell-shocked after being bombarded for four consecutive nights. Not one of my starters lasted more than five innings in the four games we lost to Gainesville. I call timeout and slowly climb the dugout steps.

After a brief reprieve the insects have returned with a vengeance. Wave after wave of the tiny winged missiles pelt my face as I cross the chalked third base line and walk toward the pitching hill. I'm forced to cover my nose to keep from inhaling the bothersome little brutes. Davis suffers a similar affliction. Using his gloved hand, he bats at the air and leaves the mound to meet me halfway across the infield.

"What's the problem, Coach?" Davis questions.

"You look tired, Charlie. Reckon we better take you out."

"But I'm not tired. My arm feels fine. Lemme stay in. This next batter is a sucker for a curve. He oughta be an easy out."

"You sure you're okay? From the dugout you look like you're outta gas, stumbling around the mound, kicking at the dirt. Thought maybe you were wasted and trying to buy some time."

"Naw, I'm fine. I'm just worried about where I'm gonna sleep tonight. My wife's folks drove in from Arkansas today. Gonna be staying with us a few days. My mother-in-law's a real doozie. She ain't too happy about her daughter marrying a baseball player. You get along with your mother-in-law, Skipper?"

"No, my wife's mother died before we met."

"You're dang lucky. A bitchy mother-in-law can make a man's life downright miserable. I sure wish the team was bunking here in Sherman tonight instead of driving back to Tyler. Make my life a lot less complicated."

"Yeah, me too. Now how about we get this next man out."

Mothers-in-law, I think to myself as I walk back to the dugout. Perhaps I should be more sympathetic with Davis, but I'd trade my conniving father-in-law for two interfering mothers-in-law any day.

"Charlie all right?" Whitey asks when I return to the dugout.

"He's fine. Just worried about his mother-in-law. She's in Tyler, visiting for a few days."

"Oh," Whitey responds knowingly.

❖ ❖ ❖ ❖ ❖

A LOUD SNAP succeeded by a moaning wail, follows Davis' delivery. Sherman's hitter backpedals out of the batter's box to reveal a sweat-soaked body writhing on the ground. The contorted body belongs to Jess Nelms.

Whitey and I leap from the dugout and run to check on him.

"What's wrong, Jess?" I ask, pushing a curious umpire aside and squatting down beside my injured receiver.

"My hand. I busted my hand." Nelms' distorted face is laced with deep lines of intense pain.

"Here, let me see. Maybe it's just a bruise," I say, taking his left hand and gently running my fingers across the callused palm. A sharp bone straining hard against the thick skin confirms my worst fears. The bone directly beneath his thumb is broken.

"Dang mayflies. One flew up my nose. Made me lose my concentration," Nelms groans.

"Whatta you think, Rick? He gonna be okay?" Whitey asks hopefully, kneeling down beside me.

"No, his hand's broken. We'd better call an ambulance. Looks like Jess is gonna be outta commission for a spell."

"I knew it. I knew them darn bugs was a bad omen. Didn't I tell you they was a bad omen? Damn."

"Yeah, Whitey, you told me," I concede. "Damn."

"And me smack in the middle of a six game hitting streak," Nelms grumbles sadly and adds his exclamation mark to the profane oratory. "Damn!"

❖ ❖ ❖ ❖ ❖

EXCEPT FOR the late innings of a few games when we've held a commanding lead, Jess Nelms has been behind the plate to receive every pitch this season. His quick arm, his dependable bat and his durability have been a major contributor to the early success of this ball club. His absence will leave a huge void.

Nonetheless, injuries are a part of baseball. How a manager handles the loss of a key player is a measure of his managing ability. While we wait for an ambulance to transport our catcher to the Denison hospital and while Whitey helps Nelms ice down his hand, I cross my fingers and survey our bench. There's not a quality catcher among the group. My surveillance stops when I come to a boyish face partially hidden behind a neatly trimmed mustache.

"Frank, you ever catch a ball game?" I ask my multi-talented Cajun player.

"No sir, but I'm willing to try," Johnson responds optimistically. Like any reserve, he's anxious to play no matter what the position.

"Find yourself some catching gear then. You're our catcher."

"Yes sir," Johnson answers, leaping to his feet. In his eagerness Frank trips over his cousin Herb Cates, but eventually, he makes his way down the bench to the equipment bag.

❖ ❖ ❖ ❖ ❖

EVEN THOUGH we have runners in scoring position in both the eighth and ninth frames, somehow we manage not to score. A double play and a pop fly terminate two crucial opportunities to cushion our one run lead.

Only a handful of fans remain in the bleachers to watch the Twins take their final turn at bat. In spite of the close contest, the insect invasion has discouraged all but a few die-hard Sherman boosters from braving it out to see the game end.

With Davis running on empty, I go to my bullpen, bringing in Matt Burns to pitch the final frame. A ground out to French at second and a sky high blooper to Akins in short center leave us one out away from our first victory in almost a week.

Then Bo Dyer, who jump-started the Twins' fourth inning rally, collects his second hit of the night, sending a two-hopper up the middle to put the tying run on first.

"Stafford's up next. Maybe we oughta walk him and pitch to Hawes. Remember, Stafford hit a homer back in the fourth," Whitey cautions, checking the scorebook in his lap.

"No, Hawes is dangerous too. Already has two hits tonight. Let's pitch to Stafford. Davis struck him out his last time up. Burns can handle him. One more out and we'll have our losing streak behind us."

To make certain Burns understands my intentions, I call timeout and trot out to the pitching mound.

"High and inside. You got that Matt? High and inside."

"Yes sir. He won't see nothing but fastballs from me. He won't see nothing if he don't duck fast."

Burns' first pitch is a magnificent example of perfect control. The baseball whizzes by Stafford's head at eyeball level, but in spite of the bad location, the Twins' slugger takes a half-hearted swing anyway.

A second pitch in the same location yields the same result. Stafford is off balance and halfway out of the batter's box when he swings, running the count to 0 and two. I cross my fingers and hold my breath. One more strike and this miserable losing streak is over.

"CRACK!" I gasp in disbelief as the hitter steps back and swings at a pitch six inches above his head. At first the baseball appears to be an easy pop fly to right field, then it gathers momentum. Hal Epps, playing right field, gives chase until the ball clears the fence. My players stand with mouths agape and watch our victory slip away, dumfounded by our sudden change of fortune.

"That ball was way over his head, nowhere close to the strike zone. Why would he swing at a bad pitch like that?" I lament. My stomach churns with a sinking feeling of despair.

"Danged if I know, Rick. Seems like we can't do nothing right. Looks like we're caught in an endless quicksand of losing. The harder we struggle, the deeper we sink."

❖ ❖ ❖ ❖ ❖

THE MORNING TELEGRAPH tells the whole story. How, after a surprising start, the East Texans have reverted to their losing ways. How, after the loss of their starting catcher who was in the midst of a six game hitting streak, there's little hope the team can get back on track—not unless the owners bring in some new talent and replace their inept manager.

I sip my coffee and do a slow burn. What does it take to please this town? Okay, so my baseball team has lost five in a row, but three of those losses were in the final inning, and by only one run. Sure we're on a losing streak, but we're still in third place. We've won more games than five other Big State clubs. And third place is a darn sight higher than where the Tyler franchise was this time last year.

Frustrated and upset, I fold the paper and shove it toward the man sitting next to me at the quick service counter. I chug down the last of my coffee and storm out the front door.

Mary has to flag me down in the parking lot to remind me I haven't paid.

❖ ❖ ❖ ❖ ❖

"SMITH COUNTY sheriff's office," a deep voice answers.

I'm calling to check on the status of the two killers we arrested night before last. Strangely, there was no mention of our Kilgore adventure in this morning's newspaper. Sheriff Grimes is generally anxious for any kind of publicity. Normally after an arrest of this magnitude, you'd see his picture plastered all across the front page.

"Hello. I'd like to speak to Deputy Mike Harris," I say, leaning back in my chair and propping my feet on my desk.

"Sure thing," the voice replies pleasantly. "Can you hold a minute? Mike's back in the storeroom. Can I say who's calling?"

"This is Rick Mason. Tell him I'm calling to inquire about the fellows we arrested in Kilgore."

"Oh, yeah, I've heard about you. You and Mike caused quite a stink. Never saw Sheriff Grimes so mad before. Hang on. I'll see if I can locate him."

"A stink? Whatta you mean a stink. . . ," I question angrily, but no one hears. The voice on the other end has gone to search for Mike Harris.

While I wait for Harris to come on the line, a thousand questions race through my mind. In the background I hear the repetitious pecking of a typewriter and muffled voices. Occasionally the ear-piercing squawk of a mobile radio dispatch interrupts the monotonous tranquility.

"Hello, Deputy Harris speaking. How can I help you?"

"Good morning, Mike. Rick Mason here. Thought I'd check in. See how things were going."

"Oh. Hi, Coach. Well, to be honest, not real good. When Sheriff Grimes came back from Dallas and found out one of his deputies was shot, he threw a hissing fit. Blamed me for acting impulsively. He's put me on administrative leave. Looks like I may lose my job. I was packing my things when you called."

"Mike, I'm sorry. I figured the sheriff would be delighted to see those two killers behind bars."

"Yeah, me too. But instead, he was mad as hell. I don't know what's going on. We haven't brought charges against either of them yet."

"No charges? Mike, that doesn't make sense. Those guys murdered Max Wagner, and they tried to kill me. No telling how many other murders they're responsible for."

"That's the way I see it, but the sheriff, he sees it different. Says we got no proof they killed anyone."

"What about the Willis Jeep we found in their garage? That should be plenty of proof. That's Wagner's car, at least it was before those two bushwhacked him and dumped him in the river."

"The jeep may not be much use as evidence. Seems like Wagner sold the vehicle to your buddy Alvin before he disappeared. A bill of sale and a request for change of title were filed with the county clerk's office two weeks ago."

The deputy's information stuns me. My feet topple off the desk. I sit up straight and lean forward, using body language to express my outrage.

"What about me? I can testify against them. That oughta be enough to convict them."

A long pause develops while Harris considers his response.

"My testimony should be all you need. Don't you agree?" I repeat.

"I'm sorry, Coach. The sheriff doesn't think he can get a conviction on your testimony alone. Says you have too much history."

"History?"

"You know—brawling, drinking. I'm not saying I agree with the sheriff, but you do have a reputation."

"I suppose I do. But we need to make sure those two stay in jail. So what about the deputy they shot? Can't we hold 'em for that? By the way, how's Ronnie doing?"

"Ronnie's gonna recover. Should be back to work in a week or so. The sheriff plans to move him and Alvin to Mother Francis Hospital here in Tyler. May be a few more days before we can move your friend Alvin. You shot him up pretty bad."

"Yeah, but now I wish I'd finished the job while I had the chance. If the sheriff cuts him and Oscar loose, my life won't be worth a plug nickel. What about shooting the deputy? Can't we press charges for that?"

"I'm not sure. The sheriff says the D.A. may not be able to make that stick. Says Alvin and Oscar have a plausible case for self defense, on account of us kicking down their door without notifying them who we were."

"If you'd warned them you were coming, we'd all be dead. Those men were armed to the teeth. We're lucky Ronnie Dobbs was the only one got shot."

"I agree, but Sheriff Grimes makes the calls around here. Right now, I'm worried about keeping my job. I got a wife and three kids to feed, so I'm not gonna argue with whatever he decides. Listen, Coach, I need to go. Sheriff Grimes wants me outta here before noon."

"Sure, I understand. But before you hang up, answer one more question. A bill of sale—doesn't someone have to notarize a bill of sale, before it's legal?"

"No, not always, it depends on the item sold, but I see your point. A bill of sale for an automobile is almost always notarized, especially if someone's applying for a new title."

"Did anyone notice who notarized the transfer papers for Wagner's vehicle?"

"Oh, sure. That was the first thing the sheriff checked out."

"You remember the person's name who performed the notary?"

"Sure do. Sharon Williams notarized the sale. I know her. Goes to my church. A real fine lady."

"So you believe the signatures and the notary were legitimate?"

"No question about it. Sharon works for your father-in-law at the DeSoto Mart. She notarizes car sales all the time. Nobody could make her do anything that wasn't strictly on the up and up."

❖ ❖ ❖ ❖ ❖

OUR DAILY COMMUTE to Texoma and back doesn't allow much time for playing detective. It's a quarter to twelve when I finish my telephone conversation with Mike Harris. Our bus leaves at two. Whitey should be here any minute to help re-pack our baseball gear, but maybe I can squeeze in a quick call to Paul.

"Operator, I want to place a collect call to a Mister Paul Matlock in Dallas. The number is Emerson 4477. My name is Rick Mason." I feel guilty about calling collect, but charging the call to this phone makes it too easy for someone to trace. It's bad enough my life is in danger. No point in jeopardizing Paul's life too.

I wait patiently while the operator negotiates through the telephone receptionist, talks to Paul, and obtains his approval to reverse the charges.

"Your party is on the line," the operator advises.

"Hey, Paul. Thanks for accepting my call."

"Rick, I've been worried about you. Are you okay?"

"Except for getting my butt kicked on the baseball diamond night after night, I'm fine."

"Yes, I know about your team's troubles. I've been following your games in the Dallas paper. How'd the caper in Kilgore turn out? Hope you have those two hoodlums in jail."

"Oscar's locked up in the Smith County jail. Alvin's in the Kilgore Hospital. That's what I called about. . ."

Quickly, I fill him in on the events which occurred after his departure—the pre-dawn raid in Kilgore and the gunfight which produced a wounded deputy and ended with me gunning down Alvin on the unpaved street. After I relate the details of this morning's conversation with Mike Harris, Paul interrupts.

"Rick, this is much too big for the two of us. Sounds like the sheriff might turn those killers loose. If he does, they'll probably come after you."

"That's what I think. That's why I called collect. They might check my telephone calls to see who I've talked to. I don't want to get you involved."

328

"But I am involved, and with my testimony and the evidence we discovered at the oil lease, we can put those two and your father-in-law away for a long, long time."

"You sure, Paul? I wouldn't want you to get any deeper in this mess, not unless we're absolutely certain we can nail these guys."

"I've got it—everything we need. Yesterday, after we signed the contract on that big project, I stayed late and put it all together."

"But who can we give it to? Who can we trust?"

"I know a man. He belongs to our South Dallas Chapter. He's strictly AA, so he knows how to keep his mouth shut. Works for the State Railroad Commission. Just say the word, and I'll call him."

"Do it, Paul. Do it right now, before I change my mind."

❖ ❖ ❖ ❖ ❖

ON THURSDAY NIGHT Sherman-Denison ekes out another one run win, coming from behind to score three runs in the bottom of the eighth. We load the bases in the top of the ninth only to have Peppy Swanson hit into a double play and end the game.

After suffering six consecutive losses, my once-confident gladiators are completely decimated. An afternoon in the Tyler Public Library would seem like a wild orgy compared to our post game bus ride back home.

❖ ❖ ❖ ❖ ❖

AS USUAL, I'm running late. Our bus for Texoma leaves at two. I swing the Pontiac into the parking lot and brake to a stop near the front entrance. A black four-door sedan is parked a few spaces away. The automobile faces the street, its rear bumper only inches from the stadium fence. While I slide out and lock my doors, a rear window on the sedan cracks slightly.

"Coach Mason," a deep throaty voice beckons from within the darkened interior.

"Yes," I answer, absentmindedly glancing toward the locker room, checking to see if the door is unlocked. Looks like Whitey's late too. Most likely the entire squad will wait until the last minute to straggle in today. None of us are looking forward to another long bus ride.

"Could you spare a few minutes? We need to talk."

"I'm kinda busy. What's this about?"

The rear car door swings open. Two men dressed in western attire occupy the back seat.

"Listen, Mason. We ain't got all day. Either get in the car, or we'll come throw you in."

"Hey, I'm not looking for trouble. Who are you guys anyway?"

"Texas Rangers. Now get in, before Joe here gets nasty."

For a second I consider making the men show me some identification. Why should I believe they're Texas Rangers? An angry scowl on Joe's face convinces me to dismiss the idea. I circle the car and crawl into the front seat.

"Frisk him, Joe. Make sure he's clean," the man sharing the back seat with Joe commands.

"There's no need for that. I don't carry. . ." Before I can complete my sentence, Joe has an arm around my throat, pinning my back against the backrest.

"Hey, you're hurting me," I complain. "Let go and I'll cooperate."

"Shut up and keep still, Mason. Let Joe finish. Then you can talk all you want."

Keeping me pinned tightly against the seat, Joe uses his free hand to pat at my shirt and check my trouser legs for weapons. When he's satisfied I'm unarmed, he releases his strangle hold and slumps into the back seat.

"He's clean," Joe advises.

"I coulda told you that, if you'd asked," I object angrily. Joe's throat hold was like a vice, temporarily cutting off my circulation. I move my arms and shift around in the seat, trying to get my blood moving.

"Sorry, Mason. We deal with a lot of weird characters. We have to be careful."

"You mind if we introduce ourselves? My name is Richard Mason. You can call me Rick. If you're gonna joust me around, I'd at least like to know your names."

"Great, now you wanna get friendly. Alright, the fellow there next to you in the front seat is Tom. You already met Joe. My name is Sam."

"No last names? Don't you people have last names?"

"Of course we do. But for the time being, it'll be better if we keep our business on a first name basis."

"That's fine with me. How about showing me a badge, so I'll know you're who you say you are?"

"Dammit, Mason. You're sure a pain in the ass," Sam growls and turns to his companion in the back seat. "Show him a badge, Joe, so we can get on with this."

"Rick. My name is Rick," I declare. Joe produces a badge, and I examine it carefully. When I reach to touch it, he quickly withdraws the shiny medallion and hides it away inside his coat pocket.

"You satisfied?"

"I suppose so. Okay, tell me what you wanna know."

"We have in our possession information concerning an oil skimming operation here in Smith County. We have sketches, drawings, itemized lists of equipment, and detailed calculations. Even have a graph showing a monthly estimate of oil barrels pirated. What we don't have are names and places. We understand you're the man who can supply that information."

Paul is so meticulous, so damn thorough, always the prolific engineer. I can only imagine how confusing the materials he prepared must be to this group of rough and tumble lawmen. A vision of these three diligently pouring over Paul's charts and diagrams strikes me as terribly funny. I cover my mouth with my hand, trying not to laugh.

"What's the matter, Mason? You think this is some kinda joke?" Tom asks harshly, breaking his self-imposed silence. His somber expression assures me there is no room for humor in this conversation.

331

"No. No. Just a gas pain. Reckon I ate something that don't agree with me," I stammer, trying to look serious, but inside I'm laughing my ass off.

In a matter of minutes I retell my story of Max, Alvin, Oscar, Clyde, Paul, and the sheriff. When I imply the oil theft and Max's murder both point to a crime syndicate based in New Orleans, Sam scoffs at my suspicions. However, when I suggest the sheriff might set Alvin and Oscar free, his reaction is loud and immediate.

"Like hell he will. You say he hasn't charged either of these scoundrels with a crime?"

"No. Alvin's still in the Kilgore Hospital. Oscar's incarcerated in the county jail. But as far as I know, neither of them has been officially arraigned."

"Now what about the property? Can you give us an exact location?"

"Sure. The property is deeded in the name of C. S. Enterprises. Tract 36G, George Maxwell Survey, Abstract A-14. I don't know what that means, but it's etched in my mind. Doubt if I'll ever forget it."

"Tract 36G, Maxwell Survey. Write that down, Joe," Sam instructs his backseat partner then looks at me. "Okay, Mason. That'll give us enough information to get our investigation started. We'll get back to you in a few days."

"What about Alvin and Oscar? Any chance you can convince Sheriff Grimes to keep them in jail?"

"That's our next stop. Once we have a friendly little chat with your sheriff, I doubt if Alvin and Oscar will be bothering anyone for a long time."

The ranger's declaration is like music to my ears.

❖ ❖ ❖ ❖ ❖

UNFORTUNATELY, I have plenty of other worries. On Friday night the Twins harness my East Texans again, concluding a three-game sweep and shoving us deeper into our sea of misery.

CHAPTER SEVENTEEN

A FLAT TIRE ten miles south of Greenville compounded our frustration of dropping three straight games to Sherman-Denison and added an hour to our travel time. It's almost three in the morning when the bus pulls up alongside our home ballpark's front gate. Dog tired and discouraged, the men disembark slowly, funneling out the bus doorway with heads lowered to greet anxious wives and family members in hushed whispers. A quick kiss, a half-hearted hug, then they scurry to their cars, perhaps hoping a hasty exit will somehow dissociate them from the awful stigma of losing.

Whitey and I are also anxious to leave. We unload our equipment and stash the bags just inside the locker room door.

Tired as we are, there'll be no rest, no time to regroup. The red-hot Texarkana Bears will be in town tomorrow night. This past week they've been on a tear, winning four in a row to move into third place, a game ahead of my fading East Texans.

With a heavy heart and eyes I can hardly hold open, I round the corner at Houston and Vine, turn left on Williams Court and coast to a stop at the curb in front of my rented duplex. Inside, Kaye will be asleep. I cut the lights, turn off the engine and consider whether I should wake her. I need to hold her, find solace for my tortured soul.

"Don't get out. We need to talk," a raspy voice whispers through the open window on the passenger side.

"Clyde! Where did you come from?"

"My car's parked down the street a piece. I need your help, Rick. You're the only one I can turn to. Will you help me?"

"Sure, but can it wait 'til later? I'm beat. We got our butts kicked again tonight."

"Yes, I heard. But no, this can't wait. We have to do it tonight."

"Do what, Clyde? What could be so important it can't wait until tomorrow?"

Even in the darkness I can see the anguish on Segars' face while he considers his answer.

"Rick, I wouldn't be here in the middle of the night begging you to help if this wasn't urgent. My future, your wife's future, my whole family's future depends on the job we have to do. Believe me. We either do it now, or everyone associated with me gets hurt—Kaye, Vickie, Ted, Felix, Vic, even you."

"When you put it that way, Clyde, I guess I can't say no."

"Fine. Now listen carefully. . ."

Segars instructs me to wait five minutes, allowing him time to reach his car which is parked behind a commercial strip center on the opposite side of Houston Street. Then I'm to climb out, leaving the car door open and the dome light lit, raise the hood, inspect the engine and slam the hood shut. He says I'm to make enough commotion to wake my neighbors and establish a definite time I arrived home.

Following his instructions, I do exactly as he says. When a light in the house next door flicks on, I march to my front porch and stomp loudly on the wooden floor. The screened door screeches angrily when I yank it wide open and let it swing back to slam against my shoulder. I unlock the front door and noisily shove my way inside.

Once inside, I immediately modify my demeanor to mouse-like quietness. I slip off my shoes and tiptoe to the bedroom door to check on Kaye. In spite of my clamorous antics, she is still asleep, curled up on our bed in childlike innocence. Silently, I work my way through the kitchen, slip out the back door, slink across the back yard and hurry down the alley.

A dark-green two-door Chevrolet waits for me at the end of the alley. Most likely the automobile, which bears no license plate, was borrowed off Segars' used car lot. When I open the passenger side door, the inside of the car remains dark. My father-in-law has removed the bulb in the dome light.

"Everything go okay?" Segars asks.

"Yes. Woke up my next door neighbors. They'll probably complain to my landlady tomorrow."

"What about Kaye?"

"Never heard a thing. She's still sleeping like a baby."

"Good. I wouldn't want to drag her into this mess. No matter how this turns out, Rick, I want you to promise you'll never tell her."

"Tell her what? Clyde, I want some answers. Where are we headed?"

"I'll explain everything while we drive, but first, I want your promise that you'll never tell Kaye what we did."

"How can I promise something like that? Dammit, Clyde, what's going on here?"

"Promise me first. Then I'll tell you."

"I promise. Now tell me," I say, yielding to his dogged resolve. My promise should be easy to keep. Whatever he's up to, I'm certain it won't be something I'll be anxious to talk about.

Since Segars picked me up, he's avoided the major streets. A left on Rusk, a right on Chilton, we snake our way through Tyler residential neighborhoods toward some unknown destination. When he slows, to stop at the intersection of West First and South Broadway, I ask again.

"Answer me, Clyde. Where we headed?"

"Mother of Francis Hospital. A friend of yours checked in there today. Name's Alvin Crenshaw." Segars turns to watch my reaction. A sly smile creeps across his face.

A cold shiver runs up my spine. When Segars says the name, it's like I've stepped into an ice cold shower. A sour taste fills my mouth. I need to spit, but instead I swallow.

"Alvin? You mean the fellow I shot? I thought he was in Kilgore."

"He was. Sheriff Grimes and a couple of his deputies moved him to Tyler late this afternoon. Tomorrow morning the sheriff plans to turn Alvin and Oscar over to the Texas Rangers."

"If you expect me to help Alvin escape, you can forget it. That man tried to kill me. He deserves everything he gets." I want to tell Segars I know all about his oil skimming operation and how he's connected to Alvin but decide against showing all my cards. Besides, accusing my father-in-law would only complicate our delicate conversation. I want to know what he's up to.

"Alvin's shot up too bad to turn loose. I have another plan in mind."

"I don't get it. Quit being so damn secretive."

"You and me, we're gonna put Crenshaw out of his misery. Fix it so he'll never harm anyone else."

"You mean kill him? Come on, Clyde. Surely you don't mean that."

"We really have no other choice, Rick, and we have to do it tonight. Tomorrow he and Oscar will be in the custody of the Texas Rangers. Sooner or later, one of them's bound to break down and tell everything they know."

"And you'll be implicated. You'll go to jail. Is that what's worrying you?"

"You know everything, don't you, Rick? After you and the sheriff's deputies raided the house in Kilgore, I figured you knew—about the oil skimming and why your friend was murdered. I'm truly sorry about your friend. I'm sorry for the pain my indiscretion has caused you."

"Indiscretion? You call cold-blooded murder an indiscretion?"

"I never intended for anyone to get hurt. The oil skimming operation was intended to raise some quick cash. The New Orleans people do it all the time. Move in, set up a phony oil well, skim off a few thousand barrels of oil, and sell it back to the same people you stole it from. And with the depletion allowance, no one pays any taxes. You know how I've been strapped for cash lately. So when they approached me, I went for it hook, line and sinker. It seemed like the perfect solution to my problems. We were in the process of shutting down the operation when your engineer friend showed up."

"So you had Alvin and Oscar kill Wagner. You're the one I should've shot."

"No. No. Please believe me, Rick. Those two scum bags work for the syndicate. What they did was without my knowledge or approval. I had nothing to do with your friend's death, or with their attempt on your life."

"But you went along. Even after you knew they'd murdered someone, you kept quiet."

"Yes, and it almost cost you your life. Maybe, if I had it to do over, I'd react differently. It seemed the right thing to do at the time. So much was at stake. My business, my reputation, and it was only a matter of days before the whole oil scheme was finished. I'd have the cash to pay my debts, and they'd be gone forever."

"People like that don't go away forever, Clyde. Once you do business with crooks, they never let go."

Segars is such a fool. Heck, it's elementary. Every kid who's ever seen a gangster movie knows better than to get mixed up with the mob.

"I admit it was a bad mistake. A mistake I expect I'll pay dearly for. I don't mind so much for myself, Rick. It's my family I'm worried about. So many people depend on me."

Segars guns the motor, and we sail across Broadway. He turns left on Donnybrook, drives two blocks and hangs a right on Lake Street.

"Why me, Clyde? Why not Vic?"

"Vic has a record as long as your arm. Once they connect me with the oil skimming operation, he'd be the first one they'd try to pin Alvin's murder on. I sent Vic to Dallas to stay with his sister for a few days, so he'll have an air tight alibi. Sent Felix to Marshall to visit his brother. Ted's in Houston interviewing for a job with that law firm that's been after him."

"And I'm supposedly at home in bed with my wife. But why me? I'm no killer."

The Chevy bounces as we cross the railroad. Segars pulls to a halt at South Beckum. His head turns slowly until his eyes look directly into mine.

"I know you, Richard. I know everything about you. The man we'll kill tonight is a no account low-life who don't deserve to live, and you've got plenty of reasons to want him dead. This is a job you can handle. You've done it before."

My initial inclination is to object strongly, tell him he's wrong. Then I remember the secret room and the private files. I never suspected my name would be posted on one of those files.

"So you know about my grandmother?"

"Yes, I know. I've known everything about you since the day my daughter called from college to tell me she'd enticed you into swimming naked in an ice cold lake."

❖ ❖ ❖ ❖ ❖

SEGARS WHEELS the Chevrolet slowly into the hospital employee parking lot. At three-forty in the morning, the hospital is manned with only a skeleton staff. Hardly a dozen cars occupy the numerous spaces.

We settle on a parking space near the perimeter, next to a hedge which will shield our vehicle from street view. Clyde signals me to remain inside while he walks around to the back of the car and retrieves something from the trunk. When he returns, he's holding a short rope and a sample piece of seat cover plastic.

"Let's get it done," Segars commands.

Side by side we step briskly across the asphalt paving to an unlit employee entrance. The door is locked, but Segars produces a small screwdriver, shoves it into the narrow sliver between the door handle and the jamb, twists gently, and the door swings open.

"He's on the third floor. Room 308. Watch yourself climbing these steps. Don't touch anything with your hands. I doubt if the Tyler police would ever think to check for fingerprints, but there's no sense taking chances," Segars advises.

While we scale the stairs to the third floor, I search my mind for reasons to justify my participation in the dastardly task ahead. Reasons to kill Alvin are easy to come by. He's a killer. He murdered my friend. He tried to murder me. Even if he stands trial, there's a chance he'll go free. He could kill again.

Finding a reason to justify my participation is more difficult.

We pause at the third floor landing while Clyde surveys the hallway. Seeing the passageway is clear, he turns back and shoves the rectangular section of plastic seatcover into my hands. Segars' eyes divulge his anxiety. Reluctantly, I accept his weapon of death and hide my hands behind my back. I don't want him to see how badly they're trembling.

"I'll tie his feet to the bed so he won't kick. He's a big man, Rick. You may have to cold cock him to keep him down."

"No, we gotta be careful not to leave any bruises. I can handle him," I boast. Suddenly I'm confident and strong, equal to the job ahead. An incredible rush of adrenaline whets my senses.

My heart pounds like a bass drum as we scurry down the corridor and sneak silently into room 308. Inside the room the smell of antiseptic hangs heavy. A dim night light is the only source of illumination. Alvin's oversized body lies stretched out on a bed in the center of the room. A tiny plastic tube connects a bottle suspended above the bed to his left arm. Alvin appears to be asleep.

Even before I reach the head of the bed, Clyde grabs Alvin's legs, quickly binds the thick ankles together with his rope and hog ties them to the bed rail.

"Whatcha waiting on? We ain't got all night to get this done."

"You'd better take the I.V. needle outta his arm. He might put up a fight. Wouldn't want that gooey liquid all over the bed covers. Someone might get suspicious."

"Alright, but hurry up. You act like you're enjoying this," Segars grumbles, impatient because I haven't finished my portion of the work.

"Maybe I am. Before this perverted bastard shoved me off the Deep Eddy Bridge, he threw water in my face to make sure I'd know

I was dying. Then he kicked me off the bridge and laughed while I sank to the river bottom."

"You're scaring me, Rick. This was supposed to be quick and easy."

"Just a slight change in the plan, Clyde. Before I kill him, I'm gonna wake him up. Now jerk out that feed needle and come help me hold him down."

I bend over the bed and slap at Alvin's face. "Hey, you ornery jackass. Wake up. You've got company."

"Rick, don't do it this way. You'll be. . . ," Segars begs, but his plea is cut short by Alvin's hoarse voice.

"What? Whatta you want?" Alvin groans. He blinks his eyes, trying to wake up.

A split second after he recognizes me, I cloak his face with the clear plastic sheet, shutting off his air supply. Underneath the sheath of plastic, I watch Alvin's distorted face. His eyes widen as his sluggish mind slowly comprehends my intent. He twists his head back and forth, fighting for air, but in his weak condition and with his feet tied to the bed, there's no way he can escape his airless cavity. I press down harder, and the plastic sheet expands, tightly tailoring itself to the configuration of Alvin's ugly mug.

"You remember me, big fellow? I'm your worst nightmare. I'm the smart ass you dropped off the Deep Eddy Bridge. I'm the one who shot that bloody hole in your chest, you murdering slime ball."

Even with Segars holding his left arm, Alvin puts up a magnificent fight. His right arm flails wildly and beats on my shoulder. He tries to sit up. I push him back. Squirming, turning, using all sorts of contorted body gyrations, he tries to escape. But two healthy men are stronger than a sickly one. Segars and I restrain Alvin's wild movements and keep him lying belly up on the bed. Eventually our prey gasps for a last breath and succumbs to the inevitable.

"He dead?" Segars asks, his voice quivering.

"I think so. Check his pulse."

While Clyde fingers Alvin's wrist and checks for a heartbeat, I walk to the end of the bed to untie the feet and straighten the sheet over the limp carcass.

"No pulse. I reckon our job's done," Segars says wearily.

"Good. Stick that I.V. needle back in his arm, and we'll clear out of here."

Before leaving the crime scene, my comrade and I carefully police the floor and bed, making sure we haven't left even the tiniest clue. When our inspection is complete, I hand the rope to Segars and grab the plastic wrap. My father-in-law grins and pats my back as we head for the door.

❖ ❖ ❖ ❖ ❖

"WHAT ABOUT OSCAR? Won't he talk?" I ask as we reach the intersection of Houston and Vine. A faint glimmer on the horizon hints that sunup is minutes away.

"No, soon as Oscar hears his partner is dead, he'll get the picture. He's a cowardly wimp, but he'll keep his mouth shut. He'll understand his life won't be worth a rat's damn if he talks."

Segars steers the Chevy to the alley entrance and stops.

"Reckon this is where you get out, Rick. I'll see you at the ballfield this evening. Maybe we can break out of our losing streak tonight."

"I hope so. This constant losing has the whole team in the dumps. . . . I've been thinking, Clyde. Vic, Felix, Ted and me, we're covered. But what about you? Everybody has an alibi except you."

"Good question. I've figured a way to wiggle out of this mess without hurting the girls. It may take a couple more days, but I'm working on it. When I have all the pieces in place, I'm gonna need your help again."

"And how's that?"

"It's amazingly simple. Soon as everything is set, we're gonna kill me."

CHAPTER EIGHTEEN

"HEY, SKIPPER, wait up!" a voice calls, startling me and causing me to almost leap out of my skin. After last night's hospital affair, I'm a bit jumpy.

I'm running late. I promised to meet Whitey at noon to sort through the equipment we hurriedly stashed in the locker room late last night.

I stop and turn back to watch Henry French climb out of a faded maroon Ford pickup. He waves, slams the cab door shut and hikes rapidly toward me. Judging from his troubled expression, Henry won't be bringing good news.

"How you doing this morning, Coach?" Henry asks, shoving his hands into his trouser pockets.

"Not too bad," I say, responding with a lie. Actually, I feel like I've been marched on by the Chinese army. It was almost five o'clock when Segars dropped me off at the Houston Street alleyway this morning. Kaye was still asleep when I slipped into bed beside her. But tired as I was, I couldn't sleep. Every time I'd doze off, the grotesque, lifeless faces of Max, Alvin and my grandmother would invade my dreams and wake me up.

"I hate to bother you when we're in the middle of a losing streak, Skipper, but I have a problem."

"What's the problem, Henry? Maybe I can help."

342

"I haven't had a hit all season. My friends are teasing me. My dad says if I can't hit, I ain't going nowhere in baseball. He thinks I oughta quit the team and get a job."

Henry's story jolts me. I halt dead in my tracks and turn to face the stunted rookie. Using both hands, I grab him by the shoulders and look straight into his eyes.

"Why would your father say that? Doesn't he know you're leading the league in walks and runs scored?"

"Sure, he knows that. But daddy claims that won't swing much weight with the scouts. He says next year or the year after that, I'll be looking for a real job. Says I should save myself a lot of heartache and quit now."

French's father is a wise man. His argument makes a lot of sense. I release my grip on Henry's shoulders and drop my hands.

"Your dad's probably right, Henry. Not more than one or two guys on our club have any chance of moving up to a higher league. Look at Peppy Swanson. He's a perfect example of a player hanging on too long. But Peppy has so many friends, men he's played with and against, and when his playing days are done, he'll have hundreds of great memories—memories that ordinary men can only wish for. That's what playing baseball at this level is about. Sure, every player in the Big State League is hoping to get lucky and catch the eye of some scout, but except for a select few, that'll never happen. Playing baseball here, for Tyler, you have to be satisfied with playing for the fun. If that's not enough, maybe you should hang 'em up. I'd hate to see you quit though. You play a really important role on our baseball team."

"You've got it all wrong, Coach Mason. I'm not thinking about quitting. I know I'll never make it to the big leagues. I can handle that, but I want to prove to my dad and my friends that I can hit. What I'm after is your okay—to take my cuts in tonight's game."

❖ ❖ ❖ ❖ ❖

"YOU PROMISED him what? Have you lost your cotton picking mind? French can't hit his way out of a paper sack. You said

343

so yourself," Whitey chides, his raised voice scolding me for my stupidity when I tell him about my conversation with Henry French.

"But I don't see how it can hurt. We're getting our tails kicked night after night. Maybe Henry will get lucky. This team needs some sort of boost to lift its spirit."

"You're losing it, Rick. You're letting this darn losing streak affect your judgement. A manager can't let his players dictate the way he runs his team. That's a sure path to last place."

❖ ❖ ❖ ❖ ❖

WHEN THE MAN I know as Joe appears in the locker room doorway, I'm not surprised. I've been semi-anticipating his visit since the moment I arrived. Discovering Alvin's dead body must've been terribly distressing for the three Texas Rangers. Sooner or later, this visit was inevitable.

"Whitey, I'll be back shortly. That man at the door is here to see me."

"Sure, and leave me with all the work, while you go traipsing off," Whitey barks.

"I'm sorry, but this is important. I'll be back as soon as I can," I explain, feeling guilty for leaving when there's so much to do.

"Hey, I'm only teasing. Go on. Get outta here. You're mostly in the way anyhow," Whitey grins.

"Gee thanks. You make a fellow feel so important," I laugh, firing a dirty jersey in his direction. With amazing dexterity my unappreciative friend dodges the flying object. He sticks out his tongue to humorously display his defiance while I turn and stride across the dressing room to greet Joe.

"Hey there, Mason. Can you spare a minute? We need to talk," Joe says when I get close.

"Sure. My assistant can finish up here. We can talk in my office. How've you been?" I say, offering my hand in a gesture of friendship.

Joe glances at my outstretched hand and decides to ignore it.

"You'd better come outside. Sam and Tom are waiting in our car."

344

"My office would be much more comfortable. Why don't we invite your partners to come inside?"

My reluctance to do exactly as the ranger suggests triggers some kind of mental eruption.

"Dammit, Mason. You're such a pain. Are you gonna come out to the car peaceable, or do you want I should break both your friggin' legs and drag your contrary butt out there?"

"Alright. Alright, Joe. There's no need for rough stuff. Look, I'm not arguing. We'll do it your way."

Tom and Sam are waiting inside the car when I scoot in. Joe slips into the back seat next to Sam so that each of us occupy the same seat as during our initial meeting. After having Joe decline my handshake, I don't bother with friendly overtures.

"Maybe you should frisk me, Joe. I might be carrying a weapon."

"And maybe you better keep your smart mouth shut, Mason, before I rip out your tongue," Joe growls and turns to Sam. "He gave me a hard time in there. Had to threaten him to make him come talk. He acts like he's hiding something. Maybe we oughta run him downtown. With a little persuasion, me and Tom will have him singing like a canary in no time."

"Hey, that's a bald-faced lie. All I did was invite. . . ," I argue, but a bony knuckle slamming hard against the back of my head terminates the discussion.

"Dammit, Mason. I told you to keep your mouth shut. Now keep quiet. Sam here will ask the questions. You're to speak only when you're spoken to. You understand?" Joe says, leaning over the seat to bark in my ear while I hunch forward and rub at the spot where he popped me.

When I don't answer fast enough to suit him, he draws his fist back, apparently anxious to pound on me again. "You hear me? I asked if you understand."

"Yes, I understand," I growl. My head throbs with pain, but my temper is rising. Texas Ranger or not, I've had enough of his abuse. I whirl around to gaze directly into the surly ranger's eyes. "And if you so much as touch me again, I'll crawl over this seat and beat your brains out. Do you understand?"

Joe surges forward, anxious to accept my challenge, but Sam grabs his arm and pulls him back.

"Take it easy, Joe. Let's get our business done. Then you two can settle your differences," Sam advises, assuming the role of mediator.

Yielding to his superior's firm suggestion, my adversary relaxes and leans back in his seat. While Sam continues, Joe's angry eyes glare at me.

"How about we all calm down. We're here to talk, not fight. We're all on the same side here."

"You keep a leash on your hatchet man back there, and I'll talk. Otherwise you'd better haul me downtown and let me call my lawyer. After he sees this knot on my head, I expect he'll be anxious to sue your butts off. Here in Tyler, our judges don't take kindly to law officers who beat up on private citizens."

"Alright, Mason. So you know your rights. Big deal. Maybe Joe came on a bit strong, but we're all on edge. That man you shot the other night—Alvin Crenshaw. He died last night," Sam explains then pauses and waits for my reaction.

A crafty lawyer would never blurt out the whole story. No. A lawyer would be more cunning, feed me bits of information and try to trick me into saying something I shouldn't. Obviously, Texas Rangers aren't so subtle. Perhaps Sam expects his information to shock me. He's wrong of course. That strategy won't work on me. When I respond, I choose my words carefully.

"Dead? But I thought he was doing okay. Last time I saw you fellows you were on your way to confront the sheriff. You promised to get those two killers charged with murder."

"That was the plan. Sheriff Grimes moved Crenshaw from Kilgore over to the hospital here in Tyler late yesterday afternoon. We were supposed to assume custody of Crenshaw and the man in the county jail today, but Crenshaw apparently died in his sleep. He was stone cold dead when the night nurse checked on him early this morning."

"That story sounds mighty suspicious. You sure Crenshaw died from the gunshot wounds?" I ask, attempting to sound keenly interested and totally innocent.

"That's what we think. The sheriff had a deputy posted to guard the patient, but the deputy was called out to handle some sort of family ruckus over in Lindale. Seems the sheriff is shorthanded. He claims you're the one who's responsible. Says he has one deputy in the hospital and another on suspension, all on account of you."

"Hey, don't blame me for the sheriff's problems. All I did was locate the killers' hideout. Without me, those guys would still be running around loose. What about Oscar? Is he still in jail?"

"Yes, and he was right on the verge of talking. Now he's clammed up. Won't say a word to nobody. That's what makes us suspicious. We think maybe someone sneaked in and killed Crenshaw while the deputy was out on call. Somehow, our man Oscar heard what happened to his running buddy."

"Whatta you mean killed him? I thought you said Crenshaw died in his sleep."

"Well, there was no evidence of foul play. Nobody shot him or slit his throat. There was no sign of a struggle."

"So you've found nothing to support your suspicions?" I ask and hold my breath, waiting for an answer. Clyde and I inspected the room thoroughly before we left. There's no way we could have overlooked some piece of tell-tale evidence. Still, I'd like to hear the ranger confirm that.

"Well, not yet. We've asked the county coroner to do an autopsy to determine the cause of death."

"So what's the purpose of this conversation? Surely you don't suspect me. Hell, if I wanted Alvin dead, I'd have finished him off the other night in Kilgore."

"No, you're not a suspect. We're simply checking on everyone's whereabouts at the time of death. You mind telling us where you were around four o'clock this morning?"

Sam's question prompts an immediate constriction in my chest. I try to breathe normally, and hope my face won't reveal my guilt.

"In bed with my wife. My team played an out of town game against Sherman last night. They beat the snot out of us for the third night in a row. Our bus dropped us off here around 3:00 A.M. I went straight home."

"So your wife can confirm you were home in bed—at four this morning?"

"Yes. Well, she was asleep when I got home. I didn't think to wake her up so she'd remember the exact time. Didn't know I'd be needing an alibi."

"Mason, we'd get along much better if you'd cooperate and not be such a smart mouth," Sam scolds. He nods at Joe as if to agree with his assessment of my attitude and continues. "How about your father-in-law? You know where he was this morning?"

"I'm sorry. Guess we got off on the wrong foot, but I'm trying to cooperate," I apologize and cut my eyes in Joe's direction. "No, I have no idea where my father-in-law was at four this morning. You'll have to check with him."

"That's all we need for now," Sam advises, dismissing me like a schoolchild.

"Fine. Am I free to go?" I ask. When I get no response, I open the door and slide out. The rear window rolls down as I'm about to walk away. Joe's smug face appears in the opening.

"You still want a piece of me, Mason? If you do, I'm available."

"What is it with you, Joe? You pick a fight with everyone you guys question, or is it just me?"

"You're hiding something. I can smell it, and I intend to nail your lying ass before we finish with this case."

"Okay, tough guy, you're on. Get out, and let's get this settled. I'd rather take a face to face licking than have you hitting on me from the back seat."

"I thought you'd never ask," Joe grins and quickly rolls up the window. Inside the car I can hear the men talking, perhaps discussing the pros and cons of Joe's impertinent behavior. In a few seconds the car door opens.

"You wanna fight here, or you wanna move somewhere more private?" Joe says, crouching low and raising his fists.

"This'll do fine. Probably won't take long. You hit me. I'll hit the pavement."

"You got that right. You ready to dance?" Joe asks. His jaws are set, his eyes narrowed.

"You damn right I am," I answer, also crouching to a fighting stance, elevating my fists, and moving closer. "But how about your gun? You mind putting it back in the car, so I don't get shot?"

My seemingly innocent request prompts my adversary to commit a novice-like mistake. He glances down at the pistol strapped to his waist, taking his eyes off me. That's when I bust him square on the end of his nose with my clenched fist. Joe's an experienced fighter. I may get in only one blow before he whales the daylights out of me, so I hit him with every ounce of strength I can muster.

His neck snaps backward, and his nose collapses beneath the force of my knuckles. A bone in the back of my right hand pops loudly. A sharp pain races through my right hand and up my arm.

Joe's glazed eyes express his surprise and shock. My lightning strike caught him totally off guard. A second later his eyes roll back, and his knees buckle. He drops to one knee, but he's a tough nut. He's struggling to stand when I land a hard left to his temple. My second punch does him in. He's out cold even before he falls forward to bounce his head against the asphalt pavement. He lies there very still, unmoving. Bright red blood oozes from his broken nose.

For a short moment I stand over Joe's unconscious body, savoring my victory and watching while the blood from his nose slowly forms a pool around his face. The car door on the driver's side opens. Tom hops out and runs around the car. When he spies his friend's body lying sprawled on the ground, he stops abruptly.

"You want some of me too? Come on. I'll whip the whole stinking bunch of you," I shout, raising my fists.

Tom raises his hands to wave me off.

"Hold up, Mason. I'm no fighter. That's Joe's department. Man, I never thought I'd see anyone whip Joe so handily."

"I'm surprised he went down so easily myself. But the insolent schmuck was asking for what he got. Maybe next time he'll think twice before he starts throwing his weight around."

"Looks like he's hurt pretty bad. You mind if I take a look at him? We may need to run him to the hospital."

"No, go right ahead. I'm done with the arrogant jerk. I'm fairly certain I busted his nose. You'll need to get that fixed," I tell Tom with an unsteady voice then spin around and head for the locker room while I'm able to make a dignified withdrawal. I need some doctoring myself. My right hand hurts like the dickens.

❖ ❖ ❖ ❖ ❖

"I THOUGHT that fellow was a friend of yours, Rick," Whitey grumbles while he dabs a soothing salve to my aching hand and gently rubs it in.

"No, I said he came here to see me. I never said we were friends."

"So you took him outside and beat him up. Rick, this ain't like you. I never knew you to fight, even when you was in high school. Now lately, you're going around shooting and beating up on people."

"You're right, Whitey. I hate to fight, but this fellow really ticked me off. So I busted him in the nose. Guess I busted my hand too. Can you fix it so I can handle infield warm-ups tonight?"

"I doubt it," Whitey replies. He lifts my arm and begins wrapping a triple layer of gauze around my swollen hand. "Soon as I tape you up, I'll rig up a sling. That oughta ease the pain so you can make it through the game. Who was this man you beat up on? Anyone important?"

"He seems to think he's somebody important, but to me, he's just another bully throwing his weight around. I'm sick and tired of people pushing me around. I ain't gonna take it lying down no more."

"Who was he, Rick? He have a name?"

"Calls himself Joe. Never would tell me his last name. You know, Whitey, Texas Rangers must all be paranoid. They only give out their first names."

"You whipped up on a Texas Ranger? Aw, Rick, you ain't supposed to beat up on Texas Rangers. You're liable to land us all in the hoosegow."

❖ ❖ ❖ ❖ ❖

SATURDAY NIGHT baseball usually plays well in Tyler. Some Saturdays we'll attract as many as three thousand fans. Tonight, with
350

the third place Texarkana Bears in town, it's possible we'll surpass our best attendance figure of the year.

Up in the grandstands, home fans continue to filter in as Nick Bounato rifles his final warm-up pitch to recently acquired catcher Joe Kracher. With Jess Nelms injured, Ted was forced to negotiate an emergency deal. On Friday he traded Jake Christie to Abilene for their number one catcher. Kracher arrived in Tyler late this afternoon.

A gentle northerly breeze ripples across the ballfield as I survey the bleachers for familiar faces. The wind contains a faint musky odor, hinting of rain, but there's not a cloud in the sky. It's a perfect night for baseball.

My surveillance ceases when I come to the owner's box which contains only two occupants, my wife and Ted Gooding. Conspicuously absent is my father-in-law.

"Steeee-riiiike one!" the umpire bellows, interrupting my speculation about Segars' whereabouts. Kracher pops up, jerks the catcher's mitt off his left hand and wiggles his hand like he's in pain. He shouts something to Bounato, reaches down to pick up the baseball and fires it back to our right-handed ace. Bounato catches the ball and nods affirmatively.

"What's the problem with Kracher? Looks like he's mad about something," I muse, curious about my receiver's behavior.

"Darned if I know. Acts like Bounato's pitch hurt his hand. Maybe we should've checked him out before we let him catch tonight," Whitey replies.

Bounato toes the rubber and checks the sign from Kracher. Satisfied with the signal, he raises his left leg and begins an off-balance windup then lunges forward to deliver a hard fastball. Texarkana's lead-off batter starts to swing, changes his mind and steps back. The baseball whizzes across home plate an inch above the batter's knees.

"Steeee-riiiike two!" the umpire shrieks loudly. Again our newly signed catcher jumps up and yanks off his mitt. He grasps his catching hand and turns to glare at Bounato.

"Time out. Time out," I shout to the home plate umpire. Kracher acts as if he's about to charge his pitcher. Disregarding a throbbing right hand suspended in a cloth sling hung around my neck,

I charge up the dugout steps. In my haste I bump against the handrail. The slight impact sets off an explosion of pulsating pain. I grit my teeth and try not to scream out. I press my hand tightly against my chest and hurry toward home plate.

"What's the matter, Joe? You and Bounato have some kinda problem?" I ask when I arrive. Kracher is clearly in agony. He holds his catching hand behind his back, away from my view.

"You darn right we got a problem. I keep signaling for a curve ball, and that stubborn so and so keeps throwing me fastballs. He ignores my sign one more time, and we're going straight to fist city," the catcher answers. His dark suntanned face is pleated with taut wrinkles of pain.

"What's wrong with your catching hand? You hurt?"

"Nothing. Nothing's wrong with my hand. It's your pitcher. He won't follow orders."

"Lemme see the hand, Joe," I insist. When I reach out, he jerks back.

"Ain't nothing wrong with my hand. Talk to your pitcher. He's the problem," Kracher argues.

"The hand, Joe. Lemme see your hand," I demand.

"It's not bad, Coach Mason. Just a little burn. Me and the wife was horsing around last night while she was ironing. I accidentally set my hand down on her hot iron. I can play. Honest I can." Kracher timidly extends a gnarled left paw and places it in my outstretched hand. He winces as he unfolds his fingers. A creamy white layer of dead skin extends across the palm of his hand from the base of his thumb to the bottom of his little finger. Once, the loose skin covered a huge blister. Now with the blister burst, the raw red skin underneath is exposed. A syrupy body fluid seeps from the open sore.

"Joe, that looks bad. Real bad."

"It don't hurt so much on curves. It's fastballs that give me trouble."

"So that's the problem. For Pete's sake, Bounato can't throw curve balls all night. Why didn't you say something?"

"Didn't want you to think you'd traded for damaged goods. I was afraid if you found out I was hurt, you might send me back to Abilene. Please don't send me back, Coach Mason. This is my big chance."

"I'd like to know where you expect to play. You darn sure can't catch with this piece of raw meat. Hell, man, you not only can't catch. I doubt if you can handle a bat."

While we talk, the home plate umpire silently scrutinizes our conversation. Finally, he's heard enough. Stepping forward, he forcefully exerts his authority.

"When you two decide which of you is hurt the worst, there's a few people here who paid to watch a baseball game. I'll give you fifteen seconds. Then I'm removing you both from the game."

"But this man is hurt. I need to sub in another catcher," I argue.

"Ten seconds!" the umpire barks, raising his arm to study the watch attached to his wrist.

"I know you're hurting, Joe, but can you make it through this inning?" I ask hastily.

"Sure. I'll make it. Don't worry about me, Coach. I came to Tyler to play baseball, not watch it from the bench," Kracher responds, eagerly pulling on his glove and crouching down behind home base.

"Five seconds!" the umpire howls.

"Okay. Okay, ump. My catcher's ready. Batter up. I'm outta here."

"Humph!" the umpire snorts, plainly disappointed.

❖ ❖ ❖ ❖ ❖

"I GOT JUST the thing to fix him up," Whitey brags after I describe the enormous blister on our catcher's glove hand. "Ran into Coach Prejean over at the high school field house yesterday. He loaned me a bottle of a new liquid bandage called *Tuf Skin*. Burns like blue blazes when you brush it on, but after the stuff dries, it acts like a protective coating. Prejean claims it works great on scrapes and skinned places. Oughta do the trick for Kracher."

353

"I hope you're right. Otherwise, we're down to having one of the Johnson boys catch."

"Don't you worry, Rick. This stuff will work. Trust me."

Using only twelve pitches, Bounato sets the Bears down in order. A ground ball to Bruzga at short, a high fly to Epps in right. The third Texarkana hitter strikes out, chasing after a slow, sinking curve. Our defensive starters sprint to the dugout with spirits high. It's been a long time since they've enjoyed such an excellent start. While Whitey hustles Kracher into the locker room for a catching hand retread, I collar Henry French.

"Be patient, Henry, and swing level. Don't try to kill the baseball, just grip the bat tight and meet the pitch solid. You have a much better chance of getting your hit if you put the ball on the ground," I instruct my anxious rookie.

"Yeah. Sure, Coach. You know, I've only made two outs all season. If I get a hit, my batting average will zoom up to over three hundred. Ain't many batters in this league hittin' over three hundred," French answers. His face is flushed. His dilated white eyes are focused on the man warming up on the pitching hill.

"You're right, Henry. There's not many batters in any league with a batting average over three hundred. Now go get your hit," I say, encouraging him with a swat to his backside and pointing him in the direction of the on-deck-circle. He hasn't heard a word I've said. No sense in wasting my breath.

A sudden gust of cool wind ripples through the ballpark while French taps at his cleated shoes with the end of his bat and steps into the batter's box. Paper cups and pieces of trash tumble across the infield as the Bear hurler winds and delivers. The pitch is outside and eyeball high, an offering French would normally take for a ball. My lead-off batter swings at it mightily, loses his balance and falls to the ground. Home fans display their amusement with hoots of hilarious laughter.

"Patience, Henry. Be patient. Make him throw you a strike," I call, using cupped hands to project my voice.

French nods to acknowledge he's heard my advice, dusts himself off and steps back into the batter's box. He bends his knees and crouches low. He holds his bat high and moves it slowly in a tight circle. He narrows his eyes and concentrates on Texarkana's pitcher.

"CRACK!" Like a sharp clap of thunder, the noise rings through the ballpark. French stands at home plate and watches the baseball sail over the surprised infielders.

"Run. Henry, you gotta run. Run the bases," my players and I bellow from the dugout.

Jess Nelms, who is coaching at first base, is waving both arms wildly, trying to gain French's attention. Eventually French heeds our anxious cries. Lowering his head, he scampers up the first base line. Out in left center, the baseball hits the fence railing and bounces back past two converging Bear outfielders, allowing Nelms to wave French on to second. An instant before the ball arrives from the outfield, Henry slides safely into second base.

A huge grin decorates the rookie's face. Raising his arms high, he jubilantly hops up and down on the second base bag. His accomplishment does not go unnoticed. Tyler boosters, realizing this is French's first hit of the season, rise to give him a standing ovation. Wild whoops and loud animated screams of encouragement from his excited teammates broaden Henry's happy smile.

French's lead-off hit ignites a flurry of batting fireworks. A long double off the center field scoreboard by Merv Connors drives in French. Akins follows with a sharp single into right field, allowing Connors to score. Then Hal Epps bloops a Texas Leaguer into short center.

"You ready, Peppy?" I call in the direction of the bench. With runners at first and second and nobody out, I want my number one slugger to take his cuts. A big inning here could signal an end to our losing streak.

"I'm always ready, Coach Mason. You want some runs. Let ol' Peppy handle the chore."

"You'll be batting for Gregory. I'll sub in Johnson next inning to take Nick's position in left field."

"That's fine with me. You want two or three runs?" my veteran fence rattler inquires, demonstrating his confidence by showing me a wide toothy smile.

"Three would be nice, but I'll settle for one," I respond seriously, resisting an urge to join in the jovial mood which has unexpectedly enveloped our dugout.

"Three you want. Three it'll be then," Peppy advises and tramps up the dugout steps.

While Swanson swings the leaded bat in the on-deck-circle, I call in our batting change. As I hang up, Whitey and Kracher return from their visit to the locker room.

"How's the hand, Joe? That miracle ointment of Whitey's gonna work?"

"I believe so. Darn stuff burns like fire when you swab it on, but it acts just like skin once it dries. Right now my hand's numb as a stump. Can't feel a thing," Kracher replies.

"I'll tape some foam rubber on his palm before he goes in to catch next inning. Joe oughta make it through the game. His hand will probably be sore as all git out tomorrow though," Whitey advises. "How we doing in the ball game?"

My answer is curtailed by a resounding blast from Peppy Swanson's bat. Whitey, Kracher, and I turn to watch a hard hit baseball soar down the third base line and clear the left field fence. As Peppy trots toward first base, he pauses briefly to grin at me and politely tips his hat.

Peppy's home run propels my East Texans to a five run lead. It also marks the end of the evening for Texarkana's starting pitcher. The Bears' manager calls timeout and signals to his bullpen. While he and his catcher stand on the mound and wait for the arrival of a relief pitcher, the wind picks up. Seconds later raindrops begin to patter on the dugout roof. Several spectators in the bleachers abandon their seats and rush for cover.

"Oh, no. Not rain. Not tonight. Not with us off to a five run lead," I wail.

My team members express their frustration in silence. With long faces we watch Texarkana's manager and his catcher slap one another's back and dash for shelter. The light drizzle evolves into a bone-chilling downpour even before they reach the steps to their dugout. What started out a pleasant summer evening has become another night of bitter disappointment for my East Texans.

"Coach Mason, does this mean my hit won't count?"

"Naw, it don't count, Henry. Neither does my three-run dinger," a devastated Peppy Swanson answers for me. Slumped forward on the bench, Peppy's elbows rest on his knees. His face is pressed between cupped hands—hiding his tears from his teammates.

❖ ❖ ❖ ❖ ❖

WHEN THE DOWNPOUR escalated into a deluge, the umpires called the game, solemnly dispatching both teams to their dressing quarters and counseling the Bears' manager and myself that, if the league office approves, we'll make up tonight's game with a double header Monday evening. At the moment that hardly seems possible. With the rain arriving so unexpectedly, there was no chance to cover the infield. Even before the heavy rain set in, the baseball diamond resembled a muddy river. My downhearted troops were in a hurry to leave. With many players choosing to forego a post game shower, most of the men had changed to their street clothes and were ready to leave when I returned from meeting with the game officials. I advised my despondent players of the possibility we might play a doubleheader on Monday and cut them loose.

A faint rumble in the equipment area catches my attention as I'm preparing to leave.

"Matilda, is that you?" I ask, trying to steady my composure. I should be used to her unexpected visits by now, but for some reason, her appearance always causes my hair to stand on end.

"Yes, it's me. I'm so sorry about the game tonight." Matilda's eyes are red and swollen, like she's been crying. Her voice is weak, her words slightly slurred.

"Me, too. Seems like we can't get anything to go our way lately. I'll sure be glad when we have this bad luck streak behind us. It'll be nice to start winning again," I state bravely, trying to be positive. Matilda looks so sad. I try to think of something to say which might cheer her up. When I can't, I blurt out, "Are you all right, Matilda?"

357

"I'm so sick of watching you lose. I wish I could be here to see the team win again."

"But you will. Remember our agreement. If I stop drinking and treat my wife better, you'll help me have a winning season."

"I remember. That's another reason why they're removing me."

"Removing you? Then you really are my guardian angel?"

"Yes, at least I have been since that day I convinced the judges not to send you to hell, that I could straighten you out. I've done a very poor job. The judges think I got too caught up in the baseball situation and haven't paid enough attention to your soul."

"But you can't leave. You promised me a winning season. I've kept my end of the bargain. I expect you to keep yours. Angels can't back out on a promise. That wouldn't be kosher."

"Kosher or not, I have no choice in the matter. I mistakenly assumed your troubles were related to your drinking and to your wife. I was wrong. I should have watched you closer. Last night you killed a man. You heard what the judges said. Murder is the one thing they can't forgive."

"Alvin Crenshaw was a no account slime bag. He deserved exactly what he got. I'm not sorry for what I did."

"I can't say I don't agree. Alvin was a horrible man. I'll never understand where monsters like him come from, or why God allows them to go around killing good people. But I've always questioned the establishment. That's another reason I'm losing my job."

"Listen, Matilda, why can't we can work something out? Even if you can't be my guardian angel, maybe you can hang around. You know, and help with the team. Whitey and I really value your advice. We still have more than a hundred games to play. There's plenty of time to turn this thing around, make the playoffs, and end up with a winning season."

"Oh, I wish I could. We could have so much fun."

"Then stay. Heck, we got along a whole lot better before you became my guardian angel. I'd much prefer having you as a member of my coaching staff."

"I wish I could, Richard, but I can't. The judges are very put out with me. They only let me stay long enough to tell you and Whitey goodbye."

"That's so unfair. I'm the one to blame. Isn't there some way we can change their minds? Maybe I could talk to them and explain."

"I'm afraid that's not possible. They're awfully hard-headed. Once they make up their minds, they refuse to listen to any more argument."

"Any chance the judges might assign me another guardian angel? Maybe one who's not so distracted by baseball?"

"I doubt it. They've pretty much given up on you."

"You mean they've already decided? I'm going to hell?" I stammer, irritated that the judges would decide my fate without giving me a second chance to plea my case. I can't say I'm completely sold on spending eternity in Heaven, but I'm absolutely certain I don't want to go to hell.

"Maybe, maybe not. It's not for me to decide. You have a long life ahead. Perhaps you'll find a way to convince them otherwise."

"I'm sorry the guardian angel thing didn't work out, Matilda, but you shouldn't blame yourself. My life was an absolute mess long before you got involved. Actually, you've been a big help. I've stopped drinking, and I'm back together with my wife. I'm in much better shape than when we first met. I don't have many friends who care what happens to me, so just knowing you cared enough to try means a lot. I'm gonna miss you, Matilda. You sure know your baseball."

"I'll miss you, Richard, and Whitey too. I don't have many friends either. Maybe after they cool off, the judges will allow me to come visit occasionally. I'll be checking the standings to see how your season goes. Even with all the turmoil, it really has been fun, hasn't it?"

"You're dang right. That's what baseball is all about. If you miss the fun of it, you kinda miss the whole point."

❖ ❖ ❖ ❖ ❖

HEAVY RAIN continues to pour down as I fumble with the locker room door lock. The ballpark is empty. Except for a night light underneath the bleachers, the stadium is completely dark. My heart skips a beat when I notice a dark figure moving through the concession area toward me. Then I recognize the walk.

"Clyde? That you?"

"Yes. Sorry about your game tonight. I was listening on the car radio. I was so certain we were going to pull out a win."

"Yeah, me too. Seems like nothing goes our way anymore. Even the weather's against us. Where were you tonight?"

"Been setting everything up. You gonna help like you promised?"

"I helped you kill a man last night. I suppose I'll do whatever you want."

"Good. Tonight oughta be easy." Segars cuts his eyes to the left then to the right, like he's making sure no one will overhear. His voice changes to a hoarse whisper when he continues, "What we're gonna do tonight is—steal a body."

❖ ❖ ❖ ❖ ❖

RAIN DROPS PEPPER at the windshield of our borrowed Chevy as Segars turns off Highway 64 and rolls to a stop facing the cemetery's front gate. Arched above the entrance gate is a wrought iron sign with the words TYLER MEMORIAL CEMETERY spelled out in metal letters between the top and bottom chords. On each side of the driveway, the entrance archway is supported by a tall masonry pilaster. Five-foot-high stone fences extend out from both sides of the pilasters to border the cemetery from the highway right-of-way.

"Here's the key, Rick. You unlock the gate."

"Good grief, Clyde. I hope you're not planning to rob some-one's grave. I thought you said this would be easy."

"No, it's nothing like that. The body we came for is stashed inside the mausoleum."

"Whose body is it? Anyone I know?"

360

"No. No one knows who it is. That's the reason we're here. It's one of the dead John Does that turns up every now and then here in Smith County. If no one claims the body, it becomes the county's responsibility to see it gets buried. The coroner had the body shipped out here late this afternoon. The plan is to bury this poor soul tomorrow morning."

"I don't get it. If we steal the body, won't they miss it tomorrow morning? It'll be all over the papers."

"Open the gate, Rick, before someone sees us. I have this all planned out. I'll explain everything as we go along."

I unlock the gate, hold it open while Segars pulls through, shove the gate closed and lock it shut. I hop back in the car, and we meander along a narrow roadway toward the middle of the cemetery. My heart beats faster as we pass row after row of tombstones. I never cared much for grave yards even in the bright light of day. I darn sure never thought I'd find myself inside a cemetery on a dark, rainy night.

"Where did you get the keys? From the coroner?" I ask, answering my own question.

"Yes. I've known Fred Varner for a long time. He and I go back a ways."

"He the only one who knows we're stealing a body tonight?" I ask stupidly.

"Yes, only the three of us. Fred will perform the examination to positively identify me after we kill me." Segars chuckles at his statement, but I'm not so easily amused. I'm about to ask if we can trust the coroner to keep his mouth shut. Then I remember Segars' secret file room. No doubt Fred Varner's name is there too, along with mine.

The roadway terminates at a small building. Segars brakes to a slow stop, allowing the Chevy to coast to within a few feet of a wide doorway before he turns off the ignition and cuts the lights.

"There's a flashlight in the glove compartment and some sheets in the back seat. The rest of what we need is in the trunk. Dig out the flashlight and bring the sheets while I unlock the door. We'll come back and get the bags outta the trunk after we check on Mister Doe."

Still a bit uncertain as to my role in this sinister scheme, I keep quiet. I snap open the glove compartment, grab the flashlight, and reach back to yank the folded sheets off the back seat. Taking Segars' lead, I follow him to the door of the building. He's fumbling with the keys when I arrive to shine the flashlight on the lock. An instant later we're inside.

The bright beam from my flashlight dances up and down the interior of the building as I quickly inspect to make certain we're alone. Satisfied the room is empty, I breathe a sigh of relief. What I do discover is an undersized tractor, a few miscellaneous garden tools, and a wooden casket perched atop a portable dolly.

"Let's check the body," Segars whispers and steps swiftly to the casket. He lifts at the lid, but it doesn't budge. "You know how to open one of these things, Rick?"

"There's a lever at one end. You gotta pull it out first. Then you can raise the top." My recent experience transporting Max Wagner's remains to Houston taught me a lot about caskets.

I shine the light so Segars can see. He finds the lever, releases the latch and shoves the casket lid open. The two of us move closer. I hold the flashlight so we can get a good look. Inside the casket lies a dead man who, if you don't look too close, might conceivably pass for my father-in-law.

"There, now don't he look a lot like me? Same build. Same height. We got lucky. Fred came up with the right body in less than a week. That's one of my suits he's wearing. Whatta you think, Rick? We could pass for twins, don't you think?" Segars proclaims proudly.

"I'll take your word for it," I say, turning away. "You think we could get this done and get outta here? I've never been real keen on hanging out in grave yards."

"No need to be afraid, Rick. The people here are all dead. They can't hurt you."

"You believe what you want, Clyde. I choose to believe in ghosts. Whatta we do now?"

Segars has every step planned. First, we lift John Doe's body from the casket, wrap him in the bed sheets, tote him to the car and shove him into the back seat. In the car trunk are four bags of sand which we unload and carry back inside. Segars carefully places each sand bag inside the casket so the weight is evenly distributed. When he's finished, he closes the lid, latches it tightly and steps back to admire his work.

"Take a look around, Rick, while I wipe off the casket. I wanna make sure we don't leave any finger prints."

While my father-in-law rubs at the casket with one of the unused sheets, I carefully scour the premises for any sign which might suggest we've been here tonight. When I'm satisfied, I point the light on Segars. Tiny beads of perspiration cover his face.

"We're okay, Clyde. You done with the casket?"

"Yes, wiped it clean as a whistle. No one will ever know we've been here," Segars replies. He uses the bed sheet to dab at his sweaty cheeks.

Seconds later we're in the Chevy and headed for the front gate. Segars turns to me and winks. A smug smile graces his face. "This is gonna work, Rick. It's really gonna work."

❖ ❖ ❖ ❖ ❖

ONCE WE'RE OUTSIDE the cemetery, we turn left and head north. We hardly reach the pavement before another heavy wave of rain arrives to angrily pound at the Chevy's windshield.

"Can you see all right?" I ask when Segars leans forward to squint and wipe at the condensate on the inside of the glass. The sudden massive downpour totally obliterates the painted center stripe dividing the two lanes.

"Barely, but we'll be fine. It's only a few miles to the airport."

"Man, this rain is something else. Hope it lets up before we get where we're going."

"No, we want it to rain, Rick. It makes perfect cover. We couldn't have picked a better night. No one in their right mind would be at the airfield on a night like this."

My father-in-law is right. This is perfect weather. Perfect for a murder. I twist around to glance at the gruesome sheeted corpse stretched out on the back seat. My back muscles quiver, and a cold chill creeps up my spine.

❖ ❖ ❖ ❖ ❖

A PAIR OF TALL brick columns constructed like bookends on each side of the access lanes mark the entrance to Pounds Field. Two distinct entrance and exit roadways are separated by a curbed median strip.

Segars carefully guides the Chevrolet into the entry side drive and proceeds slowly past the tall air control tower which protrudes high above the passenger terminal roof. When we come to a wide chain-link gate, he stops, cuts the headlights and commences to sort through a ring of keys on the seat beside him. The gate provides access to the private hangars located at the west end of the airport.

"Here's the key to the gate lock, Rick. I'm sorry, but looks like you're the one who's gotta get wet," my comrade in crime says, offering an apology when he hands me the key.

"No problem. A little rain never hurt anyone," I answer cheerfully and accept the key, but when I open the door and step outside, the cold driving rain hits me like an ocean wave. By the time I unlock the gate, wait for Segars to drive through and crawl back inside the car, I'm soaked to the bone, and my shoes are full of water. Clyde scrutinizes my wet clothing and smiles, perhaps pondering whether he should comment. He decides against it and shifts into low gear. The car lurches forward, and we head for the hangar buildings.

"You gonna tell me what we're up to?" I ask. Using both hands to squeegee the rain from my wet hair, I lean forward so the water will fall on the floorboard.

"All in due time, Rick. Let's get the car out of sight and unload our passenger. Then I'll lay out the whole plan for you."

"Tell me now, Clyde. I'm tired of playing this lunatic game," I state emphatically.

Seemingly, Segars ignores my firm demand. Staring straight ahead, he steers across the asphalt pavement until he reaches the hangar complex where private aircraft are stored.

"Clyde? You wanna say something?" I snarl impatiently.

"I hear you. You'll get your answer. Let me park. Then we'll talk."

"Okay," I concede, nevertheless pleased that I've prevailed.

Segars squeezes the Chevy into a narrow opening between two of the hangar buildings and parks. He shuts off the engine and swivels around to face me.

"Alright, Rick. Here's my plan. . . ," he begins.

Chilled and with water dripping from my rain-soaked clothing, I sit spellbound in the front seat across from my father-in-law while he explains why he's forced to launch this desperate scheme to fake his death. He's in hock up to his neck to the New Orleans organization. They've been financing his car business for a number of years. Segars says their terms seemed very reasonable in the beginning, but once they got him hooked, they raised their rates and began to suck him dry. Now it's only a matter of time before they call his loans. Segars is convinced the consequences for being unable to pay will be quite severe.

Even more distressing is the recent arrival of the Texas Rangers and their plan to investigate the oil skimming operation. Despite his friendship with Sheriff Grimes, Segars believes the rangers will eventually put two and two together and issue a warrant for his arrest. Even with Alvin out of the way, there's always the possibility of Oscar cutting a deal to save his own hide. Clyde contends if it was only him, he'd stay and face the music, but he's afraid the shame and embarrassment will destroy his two daughters.

Segars' plan for dying is simple but imaginative. Tonight he and I will load the body into the cockpit of his private plane. Tomorrow morning he'll file a flight plan showing New Orleans as his proposed destination. Somewhere between Longview and Marshall he'll saturate the cockpit with gasoline, set fire to the aircraft and bail out. By his calculations the airplane should go down in a sparsely populated wilderness area about thirty miles east of Marshall. When the plane crashes, the fire should detonate an explosion and burn John Doe beyond recognition. If the question of identity arises, or if an autopsy is required, he has that covered. Harrison County currently operates without the services of a coroner. Fred Varner will insist his Smith County coroner's office take possession of the body. If anyone objects, Fred's prepared to file for a court order, claiming the deceased is a bonafide resident of Smith County, and he has jurisdiction.

When he's finished, I'm still not satisfied. A thousand questions inundate my brain.

"You sure you can handle a parachute, Clyde? That's pretty rough country. You could break a leg or wind up in a tree top . . ."

"Not really. That's the scary part, but I can't come up with a better idea. Vic will be following me in his car. If I get in trouble, he'll find me."

"So Vic knows about your plan. Who else knows?"

"Only the four of us know—Vic, Fred, you and me. Vic wants to stick with me. He's a loyal friend. We've been together a long time. If you're worried about Fred—don't. He can keep a secret."

"What about Kaye and Vickie? Shouldn't we tell them? They'll be devastated."

"No, they mustn't know. Believe me, Rick. I've thought this thing through. My death will hurt the girls, but they'll get over it and get on with their lives. Both my girls are weak and much too proud. The shame of having their father convicted and sent to prison would grieve them much more than my death."

"What about the New Orleans Organization? They might come after the girls."

"My insurance policy should cover what I owe them. It's all in my will. Ted is named as the executor. He's to pay off the New Orleans' debt before he disperses any other payments."

"What about the car business? Your house? All the people who depend on you?"

"Everyone will be taken care of. It's all in the will. Most of the new cars are on consignment from the manufacturer. Ted will return those. He'll sell off the rest and dispose of the property and equipment. The proceeds should just about cover my bank loans. Peoples National holds the mortgage on my house and estate. They'll make a few bucks when they foreclose, but they've been good to me.

The house is so expensive to maintain. I couldn't have held on much longer anyway."

"And the people who depend on you? What about them?"

"There should be enough insurance money left over to see that everyone receives a small severance—maybe a hundred or so for each employee. Of course Felix and my house people will receive a few dollars more."

"The airplane. What about the airplane?" I ask, getting near the bottom of my list. Actually, I'm only interested in one of his assets.

"The airplane is owned by the bank. At least they loaned me the money to buy it. The plane is fully insured, so the bank won't lose a dime."

"And the baseball club? What will become of us?" I inquire meekly. Most likely I won't like the answer, but I have to know. I can hardly breathe while I wait for his response.

Segars frowns and fidgets with the steering wheel while he considers my question.

"You really care for that baseball team, don't you Rick?"

"Except for your daughter, it's the most important thing in my life. Yes, I love my players. I love the fans. I love the excitement. Heck, I even love that old man who coaches with me."

"I love the ball club too. That's another reason I hate to leave. I'm truly sorry, Rick."

"Ted will have to sell it, won't he?" I say, stating my worst fear.

"It's worse than that. Upon my death, the franchise automatically reverts to my partners. Biff and Garry have never properly appreciated you or your baseball tactics. You'll probably be fired the day they take control."

❖ ❖ ❖ ❖ ❖

MY DISAPPOINTMENT weighs heavy as we drag John Doe from the backseat, carry him inside the hangar and load him onto Segars' twin engine Cessna. Clyde insists we strap the body into the pilot's chair on the left side of the cockpit. He intends to fly the plane from the co-pilot's position on the right side. We also bring on-board two five-gallon containers of gasoline which my father-in-law stashed in the hangar earlier this afternoon. The gas will be used to douse the interior before Segars sets his fire and bails out.

"Reckon that about does it. It's been a long night. What say we head for home?" Clyde sighs after he secures the cabin doorway. Quietly, he disengages the portable metal access stair and pushes it to one side.

"Dammit, Clyde. Why does it have to end this way? You had everything going for you—a prosperous business, a wonderful family, lots of friends, and we were just getting started with the baseball franchise. We could've worked through this losing streak and made the playoffs. I know we could."

"You're right, Rick. I had it all. Now I'm about to lose it. I made a mistake climbing in bed with thieves. When you hook up with evil people, you're bound to pay somewhere down the line."

"Are you sure there's no other way? This seems so final."

"I wish there was. I'm gonna miss you, Rick. You've given me some tense moments, but you're a good friend, and you're one hell of a baseball manager."

"I'm gonna miss you too, Clyde. Could we shake hands?"

"Yes, I'd like that. Shaking hands would be a fitting way to say goodbye."

Our hands touch and clasp firmly. Segars' sad eyes meet mine. Then we give way to our emotions and throw our arms around one another. For a moment we stand there hugging each other tightly.

"We'll both go to hell for what we've done. Maybe we'll see each other there," I say with tears in my eyes.

"You'll be the first one I look up, Rick. And that's a promise."

"You think they play baseball in hell, Clyde?"

"I wouldn't think so. If they played baseball in hell, nobody would want to go to Heaven."

❖ ❖ ❖ ❖ ❖

KAYE IS ASLEEP when I peek in to check. Not wanting to wake her, I tiptoe to the bathroom and start the bath water running.

Then I go to the back porch, slip out of my wet clothes and hang them to dry. The tub is almost filled when I return to the bathroom.

Hoping the cleansing hot water will rinse off the stench of death, I lay soaking in the tub for a long time and let my mind ramble, wondering what will happen tomorrow, what fate lies in store for my baseball team, how Kaye will react when she learns of her father's death, how this will all play out.

When I wiggle into bed beside her, Kaye moans softly and snuggles up against me. I wrap my arms around her, pull her close, and gently rub her stomach. Kaye hasn't mentioned the baby. She may not know she's expecting yet. But I know it's there, and it's a boy.

I wonder if he'll grow up tall and strong? Will he be smart and clever like his grandfather, or will he be slow to learn like me? I wonder if he'll learn to love baseball the way I do?

Yes, I'll definitely want my son to play baseball. I'll teach him everything I know.

CHAPTER NINETEEN

E VEN AFTER Segars' airplane is reported missing late Monday afternoon, no one seems concerned. Much of the colonel's mystique is moored to his reputation as a totally independent individual. He'd never feel constrained by something so petty as a flight plan. It's not at all unusual for him to charge off in one direction, change his mind, and wind up somewhere else without checking with anyone.

It isn't until Tuesday morning, when a couple of teenagers stumble across the plane wreckage in a wooded area thirty miles east of Marshall, that things heat up. Word of the young campers' discovery prompts a flurry of activity inside the Smith County courthouse with both the sheriff and the county coroner immediately dispatching crews to the scene of the accident. According to a recently reinstated Deputy Mike Harris who shows up at my door around three o'clock Tuesday afternoon, Harrison County law officers offered little resistance when Fred Varner insisted on taking possession of Segars' body. In fact, the officers helped load the badly burned corpse into Varner's ambulance, evidently relieved they wouldn't be burdened with the responsibility of identification. Mike's sad duty is, of course, to inform us of Kaye's father's death and to transport us to the county morgue to positively identify the charred remains. When I volunteer to save Vickie and Kaye from the grief of

370

viewing their father in such a pitiful state, they each immediately agree to let me handle the distasteful task. I take my time, studying the carcass carefully. Finally, choking back crocodile tears, I hang my head and nod affirmatively, verifying the dead body is my father-in-law.

Naturally, Kaye and Vickie are devastated by my confirmation of their father's gruesome end. Before we leave the morgue and amidst profuse crying and mournful wails, I telephone Ted to inform him of Clyde's untimely death and ask him to meet us at the Segars' mansion. The colonel's house people and his employees need to be notified. Funeral arrangements must be decided. Neither of the two women seem up to handling the hundreds of decisions which need to be made in the next few hours.

With Monday night's contest canceled on account of wet grounds, my East Texans have a twi-night double header with the Texarkana Bears on tap this evening. The first game is scheduled to begin at 5:00 P.M. So, despite the sorrowful family situation, my presence is required at the ballpark.

It's a few minutes past four when Kaye, Vickie and I wheel onto the circular driveway fronting the Segars' Estate. Ted and Felix are waiting outside the front door anticipating our arrival. For a few moments I watch as everyone exchanges tearful hugs, but when the mourning party advances to a prolonged crying session, I exit as gracefully as possible. This may seem callous, but when you know the whole thing's a sham, it's difficult to act sad. I leave the sobbing sisters in the custody of a more sensitive Ted Gooding.

❖ ❖ ❖ ❖ ❖

WORD OF THE COLONEL'S DEMISE spreads through the city like wildfire. By the time I reach the ballpark, several hundred fans have congregated at the front gate. Recognizing my Pontiac, the anxious mob scurries toward me. Even before I crawl out people begin to inundate me with questions.

"Coach Mason, are you gonna cancel tonight's games?"

"Who'll be running the club now that the colonels gone? Are you gonna be the manager?"

371

"Did the team's losing streak have anything to do with the colonel's death?"

"You think we oughta cancel the season?"

"Hey, meathead! How long you think you'll last before the new owners fire your sorry ass?"

I hold up my hands and try to explain that the ballclub will issue a statement to clarify the situation as soon as possible, but my voice is drowned out by the crowd. When I realize no one actually cares what I say, I shove through the restless multitude and head for the locker room. Whitey is waiting for me outside the front door.

"Is it true, Rick? Is the colonel really gone?"

"I'm sorry, Whitey. You and Clyde have been close friends for a long time."

"He was more than a good friend. There've been several times I might have starved to death if he hadn't intervened."

"I know what you mean. He bailed me out of more than a few jams too."

"There's a bunch of folks here in Tyler who owe him, but not many people knew him the way you and I did, Rick. A lot of Clyde's friends were the fair-weather type. They'll mostly miss his deep pockets."

"I hate to admit it, Whitey, but I know you're right. Even for you and me this may not be all bad. According to Matilda, it's Clyde who's been causing our bad luck. Maybe now that he's out of the picture, we can start winning again."

"I wouldn't count on it, Rick. Biff Crawley showed up about ten minutes ago. He wants to talk. He's waiting for us in the manager's office."

❖ ❖ ❖ ❖ ❖

WITH A STADIUM already half-filled with curious fans and a ballgame scheduled to begin in less than an hour, it takes only a few minutes for the three of us to agree to play tonight's twin bill. We hastily prepare a statement for the press which conveys the club's firm intentions to play out the baseball season.

That's where agreement ceases. When Crawley suggests I start rookie pitcher Matt Burns in the first game, I blow my stack.

"Start Burns. Why would you wanna do that? Davis and Bounato, our two best arms, are ready to go."

"That's what I want. Burns is one of the players we intend to keep. We expect him to be the ace on next year's staff."

"Next year. But we're still in the hunt for the playoffs this season. We can win with the crew we have on board right now. I know we can."

"That's one of the problems we have with the way you manage the ball club, Mason. You're short sighted, and you're so damned obsessed with the notion you have to win right now. Now in the second game, I want you to start our other rookie, Morgan."

❖ ❖ ❖ ❖ ❖

TO HOME FANS' dismay, Texarkana pounds Matt Burns for twelve hits and seven runs before I replace him in the fifth inning with Paul Walker. Irate Tyler supporters, exasperated by my weird pitching strategy, scream obscenities at me each time I show my face outside the dugout.

Fortunately, my East Texans also have hot bats. In the bottom of the third, taking advantage of a Henry French walk and back to back singles by Bruzga and Connors, Dub Akins drives in three runs with a clutch, base-clearing double. We score two more in the bottom of the fourth after Epps reaches first on an infield error, and a rejuvenated Joe Kracher clobbers his first home run for his new team. In the seventh, Gregory smashes a line drive triple which ricochets off the left field fence. Then Neuendorff brings him in with a looping single to right, leaving us one run behind.

Walker stifles the free swinging visiting batters until the top of the ninth when he gives up a lead-off single to Bears' shortstop Irv Carlson. Texarkana's center fielder Milan Vucelich follows by drilling Paul's second pitch over the right field fence. Even though Philip Johnson comes in to douse the fire, Tyler is three runs down when we go into the bottom of the ninth.

East Texans   6   Bears   9

❖ ❖ ❖ ❖ ❖

"OKAY, LISTEN UP. This is our last chance. We're gonna win this game, so we need some base runners. You batters be patient. Make their pitcher throw you a strike before you swing," I yell, clapping my hands and shuffling along in front of the bench, encouraging my players. When I reach the end of the bench, Philip Johnson grabs my arm.

"What makes you so positive, Coach Mason? Don't you know this team's lost seven games in a row? And now the colonel's gone. How can you still believe we'll pull out a win when we're three runs down?"

His question takes me by surprise. It never occurred to me a member of my team might not share my optimism. I consider my answer carefully before I respond.

"You believe in a life hereafter, don't you, Philip?"

"Sure. That's why I decided to be a preacher—to tell the whole world about it."

"But you've never seen it, and you've never known anyone who's been there?"

"No sir. I haven't actually seen it, but I know it's true. There is a life after death. I'll bet Colonel Segars is up there in heaven right now, singing with the angels and having a gay old time."

"Well, maybe. But how do you know? What makes you so certain?"

"Faith. I got faith."

"That's what I have, Philip. Faith—faith in you men, faith in this team, faith that if we stick together we'll break out of this lousy losing streak. And if we can just get some kind of lucky break, we're gonna do it here in this ballpark tonight."

"This team needs a lot more than luck, Coach Mason. What this team needs is divine intervention. Would you mind if me, Herb and Frank get together to say a prayer and ask for some extra help from up above?"

374

"No, not at all. You can tell your man upstairs that I'm not greedy. I'll settle for a smidgen of luck and a plate umpire with a constipated strike zone."

❖ ❖ ❖ ❖ ❖

WHILE OUR THREE preachers huddle in prayer near the water cooler, Dub Akins leads off with his second hit of the night, a golf shot which falls into short right field. Dub makes the turn at first, stops and trots back to stand on the base. A satisfied grin adorns his face as he glances back at his teammates in the dugout.

"That's the ticket. Now remember, we're three runs down, so we need base runners. Watch what you swing at," I yell to no one in particular, but my words seem to stimulate a sense of excitement on our bench. Several men leave the bench to stand and lean against the front rail, shouting words of encouragement. After Gregory works the pitcher for a free pass to put runners on first and second, our dugout becomes a noisy cheering section. Every Tyler player is standing, hollering, whistling, waving their arms.

"Peppy, you ready?" I call, turning to search for my veteran, but Peppy is already climbing the dugout steps. "Go get 'em, slugger," I say and reach for the dugout telephone to call in my batting change, substituting Swanson for Neuendorff.

Peppy runs the count to 2 and 1 before he gets a pitch he can hit. "CRACK!" he sends a high fly ball soaring into deep right center. Two fleet-footed Texarkana flycatchers give chase.

"It's gone. That ball is long gone," I scream enthusiastically, but at the same time I realize the ball is hit much too high. I cross my fingers and silently pray for a miracle. My prayer goes unanswered. With his back against the outfield fence, the Bears' center fielder snares the baseball and rifles it to second base. Akins barely slides back in time to keep from being thrown out.

Our two base runners advance to second and third after Hal Epps lifts another long fly to right field for the second out. That's when Joe Kracher abandons his station in the on-deck-circle and comes running to talk to me.

"Coach Mason, you ever hear of the bait and switch tactic?"

"No, don't think so, but if you've got an idea how we can score, I'm darn sure willing to listen."

"We used it a lotta times out in West Texas. Here's the way it works. . ."

❖ ❖ ❖ ❖ ❖

BEFORE KRACHER squares around to bunt, we signal our runners to take a long lead and be moving on the pitch. When Joe jerks his bat back and takes the pitch, they each throw on their brakes and scamper back to their respective bases.

"Steerriikee One!" the umpire declares decisively.

After the pitch Texarkana's infielders inch forward a few steps in anticipation of a bunt. Kracher glances at me and nods his head. I signal my base runners to be off and running with the next pitch. We're pulling out all the stops. What's the sense in being conservative when you're three runs down with two out?

As the Bear hurler toes the rubber, Kracher squares around again, foregoing any pretense of fooling the defense.

"Bunt! Watch out for the bunt," Texarkana's manager screams from the visitor's dugout. Bear infielders move forward as their pitcher winds and delivers.

A split-second before the pitcher releases the ball, Kracher hops back into his normal batting stance.

"CRACK!" A sharp ringing sound echoes across the diamond as Kracher's bat connects. A surprised, hard-charging second baseman tries to recover as the baseball whips past. He skids to a stop, almost losing his balance as he whirls around to give chase. Eventually the Bears' infielder runs the ball down on the outfield grass, grabs it with his bare hand, and turns to fling it in the direction of home plate. His throw arrives too late. Gregory kicks up a cloud of dust as he slides in feet first to score, leaving us one run down. On the throw to home Kracher advances to second.

❖ ❖ ❖ ❖ ❖

"I'M READY, SKIPPER. We got it all worked out," Philip Johnson informs me while I consider my options. I'm thinking about subbing in Herb Cates to bat for his cousin Philip.

"What are we talking about, Philip? You mean you wanna bat?"

"Yes sir. After I get on base, Henry's gonna bring me and Joe in. I'm gonna score the winning run. It's all decided."

Every hair on my body bristles. I'm the manager. I'm supposed to make the coaching decisions. Why should I listen to a bunch of green rookies? Then the humor of the situation strikes me. Why not? Hell, it's been more than two weeks since this team won a game. Every crucial coaching decision I've made has gone sour. Why not step back and hope for divine intervention?

"Lemme get this straight, Philip. You're gonna get a hit? Then Henry is gonna drive you in?"

"That's the plan, Coach. All we need is two runs. I guess we could refigure everything if you want more than two."

"No, two will be plenty, Philip. Two runs will do just fine."

While the young preacher strolls casually up the dugout steps, I plop down on the bench and bury my face in my hands, trying not to giggle out loud like a silly school girl.

❖ ❖ ❖ ❖ ❖

EVEN THOUGH the first pitch is eyeball high, Johnson swings away, lacing a sharp single to right center and advancing Kracher to third base. Sensing an amazing come-from-behind victory, every spectator in the grandstands leaps to his feet, whooping, hollering, screaming, stomping his feet, clapping, encouraging the team while Henry French takes his final practice swings and steps to the plate.

"You sure about this, Rick? You're gonna let Henry hit away and not try for a walk?" Whitey inquires, ambling up to sit beside me.

"That's the plan. Bruzga would bat next, and he's in a slump. Except for that bloop single in the third, he hasn't hit the ball out of

377

the infield in over a week. Only other choice we have is to sub in Cates or Frank Johnson to bat for Henry. They seem to like this plan better."

"I reckon we can't do no worse than we've been doing."

"That's the way I see it, Whitey. Whatta we got to lose?"

French fouls off the first two pitches. The count is 0 and two when Texarkana's chunker decides to brush Henry back with a high inside pitch.

"CLUNK!" a sickening dull thud transmits the bad news as the wooden bat held by a dodging Henry French collides with the baseball. Henry lies stretched out on the ground while the slow-rolling ball meanders across the left side of the infield.

"Run, Henry. Get up and run," our players scream from the dugout. Kracher and Johnson are already off and running. Fans up in the bleachers leap from their seats, shouting, yelling at the top of their lungs.

Continuing on a wobbly path past the pitching mound, the baseball rolls innocently toward a hard-charging third baseman. Henry jumps to his feet, his face strained with anxiety. While he's hightailing it up the first base line, a crazy thing happens. As the Bears' third baseman stoops down to field the slow-moving ball, it careens off in a different direction, almost as if it's purposely avoiding the Texarkana player's glove. A second later the bewildered infielder tracks the ball down and lobs it toward first base where it bounces three feet in front of the bag. Texarkana's first sacker bobbles the baseball then recovers at the exact same instant French's foot touches the bag. Every person in the stadium holds his breath while the field umpire makes up his mind.

"Safe! The man is safe!" the umpire cries, waving his hands horizontally to signal his call.

The Bears' first baseman's initial reaction is to turn and dispute the umpire's call. Then he notices Philip Johnson. Starting from first at the crack of the bat, the fleet-footed preacher never slowed down. Philip has rounded third and headed for home when the first baseman realizes his team's perilous situation. The crowd is howling. Every player in both dugouts is yelling. The thunderous roar of two

378

thousand screaming fans rocks the stadium as Philip kicks into high gear, leaving his feet some twenty feet up the base line to dive at home plate and arrive at the same time as the baseball smacks against the catcher's mitt.

Abruptly, the screaming stops. For a moment the stadium is deathly quiet while the crowd awaits the call at home.

"Safe! He's safe!" Total bedlam erupts as the umpire hops back and signals safe.

When his teammates mob him at home plate, Philip Johnson is still lying on the ground blanketed in red dust. Pandemonium envelopes the ball diamond as the home crowd cheers wildly. Every person in the stadium is on his feet to clap and offer verbal approval while Philip's teammates hoist him on their shoulders and parade him around the infield.

Whitey and I stand side by side savoring the jubilant celebration. Our hearts are pumping. We're both grinning from ear to ear.

"That's the end of it, Whitey. I think we finally have the bad luck streak behind us."

"Yep, we're back on track. That hit by French was nothing but luck—pure, dumb luck."

"You're wrong there, old timer. That wasn't luck. What these Tyler fans witnessed here tonight was divine intervention."

❖ ❖ ❖ ❖ ❖

AFTER WINNING the first game and putting a definitive end to our dastardly losing streak, I'm both elated and fearless. I disregard Biff Crawley's orders and pick Charlie Davis to hurl the nightcap.

Charlie shuts out the Bears for seven innings. Meanwhile, our bats continue to sizzle. We're leading by six runs when I replace Davis with Bounato to close out the final two innings. In the eighth frame an infield error, a wild throw past second base, and a long fly ball allow Texarkana to scratch out a lone tally. Merv Connors immediately recoups our run margin with a mighty home run wallop which he air mails over the center field scoreboard. When Jim Matthews, the Bears' catcher, grounds out to shortstop for the third out of the ninth inning, Tyler supporters squeal with delight and reward us with a loud, ear-piercing and prolonged cheering session.

Final Score: East Texans 7 Bears 1

Unfortunately, that's the last game I manage for Tyler's baseball franchise. Even before Whitey and I can gather our gear, Biff Crawley storms into our dugout and pulls the plug on our joyful mood. First, he bludgeons me with a thorough tongue lashing and tells me I'm through. When Whitey tries to intercede, Crawley fires him too. Ten minutes after our East Texans win both ends of the twin bill and break out of their losing streak, both of us managers are unemployed.

❖ ❖ ❖ ❖ ❖

DESPITE MY FRUSTRATION at being so maliciously relieved of my managerial duties, there's another situation which demands my immediate attention. Not bothering to shower, I change to my street clothes and drive straight to the Segars' mansion. When I arrive, Felix informs me Ted is upstairs in the study. I scale the stairs and enter without knocking. Ted is sitting behind Clyde's desk talking on the telephone.

"Whoever you're talking to, tell them you'll call 'em back later. You and me, we've got work to do," I instruct Ted harshly.

Ted nods affirmatively and waves a hand to shush me then uses the same hand to cover the mouthpiece. He tells me with a hushed voice, "Hang on, Rick. I'll only be a minute."

"No, hang up now," I demand and reach across the desk to press the receiver lever and disconnect his call.

"Why'd you do that? I was talking to the funeral home director."

"That can wait. There's something more important that needs doing right now. You know about Segars' file room?"

"Yes, I've been wondering what we should do with all that information. Might be worth a lot of money if we could sell it to the right person."

"We ain't selling. We're gonna haul the files outta here and burn 'em, before someone outside the family finds out what's in there."

"Let's not be hasty here, Rick. Maybe we should go through the files first. Who knows what we might discover."

"We're gonna burn 'em, Ted. You gonna help me or not?"

It takes three trips up and down the stairs for Ted and me to tote the files down to my Pontiac and load them into the backseat. The two of us drive to a roadside park out on the Troop Highway where we use a metal trash barrel to burn the files. Ted heaves a deep sigh as we stand back and watch the fire blaze away.

"How'd our baseball team do tonight?" Ted asks when the flames begin to die down.

"We won. Broke out of the losing streak and beat the Bears both games."

"That's great, Rick. Maybe we can still make the playoffs."

"If they do, it'll be without me. Biff Crawley fired me right after the game."

"Oh," Ted says and turns back to stare at the fire. While we stand silently side by side, I can't help but wonder if Ted's name wasn't also posted on one of those files.

❖ ❖ ❖ ❖ ❖

FUNERAL SERVICES are held in Tyler on Wednesday afternoon at Marvin Methodist Church. The church is filled to capacity. Inside the hallowed sanctuary there's neither an empty seat nor a dry eye as a grateful citizenry bids a sad farewell to the colonel. A multitude of mourners are forced to stand outside on the church grounds.

Later, after a private family ceremony at Rosehill Burial Park, we lay John Doe's body to rest in a family plot next to Segars' wife and beneath a limestone marker which reads:

CLYDE SEGARS
1888 - 1951
FAITHFUL HUSBAND, BELOVED FATHER, LOYAL FRIEND

❖ ❖ ❖ ❖ ❖

WITH NO BASEBALL to occupy my time, the hot summer months drag by. Numerous phone calls and inquiries seeking another baseball job net me nothing more than a lot of empty promises. Finally, desperate for work and bored to tears from staying home, I do something I promised myself I'd never do. I take a job selling tires at the General Tire Center on West Erwin.

Near the end of May, Oscar Habegger cuts a deal with the Smith County D.A.'s office to forego a jury trial and plead guilty to a manslaughter charge. Agreeing to accept the plea bargain arrangement worked out between the attorneys, the judge sentences Habegger to ten years, with parole possible after two. Several days later, Kaye discovers she's pregnant. She seems so happy when she tells me. I try to act surprised and make a big deal out of it by taking her out to eat at Mary's Diner. She's been so depressed since her father's funeral. It's the least I can do.

By mid-July Ted completes the task of collecting Segars' insurance policies and disposing of the colonel's properties. After all the bills are paid, including the notes held by the New Orleans cartel, Kaye and Vickie wind up with a little less than fifty thousand dollars apiece. Everyone except me seems terribly disappointed with the final settlement. I don't see why. When I was playing in the big leagues, being paid top dollar, it would've taken me almost ten years to make fifty thousand dollars.

Kaye's portion of the settlement money allows us some much needed financial breathing room. For the first time since I moved into the duplex on Williams Court, we pay our rent on time.

On two occasions during mid-summer, I persuade Kaye to accompany me to the ballpark to watch the East Texans play. After that I quit going. I even stop listening to their games on the radio. It's too painful. The new owners have gutted the team, making wholesale changes and dismantling the squad under the guise of injecting youth and enthusiasm into the franchise.

By early August when Peppy Swanson is released, the East Texans have taken permanent residence in the league cellar. Hardly a trace of my original roster remains. Average attendance has dwindled to less than five hundred per game.

❖ ❖ ❖ ❖ ❖

"I'M GOING ON to bed, Ricky. It's been a long day," Kaye tells me, bending down to kiss my lips.

"Sure, hon. I'll be along in a few minutes. Wanna check through this tire catalog one more time. Tomorrow's the last day to mail in the store's order for the winter season. I wanna get it right. My boss is depending on me."

"You like your job, don't you, sweetheart? I hope you're as happy as I am. It's so nice having you home every night."

Laying the catalog on the table beside my easy chair, I swivel around to wrap my arms about my wife's waist and press my face against her swollen stomach.

"I am happy, Kaye—as happy as any man deserves. I've got everything a man could want—a steady job, a terrific boss, good friends, a beautiful wife, a great life. When the baby comes, my life will be complete."

"Are you sure, Ricky? I hope you're not just saying that."

"No, I really mean it. I've never felt so content. A home and family—that's what's been missing. That's what I've been searching for all my life."

"Come to bed, darling, and hold me. Hold me and the baby. You can finish with the catalog in the morning."

❖ ❖ ❖ ❖ ❖

OBNOXIOUS RINGING wakes me from a deep slumber. I open one eye, trying to come fully awake. Kaye is sleeping peacefully beside me.

The ringing commences again. I roll over and grab the telephone.

"Hello!" I answer sharply, wondering what inconsiderate fool would call in the middle of the night. Most likely it's a wrong number.

"You staying sober, Richard?" a voice on the other end inquires. The voice sounds familiar, but I can't quite place it.

"Sure, of course. Who is this?" I ask, while my groggy mind searches through the directory of voices stored inside, trying to match a name with the voice.

"I'd prefer not to say. You can never tell who might be listening, but you know who I am. Listen, I met this fellow at the racetrack, named Stoneham. Owns a National League franchise. Tells me his team is making a last minute run for the title."

"Yeah, Charles Stoneham, he's the Giants' owner. I've been reading about him in the paper, but it's too late. No way New York can catch the Dodgers. They're thirteen games back. Don't have but forty games left to play. It would take a miracle for the Giants to catch up."

"That's exactly my point. My man's ball club needs some luck—a whole lot of luck. I told him I'm closely related to the luckiest man in baseball. There's a train leaving from Union Station in Dallas at six o'clock this morning. Runs straight through to Grand Central Station in New York. When you arrive Tuesday morning, Vic will meet you and drive you to the Polo Grounds."

"Who is this? This is some kind of perverted joke, isn't it?"

"Let me assure you, son, this is no joke. This is business, and a lot of big bucks are riding on this pennant race. You know I never joke about business. You wanna be a big league coach again, or not?"

"Alright, I'm convinced. I'll come, but I'll need two tickets. I want to bring someone else—for extra luck."

"You got 'em. There'll be two tickets waiting. Now get your butt in gear. Coach Durocher wants you in uniform for Tuesday afternoon's game."

After I hang up, I'm fully awake, but my mind is a total mess. Every brain gear is whirling at warp speed. Kaye rolls over and lays her arm across my chest.

"Who was it, darling?" she asks sleepily.

"It was your father, Kaye—your wheeling, dealing father." The words are out of my mouth before I can stop. The startled, sad expression on my pregnant wife's face tells me I've struck a deep vein of hurt. I could bite my tongue for telling her this way.

"My father? But daddy's dead." Kaye's widened eyes are filled with anxiety, visually depicting her shock. Her lip quivers. She's close to tears.

"No, Kaye, your dad's alive, and he's up to his old tricks. It'll take a lot of explaining, but you deserve to know everything that's happened. Why don't you run put on a pot of coffee while I make a quick phone call, then I'll tell you the whole story."

❖ ❖ ❖ ❖ ❖

A BANGING NOISE abuses my listening ear as a dropped receiver bounces against the floor. Inaudible curse words and scraping sounds reverberate from the opposite end of the telephone line while the person on the other end groggily retrieves the dangling headpiece.

"Hello," a sleepy voice yawns.

"Whitey, that you?"

"Sure, it's me. Who else would answer my phone in the middle of the night? What the Sam Hill you want, Rick? It's two o'clock in the morning."

"Get your bags packed, Whitey. I'll pick you up in half an hour. You and me, we're headed for the big show."

"The big show? You mean the major leagues?"

"Yep, you and me, we got jobs again, coaching in the bigs. Say, Whitey, have you talked to Matilda lately?"

EPILOGUE I

On August 11, 1951, the Brooklyn Dodgers held a commanding 13-game lead over the second place New York Giants in the race for the National League pennant. However in the weeks that followed, New York won an incredible 37 games while losing only seven, a mind-boggling .841 percentage, making one of the most miraculous comebacks of all time to catch the Dodgers on the last day of the season and force a three-game playoff. The Giants won the playoff series and the right to represent the National League in the World Series with a ninth inning rally in the third game. The Giant's rally was capped by Bobby Thompson's dramatic three-run homer which was labeled by sportswriters as the "Shot heard 'round the World."

Some say the Giants won because they refused to lose. Some say the Giants simply had all the luck.

EPILOGUE II

The Tyler East Texans finished the 1951 season at the bottom of the Big State League, forty-two games behind the first place Gainesville Owls.

However, in 1952, the ballclub acquired the services of pitchers, John "Red" Murff and Gale Pringle; infielders Irv Carlson, Joe Campbell, Jack Louman and Bob White; outfielders Johnny Stone and Dean Stafford; catcher Ralph Fernandez; and third baseman/manager Billy Capps. After finishing second in the regular season, the East Texans captured the Big State title in a four-team playoff.

For winning the Big State League championship, each Tyler player received an extra $126 and a new billfold.